CW01024473

The Favourite

The Favourite

FRAN LITTLEWOOD

MICHAEL JOSEPH

PENGUIN MICHAEL JOSEPH

UK | USA | Canada | Ireland | Australia
India | New Zealand | South Africa

Penguin Michael Joseph is part of the Penguin Random House group of companies
whose addresses can be found at global.penguinrandomhouse.com

Penguin Random House UK
One Embassy Gardens, 8 Viaduct Gardens, London SW11 7BW

penguin.co.uk

First published 2025

001

Set in 13.5/16pt Garamond MT Std
Typeset by Jouve (UK), Milton Keynes
Printed and bound in Great Britain by Clays Ltd, Elcograf S.p.A.

The authorized representative in the EEA is Penguin Random House Ireland,
Morrison Chambers, 32 Nassau Street, Dublin DO2 YH68

A CIP catalogue record for this book is available from the British Library

HARDBACK ISBN: 978-0-241-54854-7
TRADE PAPERBACK ISBN: 978-0-241-54855-4

For Cath and Jules, and for Mum

Shit. I'm wearing the top that she 'lost' years
ago. So. This is gonna be tense.
Fleabag, Season 1: Episode 1

. . . memories form the bedrock of our
identities . . . if we begin to call our memory into
question we are also forced to question the very
foundations of who we are.
Dr Julia Shaw, *The Memory Illusion*

FISHER FAMILY TREE

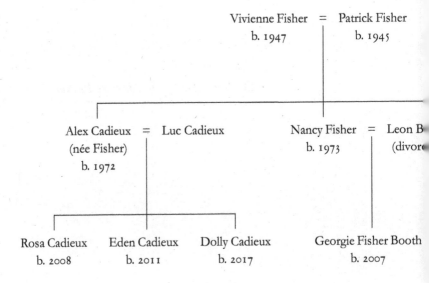

Vivienne Fisher = Patrick Fisher
b. 1947   b. 1945

Alex Cadieux = Luc Cadieux
(née Fisher)
b. 1972

Nancy Fisher = Leon B
b. 1973   (divorc

Rosa Cadieux   Eden Cadieux   Dolly Cadieux
b. 2008   b. 2011   b. 2017

Georgie Fisher Booth
b. 2007

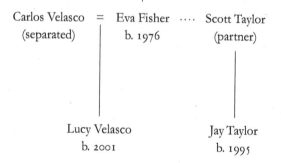

Carlos Velasco = Eva Fisher ···· Scott Taylor
(separated)   b. 1976   (partner)

Lucy Velasco   Jay Taylor
b. 2001   b. 1995

I

Vivienne, Sunday morning

Even from this distance, Vivienne can hear the cultish drone of the singing bowls, and she rolls her eyes as she comes along the dark path between the trees. The wind is pinning her skirt to her crotch, wrapping her legs in thick indigo silk, and she's hoping it will also be blowing the smell of the secret Marlboro Gold she's just smoked from her hair, her face, as she makes her way back towards the gathering at the bottom of the slope. Although she hasn't obliged, they were supposed to dress in autumn colours to match the season, and, as the path tracks to the right, she glimpses the red and yellow and orange and green of the rest of them.

The naming ceremony is over. Thank God. A tick-box DIY humanist thing that, according to Alex, all the south London 'mumfluencers' are going in for right now. *It felt like a good idea at the time* . . . her eldest daughter had murmured, as they'd lugged boxes of decorations and foldaway furniture, a bubble machine and all the rest of it from the car into the forest earlier that morning. They'd found a relatively – *relatively* – sheltered spot, and Alex and the others had wound paper lanterns through the trees, then hammered in a complicated gazebo that had whipped and snapped throughout, as if a malevolent presence was lurking. Most of the lanterns had blown away, and are tangled now in far-off branches. But for Vivienne the lowest point had come when she'd been ambushed into making a *promise* to the baby. They all had, but she'd been first up and, put on the spot like that, she couldn't remember the name of her newest grandchild. *I'd like to propose a long and happy life to . . . to our little . . . Betty*, she'd gushed finally, too loudly. It was the wrong name. There was a frozen moment until, somewhere behind her, Nancy had tried and failed to disguise a laugh as a cough. In the same moment, Alex had corrected Vivienne's mistake with a blank face – as though if she reacted minimally maybe it hadn't happened, maybe her own mum hadn't forgotten her baby daughter's name – and they could all swiftly erase it from their collective memory. *Dolly*, she reminds herself now. Like the cloned sheep. Or the country singer with boobs the size of a baby's head. She will not get away with this, she knows – Alex will be watching her, *scrutinizing* her, for signs of dementia for the rest of the week.

At the top of the incline where the trees thin out, she stops to catch her breath. It's more exposed here and her hair wraps her face, yanked diagonally like the bending trees. She imagines she looks like a forest hag, someone who would scare the grandchildren. Each time she pushes hair out of her eyes, her mouth, it thwacks right back. It's the windiest day of the year so far, of the decade, in fact. She knows this because Eva's new partner, Scott, had informed them all over breakfast that morning, before kicking off a small meteorological sermon turned climate-change horror story that had made her want to tip her glass of grapefruit juice across the vast slate table just to make him stop.

The singing bowls were his idea too. He'd produced them from his backpack in the forest, with a flourish, *ta-da!*, and the look on Alex's face had made Vivienne want to laugh. She'd seen her daughter open her mouth to say, 'No,' then watched her falter, not wanting to sour the atmosphere. Vivienne doesn't like Scott. She can't help it. Privately, she worries he's after Eva's money – a *gold-digger* – which does her youngest daughter a massive disservice, she's aware, but she can tell she's not alone. Alex and Nancy give each other significant looks whenever he opens his mouth. They're none too subtle about it either. Still, he's right, it is windy and cold and she's wishing she'd packed a warmer coat. How soon could Amazon deliver one to this middle-of-nowhere place? she wonders. One of those duvet coats like a pupa, the kind that restrict your walking. Although, of course, she shouldn't be shopping on Amazon at all, because of the shameless tax-dodging and the rest. She knows this, she means to stop.

She turns sideways to come down the slope. There's been rain in the night and the leaves are slippery under her feet. She's moving like a pensioner – Christ, she *is* a pensioner – but there's this issue with her bone density, and although she mostly tries to ignore it, she's not going to be stupid about it. She's close enough now to see that Patrick is trying to line up Alex, Nancy and Eva – their three girls – for a photograph. He's brought the huge camera, the one he spent a fortune on for the

University of the Third Age photography course. He's had it hanging ostentatiously round his neck all morning, even though she suspects he doesn't really know how to use it, beyond taking off the lens cap and clicking the shutter. She pauses in the bonfire shelter of a thick-spread beech; she can see that the little ones are in and out of Patrick's shot and he's getting nowhere, trying to shoo them to the side, and it makes her smile to watch.

Baby dispatched and standing in the middle of her sisters, Alex appears oblivious to the chaos. The only one following her father's instructions, she has one leg crossed in front of the other, her best side turned to the camera. It always surprises Vivienne, when she sees them lined up like this, that Alex is the shortest – the eldest but the shortest – of her three daughters, because even now it seems against the natural order of things. She's had her hair cut into a style that's cropped at the neck, draping at the jaw and doesn't really suit her. Streaky highlights that wash her out, or maybe she's just tired, because she's forty-five with a six-month-old baby, who has come as something of a surprise. A little disruptor, there's *quite* the age gap between Alex's middle and youngest child, but she's pushing through, or says she is. Everything is always fine, thank you, with Alex. The kind of woman who colour-coordinates her wardrobe, who has been colour-coordinating her wardrobe since the age of eleven, and Vivienne has no idea where she gets this from, none. But it impresses her still, more than three decades on. Although Vivienne's been watching her for the past twenty-four hours, she's pretty sure something's going on with her, that something's wrong.

Already she's wishing she hadn't smoked that cigarette. She taps her pocket, hears the reassuring *tock* of the cardboard packet. She'd like another, but she's restricting herself to one a day, and she has to take her moments when no one's around. Like somehow she is the child and they are the adults, a diminishing role reversal. Although, of course, she reminds herself, they are all adults now. Even Nancy, her *troubled middle one*, who is, in this moment, standing to one side of Alex with a string of paper lanterns draped around her neck. She'd appeared that morning wearing an orange dress, an emerald flower in her hair, and with her eyebrows painted on too dark. 'Full-on Frida Kahlo. Nice.' Alex had looked her up and down, as she'd spooned banana porridge into the baby's mouth. Nancy is gesticulating wildly at someone Vivienne can't see, overdoing it, and Vivienne feels a flicker of annoyance. This is the clash of them. She thinks sometimes they are too similar, other times worlds apart. Nancy, her little fuck-up. Her accident. The baby who had arrived *wham bam, thank you, ma'am* too soon into that newly vacated space – so that Vivienne had barely drawn breath between the shock of her two older daughters. And why can't the babies in this family time their arrivals more *conveniently*?

The wind drops a little and Vivienne seizes the opportunity to tug her skirt out from between her thighs. She should have worn trousers, she thinks, like Eva, who, she can see, is taking a moment – a bit of *me*-time – to do a slow roll-down while Patrick clicks his fingers trying to get Nancy's attention. Eva has her hair pulled into a ponytail, the same way she wore it through the whole of secondary school, and it's dangling upside down, like a tail. The fact is her youngest daughter would have shown up in Lululemon today if it had been up to her. She's taken to running ultra-marathons this past year – insanely, impressively, so that the muscles in her neck, her arms are like rope. There are hollows in her cheeks, too, that Vivienne acknowledges make her startling bone structure *pop*, even as it sets off all of Vivienne's mothering alarms.

Sometimes she can't believe these are her children, that these adult women, these women in their forties, have come from her. It seems a fantasy – a series of false memories – to imagine the long-ago stretched dome of her belly filled up with them. Those infants who clung to and hung from her body, and were surely entirely different people from the three women standing down there in the clearing. They are ageing, her children. Before her eyes, it seems. A kind of speeding up, these past few years, that makes her a little queasy. There's an inadvertent whisper of distaste sometimes when she looks at them now. A distaste that shames her and that she can only assume comes from her own sense of panic. Because if her children – her babies – have lines around their eyes and mouths and if their hair is changing texture, turning grey at the parting and above the ears when the dye grows out, where the hell does that leave her?

She moves nearer, not so close that they'll see her – it's

rare she gets a chance to observe them like this, free from the demands of near-constant conversation and minor domestic dramas that characterize their family get-togethers. She's thinking about the article she read a few years back in one of the Sunday supplements. The actual, physical paper that no one under the age of sixty-five seems to bother with these days, all of them too busy scrolling blank-eyed through their phones. The article about the four sisters, the White sisters, or maybe the Brown sisters. She isn't sure which, a colour anyhow. The sisters who had been photographed lined up in the exact same order once a year, every year, for four decades. *Forty* years, they kept it up. She'd been sitting in the back of the kitchen, sunk deep into the wonky armchair, reading the feature. The sun through the windows had lit up the page, sanctifying the sisters, who stared with frank faces into the lens as they turned shot by shot from young women to old. Patrick was at the stove cooking eggs for breakfast and she'd wanted to call to him, to show him the prints, but there was a swelling in her throat and she found she couldn't speak. She wanted to tell him that when the photographs were first shown in a gallery in Spain, visitors to the exhibition had stood and wept openly. Sitting there in the broken chair, looking and looking at the photographs, Vivienne had wanted to cry too. Loud, ugly tears. In the end, she'd given herself a headache from not crying.

The kids are getting restless and have moved off, away from the gazebo and the singing bowls and the champagne that's chilling in the cool box. Led by Scott, who is *performing* his role of Favourite Uncle, Vivienne sees, and tracked closely by Alex's husband Luc, who's holding the baby (*Dolly*, she reminds herself), they are trying to catch the swirling leaves, stuffing them down the fronts of their coats and into their pockets. Small figures in an autumn-shook snow globe. 'Fisher girls!' she hears Patrick call, an edge of exasperation in his voice. His trouser legs are flapping wildly, tugged into triangles, little flags in the wind. She watches Eva unfold from the waist, as Nancy turns with a grin, slinging an arm around Alex's shoulders. Then they tilt up their beautiful faces to look laughingly into their father's over-complicated lens. And suddenly the week she'll spend here with them seems impossibly short. How will she stand it when, seven days from now, this all comes to an end? How will she fill the too-big, too-quiet Dartmouth Park house when she and Patrick get home?

When she hears the sound, she thinks at first it's a gunshot. A series of gunshots. Her instinct is to duck her head, or drop to the ground because the echo is bouncing around the trees and she can't figure out where it's come from. She's scanning the space when the sound comes again and she sees sudden movement, a dark jolt, at the edge of her vision, down near the sheltered spot where her family are. Before she has time to react, there's a third crack – as if the forest floor is ripping open. Time stretches horribly, and she sees, above the heads of her children, a vast cedar pitching forwards. The three of them – *her three girls* – have their backs to the tree, and it must be the wind, or the scattered acoustics, or otherwise they're distracted by the kids, or the camera, or she doesn't know what, but why aren't they moving? '*NO!*' she screams, or maybe she doesn't, she can't be sure whether it's the sensation of her body, her flesh and muscle and bone, rearing up as the huge, dark trunk plunges through the air.

There's a moment, an absolute stillness, so that when she thinks about it afterwards, *later*, there's a strange clarity to the sequence of events. But here, now, her mind can't catch up with what her eyes are seeing, as Nancy turns her head at last to glance behind her, clocks the horrible inevitability of what is about to happen. In the same instant, Patrick lets the camera fall to his chest and lurches forward. And Vivienne is already imagining him throwing his body across his three daughters, or catching them in his arms to pull them to safety, but he doesn't do either of those things. Instead, he lunges for Eva, grabs her by the shoulders and wrenches her away, out of the path of the tree. Eva, who is standing furthest from where the tree is falling.

Then everything stops. It takes Vivienne a second – several seconds – to understand what has happened. She thinks at first that maybe she's seeing things, that her imagination has gone wild, but there's a whooping sound from below, and someone shouting, 'Fuck' – in a good way – shouting it loud and never mind the children, so that she knows she isn't making it up, it's not in her head, she has seen what she's seen. Beneath her, at the bottom of the slope, the fallen tree has lodged in the V of an oak, whose leaves look Midas-touched.

The ancient oak has stopped its fall no more than a foot above the heads of her children. It looks monstrous, wedged there, stripped-slick branches awkwardly angled, like outsized alien limbs.

Next thing, she's stumbling towards her family, bunching the fabric of her skirt up to her thighs so she can move faster, even though it goes through her mind that she's exposing her knickers under her see-through tights. She's cold, bloody cold, and it isn't anything to do with the fact she doesn't have a duck-down coat from Amazon. What has just happened? Nothing, she tells herself. *Nothing* happened. They are laughing down there already, her family. An unsteady, not-quite-convincing laughter. Standing back, necks craned and staring up at the rotten tree, the shock is printed in their expressions still. 'Woah!' she hears someone shout, one of the kids, and then Alex's voice, lifting shakily above the rest, 'Not too close, it might move again. No, further back. More. Ten steps back, you can see it just fine from there . . .'

Vivienne isn't looking where she's going and she trips on a root that's erupted through the bright smother of leaves. As she puts out a hand to save herself, the cigarettes in her pocket fall to the ground, but she doesn't stop to pick them up. The blare in her head is like radio interference, too many thoughts she can't quite grasp. Except for one clear message cutting through the noise that's repeating over and over. Something she doesn't want to know.

He chose Eva.

Nancy, Sunday morning

Nancy can't get across the car park and away from her family, from the toppled tree, fast enough. Eden, Alex's middle one, has fallen over and grazed his knee and he's screaming, even though he's seven years old now, or maybe six – she can't instantly remember her nephew's age (so sue her) – and it didn't look that bad, no blood, even, and can't he just shut the fuck up? Because now the baby's crying too and Alex has that look on her face, the pained, pinched-lemon look, like somehow this is everybody else's fault, not hers, and how is she supposed to deal with it because she's been up in the night with the *new baby* and had hours less sleep than everyone else. She's keeping a running tally of her sleeplessness, and she'll share the stats with whoever stands too close too long. Although it's *not a problem*, of course, and she's *totally fine with it.*

Nancy moves past the map of the forest with the 'You are here' sign, fires her key fob at the car. She is tempted – she's tempted but she won't – to start listing all the disorders and diseases associated with sleep loss next time Alex accosts her. To come at her sister with the full weight of her medical training. Cancer (of course) and heart disease and obesity and therefore Type 2 diabetes and blah and blah and blah. Because she herself is the world's worst sleeper and it's unavoidable, the amount of discussion on the subject. Jumping out from magazine articles and Twitter threads, TikTok memes and ten-foot-tall adverts in the bloody Tube, all informing her that her insomnia will get her in the end. If something else doesn't do her in first, it will kill her for sure – and that's the vicious circle of it, something to give anyone sleepless nights. She can feel a slight stabbing pain in her chest just thinking about it.

At the car she turns. It's just her family there, no one else, but they're clogging the space. A cacophony of family, her dad calls it. The thought of him is a jolt, and she glances across to where he's standing. Briefly, the scream of annoyance – of *anger* – in her flips to something else. To something like loneliness, or fear. The boot of the Volvo is up, and her dad has Alex's eight-year-old, Rosa, sitting on the edge, helping her off with her wellies as though nothing has happened. Has anything happened? She's had a glass of champagne and nothing to eat since breakfast, so maybe that's why she's feeling . . . How is she feeling? Slightly like the rug has been pulled out from underneath her, that's how. Except she hadn't understood there was a rug in the first place. Rather, she'd assumed something more fixed, like a fitted carpet, or maybe a parquet floor since they're back in fashion now or . . . She shakes her head, wills her mind to empty.

'I'll see you back at the house, okay?' she shouts over her shoulder, to everyone and no one, and she doesn't wait to see if anyone has heard.

As the car door clunks shut, she checks the back seat reflexively, although she knows Georgie's not there. Leon will drive her up later in the week – he gets her Friday through to Tuesday this half-term holiday, and he's not budging on it, stubbornly, stupidly, naming ceremony or not. She's accused him of using their ten-year-old child to punish her; he's accused her of being emotionally 'all over the fucking place'. The thing he knows will pierce her most. Nancy pulls her phone from her bag, remembering the whispered, spat-out conversation in the dark hallway of his new mansion block in Maida Vale. She'll call Georgie on the way back, tell her about the bunting that blew away, the tree that fell; she'll make a dramatic joke of it, regale her with how cold and miserable and *dangerous* it all was, make her daughter laugh, explain she had a lucky escape not coming. That they're saving the best bits for when she gets here.

She's about to dial the number, when the phone vibrates in her hand and Nik's number comes up. Like a gift from the gods, pretty much the only other person in the world she's happy to talk to right now.

'Hold on.' She punches the screen, drops the phone onto the passenger seat. 'I've put you on speaker.'

'Is it a bad time?' Nik's voice flares and dips.

'Nope, you've got me blissfully alone. Just be glad there's signal. I'm in the land that time forgot.' The windscreen is steaming up and Nancy leans forward in her seat, swipes at the condensation with the sleeve of her coat. She can see Eva loading the cool box into the Volvo, nodding at something her dad is saying. She feels again the thing in her that is somehow both weighted and hollow.

'Listen, I know you're on holiday,' Nik's saying, 'but I didn't get a chance to see you before you left on Friday, and I wanted to talk to you abou–'

'This isn't a holiday.' She cuts him off. 'It's an endurance test. Already. And we've only been here five minutes. Fucking families!'

He laughs. 'It's going well, then? A dreamy sunshine break?'

She's watching her dad and Eva still, deep in conversation by the car. Eva's doing a calf stretch while they talk, bouncing her leg a little like she's at the starting line of a race. Nancy has a sudden urge to confide in Nik, to tell him what happened in the woods just now, even though this isn't the kind of thing they share, but she realizes a part of her is ashamed to say it. She wants and also doesn't want to tell him; she doesn't want to think about it, but she can't seem to stop. A nasty little tripwire in her mind.

Nik is saying something about a trip to Disneyland in the eighties, but she can't concentrate, because words are packing her mouth. If she checked her face in the mirror she'd see her cheeks all puffed up with everything she's keeping in.

'There was the weirdest thing earlier,' she blurts. 'Like, seriously weird.' As she fits her seatbelt, she starts to tell him in a breathless, piecemeal way, like she's attempting to describe a dream, about the fallen tree, 'Ridiculously huge, I mean, *massive*, it could have killed someone', about where she and her sisters were standing, how her dad had grabbed hold of Eva 'and it doesn't make sense, because she was further away and . . .' Nancy lets the sentence deflate and die. 'Much like I'm barely making sense now, I do realize that.'

She's changed her mind: she doesn't want to go there after all. They've been colleagues for years, she and Nik, although they've always worked in different departments. He's a radiographer, she's a consultant radiologist – she's the nerd with the brainier job, as he likes to tell her. So there's crossover, and from time to time he comes into the breast clinic where she works. But it's only recently – since she moved one stop away from him on the Jubilee line, after her split from Leon – that they've become friends. And maybe because they work together, maybe because he's a man (which means she cares less about what he thinks of her), it's such a straightforward relationship. There are no female-friendship demands – no need for expensive spa weekends away, or anything requiring complicated emotions. It's so easy; she wants to keep it that way. She forces a laugh. 'So, yeah, long and short, I feel like I'm in *King* bloody *Lear*. Deal with it!'

'Are you making this up?' Nik asks.

'Oh okay, wow.' Nancy starts the engine, fiddles with the heating, bangs the vent with her fist when it doesn't kick in immediately.

'*King Bloody Lear* . . .' Nik says, as though it's the title of the play. 'Interesting. So which sister does that make you?'

'Well, not Cordelia, obviously, LOL. Who are the others? Gonorrhoea?'

'Yup, so that's an STI.'

'Exactly.'

In the rear-view mirror, she watches her family shrink and disappear as she drives out of the car park.

'It's no joke.' His voice is distorting a little on the line. 'Intimate infections are making a comeback.' He says the word 'intimate' as if it tastes bad.

'Ugh, Nikhil, stop.'

'I'm serious. Did you see the article in the *Standard* about multi-antibiotic resistant strains, London loo seats, all that? You should be across this stuff, Dr Fish– Shit! Hold on.'

Over the speakerphone, she hears an alarm going off. There's a sound like Nik's dropped the phone, the alarm stops, and when he says her name she can tell he's distracted. 'Okay, I'm out of here, *clients* to deal with.'

'Wait.' Nancy steers the car around a bend. She wants to keep him on the line. He feels like an island of sanity against the chaos of her family, but she won't say, 'What was it you wanted to talk to me about?' This she already knows – she's pretty sure she knows. Another thing she'd rather keep pushed from her mind. She imagines a small door in her brain, black and stamped with white words that read 'Keep Out'.

'How did your hot Hinge date go?' she says hurriedly. 'Just quickly. Snog? Marry? Avoid?'

'Yeah, well, she spent most of the night talking about her ex so . . .'

'Ah, okay.' Nancy is so far away from even the thought of dating, can't begin to imagine putting herself out there again, like Eva had done. Too many horror stories. And she's raw still, from everything with Leon. It's enough managing him at arm's length, and then there's Georgie. She presses her foot down on the accelerator. 'Well, tomorrow's another date, as no one says.'

'Yup, and I. Am. Pumped.' His voice is doubling on the line now, a ghost echo that's overlaying his words. 'Uh-huh, on my way,' he tells someone. 'Oh, and Nancy, just so you know, I'd save you, not your sisters.' She can hear him grinning as he says it.

'Aw, too sweet, but you've never met my sist–' In her ear, a series of beeps. Then the call cuts out: she's lost signal.

She's taken a wrong turn, several wrong turns, because she can't work the satnav and the roads around this place are like something out of *The Lord of the Rings*. She's three hundred miles from home, but feels, right now, like she's stumbled into a parallel universe. So that when she finally spots the sign to the holiday house, discreetly lodged in a hedge, it's almost by accident – and she brakes so violently she's millimetres from knocking out her teeth on the steering wheel. Her eyes flick instinctively to the rear-view mirror; she knows if there'd been anyone behind her they'd have ploughed into the back of the car.

Shaken, she pulls onto the long track that leads up to the house. The car rocks side to side a little where there are grassy bumps between the ingrained tyre marks, skidding occasionally in the mud. She's taking it slowly but, even so, there's a moment when she loses control of the steering and nearly hits the notice at the side of the track, warning people to watch out for endangered natterjack toads. True, she'd maybe taken her eyes off the road for longer than she should have, because the view of the house from here is astonishing. If she could inhale it, she would.

The building is made of glass, pretty much in its entirety, except for a boxed-off wooden section at one end, housing a sauna and a saltwater swimming-pool. A rectangular block of a place that's up on stone stilts so that, from a distance, it seems to have been carved into the foot of the mountain behind it. The house has featured on an episode of *Grand Designs*, which has caused an excessive degree of excitement in the family. Nancy hasn't watched it, but Alex has filled her in on the build, which was apparently started by newlyweds, finished by the newly divorced wife alone. Eva has paid for all of this – the week-long stay at the house. For seven days it'll be theirs, Eva's treat. Her present to the baby, and also to their mum, whose seventieth they'll be celebrating at the end of the week. Eva has so much money now – an insane amount – that Nancy is almost at the point where she no longer feels uncomfortable about these handouts. Almost.

Steering into the designated parking spot, she kills the engine. It's screened off from the house, but the wooden slats are angled so that, from this side, the building is visible through the gaps. There's only one other car here – her parents are back before her, and she can see them now through the glass wall, standing in the main room. It's like watching a mime show and it's obvious they're arguing. Nancy releases her seatbelt, but stays where she is. She can't take her eyes from her parents. It isn't like them to do this – to argue. Her mind jumps to the naming ceremony, to the hurricane forest, the fallen tree. Are they arguing about what happened – or, rather, what didn't happen – back there? She checks the handbrake compulsively, as if the car might be about to roll away. Another memory is tugging at her. Flashes of something that's more colour and noise and smell than anything concrete, as if she might have made it up. The sense that she's been in a moment like this before.

Nancy feels suddenly claustrophobic. This is a see-through house with no escape. It hits her that the week she's about to spend here with her family – the week she's stupidly looked forward to – is going to be interminable. Instinctively, she reaches down to the glove compartment, fishes about for her cigarettes. She's smoking menthol so that no one will know, and also so that she can pretend to herself that somehow they aren't harmful, a kind of *toy* cigarette that won't give her . . . well, that won't give her pretty much all the same diseases as her insomnia. As she grasps the packet, an envelope falls into the footwell. It's the letter from the hospital that she hasn't opened, brown with a little transparent window that shows her name, her address. Stuffing it back into the glove compartment, she tries to push it shut, but she's doing everything too fast and her hands won't work properly, and she has to try and try again, before the catch finally takes.

Alex, Autumn 1975

Alex is on her own. She's pretending she's at the circus. Like in the book with the lion and the man with the funny red coat, the tall hat and twizzly moustache. And like the circus where her mummy found her daddy, and they went on a horse with feathers. There are tents all around her, so that she can't see out, and she's walking with no shoes on. Her mummy and daddy were shouting in the car, a lot. Then Nancy was sick, and the smell made her want to be sick too. The grass here is brown and crunchy under her feet. It sounds like Rice Krispies when she steps on it, and she likes the way it feels.

She stops at the circle of stones. They are fat and grey, like the ones they use for making stone babies at Granny's house by the beach. Granny has a long packet of a hundred pens that she calls fel*t* *t*ips. She says the *t*s like she's the Queen. They draw eyes and noses and mouths for the stone babies, and colour in their blankets. Remembering the piece of pink blanket she's left in the car, Alex puts her thumb into her mouth. She can smell a hot smell. She thinks maybe the circle is something magic; she has a book about that too. About a wizard who has lost his wand. Nancy loves the wizard book. She pretends she can read it and gets the words all wrong, and it's so funny and it makes them laugh, their daddy too. The stone circle is full of dirty sand. A bit like the sandpit at the park that has twigs and pebbles and earth in it. She's thinking it would feel nice to wiggle her toes in there – and that's when she sees the shiny orange treasure. It's small, like a pea or a button, and it's how she knows it's something important. That she must rescue it.

'Abracadabra, alakazam.' She chants the wizard's spell, the words squashy around her thumb in her mouth, as she hops over the stone-baby stones. And she takes a step, two, towards the treasure, before her feet start to feel wrong. The same kind of wrong as when she fell out of the blue-and-white police car at playgroup and cut her knees. The hurting is getting worse, but it's like she's stuck in glue and can't move, and someone is shouting her name, but it isn't as loud as the noise of her feet in her ears. She thinks that just outside the circle she can see a red monster with horrible eyes, and her face is wet and she feels sick. There's a sudden hard pinching under her arms, a smell of milk and biscuits. Then she's flying up through the air, with her feet screaming and screaming and not stopping, like Nancy when her tummy hurts at night.

Eva, Sunday noon

It's better than sex. Eva honestly believes this. Maybe it's just the quality of the sex she's having (Scott likes to talk tantric, although when it comes down to it, he doesn't have the patience), maybe she's missing something. But she can't see how anything can touch the rhythmic thud thud thud of mind and body out here – even against the head-on wind that's making it hard work. But she likes that, she'll take it. *I'm going to run back to the house*, she'd told Scott, after she'd taken her trainers from the car, put them on while everyone else was looking the other way. Presented it as a fait accompli. *A quick ten K, I'll race you.* She isn't wearing the right clothes – looks, in her red satin jumpsuit, as though she's a woman running away from a wedding, or an attacker – but, relatively speaking, this is easy for her, it's nothing, especially now she's past the 'toxic ten' and her limbs, her lungs are doing it themselves: it's just her body out here and her GPS watch. And she isn't taking the roads, as she'd promised she would. She needs the forest, the trees, autumn's kaleidoscope escape. She needs not to think about what's just happened.

Lucy has gone back in the car with Alex and the kids, squeezed into the boot, and with Rosa and Eden twisted around in their seats, all the better for them to worship her, their sixteen-year-old cousin, the oldest of all the cousins, a teenage deity. Nancy was out of the car park so fast there was no chance of Lucy jumping in with her, and she wouldn't have wanted to go alone with Scott. It's tough on her daughter, she understands that. She and Scott have been together eighteen months now – since Lucy was fifteen – and there are boundaries, opaque unwritten rules that Eva must navigate, even as she doesn't want to dwell on it, would really rather not think about it at all. Especially since Scott moved in with the two of them to the Belsize Park house. She knows her child's privacy has been compromised – it's been the two of them for as long as her daughter can remember. It makes no odds that there are more bathrooms in the house than people to use them, a couple each, in fact, and a games room and home cinema in the basement that's basically Lucy's space.

If Scott noticed the snub, he didn't show it. Eyes on Eva's, he pushed his hand into the pocket of her jump-suit and extracted the keys. Took her car, although he's not insured to drive it. She isn't a hundred per cent certain he has a driving licence, come to that; she can't imagine him taking ten lessons with obtrusive L plates and someone else able to override him on the dual control. But he's a good driver: it's one of the things he does well. An iconic parker, he can slide the Tesla into the tightest London spot, like he's moulding the metal to fit the space – it's a spatial-awareness thing, she thinks. And this she does find sexy – his hands on the wheel, the deft competence of his movements, the eighties

Athena-poster vibe of it all – although a part of her dies inside each time this thought-she's-not-supposed-to-think snares her.

They don't like him, she knows this. Her family. Her sisters, at least. They preferred Carlos, although she and he were basically kids when they met, had Lucy, and he's been out of the picture for years now. They think she doesn't know but she does. *Why can't he put some fucking shoes on?* she'd overheard Nancy say the night before, as Scott had headed out into the dark after dinner, to look for endangered bullfrogs or toads or something. *And those ludicrous strap-on toe gloves don't count. Who does he think he is? Wim bloody Hof?* They have no idea she'd heard because she'd been off in the high-shine walnut and marble kitchen, making a jug of mint tea. But sound carries in the glass house.

The wind has blown itself out. In its place there's a ringing in her ears, like tinnitus, and she's alert still, wary, after what happened with the tree back there. One eye on the ground, because there are hidden dips and roots concealed like family secrets, the other on the forest. She can't afford a stumble. If she's honest her ankles are still feeling weird from the last race – that's a month ago now – when they'd swelled, like balloons, at the ninetieth mile. Not just that, but there's a fatigue in her, something she can't shake off. She's going to wind it back a bit, do a fifty K next, let her body recover, build up to the next hundred. And she can double up on the whey protein shake tomorrow morning, accelerate the healing, build up her lean muscle mass. She's brought enough shakes for the week, with a couple extra, and surely there must be a useful shop around here somewhere. They're selling them in Argos now.

Each time her feet strike the forest floor, she feels the after-echo of it in her body. As though someone else is out here, running a step behind her. Glancing over her shoulder, she sees there's no one. Of course there isn't: she's in the middle of nowhere. It's just her and the trees in their secret summits and the mulchy-damp smell, but still she's fighting the urge to increase her pace. At the runners' club, she's the only one who isn't running away from something. She hadn't realized at first, but gradually, gradually over the weeks of training, the stories came out. Michael, who's married, is having an affair, and so is Kate, who's also married. Sometimes Eva suspects they're having an affair with one another, but it could be they just spend a lot of time swapping notes. Paulo, a management consultant for a big accountancy firm, despises his job and is battling a deep-rooted anxiety he keeps from his husband; Joanne has alopecia; Balbinder lives with her in-laws; softly spoken Mark has served time for embezzlement, a nice, cosy white-collar crime, thank goodness, nothing violent or rapey. Theresa promised her son before he died that she'd run the ultramarathon for him. *I'm one hundred per cent aware I'm running from the grief*, she's told Eva, on more than one occasion. *What are you escaping from, Eva, lovely?*

A hundred miles, ten times around a ten-mile track, it does something to your mind. Shuts it down and opens it up all at once. Eva still isn't entirely sure she didn't

27

hallucinate the family of four she came across geo-caching in Hertfordshire at two in the morning as she crested the seventh hill on the seventh circuit. Or the white owl that flew just ahead of her at dusk, guiding the way for the best part of a mile. She shrugs when the other runners ask her, because she doesn't know how to tell them that there's nothing she's bolting from. She's happy. They don't know, because she's found it some-times easier that way, that she designed a board game at her kitchen table when Lucy was seven, a neat little dice game, Unfortune8!, how sales built and built and went through the roof, how she sold the company two years ago for a small fortune. A pretty large fortune, actually. How, yes, okay, it hadn't all been plain sailing: she had a 'surprise' baby – Lucy – at twenty-four (basic-ally a teen pregnancy in her family's lexicon), but that's ancient history, and the best thing that ever happened to her, obviously, and now she has Scott and her family, her house, *two* houses, holidays to Mustique, expensive laser treatment so she never needs to shave anything ever again . . . and maybe she's a little bored some days, but she's doing okay. More than okay. She just likes running. It's filled a gap where her work – her business – had been and she likes it a lot. She likes what it does to her mind, her body, which is *ripped* for someone who's forty, thank you very much.

A fly hits the back of her throat, sucked in through the vortex of her open mouth. Without breaking her stride Eva gags, hacks up some phlegm and spits on the ground, but it's too late, she's swallowed it. *All good protein*, she thinks, as she spits again, trying to clear the bitter residue that's caught in her tonsils. It's what her dad would say. *Brain food, sunshine!* His voice is in her head and the thought that's been scratching at her all this time, the thought she's been avoiding, pounces.

It was over so fast, she barely had time to register. He'd had his camera up to his face, looking through the viewfinder at the three of them and . . . Eva's GPS watch beeps. Her heart rate is up, and this means that, shit, she's out of the HR zone she's shooting for, which will skew her training stats when she checks them at the end of the run. Trying to refocus, she channels her thoughts behind her third eye. But she can't shake the images playing through her mind: the falling tree, her sisters, her dad . . . He'd had his camera up to his face, looking through the viewfinder at the three of them and – There'd been the sound like a gut punch, then he'd dropped the camera, or he'd dropped the camera and then the sound, she can't honestly remember which. She can only recall his hands tight on her shoulders, the weight of Alex's arm slipping from her. The grip of cold wind at her neck. And after that he'd – What? What had he done?

Alex, Winter 1980

Alex is bored and that's why she's in here, in her mum and dad's bedroom, going through their things. The others are downstairs playing Bird Lotto – they've only just started and she can hear the hum of their voices in the lounge, so she knows she won't be caught. Already she's taken everything out of her mum's jewellery box, tried on the long black beads and the green glass brooch, clipped the ruby earrings to her ears. *They're not real rubies, sweetie*, her mum has told her, *just costume*. But she likes to imagine anyway. The same way she likes to imagine she's eighteen years old, not eight and a half. The earrings are pinching as she pulls open the top drawer on her dad's side of the bed. It's full of pants and soft-scrunched hankies that are grey, not the white they're supposed to be, and she makes a face, shuts the drawer and opens the next one down. A smell wafts out that makes her think of boring museums, and inside there are coins and pens and old receipts. A tube of something half squeezed, yellow and crusty around the lid where it's oozed out. Prodding the tube with a finger, as if it's something dead, Alex reads the words on the side: K-Y Jelly.

The green leather book is at the back of the drawer. It's small and fat, with *Five Year Diary* written fancily in gold along the spine. She's never seen it before and she takes it out, settles on the edge of the bed. A photograph of her parents is wedged in, like a bookmark. They're squashed into a photo booth, looking at each other and laughing. It's them, but they're younger – different – and they seem to Alex like glamorous actors, like other people pretending to be her mum and dad. Her mum's fair hair is parted in the centre and splayed out over her shoulders, and she has a patterned scarf tied around her neck. There's the gap between her two front teeth. Her dad's hair is dark and wavy, down past his chin. His eyebrows are furry and almost meet in the middle. He has his arm around her mum and – she hadn't noticed this at first – his hand on her mum's boob, and he's squeezing. Alex half wants to giggle, but something else too. She feels uncomfortable, like she isn't meant to be seeing this and, anyway, doesn't want to. Like when her mum and dad kiss for too long in the kitchen. She flips the photo so it's face down, pushes it back into the diary.

The pages are thin, a bit like the pages in the Bibles at school, and there's her dad's writing on some of the days, but also a lot of blanks. As she flicks through, she's thinking how much she likes his writing: it's upright and neat and looks almost like it's been done on a typewriter. She wants to write the way he does when she's grown-up.

. . . *tennis with 'McEnroe Mark' today at Waterlow, and he does NOT like to lose . . .*

. . . *Power cut this evening. Candles + cheese + wine in the lounge and now no TV to watch so . . .*

. . . *Come in, number three! Eva Rose born today, 2 weeks early, caught us by surprise. Both still at the Royal Free, doing well . . .*

Alex opens the diary wide, smooths the page. This is what her dad wrote the day Eva was born! Four years ago now. It feels a bit magical reading it, as though she's travelled back in time. She remembers Eva coming home, the funny little knitted hat she wore. Or she remembers the photos, at least: she and Nancy meeting their baby sister for the first time, huddled in very close on the corduroy sofa.

Following the words with her finger, she reads on.

. . . *tiny, and with these huge heartbreaking eyes. A perfect little triangle mouth. She's the MOST beautiful one so far. She weighs*

And here the entry stops. As though her dad had been interrupted, called away in the middle of writing the sentence. Alex feels funny inside. The same feeling she has when she gets told off for doing something wrong. She pictures her family down in the lounge, picking cards out of a bag, matching them with the birds on their boards. She knows Eva will have chosen the board with the Lilac-breasted Roller and the Splendid Fairywren. It's her favourite and no one else ever gets to use it. *The most beautiful one so far*, Alex reads again, and she flicks her eyes upwards, studies herself in the mirrored wardrobe opposite. Her cheeks are red, like she's got an 'angry rash', as her mum would say, and she needs to brush her hair: it's in plaits that she slept in. She moves her head so she's looking at herself sideways on. Her nose seems massive like this, too big for her face and with a weird bump on the end and – There's a tread on the stairs and Alex slams shut the diary, stuffs it into the drawer, eases it closed so it won't make a sound. Then she flings herself back onto the bed, star-shaped and staring at the ceiling, as if she's just resting there. Her face is hot and guilty, her chest throbbing in a way that makes her think of the advert for Operation she's seen on TV. The electronic game with the heart that flashes and buzzes when you poke it in the wrong place, and that she's going to ask for this Christmas.

Alex, Sunday afternoon

Alex walks down the wide, light corridor, past the abstract paintings that could have been executed by any one of her children, and into Nancy's room without knocking. She's holding the baby facing outwards, joggling her, because she didn't fall asleep in the car on the way back from the naming ceremony, like they'd hoped she would, and now she's missed her morning nap and is starting to get fussy.

'Are Mum and Dad okay?' she asks, the moment she's through the door. 'There's a really bizarre atmosphere in the kitchen right now, and . . .' She clocks her sister on the far side of the room, behind the glass panel that separates bedroom from bathroom. There's a square wooden bath, a vast double basin that looks as if it's been chiselled from the mountain behind the house, and Nancy standing in front of a gold-edged mirror. Her orange dress is hoicked up around her neck and she's prodding one of her breasts.

'Ew, Nance, really?'

'Maybe knock next time.' Her sister lets the dress fall. 'Just a thought.'

Alex moves further into the room, navigates her way around the circular ottoman that's strewn with discarded clothes. 'What are you doing? Why are you checking your boobs? Like, now? Lunch is ready.'

An occupational hazard, Nancy has called it in the past. Joking, not joking. Eight, nine, ten hours a day seeing patients, women with cancer. *My perspective is shot*, she'd told Alex once, and who could blame her? Alex would never have the strength to do Nancy's job. She's in awe of what her sister does, insanely proud. She loves to drop it into conversations with friends, acquaintances, *anyone*, the fact that her middle sister is a doctor – a hospital consultant. She's forever texting her with photos of the kids' various rashes, their swollen tonsils, and once a close-up of a definitely-wasn't-there-before spot on her own vagina.

'Because they're knock-out, Alex. Not *checking* them, checking them *out*.' Nancy's looking in the mirror still when she says this, not at Alex, taking her time to adjust the dress. Taking too long over it. Alex registers the thought just as the baby lets out a colicky moan and straightens stiffly, suddenly, in her arms.

'Christ, Dolly!' She grips her daughter. 'I nearly dropped you.'

'They've had an argument.' Nancy comes through into the bedroom, takes a crumpled towel from the end of her bed, hangs it over a chair. 'Mum and Dad. I saw them through the glass from the carport.'

'What do you mean?' Alex puts the baby over her shoulder, starts to sway from side to side. 'They never argue.'

Her sister shrugs. 'I'm guessing because of the whole *fun* tree thing?' She says the word 'fun' like she's a kids' TV presenter.

35

Alex sees it happen again, the tree falling. It's been falling and falling on a loop in her mind since that morning. 'Oh, my God, I'm not kidding, Nance,' she says. 'I think I have PTSD. I'm really fucking jumpy. Rosa tapped me on the back just now and I nearly had a panic attack.'

'If a tree falls in the forest and no one's there to see it . . .' Nancy starts to say. 'No, wait. If a tree *doesn't* fall in the forest and you *are* there . . .' She stops, holds up a finger, tries again. 'If a tree *almost* falls in the forest, and your dad *chooses* to save your sister, not you, are you destined to spend the rest of your life in therapy?'

'Yeah, ha-ha, Nance. That's not what happened.'

'Do you think it's because she's the pretty one?' Nancy takes a tub of moisturizer from the bedside table, unscrews the lid.

'What – who?'

Nancy gives her a look, like, *Really?*

'It's a thing, you know.' Nancy smears two stripes of white across her cheeks, starts to rub them in. 'The pretty ones are the favourites. I read it in the *New York Times*. Or maybe *Take A Break.*' She clicks her tongue, and, as if she's been given a sign, the baby bangs her head against Alex's shoulder and starts to grizzle. 'Yes, that's right.' Nancy directs her words to her niece. 'Auntie Eva's Cinderella, and me and your mummy are the ugly step-sisters.'

'Oh, please.' Alex laughs. But it comes out a little too enthusiastic, like canned laughter.

She's the most beautiful one so far.

The sentence ambushes her. As if her brain has sifted

through the hard drive of her cerebral cortex in less than a second and produced it. She can even see her dad's neat, printed handwriting on the fragile diary page. Something she's thought about less than a handful of times in – what? Thirty years? Forty? Stumbled over it, shrugged it off, moved on. But all these years later, she still remembers how it felt. The same caved-in feeling as when she found the porn mag in his wardrobe a couple of years after that. Stuffed in a dark, musty corner at the back, behind a pair of old golfing shoes he never wore. She might as well have found a gun.

But it was the eighties, for goodness' sake, a million years ago. Pre-enlightenment. Benny Hill was prime-time Saturday-night viewing back then. People just said stuff, did stuff. They didn't overthink it. She's done it herself, made those private, knee-jerk remarks in exasperation, or as a small act of parental rebellion, or without really thinking. Without meaning it. 'Rosa's so much more confident than Eden' or 'Fuck's sake, Eden's so bloody selfish' or 'Argh, Rosa can be so goddamn greedy.' The kind of thing you're definitely not supposed to say. The kind of thing your kids overhear, then wind up damaged and in therapy twenty years down the line. The single thing they're clinging to, tripping on, over and over, disregarding an entire childhood of mothering devotion. And she isn't trying to excuse what her dad wrote, but she knows how it feels to be in the haze of a new baby. The magic of it. Or the abject exhaustion that means you're living your life like an out-of-body experience. That you do and say stupid things. Especially if . . . she thinks now . . . especially if you weren't sure you wanted the baby in the first place. Especially if she wasn't planned. Especially if, aged forty-five, and with a six-year gap between your middle and youngest child, you are way too old and tired to be starting all over again . . . Just look at Dolly, dangerously wild-eyed and dribbling and getting more fretful by the second. If this had been Eden or Rosa, one of them would have been wheel-ing the buggy out into the wilderness right now, grimly determined to get the baby to sleep, whatever it took.

As if she's read Alex's thoughts, Dolly starts to cry.

'Aw, Betty. *Bett-yyyy.*' Nancy gives Alex a slow wink as she comes towards them, strokes her niece's head where the cradle cap is showing through.

'Yeah, super-funny,' Alex says, and she shushes the baby, fixes her eyes on her sister. 'Just ignore shitbag Auntie Nancy, *Dolly*. She's got a lot of issues.'

'Still can't believe Mum did that.' Nancy shakes her head. 'I mean it was funny but also . . .' She winds her finger next to her temple. 'Is Granny getting demen-tia, Betty?' She coos the words, and kisses Dolly's face, makes her cry harder.

Alex wants to say, For God's sake, Nancy. But she swallows it. A small voice in her head: *Is* Mum getting dementia? Because, Christ, does she repeat herself these days? She's seventy at the end of the week, more and more distracted, like there's an absence sometimes, even when she's right there with you, and now this argument that doesn't fit the mould of her parents. But it's all just getting old, isn't it? It's normal. How would they know if it wasn't normal . . . ? She raises her voice above the crescendo of crying: 'I can barely remember my own kids' names most days. Constantly mixing them up.' She shushes the baby again. 'Right!' she says, like she's dusting off her hands. 'Time for lunch, and don't leave me out there dealing with the very weird atmosphere, please.'

Her sister pistols two fingers and salutes, then slides her fingers down her face, makes a V on her cheek so that she's swearing at Alex, the way they used to when they were kids.

'Nice.' Alex is almost shouting now, above the wails. 'Slick, Nance.' Then she repositions the baby, so she's lying tummy-down on her forearm. 'Now, where the fuck is your daddy?' she asks, in a singsong voice that's drowned by screams.

As she leaves the room, it's as if someone has taken a drill to her forehead, and there's the familiar dread in her, like how will she get through the day ahead? She's bracing herself for wall-to-wall whinging because it's not just the baby: Eden is overtired and over-stimulated too. So is she, and this, she knows, is not a good combination. And she's wondering whether she'll be able to slip out later, just to check in. There's no signal in the house, so she has the perfect excuse. She was going to go cold turkey while she was here, that was the plan, but her resolve is wavering. Correction: her resolve has *wavered*. A day and a half, that was all it took. Already she knows she won't keep her promise to herself.

Nancy, Sunday afternoon

They're meant to be headed to the beach to catch the last couple of hours of daylight. But while the others are running around getting increasingly antsy, finding coats and boots, filling bottles of water, and telling the kids on repeat to go to the toilet *because it's a half-hour drive*, Nancy has found some signal in the glass house. She's walked the length of the saltwater pool, and now, sweating in her coat from the damp heat, she's pressed up against the tall arched window at the far end of the building. There's a single bar on her screen – a little black rectangle of hope – and it feels miraculous, a digital gold rush, as her phone bleeps and fills with messages. And then, almost instantly, it oppresses her.

She filters them quickly, doesn't click on the ones that'll give her away, with two blue ticks, if she reads the whole thing. Ignore, ignore, ignore . . . Wait . . . Nik has sent her a gif. A bronzed, retro hunk, flexing and re-flexing his gleaming muscles, with 'You Got This!' stamped in pink lettering across his very tight trunks.

Nancy rolls her eyes. Starts to type a reply.

Yeah, not really. Please help me. I want to kill my family la la la . . .

Then she fills three lines with the scream-face emoji. When there's no response, she glances round, keeping her phone up high so that it's still in range. The pool room smells Scandinavian. Or how she imagines Scandinavia would smell. It's all the wood and water and a mineral scent, as though the outdoors – the forest – has been brought inside. Loungers sculpted like the female form, like they are all boobs-and-booty and long, long legs, are lined up along one side of the room. Outsize glazed pots, sprouting lush, glossy plants that look too healthy to be real, flank them. The pool itself is beautiful. The colour of jade and spilling at its edges, Nancy would like to jump into it right now, sink to the bottom and let the slow silence soothe her.

Lunch nearly finished her off. A strange please-pass-the-salt formality, combined with an unconvincing jollity (Alex, her dad), and the usual tone-deaf monologue about she can't remember what from Scott, and Absolutely No Mention of the morning's bizarre brush with death-and-the-rest-of-it. So that she spent the whole time fighting the feeling that she might, at any second, launch her plate across the room. Just to get a reaction.

Holding the phone up like this, her arm is beginning to ache. She's about to click back to the lock screen, to give up on Nik, when text appears beneath his name.

Typing . . .

Next to his name is the picture of him with a little girl, who she knows is his niece. The little girl is wearing football kit and has a medal around her neck, and both of them are laughing. Nancy stretches her arm up a little higher, waves the phone around so she won't lose him.

Maybe spare the children?

She grins, starts to type.

>I'd almost rather be at work

Typing . . .
Would you, though?

>Yes

Typing . . .
This will cheer you up

>What?

Typing . . .
I saw a dog on roller-skates on the tube this morning

>Noooo

Typing . . .
Tiny roller skates

>Noooooooooo

Typing . . .
You're welcome

Typing . . .
I mean, cruel, but also very much a *moment*

>Is this true, Nik?

Typing . . .
. . .

>Is it?

Typing . . .

Do you want it to be true?

Yup obvs

Typing . . .
Then it is

'Nancy, we're leaving!' Her mum's voice loops into the room.

Nancy glances round, but she's the only one in there, even though her mum sounded close by. She might be in the TV lounge that's next to the pool room, or out in the lobby at the other end of the building, Nancy can't tell. It's impossible to locate sound because of the strange acoustics in this place. On her phone, she selects the goggle-eyed emoji, presses send.

'Are you coming in our car? Nancy?'

Catching sight of her reflection in the window, Nancy goggles her own eyes. She knows she should answer, but something – annoyance, a childish impulse – stops her. How is it that her parents manage to make her feel this way, act this way? She's forty-four, for God's sake. She looks it too, she thinks, scrutinizing her face in the glass. Even though she's made an effort today: she re-applied her red lipstick after lunch, clipped up her dark hair in loose sections. But now she sees that she is garish – clownish even – not stylish, not the way she looks in her head. Fighting the urge to start tweaking and fixing, she stares through the window, through the ghost of herself, to the mountain beyond. It's a picture-book mountain, triangular and symmetrical, fading from grey to brown to luminous mossy green, as though it's been dip-dyed in sections. It even has a bright blast of snow on top. And she's just thinking maybe she'll say a small prayer, try to siphon off some of its strength and majesty and zen – so that she starts behaving less like a toddler, more like a grown-up – when a hand grips the back of her neck.

Nancy jerks forward, banging her head against the glass.

'Woah!' It's her dad's voice behind her and, as she turns, he's stepping back.

'Jesus Christ, Dad!' She has her hand up to her brow bone, which is starting to pulse. 'You scared the shit out of me. *Literally*, a jump scare. Why would you do that?'

But even as she says it, she's remembering. He hasn't done it for years, but it's the thing he used to do when they were small – it was his *thing*. The scruff-of-the-neck grab that used to make all three of them giggle and squirm. And later made her feel singled out, secure – even as she'd shrugged him off, protesting. Now she just feels awkward, uncomfortable, furious. She feels as if he has violated her.

'I just saw you in here and . . .'

He's changed his clothes and is wearing the strange knitted waistcoat he bought in Bavaria – the one her mum describes as 'very Art Garfunkel' but makes him look like a sex pest. She and Eva laughed helplessly about it behind his back when they first saw it, while Alex admonished them. Although she too, when they couldn't stop, was unable to stifle a smile in the end. Nancy can see he's overheating in it. Shiny sweat is standing out on his scalp where his hair's receded either side of a fuzzy island. His eyebrows – correction, his

44

eye*brow* – is thick and white and wiry. He's getting old, she realizes. *Old* old. How hasn't she noticed this before?

'And what?' She's got that rinsed out, bloodless feeling that comes after a shock; she'd like to sit down. 'You thought you'd give me a heart attack?'

Her dad laughs. His expression is that of a too-cheerful quiz-show host, and he doesn't quite make eye contact as he reaches out, puts a hand on her shoulder. 'Did you not hear Mum calling?'

She wants to tell him to get off; she doesn't want him near her. He's got the camera round his neck still, like it's welded to his skin, like he thinks he's Ansel bloody Adams or someone. Cartier-frickin'-Bresson! And it feels an affront to her that he's still wearing it, his pensioner trophy. *That's not what happened* . . . Alex's voice is in her head, and she's back there, posing for the shot with her sisters in the forest. The image is blurred at the edges, mixed with memories she's trying to make sense of, and the insane thing is she wants to believe it. She wants to believe that it's *not what happened*. She wants and also doesn't want Alex to be right, and her mind is twisted up with the clouded confusion, the conflict and contradiction of it. And then she does it – and it occurs to her that maybe, deep down, she's trying to force the issue: she shrugs him off with a jerk of her shoulder.

His quiz-show smile falters briefly. 'Nancy, I . . .'

She waits, uneasy.

But then he lets his hand drop, signals vaguely towards the door.

'I was just on my way,' she murmurs.

Alex, Summer 1981

Alex knows she's in the bathroom at Helen and Katy down-the-road's house, but it feels like she's in the middle of a nightmare. Helen and Katy's dad, Adrian, is usually working in his study – doing something important with maps – or else drinking wine in the kitchen with her mum and dad, but here he is with his arm clamped around her, and he's forcing her to swallow saltwater. Each time he makes her drink, she spits it out, and she's crying and she hates him, but he's telling her she has to drink it, she absolutely must, there's no choice. He's using an angry voice, and she's scared because he doesn't normally talk to her at all, except to say hello. All around her there's the sound of retching, the horrible smell of sick. Her sisters are in here too, and Helen and Katy, and her mum and dad, but she can't see the others because Adrian is gripping her head so she can't move it, he's pulling her hair by accident and it hurts. 'You're the only one who hasn't been sick yet, Alex,' Adrian says, like he's telling her off, like this is a competition and she's losing.

'Do we know how many they ate?' her mum is asking, and Alex wants to bolt across the bathroom to be with her. She'd do anything to swap places with her sisters, to get away from Adrian, who has hairy hands and smells like the dentist's.

'Does anyone know?' her mum asks again, and she sounds funny, like there's something stuck in her throat and she needs to cough.

She's talking about the Chinese lanterns. The dried ones they'd taken from the hallway table and eaten for the game. The ones they'd pretended were poisonous. It was Nancy's idea and they'd all thought it was brilliant. They'd written little notes and lain down on the upstairs landing and pretended they were dead. And now Helen and Katy's mum, Stella, is downstairs on the phone to something called the Poisons Unit for *real*, and Alex thinks the grown-ups haven't understood that the whole thing was just a joke.

Alex's eyes go wide. She's swallowed without thinking, a huge gulp. She gags once and is sick into the bath. The sick is lumpy and disgusting and she can see raisins in it from breakfast. Some of it has spattered onto the blue sponge that's wedged in by the taps, next to the bottle of Kermit the Frog bubble bath.

'Good girl,' Adrian says, sitting back on his heels and breathing his smell all over her.

He's talking like she's three years old, when she's nine, and Alex would like to bite him hard. But she's shaking too much and now her feet have started to itch, which is a thing that happens sometimes, even though it's a long time now since the skin healed over. The itching might be in her head, her mum says, although there are scars still, shiny and pinkish and wrong-looking; she tries to keep them hidden when they're doing PE at school.

There's a shout and the sound of heavy footsteps on

the stairs. Stella bangs in through the door. 'We can stop!' she yells, all out of breath, like she's run a marathon, or something's chasing her. 'Stop! It's okay, it's fine. We can stop with the saltwater. Chinese lanterns aren't toxic when the fruit is ripe. They're not poisonous. It's okay.'

'Jesus, thank fuck!' Across the bathroom, Alex's dad swears and lets his head fall back. On his knee, Eva bursts into tears.

'You silly, *silly* girls.' Stella raises her voice over Eva's sobs. 'Do you know how dangerous –?' She freezes in the middle of what she's saying and her face goes tight, like she's smiling, except she isn't. Then she looks at Helen and makes a shooing motion with her hands. 'Find the girls some clean clothes to wear home, okay?'

Alex can't wait to get out of the bathroom, away from the crying and the smell and from Adrian. And she's already on the landing outside Katy's room, when her mum catches up with her. Her mum's hair is all over the place, even more so than usual, and she doesn't smile or offer a hug. There's a dark stain on her red blouse, and her mouth, which is usually wide and soft, is a thin white line that barely moves when she speaks.

'I expected better of you, Alex.'

It's all she says, before she turns to go down the stairs. Adrian is right behind her. Glancing back over her shoulder, her mum rolls her eyes at him. 'And *she's* supposed to be the clever one.'

Nancy is coming out of the bathroom as her mum says it. She stops in the doorway, and Alex sees her cheeks go pink.

Alex knows that last term Nancy got ten out of ten for her spellings six weeks in a row. She's joint top of the spelling league table in her class, and has been awarded a new rubber for the end of her pencil. But Alex knows, too, that *she* is the one who's good at reading and writing. She's a 'natural', her mum and dad say.

'Nancy!' Alex whispers, because she wants to tell her sister it isn't true what her mum just said. It isn't fair. She wants to remind her about the spellings, about the picture Nancy drew on holiday – the one of the yellow French house with the tiled roof – that was so, *so* good. She wants to point out that Nancy can do a cartwheel with straight legs, when Alex's are all bent. But her sister won't look at her. Instead, she puts her head down and her thumb into her mouth, even though she's seven now and far too old to be doing that still, and she walks right past Alex and into Katy's room.

Eva, Sunday afternoon

The path down to the beach is a tunnel of foliage so dense it blocks out almost all the natural light. It's steep and narrow, forcing them to walk in single file, and Eva, who got her hair tangled in a branch, is the last to emerge onto the sand. The beach seems vast after the claustrophobic entrance – it *is* vast, it feels infinite to Eva – who, looking left and right, can't see where it begins or where it ends. It should be beautiful. It *would* be beautiful to run along. Alone, down on the wet sand where it's firm. But the sky is dark and sinking into the sea. It's a frightening sort of beauty, so she can't get away from the feeling that something bad is about to happen.

Eden and Rosa are dots in the distance already, headed to the water. Striding after them, Alex is calling to them to slow down, the waves are too big today and they're not to get wet or they'll feel cold and start moaning and she doesn't have any spare clothes. Alex's husband Luc is a little way behind her, the baby strapped to his front in a sling, arms and legs waggling, like she's battery-powered.

Eva touches the side of her face where the branch tore the skin as she tried to free her hair. It's sore and, when she brings her finger away, there's a bright bead of blood. It occurs to her, as she sucks off the blood, licks the salt taste from her teeth, that Alex has everything.

She's doing it right. Armfuls of babies, all with the same daddy and still living together, still making it work against the odds, which are what these days? One in three? One in two? Worse? He's been part of the family for so long, her not-quite-handsome brother-in-law, and he's taciturn, low-key, does his own thing, so that sometimes when they're all together she forgets to notice him.

She and Carlos didn't even get married. They didn't make it out of their twenties before they'd split up, and now there's Scott. Scott, who has found a big stick in the sand. A length of driftwood he's brandishing performatively, making strange, slow formations in the air, like he thinks he's a Jedi master, or frickin' Gandalf or someone. And it irritates her, because it's almost like he's *trying* to annoy her sisters, and he isn't usually this bad, she's sure he isn't. And now Nancy's turning to look at her, grinning and motioning with her arms in imitation. Yeah, ha-ha, Eva thinks, pretending she hasn't seen her. At least I'm not forty-four and alone and trying – failing – to hide my chronic health anxiety from everyone. She pinches her hand to stop herself saying it. Not the bit about the health anxiety. That's one of the unsaid things. No one mentions that.

They'd needed to get out, all of them, because of the atmosphere in the glass house. Since the ceremony in the woods, everything has felt a little unstable. Bad-tempered. As if at any moment something might blow. Eva thought they'd be the only ones on the beach, the only people crazy enough to come at this time of day, in this kind of weather. But beyond Nancy, framed in the natural arch of a hollowed rock, a lone couple are zipped smugly into the waxed green uniform of the professional pensioner-hiker. They're clomping through the sand towards them and Eva thinks it's the Wilsons, who used to live on their street. At the same time, she knows she must be mistaken. It's the thing Lucy used to do whenever they went away – *I just saw Miss Nelson from Blue Class at the tennis courts*, and *Look, there's Violet B's brother in front of the surf school.* Not understanding that they were in another country, thousands of miles away.

'Oh, fuck!'

For a moment she thinks it was Lucy who said it. Her all-too-fresh daughter, who's walking just ahead of her linking arms with her mum, the way they often do when the family's together – they find their way to each other. Eva had the swearing conversation with Lucy before they came, how it's not okay in front of the younger cousins. Or the grandparents (even though Vivienne herself is an excellent swearer, world class, *gifted*, she would say). How it's not really okay at all, and Eva's about to poke Lucy in the back, give a warning glare, when her mum puts her head down and, directing her words at the ground, adds, 'Fuckety fuck, it's the *Wilsons*. What are the bloody chances?'

'Erm, quite high, in fact.' Nancy stops in front of them and spins round to face them. She has what their dad would call a smartarse look on her face. 'This place has been all over the travel sections this past couple of years. A "hidden gem", right, Eva? A Top Ten UK Break! This is where most of London goes on holiday, these days. Anyway, didn't they move somewhere near here?'

The couple in the waxed jackets have started to wave. Arm actions that are restricted by their all-weather gear, but that are somehow, also, over the top, as though someone is drowning.

'Oh, God, they've seen us,' her mum says, without moving her mouth.

'Wait.' Eva frowns. 'I thought they were friends of yours?'

'Oh, Eva.' Her mum cups her face with a hand. 'The innocence of youth.'

'So what am I missing? What did they –?'

Eva's mum cuts her off. 'Christ, sweetheart, what happened to your face?'

Nobody can believe it. They can't believe they've run into each other here. They can't believe how much the girls have grown. They can't believe they have children. They can't believe they have children who look exactly like their grandparents, the spitting image. They can't believe Helen and Katy and their kids aren't here to see them, but they'll be up later in the week for half-term. The Larsens are coming up, too, for a few days. Do they remember them? From number thirty, moved to Bristol. They must all get together for a meal, some or all of them. There's a vegan place run by the guy off the telly, or an Italian place with enormous pizzas they can hardly fit on the tables, or a new Korean-Chinese place that's a right turn after the Jurassic gardens.

'And speaking of the Chinese place,' Stella Wilson

53

says, and pauses for dramatic effect, 'dare I mention the Chinese lanterns? One of the most harrowing incidents of my life!'

'Oh, my God,' Nancy faux-retches, 'I was just telling my daughter Georgie about that the other day. I remember it *so* clearly. Because it was so bloody awful. Me on your knee on the wooden stool by the sink, Adrian, remember? Drinking – *gagging* – from an orange mug. I wound up with you, for some reason.' She makes a puzzled face, looks from their mum to their dad. 'Probably because I'm the "difficult" one.' She flicks paired fingers, putting quote marks around the words.

'No, you didn't!' Alex has come up behind them, trailing Rosa, who's taken off her wellies and trousers and whose pants are soaked with seawater. 'You didn't get Adrian. *I* got Adrian. That wasn't you it was me.'

'It's not a competition, ladies.' Her dad stamps his feet in the sand like he's made a good joke. An eggy, seaweed smell lifts from the ground.

'No, but, seriously, I did. I know I did.' Alex is indignant. She sounds, Eva thinks, like a petulant child. Like they're back there, more than thirty-five years ago, at Helen and Katy's. 'I'm a hundred per cent. A hundred and fifty per cent! Adrian made me drink the saltwater, I puked in the bath – I remember it. I remember getting sick all over a Kermit the Frog toy. That's the level of specificity I'm talking about. You've totally appropriated this, Nancy.'

Nancy is shaking her head. 'Na-ah, I'm not giving you this one, Alex. Still living with the trauma . . .'

A little way down the beach, a pair of seagulls shriek and swoop. Their open beaks are rictus grins as they come in to land.

'Yeah, no, it was me,' Alex says, under her breath, and there's an aggressive finality in the way she says it. The last word of the older sister. The power in it still, Eva thinks. Even now they're middle-bloody-aged. Is this how it will always be? Alex will still hold the power when they're wearing elasticated slacks and subsisting on Sudoku and shortbread.

'Either way, astonishingly reckless parenting . . .' Eva unwinds her scarf from her neck, crouches and starts to rub her niece's shivery legs. She can feel the low-boil in the exchange between her sisters that she knows in the root of her is about something much bigger – more nebulous – than this. She wants to diffuse it.

'Benign neglect,' Adrian agrees.

'Ow!' Rosa makes her legs go rigid. 'The sand hurts.'

'You know, I found out later, that they probably were poisonous after all,' her mum says vaguely, ignoring Rosa. 'But look at you now!' She claps her hands together, lets them spring apart, fingers spread, as if she's an illusionist poised to receive her applause. 'Perfection, all of you. Didn't do you any harm at all.' And all the parents of the parents laugh, as they fish out their reading glasses and begin, laboriously, to swap phone numbers.

When the Wilsons leave, Eva hangs back, waiting for her mum, who's trying to extract a stone from her boot. The beach is steel-lidded now. From one end to the other, as far as she can see. She thinks she can feel it pressing thickly on the crown of her head.

'This place is bloody weird,' Eva hears her mum mutter, but she's talking to herself, not Eva. Bent over the way she is, she seems like a mad old crone straight out of folklore. 'Why does it feel like the past is treading on my heels here?'

Alex, Monday morning

Alex is moving through the house so stealthily she almost isn't breathing. She's making herself jumpy doing this. Every sound is amplified, so that when the fridge cracks as she passes the kitchen, she almost ducks, as if someone is firing at her. She has her phone in her pocket and her plan is to get to the carport before anyone else is up. Before anyone can stop her. Through the glass walls she can see that it's dark outside – the house is painted black still by the dying end of the night.

The baby's been awake since five. Alex has done two hours of the day already, and it's not yet seven a.m. It's very much Luc's turn, and she's left him comatose in the vast bed with the curved velvet headboard, one arm ringing the baby, and the Disney channel on with the sound turned down. *It's a work thing,* she whispered, her back to him while she pulled on her jeans. *The school concert rehearsals start after half-term. My maternity cover's shit, he needs some help and there's signal at the end of the drive, so . . .* but when she turned to face him, she could see he wasn't listening and, anyway, she was over-explaining, which she knows is the biggest tell of all, so she just left.

Myopic without her contact lenses, she moves into the lounge. She left her glasses in here last night, which just shows how off everything's been, because she never does that, never leaves things lying around. It's just not in her DNA. The glasses are on the arm of one of the low, wide sofas, on top of Luc's *Life in the UK* textbook, which is face-down, pages splayed. Alex puts the glasses on – she can see! – moves the book, soundlessly, to the coffee-table, tidying instinctively. Conversation was stilted after the kids had gone to bed, which isn't a thing with their family, not usually – not ever, in fact – until her mum snatched up the book, started testing them on the citizenship questions. It was a comedy quiz, basically, a deep dive into the absurd that every single one of them failed. 'Alex?' her mum or dad kept saying, when shrugs and WTFs had followed each question. As though she was maybe giving the others a chance to get it right before swooping in with the answers. And after about the tenth time, she thought she caught Eva and Nancy exchanging a look.

They all flunked, except Dijon-born-and-bred Luc, who's been studying to get his British citizenship for the past six months, feels he needs to, even though he's lived here for twenty years, married here, had three children here, works as a maths teacher at a state school in Herne Hill, et cetera, et cetera . . . And although he seems fine with it all, says he's happy to do it, she still feels indignant on his behalf. She feels this even though there's a million miles between them at the moment. They barely communicate. Their own private Brexit. The baby hasn't helped. *A Band-Aid baby*, she'd joked when they found out she was pregnant for the third time aged forty-four, and with their oldest child already in junior school.

Except it wasn't really a joke, and she doesn't even know whether he realizes this or not.

'Just what the hell, Patrick?'

When Alex hears the voice, she swings around, because it sounds like it's come from behind her. It's her mum's voice, but there's no one here. *The acoustics in this place are fucked*, Nancy said yesterday, as they were stepping into their wellies on the marble deck out front, getting ready to leave for the beach. *Sound travels in the glass house . . .* She said it as if she was narrating a thriller trailer, and Alex rolled her eyes. But now there's an unbidden flare in her, something uneasy.

There's the low rumble of her dad's response, and for a moment she daren't move. She can't make out the words and there's no sign of either of her parents; she thinks they must be in their bedroom. Like a cartoon thief, Alex starts to move back across the room, making for the front door. She has a single shining focus – to get away before anyone can intercept her. She craves what she's about to do like it's food or water, a basic human need.

'Tell me, Patrick. Enlighten me!' Her mum's voice comes again, a little louder this time. Fury with the sound turned down.

Alex stops where she is, next to the sculpture in the corner of the lounge. She doesn't want them to hear her. She doesn't want to hear them, but at the same time, she can't help it, she finds herself straining to listen.

'You want to dredge the whole thing up, is that it?' her mum hisses.

The sculpture is all angles and points and it's precariously tall. Alex is terrified one of the kids is going to break it – or impale themselves – before the week is out.

'You think that'll benefit anyone?' It's only her mum talking now, spitting the words and no gaps. 'Just a *crazy* thought, but I feel like it won't and . . .'

Standing there, Alex is overheating. The insulation in the house is off the charts, in a new eco league all of its own, so that it's airless. The family have wandered around these past forty-eight hours, stripping off layers one by one. A jumper over the back of a chair here, a shirt kicked under a table there, socks on the kitchen counter – leaving them for her to pick up, fold, place at the end of whoever's bed because, unlike the rest of them, she isn't able just to leave it.

They are arguing. She can't tell herself they aren't. The second argument in as many days and this isn't them: her mum and dad don't argue. The odd spat-out comment, *yes*, but not this. Nancy has a theory about it, that it's almost as if they know the stakes are too high. That if they started – if they got into it – they'd explode or implode and then, *bam*, there'd be no coming back from it. They'd be over. And also because of the apocalyptic argument. That's another reason. The argument that's a crumbling memory, a memory so faded she could almost believe it was a figment of her imagination that happened decades ago now, one Christmas. The one that's been pushed to the back of their collective minds, deemed too serious – too awful – to revisit. To this day, she has no idea what it was about, none. As far as Alex is aware, her parents haven't a clue that their children even witnessed it.

It makes no sense that they don't fight, her mum and dad, Vivienne and Patrick. Because they're both flamboyant characters and it seems the two things should go together. They like to say they met when they ran away to join the circus. It isn't true, but it might be. Separately, they were plucked out of the audience at Chipperfield's in Battersea one winter, chosen to ride a stallion bareback around the ring. They'd had their hands up so high, both of them, like children trying to get noticed, they'd nearly ruptured their armpits. A beautiful piebald stallion with a crimson plume attached to its bridle, that shuddered as they all but flew through the Big Top. Alex can see it all, she's heard the story so many times. Two strangers pressed up against one another, the smell of oiled leather, horse sweat and manure. Both left dangling by a safety harness at the end. With bruises on their thighs that bloomed for weeks.

It's hard to live up to – the glamorous love story of her mum and dad. In stark, unimaginative contrast, she and Luc met at work, at the school in east London where she did her teacher training. They ate their sandwiches together in the staff room and talked about . . . what? Marking? Ofsted inspections? The nightmare students? The place where music (her subject) and maths (his) met. Pedestrian, inadequate, it didn't compare. It wasn't meant to turn out that way. Alex was supposed to be a famous singer. Aged eighteen, she'd gone to the prestigious Conservatoire in Scotland. She'd spent a term breathing in and out of strange contraptions, drilling vocal exercises to grow her lungs, expand her range, but by the time she came home at Christmas, she'd lost her voice. It had vanished. She'd stayed on the sofa in the foetal position for a week, speaking in the whisper that was all she could manage. Has something happened? her mum had asked. Is it the pressure? Is it a boy?

Later Vivienne told Alex that her mouth had shrunk to the size of a pinprick. That she'd seemed to suck her words inwards, like cigarette smoke, when she spoke. As though to talk was poisoning her. That she'd been a husk, a half-presence there on the sofa. Alex hadn't gone back to the Conservatoire after the holidays. Her mum was right. It had been the pressure, but mostly it had been a boy. A boy-man. It would be called sexual assault in this enlightened age – the way one minute they'd been talking in his room, the next he'd forced his hand between her legs and clawed at her and she'd frozen. Back then no one had heard of consent. He'd kept his hand there, like she was a puppet on a stick, his eyes hard, until his roommate swung in. The roommate hadn't seen anything and, anyway, this was a pussy-grabbing time, an era of 'take-it-as-a-compliment-ladies'. So she'd never told her parents. She'd taken a year out, done a PGCE, tried not to think about what might have been. And now? Disappointed. Privately, secretly, that's what she is, because is this it?

'I can't bear it!' she hears her mum say.

And then there's the sound of her dad replying, a quietly desperate timbre, but words she can't catch.

They will be arguing about the Wilsons. She tells herself this. They were on a bad trajectory, and now this thing with their old neighbours has tipped them over the edge. The fact that, for the sake of politeness, they've said yes to an elaborate dinner date they don't want to go on. Because something obviously happened between the couples, something more than her mum is letting on. *You said, 'Oh, fuck!' when you saw them, Mum,* Nancy had said the day before, after they'd bumped into them on the beach. *You were definitely not 'just surprised'.* Later, before they'd even finished their walk, her mum's phone had pinged several times. Vivienne had checked the screen and muttered to herself, 'Oh, Christ, they actually texted. I thought we were all just being polite.' But Alex would rather not strip the rose-tint from her childhood by speculating – she was happy growing up, it was a great childhood, and she'd rather keep her version of the past that way, unsullied. They're pretty much the perfect family. Give or take. She's always thought this.

So why, then, does Alex keep seeing the tree falling in the forest? Like a meme, or a gif, or whatever, playing over and over in her mind. Even though she didn't see it fall in the first place – she'd had her back to it. She only heard the awful crack as it tore from its roots.

The voices have stopped. Alex waits for a moment, eyeing the sharp point of the sculpture, which is vibrating minutely. Threateningly, as though the breath of her mum's quiet rage is slipping out from under the bedroom door, stirring the contents of the house.

A memory. Her mum in the bedroom at Dartmouth

Park, opening drawers and banging them shut, because Nancy has ripped a hole in her new red shorts, which should have lasted her all summer, *for fuck's sake*. Then her dad coming out onto the landing, where Alex is standing with her sisters, a pantomime finger held to his lips. But he's smiling, his eyes all jokey and wide, as he leads them down the stairs and out into the street and to the park. He buys them ice creams from the van at the gates, tells Nancy not to worry, that *Mum just needs a break from us rabble, and I don't blame her* . . . And they don't have to pick from the top two rows of boring cornets and plain ice lollies so they all choose Mr Whippy 99s with Flakes – including her dad – which they're only usually allowed as a special treat.

Somewhere in the building a toilet flushes. There's a cough, the sound of running water. Then she's running herself, near silently, along the wide corridor discreetly lit with glowing floor lights, and out of the front door that breathes shut on expensive hydraulics behind her. As she makes for the carport, Alex tries to empty her mind. There's a feeling in her like she's escaping, but at the same time she's hurtling towards a gaping hole, a vortex. She pictures her mouth shrunk to the pinprick her mum described, a tiny, useless dot on her face, like her lips had been stitched together from the inside, and she knows she has to do it. She'll be half an hour, no longer – she needs this time to feed her own soul. Otherwise she doesn't think she'll be able to keep the mask on a second longer. Otherwise she doesn't know what she might do.

Eva, Monday morning

Eva is pounding the mud tracks of the drive, putting some distance between herself and the glass house. Underneath her feet, the ground is ridged and gluey, a product of the schizophrenic weather that's torrential rain one minute, sharp sunshine the next. It's hard on her ankles so she's taking it steady, there's no rush, although she does want to get her training in while she can. Scott has been checking the Met Office app hourly, and keeping everyone updated, whether they like it or not. There are severe weather warnings for later in the week – a storm with a name that's maybe Sabina, or Susanna? She can't remember which, but apparently it might blow by to the west (or possibly the east?), if they're lucky.

Eva waited for the sun to come up before she left, doing some stretches in the bathroom so she wouldn't disturb Scott. There's always the danger of him catching her with his morning erection, and then she has to endure his painful, hangdog expression as she unpicks his hands from her breasts, her crotch, explains how if she misses the window she doesn't get to run. And she has to run. This morning more than ever, she's out here trying to untangle her thoughts. Because she hasn't been entirely honest with everyone. Maybe she hasn't been entirely honest with herself. Maybe, after all, she's just like the others at the running club – trying to race in the opposite direction from the *thing* she doesn't want to think about.

She's tried to diminish it, minimize it, ignore it altogether, but she's sitting on something. She can't pretend she isn't. It's there in black-and-white, in a council storage vault somewhere in London. Or perhaps it's just a digitized copy in the cloud, these days, she has no idea, but either way it doesn't change the fact that she got married a month ago without telling her family. Without telling anyone.

One of her trainers is laced too tight. She knows she should stop and adjust it, but she won't. Is she punishing herself? Eva imagines herself an hour from now, hot and sweaty and just back from her run, bursting into the glass house, stationing herself at the slate table and announcing her news. Watching them choke on their croissants. 'I'm a newly-wed!' The expression she loves to hate. Because, yes, she's got abs like a twenty-five-year-old, quads like a much younger version of herself, but she's also got deflated tits and a leaky urethra, and it feels ridiculous to her that she's done this. That they have. She can't even claim it was spontaneous because, she's not an idiot, she went to see her lawyer first and they drew up papers. She hates the word 'pre-nup'. It's all greed and suspicion and anti-romance, envisaging the end before you've even begun. But that's kind of what happened.

They'd had a weekend away in Grasmere, she and Scott, climbed the narrow ridge of Striding Edge. Kissed

66

like teenagers at the summit of Helvellyn, high on sero-
tonin and a lack of oxygen. The fact they'd survived the
sheer drop. Then got drunk in the pub with the eleven-
course tasting menu. They'd been on to the dessert wine
when he'd asked her, and she'd tried not to notice the
piece of miso-seared kale stuck in his teeth. She'd said
yes, because why not? And the next day, when they'd
woken up with hangovers, hadn't felt able to extricate
herself . . . She'd married him out of politeness, basically. Was that true?

Her foot hits something that doesn't feel right, that's
more than mud, and there's a high-pitched sound that
goes to the pit of her. Eva stops and turns. There's
the biggest frog she's ever seen, in the middle of the
track, oozing yellow pus. She's stepped on a frog. She's
stepped with her whole bodyweight on a fucking frog
and she doesn't know what to do. The squealing noise
is going on and on and it feels like the worst kind of
omen. Squatting down, she scoops the frog that is, in
fact, a toad – it's one of the rare natterjack toads there
are signs for everywhere – and she's killed it. The toad is
dead. She knows because it's stopped making the awful
noise, and is motionless in her hands as she places it in
the long grass at the side of the track. Wiping her palms
over and over in the grass, she thinks she might cry; she
feels like she's going to be sick.

She married him because she panicked. Because she
couldn't face any more online dating. The grim, skewed
swipe-and-you're-gone façade of it. The end had come
for Eva after she'd watched a documentary about

the algorithms, made by a woman, a reporter, who'd demanded her data – her *dating* data – via the Freedom of Information Act. The reporter had the numbers analysed by experts, who found she was never matched with a man who earned less than she did, that it was policy. Eva had shrieked at the TV at this point, and spilled the protein shake she was having for dinner, staining the arm of the sofa permanently. The earnings revelation was just for starters. Eva knows it's true – she's seen it among her own single friends, the 'nice guys' over forty, who cap the upper age limit of women-they'd-like-to-meet at a whopping thirty-nine, and don't even try to hide it. Probably think they're being benevolent. Eva hadn't lied about her age online. Or about her salary for that matter, not exactly. Because by then there hadn't been one, just she'd fudged it on her income, her net worth, whatever . . . The numbers don't seem real to her anyhow.

Her satellite watch is digging into her wrist, and she adjusts it as she straightens up, smooths the pink skin with her thumb. Setting off again, she tries to concentrate on the ground underneath her feet, the air on her face, the end of the drive that's coming into view. It's no big deal, really, she tells herself. The whole marriage thing. Just a piece of paper, an antiquated ritual. It's just she hasn't quite told Lucy yet. She winces as she thinks it, squints, as if the thought might evaporate, the fact of it might disappear. There was no good way to do it, and she kept putting it off and off, and then a week and a fortnight and a month passed. Scott's son Jay doesn't know either. He's twenty-two and crews super-yachts out of Majorca, and Lucy can't stand him – he's a misogynist, she says, and a Twatty Tory. And now . . . Eva scrunches up her face. Now he's Lucy's step– No, nope! It's all just labels, and she won't go there. The fact is they rarely see him, and Eva hardly knows him and it's not her problem . . . except that it is, it *is* . . . It's a big fucking mess and how has she let this happen? She would never have allowed things to spiral this way at Unfortune8!, would never have lost control of her business like that.

There's the tok-tok-tok of a woodpecker off to her right, or maybe her left, she can't tell. A persistent, percussive beat that's like the knock of her thoughts against her skull. Tok-tok-*Scott*-tok-*Scott*-*Scott* . . . The biggest problem is Scott. Scott's excited. Scott wants to tell everyone about their great big romance – he wants to announce it to the world. Scott, sitting on this information, is like a kid with a Wonka bar (a *wanker* with a Wonka bar?) he's yet to unwrap. He's like a nervous squaddie with live ammunition. And maybe it's not that she's running away from it exactly, more that she isn't running towards it. Her family prides itself on being close. There's a smugness about it, almost, like they're better than other families. And she loves her mum and dad, her sisters, she adores them, she does. Her sisters are her closest friends, even if sometimes she'd like to bite them the way she'd bitten Nancy once when she was six – through her thick peach dressing-gown, the one with the appliquéd cupcake on the back, that Eva had coveted – and drawn blood. But she's a private person, she always has been. She doesn't want people – her family – to think she hasn't got her shit together. It matters to her that they believe she's in control. It's a youngest thing, she's been told more than once, which makes sense to her, although she can't remember the psychology behind it. The other thing – and she barely wants to think it – is that once she tells them, she'll have to admit to herself that it's true, it happened, she married Scott.

As she's thinking this, she turns onto the main road, and sees Alex and Luc's green Volvo parked on a grass verge on the opposite side. There's the Baby On Board bumper sticker, the mud splattered up the back that she knows will stress Alex out until she can get it through a car wash. What's the car doing here? Eva slows her pace, checks her watch. At this time? She can make out, through the rear window, Alex in the driver's seat, her head tipped slightly to one side. For a moment it goes through Eva's mind that her sister might be dead. But then, as she draws level with the car, she sees that Alex is holding her phone close to her face, like maybe it's on speaker, or she's studying something closely. And Eva's jogging on the spot, looking left and right, and left and right again, before she crosses the road – because cars appear from nowhere here, not like in the city – and she's starting to grin, thinking how she'll knock on the driver's side window, how it'll scare the shit out of her sister, when Alex twists in her seat as though she's sensed Eva there.

The sisters' eyes meet. Something – the patches of colour on Alex's neck, her expression that's like a warning – pins Eva where she is. And she might as well be twelve years old again because she has the feeling she's just pushed open the door to Alex's childhood bedroom, the one at the top of the house with the sloping ceilings. The room they all wanted for their own, but that Alex got because she was the eldest. There's the Indian wall-hanging draped behind her sister's bed, the Cure on the stereo, and the smell of incense that Eva pretends to like but can't stand. Her sister is in front of the mirror painting on thick black eyeliner that flicks upwards at her temples. She's standing in the middle of a pile of clothes so that Eva can't see her feet, and it's like she's growing out of the jumble, as if she's a weird kind of plant. Alex fixes her eyes on Eva's reflection behind her. 'Get out,' she says, and her voice is grey and flat – she can't even be bothered to raise it, she doesn't need to. But Eva hovers in the doorway. She's bored and she wants to ask her sister how she does her eyes like that. She wants to sit on the bed and watch her for a little while – sometimes her sisters will let her do this; she won't speak or even fidget. 'Can I just . . . ?' she starts to ask.

'No! Get out,' Alex says, and, slowly, Eva turns and leaves the room. 'CLOSE THE DOOR!' her sister yells after her. 'I MEAN IT, EVA, CLOSE IT!' And, even though Eva has the scrunched-up feeling in her stomach, the same way it feels when she gets told off at school, she keeps on walking.

A white car flashes past, momentarily blocking Alex from view. Eva decides in that moment that she's not going to stop. She won't speak to her sister, not right now. She knows it's crazy, laughable, completely nuts that Alex can still make her feel this way. That the casual cruelty of early siblinghood has tracked her down the years like this. But, anyway, it's Alex's business if she wants to come and sit in her car at the end of the drive at dawn. Who's Eva to judge? Because, facing facts, everything has gone a little weird. They've only been here forty-eight hours, and she's been trying to ignore it, but since the naming ceremony, things haven't felt right. She saw Alex coming out of Nancy's bedroom a little while after they'd got back from the forest, steely-eyed and with the baby screaming in her arms. Eva was sitting in the window seat, halfway along the corridor, watching a bird that might have been a White-tailed Eagle, circling in front of the mountains. Alex didn't notice her, and Eva got the same old feeling – the one she's had since for ever – that she was on the outside looking in, at her two older sisters, barely more than a year in age between them. Something that's always made the three-year gap between her and Nancy seem much wider than it is. *Dangerous co-conspirators*, her dad would've said. Meant as a joke, but it always made her feel worse.

Lifting her hand in a half-wave, Eva pumps her elbows exaggeratedly, like, *Can't stop, I'm training* . . . In return, Alex nods and jabs a finger at her phone, then winds it in the air above her head, and Eva understands that she's here for the signal. There's a new heaviness in her legs as she moves off, a build-up of lactic acid that she knows she'll need to outstrip. She's trying to clear her thoughts, set her mind to zen, but something's tugging at the edges of her. It's not until she's further along the road, about to turn onto the track that leads to the extraordinary waterfall she's seen in a hundred crappy photos on Tripadvisor, that she remembers. Alex was there yesterday, on the beach, when Nancy told them. They were making their way through the rock arch, the sand gloopy still from where the tide had come in, and Nancy's voice bounced around the hooded space as she announced that – *BTW, hallelujah, people!* – she'd found a way to get online: that it was possible, after all, to make contact with the outside world from inside the glass house.

Nancy, Spring 1985

Nancy and her sisters are in the waiting room at the dentist's surgery, which smells of Germolene and flowery, headachy perfume. They've come straight from school and they had to run here because her mum got chatting to Nicola's mum in the playground and it made them late for their appointment. And also late for Alex, who's at secondary now, and has come on her own on the bus. Sitting there on a padded bench in the stuffy room, Nancy is overheating in her coat. They are playing a poking game, the three of them, while their mum checks them in at Reception. There are no rules, they're just poking each other in the legs, as sneakily as they can, trying not to laugh as they do it, because the waiting room is packed with people. Even Alex is joining in, although Nancy knows there's a chance, at any moment, she'll decide it's 'pathetic' and 'immature' and then she'll stop playing and give them warning looks until they stop too.

Nancy hates and loves coming here. Their dentist, Dr Coles, wears white slip-on shoes and has a gold ring on his fat pinky finger. His voice is soft and unsettling, and makes him sound like a TV villain, and he flirts with their mum, which is gross. Especially when their mum gets all fluttery and giggly around him – even though Nancy knows she doesn't like him much either: she's heard her telling Dad – and it makes Nancy want to die, her mum acting like that. But she loves the dentist's chair that moves by itself, tipping her backwards and raising her legs. And she still loves the sticker you get at the end, from the box they keep at Reception, and sometimes even a free toothbrush and miniature tube of tooth-paste. She worries this time they might think she's too old, because she's eleven; she thinks she might be too embarrassed to take one.

They have to wait because the people with the appointment after them have already gone in, and by the time the nurse calls them through to the surgery, Nancy is feeling hungry and a bit queasy. They usually have a snack when they get in from school, but her mum forgot to bring anything with her.

The dentist is already seated in his chair as they come through the door. He's wearing a plastic apron over his white outfit and a fake smile. 'Hello, how are you all?' He's looking at her mum as he says it, and Nancy stares pointedly at his slip-on shoes, and then at Alex, trying to make her laugh. Alex flares her eyes, but Nancy can see her lips are twitching. And then they both have to look away because otherwise – and it's happened here, at the dentist's, before – they'll start giggling and won't be able to stop.

Nancy goes first, fixing her eyes on the ceiling, while the dentist mutters under his breath, letters and numbers that sound like the coordinates from a game of Battle-ships. Her jaw aches from holding her mouth open and she can smell her own breath as she breathes in and out.

'Great,' he says, once he's done, and it comes out like a grimace, with an emphasis on the *t*. Then he rolls his chair backwards a little on its wheels. He does this with his legs either side of the seat, like he thinks he's a gun-slinging cowboy, riding an impressive stallion. 'We'll sort her out with some disclosing tablets, Mum, just so we can make sure her brushing is really up to scratch. Who's next?'

Nancy pictures the horrible gummy photographs in the leaflet that comes with the tablets, all grinning children with yellow teeth dyed red at the edges. And because she knows what's coming, she steels herself as Alex climbs up onto the chair, settles her feet on the ugly plastic that protects the end from dirty shoes. Maybe this time he won't say it.

'Wow.' The dentist shakes his head in awe, the second her sister opens her mouth. Like he doesn't do this every single time, like this is something extraordinary and rare and entirely new to him.

Nancy stares at the window across the room and tries to close her ears. She can't see out because of the blind, which looks like someone has cut it into neat strips with a pair of scissors. She tries not to think about how the dentist basically ignored her, because she doesn't like him anyway, so what does it matter? *We'll sort her out with some disclosing tablets . . .*

'What beautiful teeth!' He turns to their mum, she sees out of the corner of her eye. 'Absolute perfection,' he breathes, as though he might be talking about one of the Seven Wonders of the World they've been learning about in geography.

What beautiful teeth you have . . .

Nancy sees suddenly the wolf in the Ladybird book of *Little Red Riding Hood* they used to read when they were younger. The sharp, nasty teeth, jutting out from a grey snout, a gathered cloth cap covering the wolf's ears.

'And what big eyes you have!' The words are out of her mouth before she's had time to think. Her voice is loud in the small room, and she doesn't even know who she's talking to. Alex? The horrible dentist? Her mum? She's aware that Eva has started to giggle, but she knows it doesn't really make sense, what she's said.

'Nancy! That's not funny.' Her mum shoots an apologetic smile at Dr Coles, whose hands are poised, holding a narrow metal implement just above Alex's face. His pinky finger is bulging either side of his little gold ring. Nancy can't see his nose and mouth because of the mask he's wearing, but even so, she can tell that his expression is mean.

Inside her head, it's all twisted up with anger and shame and jealousy and confusion. And now something is pushing upwards in her, something she can't stop, as if she's about to be sick, except not that.

'Maybe that isn't funny . . .' Nancy finds herself moving towards her sister in the dentist's chair '. . . but this is!' As she's saying it, she snatches up the little plastic beaker filled with pink liquid that's balanced on the edge of the stupidly small sink. It happens so fast, she doesn't know she's going to do it – she doesn't *think* she's going to do it – until she's flung the pink water at the dentist or at Alex, she isn't sure who. Then she's running from the room and down the stairs. Already the wild feeling is draining out of her so that she thinks she might be leaving a trail of something wet or violently coloured or hot to the touch on the blue stair carpet behind. She keeps on running until she's out in the street, and her legs go all wobbly so that she has to sit down on the pavement, and she starts to cry so hard that a woman with a baby in a pushchair crouches to see if she's okay. And Nancy can't speak, she's crying so much, but she's not okay, she's not, because she's going to get shouted at, and it's so unfair, because don't they understand that she doesn't feel good enough? She tries so hard, but they make her feel like everything she does is wrong, that *she* is wrong, and why don't they see that it hurts so much? It hurts in her throat and in her chest, and in her too-busy mind that feels full to bursting with all the mistakes she can't stop making.

Nancy, Monday noon

Of all the astonishing, beautiful places they could have
gone to visit around here. Of all the wild, wide-open
antidotes to the stifle of city living, they have come to
the fucking pencil museum. They've come because Eden
(and God help her, because, yes, he's her nephew but he's
also a whinging little shit), wanted to come. Seven adults
and four children – eleven of them are here – *ten* of
them flat-faced with boredom, hostage to her six-year-
old nephew, who otherwise would have thrown his toys
out of the pram. On account of her sister, who doesn't
know how to say no to her kids. *A frickin' pencil museum.*
Nancy has had to come outside before she snatches up a
handful of 5Bs and scribbles all over the walls with them.
Or karate-chops Alex in the throat. Alex, who is moving
impossibly slowly around the world's most boring exhib-
its, reading every single poorly typed museum label, as
though they've pitched up at a scene of incomparable
magnificence. Alex, who has her arm linked through
their dad's, fawning over him like she has bloody Stock-
holm Syndrome or something. Like, the worse he treats
her, the more effort she must make.

Nancy's got her cigarettes out of the car because this
is what it's come to. Slammed shut the glove-box in an

attempt to contain the throb of the official-looking letter in the brown envelope that she still hasn't opened. And now she's sitting – *hiding* – in a ditch at the edge of a field of horned brown-and-white cows that look outsized, even for cows, like they're being reared on steroids – a cocktail of steroids and antibiotics, probably – that will make their way into the food chain, meaning everyone will be swallowing mouthfuls of carcinogens and/or catching TB and syphilis they won't be able to treat and . . . Nancy takes a long, minty pull on her cigarette, flips over the packet so that she won't have to look at the horrific pair of lungs on the front. Letters in bold shout at her from the back of the packet: *SMOKING CLOGS THE ARTERIES AND CAUSES HEART ATTACKS AND STROKES.*

Knocking the packet into the space under the V of her knees where she can't see it, she tries to erase the warning from her mind. She should probably take up vaping, like the local fourteen-year-olds who waft around Archway McDonald's in sickly sweet clouds of synthetic blueberry or bubblegum or caramel. Would that be better? But, then, those reports about people's lungs exploding or the vape exploding, or something, she isn't sure exactly what but definitely something bad . . . God, why is she doing this? She, the woman who worries about the slightest itch of a mole. Neurotic but avoidant, the worst possible combination, so that most days she's living with a fizz of low-level fear, as her body continues to turn against her. Her body that's starting to make her think of something Gaudí built, drooping in places like she's melting. Nancy takes another pull on her cigarette, filling herself with smoke and self-loathing simultaneously.

She misses her daughter suddenly. Her daughter who should be here. Who would be happy to be with her cousins and her aunties and her grandparents, pencil museum or not. Georgie, her little city kid, who would be amused and astonished by these crazy-ass cows. Nancy takes out her mobile and dials her child's number. She wants to hear Georgie's voice, which sounds so much younger on the phone than it does in *real life*, soft and high and faraway, like it's been squeezed down a phone wire, although there aren't wires any more, just . . . what? Magic? Her little girl sounds vulnerable, is how she sounds, so that every word is a faint bruise. The phone is ringing and ringing and, right before it goes through to voice-mail, Nancy remembers Georgie will be at tennis camp. Tennis camp! Her daughter might as well be here if Leon is going to farm her out every day. Much like he farms out every single aspect of his life, including his wife – *ex*-wife – she corrects herself, at the same time realizing the comparison doesn't really make sense. Including farming out his own emotions, she tries. That's more like it. Not troubling himself with life's trivialities, like, say, conversation. And certainly not complicating things for himself by taking *actual* responsibility for anything.

While she's thinking this, her fingers have scrolled down her contacts, found Nik's number and dialled reflexively. She wants to talk to someone.

He answers on the first ring. 'What *now*?' he says, through a mouthful of something.

'I'm fuming, since you ask.' There's the outline of a smile in her voice as she says it.

'Again?'

She can hear the sharp echo-clatter of the canteen in the background. Smell the boiled-cauliflower smell of the food. 'You sound surprised. Because what? Normally I'm such a shot of sunshine in your life?'

'Yes, actually.'

She's waiting for the punchline, but he doesn't say anything else. 'Okay, great, can I offload, then, please? It's kind of ugly.'

Nik smacks his lips down the line. 'Let me tell you, *nothing* could spoil my enjoyment of this meal. Industrial rubber macaroni, melt-in-the-mouth canned veg, Chef's special watery sauce . . . I expect Michelin have scheduled a visit.'

Nancy almost wishes she was there, at work. She pictures Nik sitting at one of the long tables, laughter pressing at the edges of his mouth, glossy shampoo-advert hair she teases him about, and that he has to keep pushing out of his eyes.

'So talk to me. Go!' Nik says, and she can hear that his mouth is full. 'Is it the father who doesn't love you? Or everybody's favourite home-schooled piano-playing genius?'

It's what he calls Leon. Although sometimes he adds a 'faded' before 'genius'. Leon, who's a composer of obscure contemporary opera, but who subsists on the royalties of a piece he wrote twenty years ago. A piece he doesn't like to talk about, because it's the soundtrack to a long-running reality-TV show, a show that gets ever more exploitative with each passing season. The two men met only once, at a colleague's leaving drinks, which her ex-husband had endured, characteristically, in near-silence. He'd accepted three expensive single malts, stayed for half an hour, and left claiming an early start, although they all knew he only worked after two o'clock in the afternoon. She hadn't understood at the time but it was one of the key moments. The moments that had made her decide, in the end, to leave.

'Both. Everyone, everything . . .' She hardly knows where to start, but she goes with the ice cream. The fact that on the way back from the beach the day before, Alex had nipped to the little kiosk in the car park and bought a Mr Whippy 99 with a Flake for her dad and herself and no one else. Not their mum, not even her own children, who, the entire rest of the time, she can't seem to say no to. 'I can only carry two . . .' and 'It's for the memories . . .' and 'The guy was literally just closing up . . .' How in the end she'd given hers to *whingy* Eden anyhow, who'd instantly – predictably – dropped it, thrown a massive tantrum that only ended after he shocked himself by kicking a small dent in Eva's Tesla.

'Whingy Eden? He sounds a charmer.'

Nancy glances over her shoulder towards the museum, in case someone might have heard her, then hunkers further down into the ditch. She'll have to go back in soon.

'I mean, he's only six . . .' she finds herself saying. 'Plus, y'know, the usual insomnia fun for me here. The silence at night is just so . . . *loud*, so I'm knackered and everything feels a bit shit.' It's like she's making excuses. Why is she? She doesn't say she can't understand why nobody else in her family says anything, does anything about any of this. Why they all just allow it. Why none of it seems to bother them. Sometimes it makes her glad about her own bite-sized family, the fact that Georgie's an only child, that it's essentially the two of them. *Three*, she thinks grudgingly, because Leon isn't a terrible dad. Either way, contained. An uncomplicated devotion. *Hands down you're my favourite child*, she tells Georgie at least once a month, when her daughter greets her with a hug at the door, or presents her with a picture she's drawn. *No competition!* Like the Manga-style picture pinned to the cork board in the kitchen. 'Mum, Dad & Georgie', it says across the top, and Nancy is drawn much bigger than Leon, and she's googled it, analysed it, relished the science that might well be pseudo, but says it means she's a more important figure in her daughter's life.

But she feels guilt about this too, about all of it. Because she knows Georgie would like a sibling, and she's pretty sure there won't be another now, no sister or brother. Unless . . . artificial insemination. She's day-dreamed about it: picking out an Oxbridge hunk (if that isn't an oxymoron) – a dark-haired rower with a double first – from a laminated catalogue. Do they have photos? That would be good, intriguing. Like what kind of man chooses to . . . ? There are those horror stories, of course, about psychopathic infertility doctors, filling fridges with their sperm, foisting it on unsuspecting mothers, father-ing hundreds. Oh, God, it's a minefield. And, anyway, the thought of going back to the beginning is exhausting, unimaginable. She has no idea how Alex is doing it. Isn't honestly sure her sister wants to be doing it.

'Alex? Is that your older sister's name?' Nik's saying, as if somehow he's listening in on her thoughts. 'Yup, makes total sense she's scrabbling around to keep in with your dad.'

Nancy knocks the ash off the end of her cigarette, stamps on it in case there's a spark that might set fire to the ditch. 'Okay, I don't . . . What?'

'Wait, I'm sending you something.'

Her phone pings almost immediately, and she checks her WhatsApp. Nik has forwarded an article headlined **'Why Your Oldest Child Is Your Favourite (And Also More Likely To Win a Nobel Prize!)'**. She scans the opening paragraphs.

. . . the link between birth order and personality . . . Alfred Adler, middle child and founder of the school of individual psychology, argued firstborn children identify most with adults . . . dispute with (firstborn) Sigmund Freud saw Adler resign from the Psychoanalytic Society . . . Seventy per cent of fathers admitted to having a favourite child, in most cases the older one . . . fathers' favouritism has more negative effects on sibling relations, than mothers who show a preference . . . Both men and women were more likely to have a favourite child if their own fathers had favourites . . .

'You see!' she says. 'SEVENTY per cent of fathers!' and she's about to launch into it, when her WhatsApp pings again, with a link to a second article.

85

It's Official: Youngest Siblings Are Parents' Favourite

. . . the youngest child in a family is likely to be favoured over older siblings, according to new research which shows . . . a study of three hundred families . . . Mum and Dad will always love the baby of the family . . .

'Yeah, very, *very* funny, Nik,' she says. 'Side-splitting. Listen!' She holds out her phone, her arm at full stretch towards the field. 'Even the cows are laughing.'

'Cows?'

She snaps a picture of the field and sends it to him. 'Seriously, why would you do this? Search up this stuff. Do you honestly have nothing better to do with your time?'

'Er, nope.' He clicks his tongue. 'And please don't forget, I got a C in A-level psychology. I'm very much across this shit. Okay, I couldn't find anything on favoured middle children –'

'Obviously.'

'But hold on, all is not lost.' She can hear he's distracted, tapping about on his phone. 'Because I think you'll enjoy this.'

'No, stop, enough –'

Another article lands in her messages.

Study Shows Eldest Children Are Intolerable Wankers

On the other end of the line, Nik is cackling. It's a precise description – *cackling* – the exact word to capture the sounds coming out of his mouth.

86

'Isn't it brilliant? *Actual* article, sort of. A spoof Dutch thing.'

'Take me seriously!' Nancy stubs out her cigarette, launches it over the electric fence that's separating her from the farmland. 'You're enjoying this *way* too much. The thing is,' she puts on a faux-dramatic voice, 'I'm misunderstood.' She's mocking herself because she knows how it sounds, the cliché of it, but she means it.

'Me too,' he says, and she laughs.

Fixing her eyes on a brown-and-white cow in the field, as if she's about to address her comments to the animal, like they're in dialogue and it might answer back, she tells him, 'Alex is the clever one, Eva's the beautiful one, and I'm the fuck-up!' She ticks off each of them, one by one on her fingers, although she's aware he can't see her doing it. Then she snorts as if she's made a joke; she doesn't know why she's telling him this. She's tempted to double down, to quote Larkin at him, but that just seems like another cliché, so she resists. *I blame the parents* . . . It's what she and her sisters have always said to each other. Joking, not joking. It doesn't feel so funny now.

'*Eva*'s the beautiful one?' She hears the words scramble from him. He sounds indignant.

It takes her a moment to process the implication of what he's said, or rather how he's said it. For a second, maybe two, neither of them speaks. There's his breath on the line and something feels weird between them.

'Oh, okay, cheers for that, not the clever one, then?' She says it like he's affronted her. She says it to save him, to steer things back. She uses the word 'cheers', something she would never say, and the trace of it in her teeth makes her cringe.

'Hmm, I feel like there's no right answer to this.'

'Correct!' She scratches her shin. A straggling gorse twig has spiked her through her jeans, and it's irritating. 'I mean, right now I'm hiding in a ditch, while the rest of my family tours a pencil museum, so draw your own conclusions.'

There's a moment, after she hangs up, when she feels as if they ended the call too quickly. She's starting to overthink it all. Will things be *off* between them now? Or is this whole thing in her head? She doesn't want anything to change: she values his friendship – she needs it. Also, did she say too much? Because he's three hundred miles away on the other end of a line, he's a disembodied voice, basically, and she's aware that, like this, he doesn't quite seem real. Did she come off as neurotic? Bitter? Or, crime of all woman crimes, *unlikeable*? And she's about to fire off a quick text, something light and in their usual vein, when she hears a whoop, feels a thud, and her niece lands in the ditch next to her.

'Rosa!' Nancy fumbles beneath her legs, finds her cigarette packet and stuffs it up her sleeve. Like she's the child here.

'You smell funny.' Rosa frowns.

'So do you.' Nancy pokes her niece lightly in the ribs, trying not to breathe her smoky-mint breath on her. 'Plus, Rosa, that's no way to talk to your favourite auntie.' When her niece yelps, Nancy jabs a little faster. 'It's okay, you can admit it. I'm your favourite. I won't tell

Auntie Eva. Now *she* really does smell funny, especially after she's been for one of her crazy runs.' And Rosa is giggling and giggling, rolling helplessly in the ditch, and Nancy is laughing too, harder and harder, uncontrollably, until from nowhere, something slams into her. A memory.

She sees her dad and Eva walking through a field just like the one on the other side of the fence, except the cows are black-and-white, normal cows. Eva's maybe five, several years younger than Rosa is now, and they're on holiday, headed to a village pub, fuelled by the promise of a packet of smoky bacon crisps and a lemonade-and-lime when they get there. Eva has on the open-toe sandals that are new from Mothercare, and she isn't looking where she's going when she steps into the cowpat. Green and yellow gloop oozes horribly over her foot, and oily emerald-coloured flies swarm from nowhere. And Eva cries and cries, until their dad lifts her onto his shoulders. He carries her all the way to the pub like that, one sandal on and one off, cracking terrible jokes to make her laugh. Takes off his straw hat that makes him look cooler than other dads, and squashes it onto Eva's head, *So that people coming the other way will think we're an extra tall man . . .*

And lagging behind, complaining loudly about her achy legs, Nancy hadn't understood that she was jealous. Even with Eva's toes covered with shit and the ruined new sandals, which later had to be thrown away, she felt pushed out of something private between them – and, for God's sake, what is wrong with her? Why is she like this? Still now. So stupidly sensitive about every little thing.

'I'm going.' Rosa has sensed her distraction and she's bored and scrabbling up and out of the ditch, accidentally elbowing Nancy in the head as she does it. There are voices in the distance: the others must be done in the museum – it has all of two rooms after all, and a tightly focused brief. Nancy knows she needs to get up and find them, to make her excuses about where she's been. But she isn't sure how she'll muster the energy to stand. Is it true? Is she the fuck-up? Bowing her head to her knees, she imagines broken pieces of herself, like the remains of an archaeological dig, mud-crusted and fractured and strewn in the ditch. And it seems to her that, no matter how tightly she hugs her legs, no matter if she could wrap her arms all the way around her back, still she wouldn't be able to keep herself together. Because she feels, in this moment, as if she – as if *everything* – is coming apart.

Eva, Monday afternoon

There's something very weird going on with the weather. Eva is starting to think that the glass house has some kind of strange micro-climate all of its own because now, on top of the wind and the rain and the sun, it's snowing in autumn. And not just ordinary snow. Scott is beside himself with excitement at this new meteorological 'event'. They're in the lounge and he's like Tom Cruise on *Oprah*, leaping up and down on one of the endless oatmeal sofas, jabbing a finger in the direction of the wall of glass at the white-out beyond. Every few seconds there's a *boom* that sounds like a distant explosion.

'This is unreal,' he's saying. 'It's *thundersnow*. I mean . . .' And then he shakes his head, jumps a little more. If it was one of the kids, someone would have told them to get off the sofa by now. That it isn't a playground. And Eva loves snow, she adores it, but it's come from nowhere, this downfall – even the Met Office didn't predict it. She knows this for sure, thanks to Scott's rolling weather reports, which have started to unsettle her with the chaotic conditions they describe. Maybe it's because of the see-through house, which seems to bring the outside in, but Eva feels vulnerable here, more so than in London. There's no one else for miles around: it's just her family and the mountains and forests, an ocean. The natural world pushing up against them.

Kneeling at the coffee-table, Nancy is painting her nails turquoise, murmuring something about how oppressive it all is, and please, God, let them not get snowed in, and Eva's one hundred per cent sure she intends it to be audible. Rosa and Eden have their faces pressed up against the glass wall, and they're asking Alex will there be enough snow for sledging and when can they go out and can they have a snowball fight, and Luc is holding the baby up at the window so that she can see out too. '*Il neige*,' he's saying. '*Il neige, mon petit chou . . .*' And Scott is telling everyone and no one, because they aren't listening, that when thunderstorms form in wintry conditions they can cause heavy downfalls of snow, that the snow acts to dampen the sound of the thunder, that *thundersnow* is caused by an upward current of warm air rising into a layer of cold air and . . . Eva is just waiting for Alex and Nancy to exchange a he's-such-a-dick look, when from nowhere, a melody starts to play. An exquisite cadence that spreads through the room.

None of them have heard it before, and they all stop what they're doing, because it's like a Juilliard ensemble has set up discreetly in each of the four corners of the outsize space.

'What the frick is that?' Nancy screws the lid on the polish, makes wide stars with both hands.

They wait, listening, until the melody comes again.

'Doorbell, must be,' Eva says. But as she starts to move across the room towards the hallway, Scott leaps off the sofa and bounds past her. By the time she reaches the lobby, there's a man dripping onto the heated floor tiles, his hair shaggy with snow, his clothes caked with icy clumps. He's framed by the open door and a swirling Narnia snowscape beyond, an intrepid explorer who's stumbled heroically out of the wild. There's an expensive-looking leather holdall at his feet.

'Yeah, the taxi guy refused to drive down the track,' he's telling Scott. 'The pussy.'

It's a long moment – a moment of denial, she thinks afterwards – before Eva recognizes Scott's son Jay. She looks from father to son. What is he doing here? How did he know where to find them? Scott is turned entirely away from her, and there's a squareness to the set of his shoulders, a rigidity that tips her off. *Scott knew he was coming,* she thinks. He invited him here without telling her. But why? She wouldn't have said no; she couldn't have.

'Hi!' she says. 'This is a nice surprise.' Then she moves forward with a little skip, making a dumb 'oop' sound, like she's forgotten her manners. Half misses as she kisses his cheek.

'The crew docked earlier than expected.' Scott twirls a hand vaguely and doesn't look at her as he says it. 'A meeting of oligarchs or something. Which is perfect timing!' He claps his son on the arm. Pieces of icy snow slide from his coat to the floor.

'I was tempted to take a detour,' Jay says, and he laughs. 'There was some serious hotness sitting across from me on the train.' He mimes long hair, long nails.

'We got chatting, but there was a boyfriend, there's always a boyfriend . . .'

He is my stepson, Eva thinks, before she can block the thought. Her mind skids to the grey day that was how many weeks ago now? Six? Eight? She hasn't kept track. Hasn't wanted to think about it at all. About the quick vows she and Scott made at Camden Register Office. The smell of old carpet and the registrar's Burger King breath. How functional it all was, how practical. Really quite depressing, if she's honest. They were overdressed, both of them: she in a matching skirt and blouse she'd had delivered the day before from Net-a-Porter, Scott in a Hermès suit that she'd paid for. On the way in, she'd skittered her eyes past the less-than-romantic signs Sellotaped to the walls, cheap printouts in shouty capitals warning against sham marriages. Wondered, for the briefest of moments, if maybe the signs were there for her benefit. They had sex afterwards, back at the house. He went down on her at the foot of the stairs, and it felt . . . What? Unexpected? Unmarital? Hot? But then she opened her eyes and saw him between her legs, his neck stretched awkwardly, his too-eager eyes watching her face. The narcissism there. It was the over-enthusiastic pink flicker of his tongue that tipped her over the edge – and not in a good way – so she faked an orgasm to make it stop. Felt unsavoury as she smoothed down the Net-a-Porter skirt that had got all bunched up around her waist. Eva realizes she's clenching her jaw, releases her teeth. Does Jay know about the wedding? Has Scott told him? Has he kept that from her too?

There's a crowd of them in the hallway now, rubber-necking at this six-foot-tall stranger, with his super-yacht tan and asymmetrical nose. Her mum and dad have stayed in the lounge, asleep – or pretending to be – her mum in one of the mid-century-style armchairs next to the wood-burning stove, her dad stretched out on the daybed that's positioned at the far end of the room for the best mountain views. Rosa's balancing on one leg and staring, as Scott rushes through some introductions. He doesn't bother with the kids, she notices.

Behind Jay, in the open doorway, lightning slashes the sky. Eden screams and covers his ears.

'Can someone please shut the door?' Nancy says, in a tone that suggests she, too, would like to scream.

'Is it too early for drinks?' Luc is already bundling the baby to Alex as he says it. And Eva understands that this is less an act of altruism – Luc is never knowingly caught helping in the kitchen, or indeed helping any-where at all – more a reason to palm off his own child at the earliest opportunity. She's not about to complain, though. The fact is she could do with a drink right now. Hell, she could do with several.

'No, not too early,' she says quickly. 'Definitely not. This is a *holiday*!' She tries to inject the word with giddy enthusiasm, but she's aware, as she says it, that she's fallen short. Like, really, she might as well have said, This is a *shit-show*!

As they're turning to go back into the lounge, Lucy appears in the wide corridor. She's in a khaki belted bikini, the insanely expensive one from Selfridges, and her hair is wet and slicked back from her forehead. It looks black like that, her hair, and her mouth, which is Vivienne's mouth, looks full and dark and wide. More so than ever, as if she's bitten her lips to plump them up in the old-fashioned 1950s way. Eva's automatic thought is how incredible her daughter looks, and she immediately hates herself for thinking it. As if her unconscious brain – her true, shameful self – believes that how her daughter looks is the single most important thing about her child. That her daughter looking like this somehow reflects back on her. Like together they're winning the beauty contest. But still she can't stop herself assessing, rating, *comparing* her as she stands there. She has the look of Ursula Andress when she rises out of the sea in *Dr. No,* Eva thinks. And then she realizes – and she can't understand why it's taken her so long to arrive at this conclusion – that Lucy has come from the pool. Eva hadn't known she was in there.

'Jesus, Lucy!' She bolts towards her child, as though she's been pushed from behind. 'What were you doing, swimming in a storm? You don't go near water when there's lightning. You know that!' Her voice is climbing a ladder, and she tries to rein in her mind, which has jumped to an image of her daughter scorched at the edges and floating face down on the surface of the gently lapping jade-green pool.

'That's not a thing,' Lucy says, but she hugs her arms around her torso. There's a flush across her chest in the shape of a lopsided heart, a droplet of water running down her neck.

'It bloody well *is* a thing, excuse my French.' Eva scrunches her face briefly, glances at the kids.

'The chances of getting struck by lightning are higher than you'd guess,' Scott announces, in his let-me-tell-you voice. 'Between thirty and sixty people a year in the UK.' He reaches past Jay to adjust a picture on the wall, one of the scribbly paintings that line the corridor – it's been knocked slightly askew. 'That's a stat from the Royal Society for the Prevention of Accidents.'

'Do you make this stuff up, Scott?' Nancy asks, and Eva catches her middle sister flicking her eyes towards Alex as she says it.

'I knew someone who got struck by lightning in the bath once.' Eva's dad has come round the corner from the lounge. His hair, what's left of it, is all fluffed up to one side, and there's a crease mark on his cheek where he's been lying against it. 'Killed instantly,' he adds enthusiastically. 'Electrocuted. More a friend of a friend, really. I mean, I knew someone who knew someone. At university.'

He's come to stand next to Nancy, who flinches – literally flinches – and moves away from him. She doesn't even try to hide it.

For God's sake, Eva thinks. Enough already. She just wants to enjoy the holiday, and is that honestly too much to ask? This holiday that she's paid for, and it isn't the point, of course it isn't, but why can't her sister just let it go? It was an accident. Barely even that, because no one got hurt. Nothing happened. And now Jay, Jay who is a virtual stranger, is here, and she wishes with her whole heart he wasn't, and does that make her a horrible person? Probably.

'No blood at least, or I'd imagine not anyhow . . .' her dad is saying.

'Maybe not in front of the kids, Dad.' Alex makes a small 'cut, cut' motion with her hand back and forth across her throat. 'Sorry, Dad, it's just . . .' Her sister trails off, then apologizes a second time.

Eva thinks she can smell the snow, the sharp, fresh scent of it, and she'd like to get out there, see if she could run. Make some tracks and work against the cold weight of it, challenge herself. It would be the exact opposite of the desert run, the Marathon des Sables she's had her eye on these past few months, wondering if it would be a bridge too far. Too dangerous. Six days running, 156 miles, carrying everything you need on your back.

'Don't dress up on my account, Lucy . . .' Scott's son has raised his voice, and it takes Eva a moment to process what he's said. A quip he's making so far after the event, it's obvious it's taken him a good while to arrive at it. It doesn't even make sense.

'Ha-ha. Who invited you?' Lucy makes her voice go dead, but Eva notices she shifts a little, wraps her arms a little tighter around her breasts. There are goosebumps on her daughter's skin, even though, despite the snow, the house is still crazily, stultifyingly hot. She's in a bikini, but there's a nakedness to her. Something Eva wouldn't have thought twice about before Jay arrived, before he made that comment. Lucy fixes Eva with a look, like, 'Really, I mean it, who invited him? What's going on?'

'Jay's here!' Eva says limply. Because what else can she do? She has a friend, Marta, who does this, who talks in non sequiturs, so that hanging out with her makes Eva feel a little trippy, confused, like her brain is chasing round in circles. Then, as she gestures towards Scott's son, to illustrate her point, she sees his eyes all over her child's body. There's a beat before he notices Eva watching, and he looks quickly up and away. She roots her feet into the ground beneath her. Otherwise she might take three quick steps towards him and slap his wonky little face. Fuck you very much for this, Scott, she thinks.

There's a muted boom of thunder from outside, and behind her, someone squeezes her arm. Nancy. She knows before she looks. Nancy who, when Eva glances over her shoulder, gives her a wink. Not a taking-the-piss wink, but an I-feel-you wink. Because Nancy knows. She sees what's going on. Eva has confided in her about how it is between the kids, how it is with Lucy and Scott too, the unhappy tangle of it all. Because she tells her sisters everything. All the boring bits, the tedious stuff, the extensive moaning that she knows makes her look bad, bitter, mean-spirited, neurotic, unattractive. The offload. The whole shebang. The things she wouldn't share with anyone else because she would haemorrhage her friends for sure.

And now, with the imprint of Nancy's hand on her arm still, she feels guilty. Guilty because Nancy is being kind. Nancy is demonstrating the exact opposite of the uncharitableness Eva directed towards her just moments ago. Whatever this thing is with their dad, she can't tell

99

Nancy how to be, how to feel: it isn't up to her. And guilty, like she's betrayed some sort of unspoken pact. Because it isn't true that the three of them share everything, that they always have. Eva glances at Scott, at the signet ring he's wearing on the little finger of his right hand. The ring that reminds her of the one their old dentist used to wear, the dentist with the slip-on shoes that she and her sisters couldn't stand. It's the most she'd agree to for now, a placeholder, until she and Scott upgrade to the real thing – the real *rings*. Just as soon as they've told the family – just as soon as she's told Lucy, which she will do, she will. She just needs to pick her moment.

Yes, it's some kind of special bullshit, she thinks, as she takes off her hoody that she's going to wrap around Lucy, to cover her up, to shield her. It's bullshit, this notion that the three of them – Alex, Nancy and she – know each other inside out.

Nancy, Autumn 1989

She's late coming out of school, and her friends are long gone, as she makes her way along the road that narrows between concrete bollards – the ones her mum once scraped the car on (coming towards them at 30 m.p.h., according to her dad). She hadn't handed in her maths homework again and Mrs Gerard stopped her at the end of the lesson, asked her to stay behind. Nancy doesn't mind her, Mrs Gerard. She likes her, even. She's not an idiot like some of the other teachers – she's not trying to be your friend, and she isn't patronizing, or reaching round you at your desk, a little too close, breathing coffee breath all over you. She doesn't have favourites. Even so, Nancy hovered by the classroom door, making it clear she didn't want to be there.

'You're really smart, Nancy,' Mrs Gerard said, not looking at her as she wiped clean the slide on the overhead projector. She was wearing the necklace with the beads like dark plums and it banged against her chest with each vigorous movement of her arm. 'As smart as your sister.' She glanced up as she said this, and let the words hang. 'You just hide it better.' She was talking about 'All the As Alex', as Nancy has been calling her since GCSEs, trying to make it stick. And it shocked her that Mrs Gerard had just come out with it like that, because no one had ever said it to her before. Not directly. It's something she's never understood because she knows she finds things at school pretty easy most of the time, and she's interested too, in how things work, finding out stuff, so she doesn't get how her parents seem not to have noticed. Or maybe they have. It's just they've noticed Alex one hell of a lot more. 'It's not like that role is already taken, Nancy, okay?' Mrs Gerard went on. 'There's space for more than one. Do you see what I'm saying here?' And standing there, with the back of her head pressed against the rectangle of reinforced glass in the classroom door, a strange tidal wave rose in Nancy. A kind of whooshing feeling in her stomach, her throat and her ears, and it was all she could do to stop herself bursting into tears.

She's fighting to keep the swell of it down as she comes out onto the main road, across from the bus stop. And that's when she sees them. Eva and the two girls. Eva's small for her age and the two other girls are taller. As she waits for the lights to change so she can cross, she recognizes the one with the curly hair – she's the younger sister of someone she knows to avoid. She knows, too, that the girl at the bus stop is in the year above Eva. What is Eva doing with them? The older girls have cigarettes in their hands and they're waving them around, making sure people are noticing. At first Nancy thinks her sister is smoking too, and it jolts her, even though she smokes herself – at parties, and down by the old railway tracks, out the back of the flats behind the hospital, anywhere, really, that her parents or their friends won't catch her. Even though she keeps a pack of ten Marlboro Lights in the top drawer of the desk in her bedroom, she can't stand the thought that her little sister, who's only twelve, might be doing the same. They learned about it in sex education and personal development, that absolute cringe of a lesson, taken by the hideous Miss Bannister: that you're four times more likely to smoke if your older sibling smokes, the same with teen pregnancy, drugs, all of it. So it would be her fault if Eva is smoking. Well, Alex's. But as she comes closer, she understands that isn't what she's seeing. One of the older girls – the one she doesn't know – is holding her cigarette too close to Eva's face, and as Nancy watches, she thumbs the filter, flicks ash at Eva. A howl jumps into Nancy's throat as her sister jerks her head back, reaches a hand to her cheek, like she's been burned.

'OI!' Nancy yells, and runs out into the road because, sod the traffic, she needs to get to her sister. Then she's stopping, running, stopping, running in between the cars, and she knows what she's doing is dangerous. She's nearly across, when a man in a work van leans into his horn, and gesticulates at her through the windscreen. He opens his jaw wide and mouths a word that looks like *cunt*. It's obvious she's a kid – she's in her school uniform – and it shocks her, the open, ugly aggression in him. The hate in his face that makes her feel as if something is letting loose in her bladder, like all of a sudden she needs to pee.

'Eva!' she calls, as she reaches the pavement on the other side. All three girls turn to face her.

She doesn't need to say anything. One hand on the bus shelter, the other squeezing Eva's arm, she just stares the two girls down. Her heart is thumping in her body, and she isn't letting it show on her face, but it's taking her a moment to get her breath back.

'Do Mummy and Daddy know you're smoking?' she asks, after a pause. The girls roll their eyes, but she can see they're squirming. Knows they can sense she's a bomb that might go off. They can't leave, because her arm across the bus shelter is blocking their exit. 'You do know you're supposed to inhale, right? That's what the big girls do.'

'Nancy, it's all right, honestly. I'm . . .' Eva starts to say.

Nancy looks at her sister. Sees that hair has escaped messily from the two little buns knotted either side of Eva's head. Sees her too-shiny eyes, her slack mouth, the look she knows so well. The exact same way she looks when she's been told off by their mum or dad. Scared, is how she looks, and Nancy feels something tip in her chest.

They were arguing only yesterday afternoon because Eva had borrowed her Lenny Kravitz album without asking and bent the corner. Or maybe the corner was already bent, Nancy isn't entirely certain, but she yelled at Eva anyhow. Blasted away her protests that Nancy never listened to the record anyway. Snatched up the album from the end of her bed, and left her sister standing in the middle of her room, arms hanging at her sides, watching her go. Later, she saw a note Eva had left on the kitchen table, *Please buy Clearasil! The lotion in the bottle, not the weird brown cream thx*, she'd written, and drawn a smiley face next to it. Reading it, Nancy felt a strange pull of guilt. She took a pen from the pot next to the phone, inked an arrow pointing to the smiley face and wrote, *Pls don't do that rank face x*. She chuckled to herself as she did it, imagining Eva reading it. Then, when she checked the note later, there was a reply in tiny squashed writing, barely legible. *Nancy smells*. She laughed out loud when she saw it.

'She thinks she's the big-I-am just because she's got her face plastered across C & friggin' A.' The girl with the curly hair has her head down, but she says it loud enough for Nancy to hear.

Oh, okay, of course, Nancy thinks. She's talking about the modelling. Eva's famous at school for it. She's been doing it since she was six and gets a lot of work for shops and catalogues, so everyone knows, and it's her thing whether she likes it or not. Maybe related: all of the boys are in love with her; most of the girls don't like her. It's a win-lose situation. And Nancy is proud and jealous all at the same time, which is confusing and messed up. She's never told anyone how she feels, because how could she? Although she's wondered if Alex thinks the same things she does; she's almost confided in her more than once, but something's always stopped her. One thing's for sure: there's a lot of money building up in a Nat-West bank account somewhere. Eva has all five china piggybanks, which come one by one as you stash more and more money into savings and reach certain target amounts. They're lined up on her windowsill, from the baby pig in a china nappy with an outsize safety-pin, to the dad in a shiny black suit and red bow tie. And Nancy covets them, she can't help it, although she's aware she's way too old for things like that.

The girl with the curly hair is still muttering. Nancy catches the words: '... not exactly Cindy bloody Crawford ...' But she's barely audible, trailing off, unconvincing.

Nancy pictures herself lifting the largest of the pigs – the banker dad – from Eva's windowsill, and smashing it hard into the top of this girl's curly head, which looks stiff with VO5 mousse she probably buys in bulk from Superdrug. Imagines the china shards stuck sharp in her pink scalp, blood seeping at their edges. Nancy's aware of an old lady wheeling a tartan shopping trolley past the bus stop; she can feel something like sparks popping behind her eyes as she stands there, holding herself back. She waits until the woman has moved further along the pavement. Then, putting her body between the girls and her sister, she leans in close, makes her voice low.

'You touch my sister again, I'll come after you. Okay?' She smiles. A smile that isn't. 'And trust me, if I do, *your* face won't be appearing on a billboard any time soon.' She jerks her head to the side, as if she's head-butting thin air. A blunt nod in the direction of the street. 'Now fuck off.'

As soon as they've gone, she wraps an arm around Eva's shoulders. She feels strangely emptied out, a little bit weak in her arms and legs, like she needs to sit down. The same feeling she gets when she skips breakfast. Clicking the side of her mouth, she gives her sister a kind of half-hug. 'I could totally get a part in *EastEnders*,' she says.

Eva leans into her, just for a second. Her head fits under Nancy's chin, and when Nancy breathes in, she can smell the Impulse body spray her little sister has started wearing these past couple of months. Gipsy it's called, and it lingers in the bathroom, in the hall, in the kitchen, long after Eva's left a room. There's the cringiest ad campaign for it, and it's an absolute gift, just too good to pass up, so that Nancy and Alex have taken to following their sister around the house, quoting it, in silky Milk Tray voices. *When a man you've never met before suddenly gives you flowers, don't be alarmed . . .* then laughing and laughing, as they choke out the punchline, infecting each other because they can't help it, . . . *he's only acting on Impulse!*

'Thanks, Nance,' Eva whispers now.

'You're welcome,' Nancy tells her. And she checks over her shoulder, sees the red bulk of the number four coming up the road. 'But you're not sitting next to me on the bus.'

Alex, Monday evening

No one wants to admit it, but there's a bad smell in the glass house. A smell that won't go. It started in a corner of the TV lounge and now it's spread to the hallway outside the pool room. Standing at the basin in the en-suite, Alex sniffs the air. Can she smell it here too? She's had the windows open at the other end of the house all evening, but if anything it's getting stronger, and when she checked last thing there were damp patches on the walls, on the floor, where the snow has got in. Reaching into her wash-bag, she finds her dental floss. And she's about to snap off a thread, when she realizes she's too tired, she's done, it just feels too hard. Alex bares her teeth in the mirror, checking, then grimaces at her reflection: she has become a woman who no longer has the energy to floss.

As she comes into the bedroom, poking her tongue into the gaps between her teeth, as if that way she might be able to unclog them, Luc looks up from his book. He's reading *Fermat's Last Theorem* for the third or fourth time, the French edition. His *maths book*, she calls it. And he has on his polo shirt still, teal with a little pink logo. He owns the same shirt in several different colours – and none of them make him look like Paul Weller. Luc puts a finger to his lips, points at the baby, who's asleep in the travel cot on his side of the bed. Through the white netting, she can see a small hump of sleeping bag. The one with the tiny yellow armadillos that has press studs decorated with tufts of grass on each shoulder. Her baby's head is turned to one side, and Alex has no desire to move closer, to creep around to the side of the cot to observe her sleeping. It's the best bit – one of the best bits – she knows this. You can just watch and enjoy and you don't have to *do* anything, give anything, but she isn't interested; she feels almost nothing at all. Was it like this with the older two? She doesn't think so. She glances at her husband. He's eyeing her oddly. Does it show on her face, these thoughts she's having? Is he noticing?

Luc props himself up a little higher on his pillows. 'You look beautiful,' he whispers. And it's so unexpected – he isn't one to throw a compliment around, neither of them is, really – she wonders how much he's had to drink. He's been at it pretty steadily since late afternoon, and he doesn't usually drink much at all.

Alex glances down at herself, at the washed-out Coca-Cola T-shirt she's wearing, at her legs she hasn't shaved since she can't remember when. Since they'd spent a fortnight at Center Parcs at the beginning of August, probably.

'Where's Scott's son sleeping?' she asks, and sits on the edge of the bed, ignoring the comment he's just made.

'In the TV lounge? The laundry room? The carport? I don't give a fuck,' Luc answers, and he has that look on his face. The dopey, lopsided look. She thinks maybe he's slurring his words a little. He reaches for her with one hand, splays his book on the bedside table with the other. 'Alex, we're on holiday . . .'

She wants to say, Ha! This is not a holiday! Because she's completely drained from being away from home with kids this age. It's not even close to being a holiday. It's harder work, in fact, just that the domestic drudgery has shifted from one location to another *temporary* – and therefore more difficult to manage – location. And there's an audience so you have to smile through it. But she knows that what Luc means is we always have sex on holiday.

Tugging down the hem of her T-shirt, she covers the tops of her thighs. 'You literally just told me to be quiet,' she says, aware that she's stalling. She thinks they've had sex maybe twice since the baby was born six months ago. Three times at a push. And she doesn't want to go there now. It's the last thing she needs. Or maybe it's exactly what she needs. It's just that when it comes to Luc, there's a void. A void where her desire used to be. And, anyway, her mind is crowded with all the things she's been keeping in. For a start, she wants to talk about Scott's son, to dissect the feeling in the room. Like: Eva *did not* look pleased when he showed up – the words out of her mouth in no way matched the expression on her face – and she wants to know if her husband saw it too.

'Luc . . .' She nods in the direction of the cot, wrinkles her nose in a way she hopes makes her appear regretful.

'We can be quiet.' Moving towards her, he starts to kiss her neck, slides a hand up under her T-shirt, finds her breast. 'See?' he whispers. 'I don't hear a thing.'

Her whole body tenses. She doesn't want to do this. There's the baby right there, all the stuff with her dad, her mum, Nancy, the smell in the house, and . . . and there's Matt. Her fingers twitch. Like his name – the name she's been trying to keep pushed down in her – has set off a body response. Something involuntary that's zipped from the root of her brain and along her spinal cord, through her nervous system to the tips of her. And it's all she can do not to wrestle her husband off, bolt from the bed and snatch up her phone that's plugged in at the other side of the room.

Alex's mind jumps to that morning. The clear early light, her hot breath in the cold car pulled up on the verge at the side of the B road. She can't call him, so she does the next best thing; she jumps on Facebook, Twitter, Instagram. Matt is prolific on social media, constantly posting. And as she scrolls through his past twelve, twenty-four, forty-eight hours, like she's feeding an addiction – she *is* feeding an addiction – she's aware she both loves and hates seeing him like this.

He's uploaded a bunch of new posts to Instagram. The first is a picture of him in his garden. He's holding a basketball, making as if he's about to pitch it at who-ever's taking the photo. It's one of those contemporary concrete gardens that make her thirsty to look at. Matt's wearing chinos and a white shirt that's untucked, and his hair is pushed back off his face. It's thick still, his hair, unlike Luc's, which he has to cut close to his head now. And it's mostly dark brown – just a little grey here and there, which doesn't matter because he's a man so it's 'acceptable', attractive even. She certainly finds it attractive. *Salt and pepper.*

Reflexively, Alex flicks to the next post, feels her stomach swoop. And she knows she should stop right there, because Zoë is in this picture. Matt's wife is looking at her husband and smiling. Alex pinches the screen, enlarges the image, until Zoë's face fills her phone. She isn't as beautiful close up: there's a hollowing in her cheeks that ages her, and her eyes are on the small side, sort of fading out. And she's very thin. Is she too thin? Alex zooms out a little, pushes the picture around the screen with her finger. Are those marks on Zoë's arms and legs? They look like marks, suspiciously regular ones, and there's quite a few. She's exactly the sort of perfect woman who would self-harm. But she *is* pretty, Alex can't deny it. Is Zoë prettier than her? She thinks yes, then no. She zooms back in. Zoë has good hair, perfect balayage that fades light to dark in salon waves (which gives you an idea of their income, because that is a professional blow-dry in a day-to-day setting for sure), and she has a strong nose, not too narrow, not too wide and not at all sharp, or bumpy or hooked in profile. It's a thing on Instagram now, what you look like from the side. All the kids are doing 'profile checks', which is as horrendous as it sounds – Lucy was talking about it in front of Rosa yesterday, and she'd had to steer her daughter away. Made it very clear that it was stupid teen stuff, definitely not something to aspire to.

Alex twists in her seat, elongates her neck, so she can see her face sideways on in the rear-view mirror. She's at an awkward angle and it's difficult to assess. Plus, she can't look in the mirror and see the whole of her profile at the same time. She adjusts her head down a little, up a little, eyes her chin, which recedes in a way she hates. It's a weak chin, sloping backwards like an apology. It's part of the reason she's had her hair cut as she has, longer in the front to try to make more of her jaw. *Alex! Did you lose something?* Nancy or Eva used to ask her when they were teenagers. And they'd come towards her, hands cupped in a careful ball, like they were holding something precious – a live creature or a rare jewel. *I think I've found it! I've found your chin, Alex* . . . She could almost laugh about it now, and does with her sisters sometimes, marvelling at the casual cruelty of it; strange to think there was once a time they felt so close – so *safe* – they could just come out and do those things, say those things. How could they have known this kind of brutal scrutiny would sink its teeth in, stay for life?

Alex squints at the screen. Zoë is definitely prettier. But Alex knows that her own eyes are striking. Matt has told her this. They're her dad's dark brown eyes, but with flecks like spattered gold. And eyes are most important, right? Windows to the soul and all that. Eyes trump everything. Trump. She can't bear to use that word any more, not even in thought. Is it true that eyes *beat* everything? She would like to ask someone. She would like to ask Matt, but how can she? Behind his wife in the picture, there's a single olive tree bent like a stooped widow, like there's a third person in shot. Alex shrinks the image back to its original size. Zoë is wearing a loose dress with clogs; she's stylish in that moneyed west London bohemian way. Alex wonders where the dress is from, how much it cost. She glances down at her feet in the wheel well, at her Adidas trainers that she'll need to go over with the whitener when she gets home because of the crazy weather and all the mud here. Could *she* get away with wearing clogs?

Luc has pushed her T-shirt right up. He has his mouth on her breast now, a hand between her legs, and she's half in the room, half not. Despite herself, she's starting to feel it, as if the surface of her skin is on high alert. Tipping back her head, she lets her throat stretch long. She's picturing Matt. Imagining it's him bent over her like this, tracking a slow hot line down her ribcage, her stomach, her abdomen –

'*Merde!*' Luc whispers, and he freezes, his face inches from her body.

It's a moment before she realizes the baby has cried out.

Stealthily, Luc takes his arm from her, puts a finger to his lips, which look wet and swollen, although he is the one who's spoken, not her.

The baby cries out a second time. Alex experiences the sound in the pit of her body. She closes her eyes, wills the baby back to sleep. She can feel the pulse between her legs still.

Matt does not have a baby, she thinks. He's out the other side of the nappies and reflux and teething. He doesn't even have a child at primary school. The family spent the bank holiday weekend in Amsterdam. She's seen photographs of the four of them – Matt and Zoë and the two girls – posing on old-fashioned bikes next to a canal, flicking peace signs outside the Stedelijk Museum. Eating sushi at an outdoor table, a bottle of something cooling in a silver bucket on a stand. Photographs she resented – no, *hated* – but couldn't take her eyes off. She thinks of their own mealtimes: melamine plates and beige chicken pieces from the freezer. Almost always a cup of juice knocked over, pooling stickily under the table because Eden is left-handed. Amsterdam was the second holiday they'd had in quick succession, Matt and his family, after July in the Seychelles. That one was all infinity pools and langoustine platters, sunshine trips on catamarans. The girls are tall and slim and tanned and look like their dad. She wishes she didn't know their names, but she does. The older one is Sadie, the younger Coco.

Luc has started to kiss the skin at the top of her thighs. She opens her eyes, glances at the cot, sees that the baby has settled. Then she lowers her head back onto the bed. Did Matt and his wife have sex in the Seychelles? The thought of it assaults her. It's an island stuffed full of besotted honeymooners, after all. Floaty white dresses and barely there bikinis, the hiss of the dark sea at night. They probably did it everywhere: on the beach, in the sea, in the shower. In the super-king-sized bed that could house a family of five, while he licked white rum from her flat stomach, speciality of the island . . . Alex squeezes her eyes shut, feels a line of pain shoot from temple to temple. Blindly, she reaches down and finds her husband's shoulders, grips them, trying to anchor herself, like that way she might nix these thoughts she doesn't want to be having.

She panicked when she saw Eva across the road, running on the spot and staring hard in through the car window. She had a photo up of Matt – a selfie – with a tall, modern building in the background, and was thinking how much he'd changed since they were teenagers, and also hadn't. There were the grown-up clothes – the dark grey chinos he always wore, and an ironed T-shirt that she knew would smell of washing powder – but his expression was the same. The same serious eyes, that looked sad even when he wasn't. They'd started dating – *going out*, they called it then – after she'd met him at the Dartmouth Arms, one of the pubs where the bar staff didn't look too hard at your fake ID. They'd never spoken before, but she knew who he was, of course she did. He'd come up to the corner table where she was sitting, and bummed a cigarette from her. He could have asked any one of her friends, but he'd acknowledged only her, like the others didn't exist. They'd passed the cigarette between them, smoked it down to the butt, and then he'd said did she want to come outside? It was kind of loud in there with the music.

Matt Dempster. The boy she's loved since she was seventeen, the boy she's been *obsessed* with since then. Man, she corrects herself, the man she's loved. She does the maths. Seventeen . . . twenty-seven . . . thirty-seven . . . forty-five . . . For nearly three decades. And who has come back into her life this past year. Showing up again at the exact same time as the baby – like somehow it was ordained – and splitting her soul. In the picture on her phone she could just make out his tattoo, showing at the edge of his T-shirt sleeve. The Japanese symbol he'd had done in Camden, after they'd been seeing each other for a couple of weeks. *Live for Today*, it meant. They were basically kids back then. And this is why – okay, yes, he and Zoë have children together – but this is why Zoë can never know him as Alex does. Because of this shared history, the days spent down by the canal at the edge of the market, nights drinking cider in Waterlow Park. Midnight cheeseburgers at Archway McDonald's, and Southern Comfort at Quinns on Kentish Town Road. Hands inside each other's clothes in the shadows of the Heath. Underage clubbing at the Dome. Matt had kept the tattoo hidden from his parents until the scab got infected, and they'd been furious, cut off his allowance indefinitely. He was in the year above her at school, but didn't go much: he was planning on being Jon Bon Jovi back then, not a management consultant.

It looked as though Eva was going to cross the road to the car, and Alex felt a sudden speeding up in her body. She almost dropped the phone as she fumbled to swipe away the post she was looking at. Watched, with her face on fire, as Matt vanished and the screen turned black. But then her sister pumped her arms, flashed a comedy grin, like *Can't stop, I'm training!*, and moved off. Staring through the windscreen, Alex felt winded, weak. As if she, not her sister, was the one out there doing the exercise. And as Eva disappeared into the trees, she laid her head on the steering wheel, felt the knobbled plastic dig in at her hairline. Because had her sister seen anything? Had her alarm shown in her face? Her shame? Her guilt? But even as she was thinking it, her fingers were grappling with her phone. She knew she should go back to the glass house – she'd already been gone too long. She knew she should stop, but she couldn't. Just five more minutes, that was all she wanted, five more minutes with him, with Matt.

Alex is vaguely aware of the loveseat on the other side of the room, and on top of it their tech lined up neatly, their laptops and iPads and Kindles and phones . . . but something is happening to her body. So that she isn't thinking about Matt any more, or his wife, or Luc, or anyone or anything. She's somewhere else altogether. A tunnelled place that's at once shut down and wide, wide open. Alex is entirely inside her own mind, and she's given herself over to a force that seems to have nothing to do with her. All she cares about is the moment she's in.

But as she comes (noiselessly, so she won't wake the baby) – even as she's a split second past the tipping point, even as the muscles inside her are still contracting – she already feels horribly empty, as if something has been stripped from her. As Luc smiles up at her, a sleepy, self-satisfied smile, she couldn't feel further away from him. She couldn't feel lonelier. Lying there on the bed, her feet start to itch, the too familiar feeling that starts at her heel and moves up along her sole, or maybe her soul. And she grinds them against the sheet, but the sensation won't stop.

Vivienne, Autumn 1990

It's half past one in the morning and Vivienne is sitting in the armchair at the back of the kitchen, a cup of tea at her feet that's gone cold. Patrick is out, driving the streets, looking for Nancy, who should have been home an hour and a half ago. He's desperate with worry, more so than she is, because it isn't the first time their middle daughter's done this, far from it – especially since she started a new school year, turned seventeen. But Patrick's anxiety has infected her, because *what if* . . . as he keeps saying, and now Vivienne can't sleep.

There'd been another phone call from the school this week, this time from the physics teacher. 'She's a really bright kid and her scores are good *but* . . .' the call had started.

'Me? Rude?' Nancy raged afterwards. '*Sir* was rude. He read out the test scores, right the way to the lowest mark, and made Shiloh cry. So I told him that was shit, and *big deal* I swore. I'm not a child!' And a part of Vivienne – the part that isn't worried about her daughter dropping out of A levels 'because it's all bullshit', the part that knows she's ambitious, and is thinking about studying medicine – wanted to applaud her.

Vivienne hears the key in the lock – the lock she had to have changed last week because, between them, the girls have lost so many keys that she was scared they'd be broken into. She's up and out of her seat straight away, adjusting the cord on her dressing-gown. But it's Alex in the hallway. Alex and her boyfriend Matt, who's a year older, and who has his hand wedged in her daughter's back pocket, as they pass a McDonald's hot apple pie between them. They seem to be touching at all times, Vivienne thinks, whenever she sees them together. Different bits of their bodies pressed one against the other, permanently, like they've been glued. She remembers how that felt. A compulsion. Right now, Alex is wiping a flake of pastry from Matt's chin. 'You are disgusting . . .' her daughter is telling him, in a tone that makes clear she thinks the opposite. It's like they've hardly noticed she's there.

'Have you seen your sister?' Vivienne asks, and as she says it there's the sound of a car door slamming on the street, a girl's voice raised, indignant.

A moment later Nancy is stepping too carefully into the house, with Patrick behind her. 'Coming out of Camden Palace with Aimee,' he mutters, as Nancy steadies herself against the wall. His face is flushed, and his eyebrows all crazy, the way they get when he's been working on a difficult project. He's pulled on a jumper, over the T-shirt he sleeps in, and it's inside out. He looks exhausted, Vivienne thinks. But she sees too, in the looseness around his jaw, a slackening in his cheeks, that he's relieved. That her husband has breathed out for the first time since midnight, since before then.

'Tut-tut, Nance . . .' she hears Alex say, then catches

her winking at her sister. Alex, who would never do this, who comes home when she says she will. So that whatever else she gets up to, they don't have to ask.

'You smell like a brewery,' Vivienne tells her middle daughter. She wishes Matt would leave: she would love to be doing this without a spectator.

Nancy throws out an arm in Alex's direction. 'Why's my curfew so much earlier than hers? She's not *that* much older than me.' Her words are running one into another, and her eyes have that heavy, sleepy look. Vivienne can hardly stand it. She hates seeing her children drunk. She'll never get used to it. Even though she's seen a lot worse, done a lot worse. Out of the corner of her eye, she registers Matt burying his head in Alex's neck, trying not to laugh.

'Oh, my God, get a room, you two!' Nancy starts tugging at her sleeve, attempting to take off her jacket. Stumbles forward as her arm comes free.

'Can you all just be quiet!' Eva has appeared on the upstairs landing, and she's shouting. She has on the pyjamas with little pink love hearts, and her hair is all static at the side of her head.

'Oh, Eva, darling, sorry . . .' Vivienne says. It goes through her mind to tell Eva to be careful, because her youngest daughter looks half asleep, and there's the gap in the staircase still, between the banisters and the treads, that's been there since the house was in flats, since before they moved in. But Patrick has already started up the stairs.

'She's thirteen years old!' Turning back, like there's

something he's forgotten, he fixes his eyes on Nancy. '*Thirteen.*' His voice is a sharp slap. 'How do you think she feels, seeing you like this? Look at the state of you.'

And even though Nancy probably deserves it – she does deserve it – Vivienne winces. It's the way she always feels when Patrick shouts at the kids: it wounds her. Because it seems so harsh when you're the parent on the outside looking in. Even though on a different day, she knows she'd do the exact same herself. But there's something else too, the thought she won't allow herself to think, still now, all these years later. That maybe, somehow, he forfeited this right. She wants to say, 'He's upset because you scared him, Nancy.' But she's upset herself, and tired, and they're having people over for dinner tomorrow evening – which is now *this* evening – and she hasn't even started to think about what she might cook, let alone when she's going to find the time to sort out the house, which is littered from the front door to the attic with teenage crap . . . and she could have done without all of this.

'Okay, I'm going back to bed,' she announces. There's nothing more she can do here. 'Nancy, take the sick bucket up with you when you go. It's under the sink.'

As Vivienne walks down the hall towards the stairs, she sees Alex extract her boyfriend's hand from her pocket. Then – and something about this makes Vivienne feel shame and solace all at once – Alex moves towards her middle sister and, without speaking, starts to rub her back.

Eva, Tuesday morning

They are lost already in the dark green tunnels of the maze. The hedges are so high, there's no question of cheating, and they're sticking together all eleven of them, like pack animals. Twelve of them, Eva corrects herself, frowning. Now that Scott's son – her *stepson* – is here. She swallows, glances at her sisters, in case somehow she's leaked the thought. But Nancy and Alex are laughing together, talking about cold-water swimming and whether or not it could literally freeze your tits off, like how cold would it have to be. The snow from the night before has melted. As though Eva dreamed it up. As though it was never really there at all, and it's almost as if, with the thaw, something has lifted. The atmosphere in the glass house that morning, the atmosphere between them all, seems altered entirely.

Her mum is up at the front of the group, leading the way theatrically. Being very Vivienne. Being the most 'Vivienne' she's been all holiday, in fact. *Making the whole thing feel like a fucking school trip*, Nancy had muttered, as they'd queued for tickets at the little kiosk on the way in. But Eva is relieved to see her like this. Relieved about something she hadn't even known was bothering her. Because her mum has seemed a little distant these past couple of days, in a way Eva hasn't really noticed before.

Her mum who, her whole life, people have described as vibrant or vivacious or vital, all the V for Vivienne words. Maybe it has to do with the argument after the naming ceremony (the argument that, let's face it, Nancy reported back. Nancy who isn't exactly averse to a bit of drama), or maybe not. Either way, Eva hadn't realized how unsettling she's found it, this almost-absence, until now.

They've dropped to the back of the group, she and her sisters, and she's got that familiar feeling of rebellious solidarity. Like they're teenagers again, being forced into something outdoorsy that will *do them good*. The irony is that Eva would love to do something outdoorsy, just not this. She's tried to find the fun in it, to access her 'inner child', as Vivienne had suggested in the car park, but they've been in here for half an hour already – it's a claustrophobic shuffle and it's essentially pointless. A bit like when they were kids, and used to go head first inside their sleeping bags, the breathless, hot panic of it. Although, if she was by herself, she could do some good short interval training in here, a bit of agility stuff. And they're having a laugh, she and her sisters. They're slagging off the kids, basically – with the occasional detour into something else – which is always cathartic. Only their own kids, though, not each other's. They're not dumb: they know not to go there.

'We've been this way already!' Scott shouts.

'How can he possibly know that?' Nancy says. 'It all looks the fucking same.'

Eva eyes Scott's back. He has an arm raised, and he's

gesturing expansively, authoritatively, describing the route in the air, she assumes. 'I'm trying to remember what I saw in him,' she murmurs. She intends to say it laughingly, as if she's joking – or half joking, at least, but it comes out like she means it. Does she mean it?

Alex shoots her a look.

He took her to see the Northern Lights. That was one of the moments. He'd booked it for their anniversary, a year after they'd met, arranged for Lucy to stay with her grandparents. And he didn't tell her where they were going until they got to the airport. They bathed in the blue lagoon, smeared their faces with white mud, and he came out in a skin rash, laughed it off. The lights, when they saw them, weren't multi-coloured: they were green. The whole thing was green, unless you looked through a camera lens, and it was only then that the sky turned violet, fuchsia, turquoise, lemon. According to their guides, they were lucky enough to witness a 'good display', but she couldn't help feeling it was the biggest swizz. 'This is it?' she'd wanted to say. But if Scott felt it too, he was the world's greatest actor, he seemed to be having the time of his life. His positivity, his energy, his outdoorsiness, that was what she'd liked about him. *Likes* about him. And also she feels safe, emotionally safe. She knows he won't hurt her, she's pretty certain of that. She just doesn't know whether that's enough.

Someone – Scott, or maybe Vivienne – has decided they're going to turn around and go back the other way, try a different route. 'Fuck's sake I need some caffeine,' Nancy says, under her breath, as the sisters press themselves against the hedge to let the others come through. Lucy comes towards them holding Dolly, and flashes a goofy grin in Eva's direction. She has her arms wrapped around the baby, who's facing outwards, eyes bright. Lucy looks expert, Eva thinks. She looks like a young woman, not a child, and it makes her suddenly proud.

'Can we get one?' Lucy shouts as she goes by, jutting her chin towards the baby, and Eva rolls her eyes.

'You see? They're not all bad, our kids.' Nancy nudges her as she says it. Nancy, who's noticed again. Nancy, who always notices. 'It suits her,' her sister goes on. 'I mean, how old is she now, sixteen? Never too soon to start popping them out, I say. Get a jump on it while your vagina'll ping back to perfection! I bet you're pretty much *intact* in that department, aren't you, Eva?' Nancy presses her thumb and forefinger together at her lips, performs a small chef's kiss.

Laughing, Eva gives Nancy a shove. Only her sister – her *sisters* – could get away with talking to her like this. Only they would say it. They were there from the start with Lucy. From the moment she found out. Fiercely and without question, they were there. The very first people she told.

'Never too late, for that matter, eh, Al?' Nancy says now.

'Oh, God, don't, I can't bear it,' Alex covers her face with her hands. 'I'm going to be ancient in the school playground. The old bag, with no friends, who everyone avoids. Just me, my saggy cervix, and a daughter telling me how young all the other mums are.'

There's a strange symmetry to their children, their babies, hers and Alex's. That the youngest child should be mother to the oldest, and the oldest child mother to the youngest. It's even more pronounced since Dolly came along, because there's a decade and a half separating Lucy from the baby. *It's out of the order of things*, her mum would say. A part of her – a small part of her that wasn't the scared, ashamed part – had recognized at the time, all those years ago, that for once she was leaping ahead of her sisters. For once she was doing it first.

'And I s'pose Luc's having all these same concerns?' Nancy tilts her head at Alex, her mouth twisted to one side.

'I do think he's pretty worried about his cervix . . .' Alex says.

They stand and watch as Lucy disappears round a corner, joggling her smallest cousin in her arms. The voices of her family are growing more distant, and suddenly they're the only ones left. Three sisters lost in a maze . . . it's the start of a fairytale, or a sexist joke, Eva thinks.

'She's beautiful, you know, Alex,' she tells her sister. 'I'd give anything for a single day with Lucy that age again. Anything.' She casts her eyes upwards, as if she's religious or superstitious, and someone or something might be listening, poised to grant her wish. And it's true, she'd give away all her money – her *fortune* that's invested in stocks and shares and property and God knows what because someone else deals with all of it – if science could find a way to do it. 'I do mean a day, mind you, just to clarify. Definitely not a night.'

'Yup,' Alex says. 'Thanks.' But her voice is all zipped up, which makes Eva turn to look at her. She'd been about to say, 'Yeah, she's a beauty, *my* niece . . .' like it's all down to her. The words are in her mouth already, the joke is. But something in Alex's expression stops her.

Next to them, Nancy is brushing leaves from her coat. She's doing it vigorously, a little crossly. 'Right!' she says, glancing up. 'I'm deadly serious about that coffee, Diet Coke whatever, and I'm so done here. Can you two give me a leg up? I'm going over the top.'

They're here finally, in the centre of the maze – Nancy included because, in the end, they'd been too weak with laughter, the three of them, to get her over the hedge – and there's no getting away from it, it's a massive anticlimax. It's impossibly British. There's nothing here except a shitty statue of a little girl holding a lamb – literally shitty, as in covered with bird shit – and most of the adults are standing there, embarrassed almost, like they're waiting for something to happen. The kids are bored already; she is bored. *What did you expect? Dancing clowns?* her mum said to Rosa and Eden, when they started to moan. *Lost treasure? The journey is the thing . . .* But she might as well have been talking to all of them, and Eva felt told off. She's retreated to a small stone bench dug into the hedge to one side. It's grown over with spiky greenery, and she's hunched into the space with one shoe off, sticking a plaster to the weeping sore on her heel. A plaster that ultra-mum Alex had produced miraculously from a pocket. Her ankles have swelled again, more so even than yesterday, and the cool air feels good against her bloated skin.

Sitting here, it's making her think of the den she and Alex and Nancy made in a cupboard, at the top of the house in Dartmouth Park. There was a narrow shelf all the way round, and they decorated it with little china animals they'd saved from Christmas crackers. A lion and a monkey and an elephant and . . . She can't remember exactly, just that she knows they were precious and she loved them with her whole child heart. It was so dark with the door shut, she could hardly see, hardly breathe, and they never quite knew what to do when they were in there, but it was theirs, their secret, and that was worth the almost-boredom, the almost-asphyxiation. 'Do you remember the den?' she says now, looking up. But no one hears. 'Guys?' She tries again, a little louder this time. No one even turns towards her.

For a moment she thinks maybe they've found something worth finding after all. Either that or there's been an accident, that someone – her mum, her dad – has keeled over in the middle of the maze. Because her entire family are gathered in a haphazard circle beneath the statue, all of them focused intently on something she can't see. 'What's going on?' she calls, struggling to pull on her sock. And she can feel her heart speeding up a little. When she stands, she sees that Jay is in the centre of the circle, and he's holding his phone up and out. There's a stillness about her family, grouped around him. It goes through her mind that somehow he's got a recording of her wedding – her wedding to his dad that he wasn't invited to. Is he showing them a video of the vows? she thinks crazily, blowing the whole thing wide open before she's ready to tell them.

But then Jay starts to laugh. He's laughing and laughing, like he's never going to stop, and he doesn't seem to notice that, around him, the family have gone quiet. All the family, except the kids, who are complaining that he's holding the phone too high and they can't see the screen. Something is wrong, and Eva's still trying to jam her foot back into her shoe, wincing at the pain that screams in her heel, in her ankle, as she does it.

'Fuuuuck . . .' she hears Scott's son say, drawing out the word, like he's a stoner or something. And no one makes to cover the kids' ears, or admonish him. Not even Alex. 'Damn, I could watch this thing on a loop. *Man*, I could watch it all day!'

He starts to laugh again, as Nancy peels off from the circle, and her face doesn't look right as she crosses the little courtyard, headed towards the way they came in, the only way out. 'Who needs dancing clowns?' her sister says, as she passes, and her voice is flat, sarcastic, but she's staring straight ahead towards the exit, and Eva has no idea whether Nancy is talking to her or not.

'What?' Eva calls after her, or to anyone who might care to answer, because she's really starting to feel anxious now, paranoid. 'What is it?' It's like she isn't there, or she's invisible. Nobody's listening to her and she knows this feeling too well. Abandoning her shoe by the bench, she starts to hobble towards where the others are standing. She knows she looks ridiculous, and there's grit pricking through her sock, so that after a few steps she has to stop, dust off her foot. When she glances up, she notices Alex, who's moved to the edge of the circle, and is frowning, shaking her head. Eva watches as her sister looks from the screen to her mum, then back again; she looks confused, as much as anything. More confused than angry, which was how Nancy seemed. Angry, or maybe – Eva isn't sure – *upset*?

There are too many people in the way still, so Eva can't see the little screen from where she's standing. She has no idea what's going on, and it's as if someone is playing a practical joke, because it can't have been more than fifteen minutes since they were helpless with laughter, she and her sisters, trying – *failing* – to get Nancy over the hedge. She's got the scratches to prove it. A rare shot of joy had gone through her, as she'd grappled with Nancy's muddy boot in her hand, whipped her head away just in time not to get kicked in the face. *They are my favourite people in the world*, she'd thought, her nose up against the dark green leaves that smelt of afternoons building grass houses when they were kids. *Friends don't come close.*

But now . . . now something has changed. 'What is it?' Eva asks again, and she's raising her voice, as she approaches the group. And it's only then that someone – her dad – turns towards her, at last. He's trying to smile, but Eva isn't buying it, and she's suddenly afraid. 'What's happened?' She can't look in his eyes as she says it. 'What's going on?'

Vivienne, Tuesday afternoon

Vivienne is having another cigarette and she doesn't care. It's her third of the day and she's going to smoke the whole thing *no matter what*, and if someone catches her doing it, well then, they'll just have to deal with it. She's at the back of the glass house – behind the wooden pool room where she can't be seen – and she's got her eyes on the triangular mountain, which seems impossibly huge from this vantage point. She's trying to seize some kind of perspective, trying to process her pinballing thoughts. She can't believe what's just happened.

Scott's son. She'd known from the moment he showed up that he was bad news. She has that intuition – she's always had it. Although it isn't hard to see that the kid is a pain in the backside, much like his father, just a different flavour of bad. She's seen him looking at Lucy too, *looking* looking. As if her granddaughter is an ice-cream to be drooled over, a triple scoop with sprinkles and a Flake and . . . He looks at her like she's a grown woman, when the fact is she's barely sixteen. He looks like a predator, is the point. And it's making Lucy uncomfortable – she sees it. She's going to say something to Scott if it carries on. Because this is Lucy they're talking about. Lucy, who lived with them for the first eight years of her life. Lucy, who's as much a daughter to her as a grandchild.

She's thinking this – poking at it like toothache – because she doesn't want to think about the other. About the rest of it. She turns seventy at the end of the week: it's fair to say she's too old for all this. This thing that, somewhere in the pit of her, she's been expecting, anticipating for the longest time now. *How have you all not seen this before?* The words ring in her. *Where've you lot been? Under a rock? She went viral on TikTok with it!* He'd nodded in Lucy's direction as he said it. Scott's son, whose name she's misplaced just at this moment, and that, anyway, she's none too keen to retrieve – she's not even really trying. *I saw it when I was on the boat. It blew up FAST . . .* He'd fiddled, infuriatingly, with his phone at this point. *How many views, Luce?* He'd called her Luce, and she's convinced his tone had been mocking. Luce. Loose. And Patrick, as far away from the point of things as he could possibly have been, had started to say something about the pool room in the glass house and unstable Wi-Fi, then some technical stuff to do with routers and she didn't know what else, because she could feel Alex's eyes on her – the question in them. And when she'd looked up, finally, and met her daughter's gaze, she'd had to fight to stop herself looking away.

She's wandered a little way along the path that leads away from the house, and now she stops at the copper sphere that's hidden in the long grass. It's hollowed out and padded all the way round with cushions that are patched dark in places. Vivienne prods them with a tentative finger. They're damp to the touch, but she climbs inside anyway, settles herself with her feet dangling above the ground, as if she's a child. There's a smell like washing left too long before it dries. Fumbling in her coat pocket, she takes out her phone. Alex, no, Nancy, no, Eva, no, Lucy . . . Vivienne cycles through their names before she lands – and, for fuck's sake, she's acting like she does have dementia, because she knows she had her grandchild's name in her mind not two minutes before. It was *Lucy*, she thinks now, who'd uploaded TikTok for her when she'd asked. Vivienne isn't the least bit interested in social media – it's all a load of mindless crap, as far as she's concerned, mindless and also worrying – but she *is* interested in keeping in step with her grandkids, with the younger generation full stop.

She knows she should put her phone back into her pocket, leave this thing well alone. Because what's the point of looking, what can it possibly change? Is she hoping to prove herself wrong? But it's like the pull of nicotine, she can't help herself. The truth is, she's known since they got back to the house that she'd do this. Her fingers grow sweaty as she clicks and swipes, and there's a clumsiness that makes her clench her teeth. She doesn't like to see her hands against the screen, the age spots and puffy knuckles and corrugated nails that look nicotine-stained. And is she anxious? Because they're shaking too – she can't still them. Tipping forward in her seat, she glances back at the glass house. Checking. Everyone has retreated this afternoon to their own rooms, but even so she feels watched. The place is weird, and she knows it sounds mad, paranoid, neurotic – *loopy*, her friend Monique, who used to live in the flats next door to them, would say – and she wouldn't dare to articulate it, but she could almost believe there's a force working against her family here. She'd just started to breathe again this past twelve hours, started to believe that the *unravelling* wouldn't happen after all. But now she wishes they'd never come. If she could turn back the clock and unbook the holiday she would.

As soon as she finds the post, she changes her mind. She knows that once she looks she can't unsee it, but it's already started to play. Like the trailers on Netflix that won't let up for a second because of diminishing attention spans, and life at a hundred miles per hour, now that everyone is supposed to be permanently productive, constantly go, go, go. Three kids under the age of five – that's constantly productive, for you, she thinks, enough to put you off productivity for life. Lucy told her afterwards that they'd shown the video to Rosa and Eden because they were bored, because they'd been disappointed at the lack of thrill in the middle of the maze. She said it reminded her of Eva's story about the birthday present her sisters had given her. The huge box, beautifully wrapped. And when she'd opened it, she'd found another box, slightly smaller, also beautifully wrapped. And then another and another and another, until she'd got to the smallest one – no bigger than a matchbox – and opened it. And found nothing. *Auntie Alex and Auntie Nancy laughed*, Lucy said. *They thought it was the best joke ever. But Mum felt like crying, even though she didn't let it show.* She said it like she was making an excuse, like she understood that, whatever this thing with the video was, it needed an excuse.

Vivienne can't tear her eyes from the screen. She doesn't remember the empty present; she's pretty sure she'd remember something like that. But she does remember this, the scene unfolding in front of her. She was too far away to see earlier, at the back of her family grouped in the maze, and not minded to move any closer because she hadn't wanted to look. The film on her phone is overlaid with jaunty purple lettering, spelling out *IT'S BEHIND YOU!!!!* The pantomime phrase is punctuated either side, with a pair of animated googly eyes. There's her husband, camera held high, and her three daughters, arms slung around one another, and they're smiling. Vivienne watches as the tree starts to fall, and it's like she's back there: she can smell the mushroomy smell of the forest floor. Her fingers tighten on the handset, as Patrick drops his camera – his precious camera – and, although the next bit happens fast, it seems to Vivienne that it goes on for ever. She can hardly watch as her husband runs straight past Alex and then Nancy, as if they're not even there, like they don't exist, before he wrenches Eva desperately by the shoulders. And she's thinking, That's it, that the worst is over, but then the picture jerks and resets, and the tree falls again, then again and again. Because it's running on a loop, this film, and she can only watch helplessly, as Patrick chooses to save their youngest daughter every single time.

Eva, Autumn 1990

Eva's late. They are late. They missed the train at Paddington by two minutes, because her dad was buying a paper and some Juicy Fruit from WHSmith, and they had to wait ages to get the next. 'Don't worry,' her dad said once they'd settled in their carriage, and he squeezed her shoulders, until she giggled. 'We'll be fashionably late to the fashion shoot. You think Twiggy turns up on time?' And she asked, *Who?*

Now, at last, she's sitting in the chair in a stuffy tent, having her makeup done. Her head is tilted up at an uncomfortable angle towards the woman, whose black hair is studded with silver clips, and whose perfume is going up her nose, making her want to sneeze. 'Hold still . . .' the woman says, although Eva's pretty sure she hasn't moved '. . . darling,' the woman adds, tacking the word on a little late. And she flashes a brief smile too close to Eva's face, as though she's realized she's been unfair. Or maybe that someone might have overheard her. 'It's just we're on the back foot here. I'm getting this done at breakneck speed, okay?'

The other girl is already out there when Eva emerges into the open-air theatre that looks out to sea. The theatre is basically a pile of old stones on top of a cliff. Eva's wearing shorts and a striped top she wouldn't be

seen dead in – she looks young for her age, so she's still
getting booked for children's catalogues and campaigns.
She can see that the other girl has on a nicer outfit – a
mini skirt and a white T-shirt with cap sleeves. There are
heaters blasting, but it's a cold day and it's windy, and
Eva has goosebumps all up her arms. Nobody notices
her standing there, and she shifts awkwardly, unsure
what to do next. It feels like for ever before the photographer spots her, waves her over. She wonders where her
dad is, whether they might be able to swim in the sea if
they finish in time. He's promised there'll be sunshine as
the day wears on. *I can feel it in the tips of my fingers, Evie,*
he told her, wiggling his hands at her – being deliberately
annoying – as they jumped into a cab at the station. And
even though she rolled her eyes, she wanted to laugh,
and she believed him.

Eva says hi to the other model, Emma, who smiles
back, but whose eyes don't change, like, who are you?
Eva notes the girl's hair, her nose, her teeth, her skin,
which she can tell is the kind that tans the second
the sun comes out, the kind everyone wants, and she
doesn't have. Eva's skin is so pale you can see the veins
through it. Alex drew them on in biro once, when she'd
fallen asleep in front of the TV, added grass and flowers
and birds, and the first three letters of *river*, before Eva
woke up. Eva sees that Emma is eyeing her too, judging. But they both know how to set their faces, trying
not to show that they're doing it. Emma looks a bit like
Madonna.

*

Eva is hungry. She thinks maybe she missed the snacks on arrival because they were late, and she's got that sicky ache in her stomach; she feels like she could actually be sick. She's just changed into a ninth, maybe tenth outfit, she's lost count, and the sun has not come out, as her dad said it would. Another thing: she doesn't like the photographer. The woman is old, but she's wearing jeans that are way too tight for her, and a fluffy jumper that falls off her shoulder. And she has her hair tied up with a scarf in a bow, like the lead singer of Bananarama. Or, rather, Eva's desperate to make the photographer like her. Because although she and Emma are out there together, hitting poses, fake laughing, leaping, looking off into the distance, chin up a bit, down a bit . . . the photographer is taking far more photos of the other girl. She isn't even trying to hide it. The makeup woman with the silver clips is tweaking Emma's hair right now, fluffing it with her fingers, telling Emma to close her eyes as she fixes it with a blast of hairspray. Arms hidden behind her back, Eva scratches herself, just above the wrist and it hurts. It's the only way she knows she hasn't actually disappeared.

Climbing a step higher on the crumbling seating, she clears her throat, pushes out her chest. There's nothing there – she's *flat*, which the boys at school all love to laugh about, and she hates that expression, hates it so much – but she's thinking maybe this is what the woman wants. That this will make her notice Eva. 'Smile! Keep it natural!' they always say. 'Just pretend we're not here!' But she hears them talking about shaping and sculpting and knowing your angles; she sees them assessing and sizing up. She sees them picking favourites, and today it isn't her. Do they wish they hadn't chosen her for the shoot? The makeup artist tutted as she covered the spots on Eva's forehead earlier. Is that the problem? Her spots? She changes the angle of her body, pushes her chest out further. It's steep up here, making her feel a bit wobbly, and she stumbles a little as she does it, feels everything swoop before she rights herself. The photographer glances across at her. 'Can you come down to the original level, hon?' she calls. And Eva thinks, This is it – it's her turn now. But when she steps down, the woman turns her camera back to Emma.

There's a rush in her head, and she knows, the second before it happens, that she's going to cry. Horrified, she stands there, lets the tears run down her face. If she doesn't move, if she doesn't wipe them away, maybe no one will notice. She's hungry, she's cold, she feels stupid and ugly, and she's willing the tears to stop, but the more she wishes them away, the more they keep coming.

'Hey!'

It takes her a moment to realize it was her dad who shouted. Her dad, who's on the open-air stage where they were shooting earlier. There's a huge throne in the middle of the set – covered with pieces of plastic made to look like jewels – and he's been sitting in it, because he thinks he's so hilarious, with his papers out, working.

'Hey! We need to stop,' he shouts now. And as she watches, he jumps from the stage, and starts to make his way up the rows of stone seating, taking the steps two at a time. She's vaguely aware of the photographer and the makeup woman, the director and the other girl all turning to look at him. Next thing he's by her side, wrapping his arms around her. 'What's wrong, sweetheart?' he says, and then, as if he's talking to himself, 'I *knew* you were crying.'

Eva stands for a moment, unable to move; she thinks she's going to die from embarrassment. He smells of the chewing gum he bought at the station.

'Is everything okay?' one of the women is calling across to them, she can't tell which. But isn't it obvious? Can't they see that everything is definitely not okay?

Eva pushes her dad off. Snot drips from her nose and hits the ground, but even so, for a wild moment, she thinks maybe the people on the shoot haven't realized, that maybe she'll get away with it. That they can just carry on, as if nothing has happened. Nothing *has* happened. Not really, she thinks.

'I wish Mum was here,' she murmurs. It isn't true, but she's saying it to punish him. Because he made them late, because of the photographer, because of the other girl who looks like Madonna, and because she's ashamed and tired and she's had enough. Her mum has to be at the solicitor's office for work so has never come with her on a shoot. It's always her dad. He's freelance, a freelance surveyor, so he's *free* to do it, as her mum likes to say, with a little trill on the *r*. Eva tries to smile at the group of people, who are looking at her still, giving her all the attention she no longer wants. She wishes the ground would open up and swallow her; she wishes with all her heart that their neighbour, Monique, had never scouted her, suggested to her mum that it might be a laugh and she'd get to see some places, talked about saving money for college.

'You know you don't have to do any of this if you don't want to, sweetheart.' Her dad is breathing his Juicy Fruit breath all over her. 'You know that, right? It's just meant to be a bit of fun.' Then to her horror, he raises his voice. 'Yup, we need to stop guys, apologies. We need to take a break.'

'No!' The scream bolts from her, before she even understands that she's opened her mouth. 'No! I don't want to stop!' She starts to smooth down the front of the blue dress she's wearing, over and over, trying to soothe herself. There's the *sssh sssh* sound of the sea in her ears, but it's making things worse, not better, and the tears come again. She can't stop them. She's crying harder this time, gulping and sobbing, and she knows everyone's watching, but it's like something has let loose in her, something that, until now, has been folded up tiny and neat and small.

Tuesday evening

Nancy

Nancy's going to wait until the last possible minute to get out of her car. They're due to meet the Wilsons at seven and, she checks her phone, it's still only 6.58 p.m. She can see her family in the rear-view mirror, milling next to a little row of shops. The place looks like a model village. Everything seems miniature so she feels like she's swallowed the 'Drink Me' potion; she feels like she's stumbled into Wonderland, where everything looks sweet on the surface, but is actually dark as fuck. Her family are tiny too, reflected back at her like this, and although she can't make out their faces, she knows their expressions are flattened with shock. As if Lucy's dumb TikTok was some kind of revelation. Like it hadn't all been blindingly obvious before. She makes her hands into duck beaks above the steering wheel, opens and closes them like she's working glove puppets. 'That's not what happened, Nancy!' she mimics, in a voice that's crazy high, and she likes to think sounds just like her sister's.

Walking towards her family, she's got that twitchy-eye thing. A weird, fast vibration that she knows is supposed to be a sign of stress. They're grouped in front of a small door that's painted gold. Really small, like she'll have to duck to get through it. It's the unmarked entrance to the Korean-Chinese fusion restaurant the Wilsons had raved about, a sort of secret society set-up, an if-you-know-you-know scenario. Scott, alone among the adults, looks as though he's thrilled at the prospect of the evening ahead. He has on some kind of poncho, over his polo shirt, like he thinks . . . She dreads to think what he's thinking, but he's been referring to the restaurant as *Sino*-Korean, and Nancy swears he just fucking googles this shit. He's like a trainee teacher, staying one lesson ahead of his class, winging it. How can Eva stand it?

'Okay, let's do this,' she murmurs to herself, as she approaches. And she raises her hand weakly in greeting. Her dad is the only one looking in her direction, the only one who smiles, wildly, who waves back like his arm might fly from its socket. It's painful to witness, because he's sucking up to her is what he's doing, and she hates this new version of him.

Thank God for the kids because, if it wasn't for them, her family would be standing there in silence. They're not talking about *it*; they're not talking at all. Because this is what her family does. It's like they have their fingers in their ears, trying to la-la-la away the problem. A special kind of bullshit magical thinking. Still now. But there's an atmosphere. Even Jay seems to have detected this. Standing next to Lucy, he looks shorter than usual, sloped in an almost-apologetic stance that seems to have shrunk him. Maybe he feels responsible for what's happened, for what he set in motion that morning in the maze. At the thought of it, Lucy's TikTok starts to play in her head again. Nancy can see herself, hip tipped out in the woods, her garish mask of makeup, squeezed in close to her sisters, like they're three parts of a whole, and then ... *Stop it!* she tells herself, and for a second, she wonders if she's blurted the words out loud. Because she can't replay the whole thing in her mind again, she can't bear to; she won't.

Alex

'Are we going in or not?' Alex hears Nancy say, in a voice that suggests she would like to punch someone. Nancy, who's only just turned up, when the rest of them have been standing here, waiting for her, for the last five minutes. She wishes they had cancelled, can't believe they didn't cancel after what's happened, after what they've all seen. And why hadn't she made her excuses and stayed back at the glass house? She's spent the afternoon in bed, pretending to have a migraine, and now she's all blurry at the edges and sore to the touch. She feels wrong – and how's that for psychosomatic? As if she's convinced herself, tricked her own body into believing she really has been struck down. How is she going to eat anything? The restaurant has a Michelin star and it's going to cost her a fortune just to push the food around her plate. She and Luc are on teachers' salaries, and they have three kids to feed, although no one cares to notice. And the Wilsons? How is she going to speak to these people she hasn't seen in years? Ten years? Twenty? More? How is she going to keep up the façade? Why should she? Why does she even care?

She's got Dolly strapped in a sling to her front, and it's a small miracle, a minor enchantment, One Good Thing, because her daughter has fallen asleep in the time they've been standing here. Alex sends up a prayer that she won't wake up as they cross into the clatter of the restaurant.

'Can we go in, Mum?' Rosa turns as she says it. She's in front of the small gold door, staving Eden off with an elbow. She wants Alex to give her the go-ahead, and Alex nods. They file in one by one, and despite herself, Alex feels the discomfort of no one saying anything. Her own head feels empty of small-talk, and – she can't help herself – she has the urge to smooth out the social awkwardness, to cover it up. And she's scrambling for something to break the silence, anything, when she collides with the door frame. Pain smacks her forehead. 'Fuck! Ouch! Fucking hell!'

Next to her, Vivienne puts a steadying hand on her shoulder. 'Language!' she says, in a comedy voice that goes from low to high. Then she pulls a face, checks on Dolly in the sling.

But Alex doesn't laugh, doesn't even smile.

'Are you okay, darling? I can't see any damage. Shall we keep an eye on you for concussion?' She's stroking Dolly's cheek as she says it, and Alex wants to tell her to leave the baby alone because, for God's sake, she'll wake her. She wants to kick the stone door frame that's three feet thick – she's got the throb in her face to prove it; she wants to sit down where she is, put her head into her hands; she wants to rewind the tape, put everything back to the way it was. She wants it all to stop.

Eva

Eva's the last one through the gold door, and it's as if someone has waved a magic wand, or they've walked through the back of a wardrobe. Because by the time she sets foot on the other side, each and every member of her family seems to have had a personality transplant: they have put on their social masks and are presenting a united front.

'Isn't it knockout?' Adrian Wilson is up and out of his seat, and coming towards them. 'I mean, what a place, huh?'

Her mum, her dad, her sisters, her brother-in-law, all of them have slapped-on expressions that are bright with what she can only describe as abject delight. They are throwing themselves into this emotion as if it were an extreme sport. Something winnable. Eva knows her own mouth is pulled into an insane grin. The fact is, she *could* almost laugh, it's almost funny. We are one happy, *delightful* family, their faces say. It makes her think of the shows they used to put on when they were kids at the Dartmouth Park house, or sometimes at the Wilsons' too. She remembers the five of them, she and her sisters and Helen and Katy, all dressed up as Elvis on a hot summer afternoon. Hair greased into quiffs and playing air guitar and not understanding why the grown-ups were laughing because it wasn't meant to be funny. They'd been rehearsing all day, but halfway through the opening number, Eva had a nosebleed. Bright red blood down her white T-shirt, in the middle of 'Blue Suede Shoes' – and they'd had to abandon the whole thing.

'Michelin starred . . .' Adrian says now, dipping his head a little. Modestly, as if maybe he's in some way responsible for the restaurant's success.

He's right: the restaurant is unexpected and wonderful. It's large inside, and low-ceilinged. There are glass lights hung everywhere it's possible to hang them, and they cast an orange glow that makes her think of tangerines and fire and amber. In the middle of the space a kidney-shaped pool is scattered with lotus flowers, bursting white blooms. The smells from the kitchen are rich and sticky and sweet, and she's suddenly ferociously hungry. Seated at a long table across the room, she spots Helen and Katy. Nerves flicker, and it surprises her. She follows them on Facebook, although they never interact. Eva recognizes Helen's wife: she's seen photos of their wedding, their kids. She knows that Katy's husband is a lighthouse enthusiast; she knows too much. She will have to try not to leak this information as the evening goes on. Eva wonders if they stalk her too.

'Come! Sit . . .' Adrian is flapping his arms in the direction of the long table. 'The girls are desperate to see you.' The orange light catches his movement, and Eva notices his hairy hands; she remembers. A flash of memory.

Alex standing in front of the cooker in the Dartmouth Park kitchen. *Hello, my name's Adrian,* her sister is saying, and she's stroking one hand with the other, to the tips of her fingers and beyond into thin air, as far as her arm will stretch. *Who needs pets, with strokable hands like these?* And Eva and Nancy are laughing and laughing, telling her to please stop, they're going to wet themselves.

As she moves past him now, Eva's eyes are drawn to the black hairs curling over the cuff of Adrian's shirt – he has more hair there than on the whole of his head, and she knows it's childish, she knows it's mean, but she wants to alert her sisters somehow. Despite everything, she wishes she could share this with them. Glancing up, she sees Adrian watching her. She forces a smile.

'Ah, the stunning Fisher sisters,' he announces to everyone and no one, and he pats her on the back with his hairy hand. 'Each more beautiful than the last . . .'

Nancy

Nancy can't help noticing that Alex is drinking an awful lot for someone who claims to have had a migraine all afternoon. Nancy's not keeping track exactly, but she's pretty sure her sister has just ordered a fourth cocktail, and they haven't even brought out the starters yet. Her top has slipped from her shoulder, revealing her bra strap, and she's just pinged it – as far as Nancy can tell – to emphasize a point she's making to Katy. Alex can't take her alcohol, everyone knows this. Should she tell her to go easy? Her sister still has the baby strapped to her after all.

She has the urge to text Nik, to tell him about Alex's pinged bra, to describe in a few short sentences this bizarre dinner, the enforced joy-on-a-knife-edge vibe of it. She wants to share with him Adrian Wilson's Fisher sisters comment, that he no doubt considered a compliment, a witty welcome. *Each more beautiful than the last . . .* He'd said it in a jocular way, like he was finishing off the cadence in the opening line of a fairytale, but she'd had to dig her nails into the palm of her hand as she passed him. *Holy shit!* she'll start off. *Things are really cranking up to warp level insanity here . . .* and she'll punctuate the message with several exploding brain emojis. She imagines Nik smiling as he reads it. The dopamine hit she'll feel, as the three grey dots appear to signal he's keying a reply.

'Nancy!' Her dad is all of a sudden at her elbow. He's adjusting his belt like he's on his way back from the toilets, and his mouth is close to her ear. 'I know this isn't the time, but I do want to talk to you and Alex, at a point, about the whole . . .' He mimes a square with his index fingers, like they're playing charades. He's miming the TV, she thinks, and it's a moment before she understands he means to reference Lucy's video. Nancy can't quite believe he's broaching it, half broaching it at least, but at the same time she knows she's been waiting for this – dreading it. Why now? she wants to ask. Why not right after the naming ceremony? What's changed? The fact you've been *busted*?

When she doesn't say anything, her dad smiles

unconvincingly. 'I'd like to talk to you about the whole . . . silliness.'

Nancy blinks. '*Silliness?*' She doesn't bother to keep her voice down, the way he did.

He straightens immediately, casts a smile around the table, although no one's looking at them. 'Okay, Nancy,' he says, as if he's admonishing her, like she's the one who's done something wrong, not him. Then he creases his forehead, signalling he's mystified, and moves off.

Across from her, Alex snorts in laughter at something Katy has said. Nancy sees the baby jump in her sleep. *Silliness.* The word is a boomerang in her mind. Alex is throwing back her head now, laughing some more, and Nancy wonders again whether she should lean over the table, say something to her sister, point out the cocktails are pretty strong. Then she pictures Alex's response. The sucked-lemon glare she knows too well. Let her drink, Nancy thinks. Let her have her fun. How much worse can things get?

Eva

Katy's husband is fantastically boring and, of course, she's seated next to him. He's discovered that Eva is an ultra-runner, and although he is an 'armchair sportsman', this has not deterred him from telling Eva everything she needs to know about her own sport.

'So there's this incredible story,' he's saying now, 'about a guy who ran the desert race, you know the one?'

'The Marathon des Sables,' she says.

'He was running the Marathon des Sables,' Katy's husband tells her, as though he, and not she, has provided this information, 'and went off course. Was missing for days in the desert and —'

'Oh, yes, I know this story well,' she interjects, like, no need to go into detail. Because it's fascinated and terrified her, this incident. It gripped her. They've discussed it endlessly at the running club, swapping notes and theories and figuring out what they each would have done in the same situation. Would they have drunk their own urine as he did, as you should never do? She's pored over articles in the press, watched a documentary about it, scrolled endlessly online. She even knows his date of birth (July 13th) and the fact that he has three kids. The ultra-runner who lost his way, and took shelter in an ancient stone shrine in the middle of the Sahara. Miraculously alive, he'd survived by drinking bats' blood. She knows all about it, every last detail: it's her sport. But Katy's husband's telling her anyway, as if she hasn't spoken.

Eva tunes out, her last line of defence, turns her attention instead to her food. She's eating octopus and scallops that arrived at the table in a cast-iron dish, spitting hot oil that burned her mouth, her throat as she swallowed. The flavours are sublime and she wishes she could sit here alone to devour it. Forking glass noodles into her mouth, she checks on Lucy. Eva is all too aware that her daughter has somehow ended up stuck next to Jay, of all the people, and she's going to get everyone to shift places next course, because it isn't fair. Already, his arrival into the middle of their holiday has checkmated her child. Has stopped Lucy pitching back into childhood, the way she still does when they go away. Throwing off the shackles of friends and peer pressure, for sacred moments that are getting fewer and further between. A return to an easier self. For the short periods while she's off her phone, at least.

Grease dribbles down Eva's chin and she wipes it away. She's worried about Alex too. Alex who is at the other end of the table, laughing loudly. And is it just her, or does the laughter sound loaded? Is Luc going to say something, is anyone? Because her sister is drinking a lot, and Alex doesn't drink, not usually. She's slurring her too-loud words, and it's not a good look, and the kids are here and Eva's amazed that Alex would do this in front of them; it isn't like her. Eva tries to catch Nancy's eye: she wants to communicate that maybe Alex needs saving – she knows Nancy would take it on – but Nancy's looking down at her lap, thumbs flying; she's texting someone, and Eva wonders who.

Alex

Alex is chasing an ice cube around the bottom of her glass with her fingers, taking time out from the conversation that's going on around her. She's become obsessed with whatever's going on with Scott's son and Lucy. She doesn't know if anyone else has noticed, but as far as she's concerned, it's the most interesting thing happening at the table. It's something to take her mind off things. That and the Cosmopolitans she's ordering back to back, because they'll be splitting the bill at the end and she wants to get her money's worth. She's getting her money's worth: she reckons they're costing her – costing *everyone* – three quid a gulp, minimum. Worth every penny, she thinks, because they're certainly going down very smoothly. Especially now Luc has relieved her, finally, of the baby. Even if he did give her a funny look, as he scooped Dolly – quite roughly, if she's honest – from the sling.

An ice cube jumps from her fingers and skitters across the floor. She imagines one of the waiters skidding on it, cartoon-like, and the thought of it makes her want to laugh. Nancy has told her that Lucy can't stand Scott's son. But it doesn't look like it from where she's sitting. There's a flush in her niece's cheeks that she's pretty sure has nothing to do with the glow of the lights in here, and everything to do with the wine Lucy is trying to drink surreptitiously, so her mum won't notice.

Nancy

Stella Wilson has the phone out and held high, before Nancy has time to register what she's doing, to understand what's about to happen.

'I'm useless with technology,' Stella's saying. 'Lisa, can you help me here?' She waves the phone at Helen's wife, who does something in tech. 'We only saw this yesterday. Helen showed us.' Raising her voice, Stella addresses the table, 'We're amazed you agreed to meet us.' She gives a little wink. 'Now that you're all famous!'

'We couldn't believe it.' Katy looks from Nancy to Eva to Alex. 'None of you have changed *at all*! Weren't we saying, Mum?'

Nancy eyes the phone in Helen's wife's hand. *It's behind you!!!!* The words spring into her mind. She squeezes her chopsticks between her thumb and forefinger, until she thinks the skin might dent. She knows she needs to say something, do something, to stop this playing out. How have they not noticed that half the people around the table have fallen silent? The comments she can't unsee, the reactions from perfect strangers, scroll across her mind.

. . . to quote Robbie 'She's The One'! Oof. Um, no offence ladies . . . He's not dumb, he picked the prettiest lols!!! . . . Ugh dirty old man much . . .

When Vivienne stands, the whole table shunts forward dangerously, then back. Her hair is twisted up into a tortoiseshell clip, and she has on a bright patterned trouser suit she bought in Sicily. From nowhere, Nancy sees her fifty years younger, riding bareback around a circus ring. In her mind's eye, her mum is wearing a ringmaster's hat, and she's radiant, luminous, wild.

'We've seen it a gazillion times,' Vivienne says now, fixing her eyes on Stella. She has a pleasant look on her face, but something in her voice is a hard, dark line. Nancy knows that voice. It's a tone she associates with Rizlas

155

found in a bedroom drawer, a midnight curfew missed by hours. 'I think we should have a toast instead.' Vivienne lifts her glass from the table. Nancy notices her hand is a little unsteady. 'Here's to friends and family,' Vivienne smiles, 'who know us well, but love us just the same.'

There's the sound of glass shattering. Everyone at the table – everyone in the entire restaurant – turns to look. Alex is on her feet and steadying herself against the back of her chair. Red wine floods the table in front of her, chasing around the edges of cast-iron bowls, ceramic dishes, soaking into the rainbow-hued dragon fish that are stitched into the tablecloth. And it's spattered across her sister's grey dress.

'Fuck,' Alex announces belatedly. Alex who is so quick to admonish everyone else for swearing in front of the children, Nancy thinks. And Nancy's grabbing her napkin, ready to mop, already locating in her mind all the incidents of hypocrisy down the years – the ready store of resentment at this eldest-child privilege – when her phone vibrates in her pocket. She takes it out in case it's Georgie, and as she checks the screen, a photo pings through from Leon. It's a picture of his leg in a navy cast, and a message that says, in his usual exhaustive prose, Broke my ankle.

'Nancy, put your phone away!' Her dad is frowning at her from the far end of the table. She thinks for a minute he's joking. Talking to her like she's a child when she's not. Then she sees from his face that he's serious. *Are you fucking kidding me?* she wants to say, and she gestures indignantly at the *literal* shattered pieces surrounding her sister's chair, the dark stain pooling on the table. But the disbelief is so huge it silences her. She thinks again about the torrent of TikTok comments, and how dare he?

'Leon's broken his leg,' she blurts. She means to say it in a so-you-can-shut-the-fuck-up voice, but she finds she's about to cry. He *texts* to tell me this? she thinks. Because Leon is supposed to be driving Georgie up tomorrow, and Nancy's frantically counting hours, calculating dates in her head, because how is she going to get her here? She knows she can't drive to London and back in a day . . . and then it'll be Thursday – the tail end of Thursday – and what's the point? She can't see a way her daughter will be able to join them now. And she has been sitting on her hands, chewing her cheeks, trying not to miss her child, trying not to feel her absence here, and she can't bear it, the thought that she won't have this holiday, that they won't.

Eva

'Can we all swap places?' Eva's voice sounds manic to her own ears, like it might spontaneously combust. 'Since Alex has got us all on our feet anyway!'

There's a moment, the ghost of a groan, but then people start to edge uncertainly around the table. It's like musical chairs, except kind of the opposite, because the three of them are avoiding the chair next to their dad. None of them want to sit next to him. Not Alex – who's apparently so wasted Eva's surprised she even cares, not

Nancy, and not her. It's so blindingly obvious, the way they all do-si-do as he approaches, that she almost feels sorry for him. Usually, they'd consider it a prime spot, a seat next to their dad. He's funny and irreverent, *juvenile* at this kind of event. It's his thing that he likes to comment, sotto voce, on other diners, or guests at parties, trying to make his daughters laugh. Or they'll turn to see him wearing the food like a hat, a moustache, a pair of breasts. Two olives for nipples, a Lollo Rosso beard. And still no one's saying anything. Even Nancy isn't touching this. But it shows. It shows in their faces and in their voices and in their bodies. Eva knows her sisters too well. She's sure it must show on her face too, and in her bones and on her skin, which feels contorted with everything she isn't saying.

As she's thinking this, her dad calls across the table to her sister.

'I was just telling Stella about your promotion, Nancy!' He says it like he's trying to make up for something. He sounds like a sycophant, Eva thinks, and she doesn't like it; it isn't him.

'That was a year and a half ago,' Nancy murmurs. Her look says, You're confusing me with someone who gives a fuck.

Eva sees her dad glance too quickly at Stella, who smiles unconvincingly, picks at her collar with a fingernail, as though there's a mark she's trying to eliminate.

She's going to offer to pay! The idea comes to her like a small epiphany. An answer. And how soon can they wind this up? Because – very much like their mother – Alex's kids are losing it. Right now, they're under the table squawking loudly, showing off to Helen and Katy's children, three sweet little boys with sandy hair. And she isn't sure whose is which, but they are all behaving like angels, like maybe they've been drugged with that kids' medicine, the one parents used to use on long plane journeys, the one that was withdrawn from the market not so long ago. And why aren't Alex and Luc controlling their goddamn children? Eva can see people at the other tables, sliding their eyes sideways, casting glances in their direction; someone is going to make a complaint soon.

'Why so stressed, Mrs Taylor?' Scott is at her side and whispering in her ear. Barely whispering in her ear, more talking at a normal volume, and dread jumps into her throat. *Mrs Taylor*. Did anyone hear him? She checks around her. She hasn't changed her name so why would he say that? Does he think he's flirting? Does he *want* the family to find out? Now? Why would he do this?

'Don't,' she says, under her breath. And he flinches, as if she's pinched him. Smooths down the front of his ridiculous poncho, which he's still wearing, despite the heat from the kitchen.

'O-*kaay*,' he says, and his expression makes her think of Charlie Brown. 'It's no biggie, honey.'

'Just. Do. Not.' She spits the words into her lap.

Alex

Alex feels like a swan. Here she is gliding along on the surface, looking serene, and no one would know it, but underneath she's flailing desperately. Helen's wife is laughing and looking at her. She has excellent hair. A shag, Alex thinks it's called, and she's wearing an asymmetrical top you can tell is expensive.

'You don't *look* like a swan,' Helen's wife tells her.

It's a long moment before Alex understands she must have articulated her thought. Her head is hurting. She feels like a swan with an aching head, and she's glad Matt can't see her like this. Maybe she does have concussion. 'Mum!' she calls down the table. 'I think maybe I do have concussion. Do you think there's a hospital anywhe–' She interrupts herself. 'Nancy,' she hisses, because Nancy will know. She's going to ask Nancy about the concussion, *concussion con-cushion* . . . The word in her head sounds like 'cushion', and it's making her want to lie down; she'd love to lie down with her head on something soft, but now the waiters are swooping in. They're coming en masse, placing perfect origami presents in front of each person, a long curling bill in the centre of the table. Alex feels a little dizzy at the choreography of their movements, the flourish of their arms, the lights in her eyes. Her present is beautiful: a pattern of cranes on the paper, in turquoise and scarlet and black and green, and she's remembering. A door opening, and behind it, a room full of bright-coloured birthday gifts – large, small and everything in between – and her dad standing off to one side, smiling. Like something from a dream. It's one of her earliest memories, the one she comes back to most. Except for the other memory, the half-memory of her burning, burning feet that's a blare of image and sound and smell and fear. The memory she hates to remember.

Alex is trying to unpick the little paper gift, but her fingers won't do what she wants them to. She even looks like her dad, she's thinking, as she does it. Everyone tells her this. They have so many similarities, the two of them, other people's words, not hers, but she sees it too. So she can't figure out why . . . She doesn't get why her dad . . . The thing is, Lucy's TikTok showed it all clearly, it's inescapable, but she just doesn't understand why her dad chose to . . . Alex rips at the paper in her hands. She can't finish the thought. Inside, she finds a small white mint. All that promise for this? Placing the sweet on her tongue, she eyes the beautiful, ruined present.

'Let me get this,' she hears Eva say, and jerks her head up. Eva's directing her words at their mum, but she's talking to all of them, tipping her head towards the bill in the middle of the table. She's saying it in a sort of *breezy* tone, like no big deal. And Alex is suddenly incensed. She feels as if she's gone up in flames.

'We don't need your charity!' The words burst from her, and her mint flies from her mouth, like saliva. 'Maybe give some of your money to an actual charity. They could certainly use it in these dystopian times.' She's warming up now, thinks maybe she's being kind of funny. Satirical. Amusing, at the very least. Opening her arms expansively, she addresses the table; she's enjoying herself. 'I bet all her money's in petrochemicals and big pharma and despotic regimes lols. All those stocks and shares and options and futures or whatever. La-la-la *Wall Street Journal*, Dow Jones Index, FTSE 100, blah blah. You need to offset that, you know, Eva. For the future of the planet and all that jazz. Buying a Tesla – *virtue signalling* – won't cut it, sunshine.' She twiddles her fingers at the side of her mouth, as if she's Groucho Marx or someone, some cultural reference, she isn't sure what or who. Then she looks from her sister to her mum to Stella to Helen, and finally at Luc. Why is nobody laughing?

Eva, Winter 2000

Eva's standing outside the door to her sisters' Hammersmith flat. It's taken her more than an hour to get here, because the tube journey west is a nightmare, and now she's arrived, all she wants is to turn around and go back. The street is dark, and it's raining so hard her clothes are soaked, all the way through to her underwear. Her breasts feel damp, her belly, her thighs. She doesn't have the energy to push her hair from her face – she feels as if it would be too heavy to peel from her skin.

When Nancy opens the door, Eva starts to cry. Silently, so that in the rain, it could almost seem like she isn't. Except she knows that her mouth is wrong: she can't force her lips into a smile, into any kind of greeting at all.

'What's happened, Eva?' Nancy is out on the pavement, taking her hand, trying to get her in through the door and out of the rain. 'Why didn't you call?' She's wearing new slippers, Eva notices, fluffy with Snoopy motifs, and Eva wants to tell her, Don't get them wet.

'Let's get you inside,' her sister says. 'Okay?'

Alex is in the kitchen, a glass of red wine in her hand. The windows are all steamed up, and she's stirring something on the stove. There's a smell of burned garlic and hot tomatoes. Eva is relieved to see that Luc isn't there.

He has his shared house in Hackney, but most nights stays over with Alex.

'Oh, okay, hi, it's you,' Alex bangs the wooden spoon on the edge of the pan. Scratchy sounds of old-skool funk are coming from the radio. 'You should've called. I don't know if this will stretch to . . .' And then Eva sees her see. 'Hey, what's wrong?' her sister asks, and she turns down the flame, glances at Nancy as she crosses the kitchen. 'Sis?' Taking Eva's face in her hands, she kisses her forehead that's slippery still with rain. 'Is it Carlos? Work? What?'

Eva shuts her eyes, like that way she might seal everything in, or disappear. If there are words she can't find them; she doesn't want to find them. Her sisters. She tells them everything. But she doesn't know how to tell them this.

'Right, first things first.' Alex finds her fingers and squeezes. 'Let me get you a towel. You're an actual flood hazard, Evie.'

And standing there, shivering and sore, her clothes sucking at her body, Eva knows she's done the right thing in coming here. The only thing she could have done.

At the sink, Nancy pours wine from an open bottle, fills two large glasses more than halfway. 'I say, let's self-medicate . . .' Her sister smiles goofily, pulls out a chair from the kitchen table. 'Sit!' she orders, in her Barbara Woodhouse voice. 'Drink this.' And Eva does.

'You're basically the princess of "and the pea" fame,' Alex says, coming back into the room, a bundle of blue towels in her arms. They're the old towels from the

Dartmouth Park house, the ones they've had since they were kids. 'Turning up like this, in the dark, the driving rain . . .' Alex shakes out the towels. 'Remember the Ladybird book with the super-mysterious woman in the grey dress on the cover? The jumble of mattresses all stacked up on the bed behind her.'

'Yeah, Mum gave it to Oxfam.' Nancy lights a cigarette, tips back in her chair. 'That and practically everything else. For fuck's sake, I loved those books.'

'She did keep asking us to come and sort through what we wanted . . .' Alex doesn't look at Nancy as she says it. She's using the voice that makes Eva think of stripped teeth. 'And can you open the window if you're smoking?'

Eva holds still as Alex twists her hair up into a turban. She starts crying again as her sister wraps a bath sheet around her shoulders. This time she can't stop.

'Talk to us, Eva,' Alex says, or Nancy, she isn't sure who, because she can't look at them. She's pressing her fingers against her eyes, and everything in her head, in her whole body feels swollen. And it must go on longer than she thinks, the crying, more keenly even than she's aware, because Nancy is all of a sudden standing in front of her, pulling Eva's hands from her face.

'You're scaring me now,' her sister says. 'I'm thinking cancer, okay, at this point, just to give you a ballpark. Rape? Have you been home? Are Mum and Dad okay?'

'Stop it, Nancy.' Alex's voice in the kitchen is quiet, but there's the surrogate-parent power in it.

Eva listens to the hiss and spit of the sauce simmering

on the stove; it sounds too loud, angry, like a demon might be about to emerge from it, snatch them all around their necks. She pushes out a breath. She thinks she's going to be sick. 'I haven't had a period since before Glastonbury.' It's the first thing she's said since she got to the flat.

'Because why? I mean, you're very thin . . .' Nancy adjusts the towel that's slipping from her shoulders. 'Have you been to the doctor?'

'Have you done a test, Eva?' Alex asks. She says it like maybe she's just double-checking the time.

'Yup,' Eva answers. Her throat is dry. Then she holds up her hands, all the fingers splayed. All ten of them. She's done ten tests.

Alex moves across the kitchen, turns off the gas ring on the hob. 'Does Mum know?' she asks. 'Dad?'

Eva presses her lips together or she'll start to cry again. She shakes her head, *no*.

'So we'll get you the morning-after pill. Where's my bag?' Nancy is already moving through to the lounge, lifting cushions from the sofa, checking under the coffee-table. 'There's a twenty-four-hour chemist in Ravenscourt Park, I'll be, like, forty minutes.'

'Glastonbury's in June,' Alex says. 'It's December.'

Her sisters start discussing dates, counting on their fingers, and it's like she isn't here. The familiar feeling. Deep-rooted in her bones. Words above and around and off to one side of her. People talking, talking, talking, and she isn't quite in it, doesn't quite get it. Can't keep up. It's like she's three years old again, and five and ten and twelve; it's busy and comforting and frustrating all at once. Disenfranchising. Easy. It silences her.

Her sisters keep glancing at her stomach. Do they know they're doing it? Eva swallows a mouthful of wine.

'So, the A word, then?' Nancy has come to stand in the archway that separates the kitchen from the lounge.

'The *A word*?' Alex snorts. 'Christ, Nance.'

'I'm trying to be sensitive.' She looks at Eva and winces. 'Sorry . . .'

'The thing is, it's too late.' Eva shrugs. Her shoulders ache as she does it; her whole body aches. 'I've fucked up spectacularly.' She tries to smile.

'But surely –' Nancy starts to say, and Eva shakes her head again.

The song on the radio is one they used to dance to at Camden Palace when they were teenagers. Nights that were hot and intoxicating, sleazy and wild. Nights that were not all that long ago. Nights that, right now, seem like a memory she's appropriated.

'But, I mean, Carlos is nice?' Nancy blurts. 'He's ripped for a start! And those fuck-me eyes, Eva, hey? I mean, you clearly did . . . um, fuck him that is . . . unreservedly, and who can blame you?'

'Nancy, *Jesus*!'

'Have you told him?' Nancy finishes.

They're trying to hide it from her, but she sees their panic. She sees their confusion. Their pain that is her pain. They are a pair of doubles, reflecting her self back at her: she knows her sisters too well.

Has she told Carlos? Eva eyes the condensation

sliding down the dark windows. No, she hasn't. She has no idea how she'll tell him. Carlos, the other intern at the ad agency, who she's been dating for all of ten months. Carlos, who she likes, maybe loves. Carlos, who she has nothing in common with, except work. This is how it's gone for her, she thinks: school, university, a year out, five minutes in a first job and now, *bam*, the end of the beginning of her life. The beginning of the end. She's twenty-three, for God's sake. What has she done?

She doesn't realize she's crying again, until Alex leans in towards her, draws her thumbs across the skin under her eyes, trying to wipe away the tears there. 'You're not on your own with this,' her sister says. 'Okay? Come here.' She feels Alex's arms go around her. Then, a moment later, hot, muffled words in her hair, Nancy saying something, she doesn't catch what. All she knows is that her sisters' hearts are beating in her body. And they stay like that, not moving, a wrap of breath and heat and home.

Nancy's the first to pull back. 'Nobody puts baby in the corner!' Her middle sister announces, in an off-key American accent, before scrunching up her face, like *What just came out of my mouth?*

There's a pause, and Nancy looks so stricken, so unlike herself, that Eva starts to laugh. She's laughing and crying all at once – she can't help it.

Alex takes Nancy's shoulders and shakes them. 'Didn't make sense on *any* level,' she says. She's smiling too, but Eva thinks she sees tears in her older sister's eyes. 'Actually a little bit offensive and weird TBH, Nance,' Alex adds, and she moves away, towards the stove. 'Listen, there's nothing we can do until tomorrow. We'll make a doctor's appointment first thing. I can take a day off work, come with you. Right!' Alex dusts off her hands, like *That's sorted*. 'Shall we eat?' She looks at Eva, raises her eyebrows, questioning. 'You can have Nancy's . . .'

Eva thinks she could sit here for ever. She would like to stop time, in this fuggy room that smells of garlic and perfume and warm, wet clothes. With her two favourite people. Her two favourite people in the world, who won't know that, in this moment, they're wearing the exact same expression, a look that's at once fragile and fierce. They're trying so hard to make it okay, her sisters, to treat this like it's a blip. A nothing. So that she could almost believe it can be fixed. That they will fix it. They'll fix it with borrowed lipgloss and sarcasm and John Hughes films and secret smoking. The three of them, together.

Nancy, Tuesday evening

Nancy has the envelope from the hospital on the bed-side table in front of her, but she can't open it. She's thinking of the scene in a Jonathan Franzen book she once read, she doesn't remember which one, the awful, awful scene where a child is forced to sit at the kitchen table until he finishes his dinner. Forced to sit for hours and hours and *hours*, with a plate of food in front of him, late into the night. That's how Nancy feels now: she's going to make herself sit here until she opens this letter. This goddamn letter that's been burning a hole in her glove-box for too long now. Everything's gone to shit anyway – Georgie can't come up, her dad is a twat, her family is basically imploding – so, hell, she might as well pitch this into the fire. And it's not as if she'll sleep now anyhow. She's trying not to count, but she feels like she's averaging five hours a night, maximum, since they got here. She's exhausted.

The surface of the table is glass. There's a geometric pattern beneath it in blues and browns and greens that morphs into watchful eyes, if she looks at it too long. Nancy flattens out the envelope; her palms are slippery. At least for once the heat is off her. She could almost thank her older sister for that. Almost. If the entire evening hadn't been so excruciating, a stunning crescendo of shame. As far as she's aware, they're all in bed now – or, in Alex's case, probably throwing up her liquid dinner. Except Scott and his son, who've decided this is the perfect moment for a swim in the saltwater pool. *The night's still young!* Scott had declared, as he went to fetch his trunks, with a thumping tone-deafness that made Nancy feel her eyes might burst from her head. She had an argument on speaker phone with Leon in the car. Accused him of doing it on purpose, of deliberately fucking up his ankle, which she understood to be absurd even as she said it. Georgie had been in tears about not coming, Leon said, but he wouldn't let her speak to her daughter, refused to wake her up. Nancy imagines him hobbling around, ordering takeaway, feeling sorry for himself, and the thought makes her furious.

And another thing. A whole new shameful spectrum of anxiety she's concealing, since she watched Lucy's TikTok. It's like vertigo. The feeling she gets when she's at the top of something – an escalator, a cliff, in Barcelona one time climbing the Passion Towers at the Sagrada Familia – that she might not be able to stop herself jumping. Nancy keeps seeing the tree falling, except nothing's there to stop it, and she knows it's going to hit her but she can't move, braced for the impact. Knowing she's going to die. She can't stop thinking about it, about death and dying. Because life right now feels like one long hazard – or a series of hazards, like how is she even still alive? It's the reason she's drinking, one of the reasons. Straight from the bottle of vodka she's taken from the freezer – she isn't bothering with a glass. She likes the burn of the alcohol in her throat, the loosening of her mind as she swallows.

Dr N. Fisher. Her name is printed beneath the transparent window on the front of the letter. She runs her finger across it; she's going to do it.

Nancy snatches up the envelope, tears at the gummed seal. Like she's ripping off a plaster, or diving into freezing water. Is she punishing herself? There's the smell of the hospital on the letter, as if it's been sprayed with industrial disinfectant before posting. She reads it in a single photographic snap. Then line by line, more slowly. The words on the page confirm what she already knows but, even so, she can't quite process it. Nancy is all of a sudden acutely aware of her body. Too aware. She thinks she can feel the fizzing cells in her blood, in her tissue, in her bones, pushing through to the edges of her, making her skin pulse, the same way it did the day it happened. And there's the smell, the hospital smell that catapults her there.

She's working in Room Four, the one opposite the waiting area. The room no one likes because there's black mould in one corner, a patch that seems to bloom larger with each week that passes. Her patient is a woman in her fifties, who's nervous and doesn't speak much English, and Nancy's just completed a fiddly biopsy, working closer to the chest wall than she's a hundred per cent comfortable with. Her armpits smell of sweat, and she hopes her patient hasn't noticed.

'Nearly done now,' she says, and smiles at the woman, trying to put her at ease. She doesn't say she herself found something in the shower this morning, at the top of her thigh, a darkening mole that's gone crusty and that's put her on edge. She has a friend in dermatology she could ask about it, but she'd rather ignore it, doesn't want to know. 'Literally no irony I love more than a hypochondriac doctor,' Nik had laughed on the tube the other day, not in relation to her. Because she hides it, she thinks she does. But it's getting worse: she sees too much, her perspective is shot, and it's one of the reasons she isn't sleeping. One of the reasons she's smoking again – another irony, she's all too aware.

Nancy's thinking this when she hears it, a raised voice in the waiting area. It isn't much to start with, but she's on alert straight away – already she's a little tight behind the eyes, because of the mole and the nervous patient and the not sleeping. She sees her patient hear it too. Nancy wrinkles her forehead, like this is something faintly distracting, amusing even. Nothing to worry about. She's pressing the dressing into place, when the voice comes again, indignant, angry, getting louder.

'Don't tell me to sit down!'

Nancy smiles at her patient, peels the latex gloves from her hands. She knows there are two people off sick today, another on leave. She's pretty sure there's a single receptionist out there right now, trying to deal with whatever this is.

'I'm not shouting at you! You think this is fucking shouting?' she hears.

'You can put your things back on now, okay?' she tells her patient. 'Sorry about all the . . .' She loops her finger in the air vaguely, as she moves away from the bed, securing the curtain behind her.

The tirade isn't stopping. Nancy crosses to the door, hesitates. This is not her job. It's not her job to deal with these people: she didn't train six long years for this. Cutting up cadavers and mainlining Pro-Plus and racking up a student loan bigger than Bermuda. She's not a bloody bouncer. 'I've been waiting fifty fucking minutes,' she hears. 'I've waited six months for this appointment and now I'm here fucking well waiting again and . . .' Nancy feels something that's both fear and rage: she can't leave the receptionist out there dealing with this alone.

'Excuse me one moment,' she calls to her patient, her fingers on the door handle. She's going to explain to the woman in the waiting area that they're understaffed today, that she's seeing people as fast as she can, that there's nothing the receptionist – nothing *anyone* – can do. She'll use reason. She'll be professional; she will not rise to it.

Nancy sees her straight away. Someone a lot smaller and thinner than her loud voice suggests, a woman who's maybe in her thirties, and who's jabbing a finger at the clock on the wall, the clock that doesn't work. The receptionist, Divine, has her hands up trying to placate her.

'I don't give a fuck how long everyone else has been waiting. I pay my taxes! I pay for this hospital. I pay *your* wages!'

Nancy moves across the waiting area. She can feel a hole in the toe of her tights, pinching as she walks. 'Can I help?' she calls.

The woman swings round.

Nancy fixes her with a look. She's aware of the rows of plastic seats, people in them watching her. *Our clients,* Nik calls them. 'I'm afraid we're a couple of staff down today,' she tells the woman. 'And you will know that services have been cut to the bone, not our fault.' She says this through squeezed lips, and she's reminding herself of her older sister. Inside, her heart is jumping a little. 'If I can ask you to take a seat, we'll get to you as soon as is humanly possible.' She smiles, a counterfeit smile.

'This place is a joke,' the woman says. 'I want to see a doctor now.'

'I am a doctor,' Nancy says, and sees the woman stall. 'I'm the only doctor on duty, and I can assure you I'm going as fast as I can.' Reaching out, she puts a hand on the woman's arm; she intends to patronize her into submission. 'I'm afraid –'

'Don't you fucking manhandle me!' The woman snatches away her arm. She catches Nancy on the shoulder as she does it. 'Don't you dare touch me.'

A roar flares in Nancy's chest. She's been here since seven a.m., already put in a nine-hour shift, hasn't stopped except for a snatched tuna sandwich from the canteen for lunch, and screw the mercury content, the micro plastics, she needed the protein hit. She's exhausted. Physically, mentally, existentially.

'We have a policy here, okay?' She points to a poster on the wall that details, in cartoon format, a zero-tolerance policy to bullying the staff. 'So I'm asking you to moderate your language, your attitude in general.'

'*My* attitude?' The woman lurches forward. For a moment, Nancy thinks the woman is going to hit her, and flinches. 'Don't you come at me, bitch,' the woman spits.

The words when they come seem to arrive in her mouth from a higher force. It's like she's back at school. At the bus stop that one time with Eva, those girls from the year above jabbing their cigarettes in her sister's face. The flash of rage in her. Her voice is soft – she's all too aware there are kids in the waiting area – but there's no mistaking the anger. She's had it. Her ID card swings from her neck as she leans in close to the woman. 'You fucking speak to me like that again,' she whispers, 'I'll have security up here so fast you won't know what's hit you, understand?' Then she turns to Divine, tries to communicate solidarity with her eyes, a steadiness she isn't feeling, not even close. 'I'm heading back in to my patient, Divine,' she says, and she can hear the crack of adrenaline in her voice. 'Any more problems, don't hesitate to call security, okay?'

Nancy drops the letter onto the bed. This job, she thinks. The hours in A and E as a junior doctor, the on-calls, the never saying no. Literal blood, sweat and tears, and the rest. Even when Georgie was a baby, *especially* when she was a baby, there was no respite. And now this. One woman can do this to her. One wrong-headed woman. One bullshit complaint, outlined in black-and-white here: *Dr Fisher used physical force against the complainant . . . Dr Fisher used aggressive, unprofessional and unacceptable language to threaten the complainant . . . Dr Fisher threatened to employ her influence to ensure security exercised undue physical force . . . Dr Fisher caused the complainant to suffer PTSD-related panic attacks . . .* The injustice winds her. But even so she's ashamed. She's beyond ashamed. How will she tell her family? This will play into everything they think they know about her. That she's the trigger-happy fuck-up, who can't *self-regulate*, who never has been able to keep her emotions in check. And never mind Alex's performance tonight, never mind everything that's happened – or hasn't happened – with her dad, never mind any of it. The truth is, this will play into everything she thinks she knows about herself. Because a part of her believes she's the problem, at some level she always has. She pinches the skin on her arm; she pinches hard, knows it will leave a mark. Then she texts the only person she can.

So they suspended me . . .

Within seconds, her phone goes, and she answers.

'I don't want to talk about it,' she says.

'Totally your call.' Nik's voice is in her ear, and she feels something release in her. 'But for the record, they're bastards, obviously,' he tells her. 'You're one of the best doctors in that place. You've got the research track to prove it, and they know it.'

Nancy takes a swig of cold vodka from the bottle by the bed. 'They suspended me and Leon's broken his sodding leg. On purpose,' she adds, and then she laughs, because she knows how it sounds. 'So Georgie can't come up, and I am this close to –' She stops: she thinks she might cry. She's been so tearful lately – it's ridiculous, embarrassing. 'Anyway, shouldn't you be in bed? It's gone eleven. What's the cut-off?' She forces the joke, which barely even qualifies as a joke, she knows, because she doesn't want him to sense she's upset.

She could just leave, she thinks. She could pack her stuff in the morning and go, use Georgie as an excuse. But it's her mum's seventieth at the end of the week, and if she so much as dared to float the idea, the others would come for her. Not in a straightforward way. God, no. In a head-spinning, passive-aggressive cocktail of thin-lipped intimation. A read-my-facial-expressions-and-between-the-lines-of-the-words-that-are-coming-out-of-my-actual-mouth kind of a way. Something they could have stamped in Latin on a family crest.

'Georgie can't come up?'

There's a tap dripping in the bathroom. She doesn't have the energy to move from the bed to turn it off. 'Yup. She's too young to get the train on her own, and I can't make it there and back in a day, and I just can't see the point. Also the atmosphere here is . . .' She lets the sentence drop; she's given up. She doesn't say that on top of everything else she hates driving, that she's increasingly paranoid behind the wheel of a car, even though she used to love it – nudging ninety up the motorway, tunes blaring. She's aware it makes her sound neurotic, weak, a stereotype. She hadn't even known it was a thing, but it is, apparently, another joyless marker that she's now a woman of a *certain age*.

Eyeing the letter on the bed, she wonders if she could tear it to shreds without touching it, using just the supernatural force of her fury, her despair.

'Okay, I'm going to say some stuff and I want you to listen,' Nik says.

She blinks extravagantly, as if he's able to see her. 'Kind of reading like a hostage situation –'

'You see, you've interrupted there. Already,' Nik says. 'So, listen.' She hears him inhale, like he's gearing up to something. 'Number one: I'm owed a ton of leave that I have to take soon or I'll lose it. Two: I don't need cover right now because of the Kafkaesque restructure. Three: I have cousins about thirty miles from where you're staying, who I haven't seen in five years. Four: I need a break. Five: I'll bring her.'

'What? Bring who? You mean Georgie?' she asks. 'Are you drunk?'

'*Five* compelling reasons, Nancy Fisher. Count 'em!'

Her instinct is to quash the idea, to kill it dead. Because there's a dangerous hope in her. Would he really do this?

'This won't look like such a good idea in the morning,' she tells him.

'Nothing, apart from staying in bed, feels like a good idea in the morning, but I'm offering now.' She hears him whistle through his teeth, and she can picture them, his neat white teeth, the little gaps between them. Like an unzipped zip, is how he describes them. 'Do you want it in writing?' he asks. 'I can drop you a text.'

Nancy hesitates. She hasn't pulled the blinds in the room and she can see herself sitting on the bed, reflected in the night-black glass. Her knees are pulled up to her chin and she's smiling. 'She's only met you twice,' she says. 'It would be weird.'

'Very much not a problem. Kids love me, you know that. I'm a natural.'

Nancy doesn't know that, but she doesn't doubt it. And although she's never asked, she does know – she *thinks* she knows – that Nik had a girlfriend, or wife, or fiancée, she isn't sure exactly, who died. He's never mentioned anything to her, and she has no idea about the ins and outs. It's just one of those things that circulates among colleagues. Something half whispered, half remembered, the bones of a past no one wants to bring up.

'Okay, I hear from your silence you're doubting my competence,' he says now. 'How about I borrow my niece? My brother would bite my bloody hand off. Would that be less *weird*?' He puts emphasis on the word, her word.

Why is he doing this? It flits through her mind that she should refuse, that it's too much, that there's something . . . but she wants so much to have Georgie here. She conjures her child's face, feels the physical ache in her gut that is longing. How can she pass up this chance? If not for herself – and it very definitely would be for herself – for Georgie.

'Let me pay for your petrol, at the very least,' she blurts, before she can overthink it – before she talks herself out of it, before she talks him out of it. 'And next lunch in the canteen is on me. I mean, obviously, and I'll throw in a fat Coke and a side of greasy NHS chips. Once they let me back in the building that is. And no driving over eighty miles an hour, okay? Seventy, and in the slow lane, would be my preference. And I owe you, Nik. I owe you, I *owe* you for this.'

'Just know that I will hold you to the extra chips,' he says.

Nancy, Summer 2002

They took off their clothes pretty much the minute they got through the door. A trail along the narrow corridor like a bright fabric river. The temperature outside is in the nineties, stultifying, but it's more than that, the heat of them, the heat between them. Lying here in his bed, in the flat his parents own, Nancy can feel the sweat in the crease of her thighs, under her breasts, sliding down her back between her ribs. It's been all of three minutes since they came – a simultaneous orgasm, their speciality, because their body chemistry is *on point*, and she's secretly pretty smug about it – but already the shower's going in the en suite and Oliver's in there. He's a clean freak. He's OCD. Fallout from boarding school, she thinks, she knows. He hated school, won't talk about it.

He appears in the room in a cloud of steam, a magician's trick. There's a white towel wrapped around his waist, around his body that practically makes her salivate. She could take a bite out of him, he looks that good.

'Hey,' he says. And she's hoping he'll come towards her, but he stays where he is. 'So your sister . . .' He leaves the sentence there.

Pre-sex they were at the Dartmouth Park house. They dropped off the doctor's kit for Lucy, the cheap plastic set she'd found in Woolworths and couldn't resist. Her mum was in the kitchen, coffee-breathed and hairdressing scissors in hand, with Lucy sitting on a high stool, damp-haired and a towel round her shoulders. 'She has so much hair this kid,' Vivienne announced, clamping a strand between her fingers and snipping. 'Don't you?' she said, craning her neck round to smile at her grandchild, lovestruck. 'Just like Mummy, who, by the way,' she turned to Nancy, 'is having a nap. Bad night.'

Oliver leans against the wall, his mouth twisting into a smile. There are glistening flecks of water from the shower on his chest, and his eyes have that look. The you-know-I-know-you-want-to-fuck-me look.

'So . . . my sister?' Nancy says, pulling the sheet across her, because she feels suddenly exposed, lying here like this.

'Ten. Out. Of. Ten.' He articulates each word slowly, as if he's scoring a fine wine.

For a moment she's confused, and then, because of the way he's looking at her, she understands that he's changed tack: he's flirting with her. And despite herself – despite all her feminist principles, which surely are about choice and circumstance and personal empowerment and whatever-rocks-your-boat anyway – she's pleased, she can't help it. Hell, she's bloody delighted. Her boyfriend of three months, her junior-doctor boyfriend, who all the other junior doctors have the hots for – men and women both – thinks she's a ten out of ten, and she isn't going to argue.

'Yup,' Oliver says, and he half whistles through his teeth. 'She. Is. Hot. Hands down a ten.'

There's an instant when Nancy thinks he's referring to her in the third person, like he's being cute, a little kooky. Before she realizes. *Eva.* He's talking about Eva, who they've just left, lime green stethoscope around her neck, finding snail patients in the garden with her toddler. *Eva is the ten.* If Oliver wasn't across the room, if he was next to her, here on the bed, Nancy might think he'd punched her, an actual punch in the gut that's bruised her insides. She knows she should be angry, but instead she has the urge to zip herself up. Setting her face to neutral, she swallows the pain of his words.

It's true, she can't deny it, that Eva looked effortlessly beautiful when she wandered, yawning, into the kitchen in Dartmouth Park. Nancy hates the word 'sexy', makes her itchy, but Eva did look sexy. Pretty and sexy both. Like the sleep in her face worked in her favour rather than the other way around, like it did for most people.

'I thought I heard my favourite sister,' Eva said, helping herself from the pot of coffee on the side. 'You up next?' she asked Oliver, pointing to her daughter in the hairdressing chair. And Nancy noted it, absorbed it, the choreography of her sister's ease in the kitchen, the way she bumped shoulders with their mum as she joked with Oliver. Their closeness. And it's not that Nancy isn't comfortable at her parents' house, it isn't that. It's just the way Eva is there, the way her sister exists in the space, feels different. Nancy doesn't know why she even cares, because the last thing she'd want is to be living back home with her mum and dad. The last thing she'd want is to have a baby at her age. It's just still a little strange that her sister has a kid, that's all. *It's out of the order of things,* her mum would say. Which isn't to say Nancy doesn't adore Lucy – she'd do anything for her niece. It's just weird that Eva was the first, and so soon.

'You sure we can't tempt you?' Eva mimed a pair of scissors, while Oliver laughed and shook his head. And Nancy told him, good call. 'Mum's the master of the too-short fringe. Aren't you, Mum?'

At that Vivienne straightened, one hand on Lucy's small shoulder. 'Ha! Bit rich coming from you. Let me tell you, Oliver, about the time . . .' And – as if she'd never told it before – she launched into one of her select pool of *stories about their childhood,* one of her standards from the Anecdote Hall of Fame. The one where Vivienne had been on the phone, distracted, and Nancy had decided to play hairdressers. How she'd taken the kitchen scissors, along with a toddling Eva, out into the garden, washed her sister's hair in a puddle, and escalated things quickly, enthusiastically from there. 'A towel round Eva's head and great chunks of hair falling out,' Nancy registered her mum saying, and she rolled her eyes, tried to fix a humorous expression on her face. Because there's an undercurrent for her to this *Amusing Family Tale.* The fact is, she can't find it funny, can't tell anyone it's not funny for her. 'All those beautiful apricot curls, everyone used to comment on them. Lopped off!' Her mum made a sharp, chopping motion with her hand – the one holding the scissors – a little too close to Lucy's head. Then she pulled her fingers through her own hair, like maybe those long-ago curls might fall from her scalp. 'They never grew back, you know,' she added, as she always did, as though she'd never disclosed this fact before.

'I don't remember it,' Nancy murmured. Because what was her mum after, an apology? An admission that she was jealous of her sister back in a pre-memory time? That it was revenge because she'd been usurped by an interloper with great hair? She wanted to say, I was five, for fuck's sake! But, hey, I guess shit sticks, am I right? Because, surely – *surely* – if we're talking 'mistakes we've made', we might want to zero in, now and again, on Eva's ACCIDENTAL PREGNANCY. Let's be honest, that was *quite* the fuck-up. She glanced quickly at her niece as she had the thought, apologized in her head. And here's another crazy thought: I know it was the seventies, and you're all super-proud of your benign neglect, but maybe, just maybe, Mum, you should've been keeping a closer eye on your children. What with the haircut and the Chinese lanterns, the staircase with no spindles and, um, I don't know, Alex's burned feet that – unlike the hair, the unsupervised snacking, the deathtrap stairs – are *never* talked about. Even though Nancy knows, because she did part of her training in the burns unit, and because she's seen the scars a thousand times, how many hospital visits her sister must have endured, how long the skin would have taken to heal. How serious the injuries must have been.

'You don't remember?' Briefly, her mum pulled a face. 'You were fairly old, Nancy. But we often repress our memory of events that threaten to invalidate us. I read that somewhere,' she added vaguely. 'A sort of memory pick 'n' mix. It's fascinating.' Then she turned to Eva. 'We called it your lesbian trim, your dad and me. Your dyke do. I know, I know, I'm not supposed to say that –' And then she laughed so violently, Lucy jumped in her seat, a sheen of tears threatening to spill from her glossed-over eyes.

The sun through the high window in the bedroom is bouncing off the mirrored wardrobe, illuminating him. Objectively, his body is beautiful. Ridiculously, insanely so. Although, in this moment, he no longer seems so attractive to her. Digging her nails into her thighs under the sheet, Nancy forces a smile. Like this whole thing is some sort of elaborate flirtation between them. And she's trying to suffocate the knowledge that he's been thinking about her sister – her *younger* sister – in that way. She doesn't want to know. But it's fine, it's all right, she can handle it, she can handle him.

'Okay,' she says, and she knows, before the words are out of her mouth, that she's going to ask. She can't stop herself. 'So I'm a . . . ?'

'What?' he asks. She doesn't like the look on his face. The thinned eyes, the slight mirth, the twitching micro-expressions that tell her he knows exactly what her question is. He's going to make her say it.

'So what am I out of ten?'

There's a gap in things then. The hum of the fridge down the hall, working too hard in the crazy heat.

Behind her eyes, the pine-fresh smell of the shower gel he's used. Too strong, it's giving her that headachy feeling. Nancy rubs her temples. She knows what he's going to say. She knows he'll say ten, of course he will, so she doesn't understand why her throat is clogged, like she needs to clear it.

'Seven?' he says, his back to her, as he takes a pair of fresh boxers from the mirrored wardrobe, pulls them on. He spends several seconds towelling off his hair, before he hangs the towel around his neck, turns to face her. At least he has the humility to look vaguely sheepish. Not hugely. Just marginally uncomfortable, as if, really, this is a bit of a joke between them. Nancy grips the sheet, pulls it further up her body, although she's already too, too hot.

'But you're amazing, of course you are.' He says it as if he's offering her some kind of compensation. A booby prize. 'I mean you're so damn sexy, Nancy. An absolute *whore* in bed.' He winks at her, clucks his tongue, in a way that suggests he's just delivered a compliment. Is it a compliment? I mean, she hates the word, but sexy is good, right? Good in bed is good too, she thinks desperately. Then she thinks *seven*. She can see the number – tens of sevens, hundreds of sevens – cantering across her mind. Not eight. Not nine. Seven. Three fewer than her sister. Maybe the worst part is she agrees with him: she isn't as pretty as her sister, she knows this, she's well aware of it. He's only stating a fact. It's just she didn't expect him to *see* it. To say it. Nancy doesn't know what to do with her face. How is she supposed to respond to this?

'Yup.' Oliver pinches his thumb and forefinger together, like he's indicating something small, squints. 'Sexy, but just a little bit psycho . . .' Then he laughs, as if this is a joke they're sharing. 'Right, I'm starving.' He hooks his wet towel carefully on the back of the bedroom door. 'I'm going to make a sandwich, grab a Sol, cheeky slice of lime.'

He doesn't ask if she wants something to eat too and, anyway, she has no appetite. She could definitely get drunk, although he makes no noises about her joining him, and she won't go. *Psycho.* The word pinballs around her mind. She thinks of the Hitchcock film, imagines a knife with a flashing blade, her own body punctured, dark blood gushing from her. It's the middle of the day, but she's all at once exhausted. She thinks if she turns on her side and shuts her eyes, she'll sleep; she's pretty sure she couldn't move if she wanted to. Even so, as he leaves the room, she feels as though he has taken a piece of her with him.

Alex, Wednesday morning

Alex needs to block it all out; she needs an escape. She would have got into her car and driven down the track, parked on the B road again, but she's pretty sure she'd still be over the limit from the night before. And, anyway, everyone's aware now that there's signal in the pool room. Out in the grounds too, around the sculpted-copper seating area, so she has no excuse to leave. Nancy's taken pity on her and relieved her of Dolly. *Oof, that is one bad case of cocktail poisoning*, her sister said, as she scooped the baby from her arms. *You look green, almost fluoro. Go and lie down. Where's Luc?* Alex is on borrowed time and she knows it. And she's feeling jumpy – sick and tired and jumpy – as she flicks from Matt's Twitter to his Instagram to his Facebook page, and back again; at any moment, someone could walk in and catch her.

He's been to see *Cats*, with Zoë and his daughters, and she finds herself wanting to laugh, and also cry. Imagines herself teasing him about this, like, of *all* the musicals? Grown-ups dressed as *literal* pussies, and what happened to the tattooed Camden boy, who drank cheap cider down by the canal, and collected obscure LPs? What happened to the Matt who fucked her in some-one's bathtub at a house party in East Finchley? She'd been drunk then, too, had had to take the morning-after pill the next day, felt the quiet scorn of the doctor on duty. And Matt's bought some aubergines from the farmers' market. He's looking pretty pleased about it, holding them up, purple-polished and huge, like he's just won first prize at the village fête. Alex imagines herself making a good *bad* joke about this too, runs it around in her mind, something a bit *Carry On*, a bit oo-er, missus, which isn't her style at all, more Nancy's. She thinks it would make him laugh, though.

She's back on his Twitter feed, checking again, in case he's posted something new in the last three minutes, when a promoted tweet pops up, snags her.

Celebs Whose Siblings Are Way More Attractive!
20 stars you didn't know have beautiful siblings . . .

Her thumb hovers. She both wants and doesn't want to click on it. *Do you think it's because she's the pretty one?* Nancy's voice is in her head. She hears the timbre of her sister's laughter in the words, but she doesn't feel like laughing, not this morning, not after everything that's happened. Has her phone been listening to them? *The pretty ones are the favourites. I read it in the* New York Times. *Or maybe* Take a Break . . .

The thing is, if she's honest with herself, Alex always thought *she* was the favourite. The truth is she still thinks this. Does she? She eyes the pool. Her feet are itching again and she would like to dip them into the water, thinks the salt might soothe the skin, but the signal won't stretch to the edge. She has a friend, Barbara, who once confessed she had a favourite child. Years ago now. They'd been at Cally pool when she'd said it, sitting in a pair of flip-down seats, watching their kids' swimming lesson. Breathing chlorine, swapping notes, their weekly Saturday-morning ritual. Barbara had put her finger to her lips as she spoke, because she knew it was transgressive, taboo. *All middle-class parents love their oldest child the most. It's a thing,* she'd said.

Alex thinks of her children. She thinks of Rosa and Eden. She thinks of Dolly. Takes a long breath in. The timing was bad is the thing. She'd been in the middle of her grand plan, her experiment, trying to teach her A-level students perfect pitch. She'd wanted to be like the maths teacher at the state school in Wales, the one whose class had all got A*s in their GCSEs – every single one of them. She'd wanted to be Robin Williams in *Dead Poets' Society*, Tooting's very own Maria von Trapp, inspirational and brilliant. It's a thing in Singapore, higher rates of perfect pitch: there are statistics, she can't remember them. It's teachable, she really believes it is, and she was making progress with some of the students, and then, *boom*, she was pregnant. Really quite pregnant. So although it went through her mind that she could – that she had the choice to – Alex shuts the thought down. Her head, her neck feel bruised; if she were to move too quickly she's certain she'd be sick. It's not about favourites, she thinks, absolutely not. She doesn't believe in favourites. Just, the timing was off. Way, way off in so many directions, and it's an adjustment. Dolly is newer; she doesn't know her so well. It isn't wrong to think that, it's just fact. And, anyway, 'favourites' are something consigned to the past, to less enlightened, put-some-lead-in-your-pencil times. Pre-therapy, pre-pop-psychology, pre-cookie-cutter social-media self-diagnosis. Pre her own parents. Pre her dad.

Before she can stop herself, Alex has typed the words 'favourite child' into her phone, short, sharp jabs at the screen, as if the letters might burn her fingers. The page loads instantly, although the reception is usually so patchy here, as if the algorithm knows she's all set to change her mind if it takes too long.

What to do if you have a favourite kid
What it's like to be your parents' least favourite child
Do parents have a favourite child? It's not who you
think . . .

She clicks on links, scans the contents.

If you absolutely have to have a favourite – and you probably do – you're right to keep it to yourself . . .
   . . . No parents are quite as giddy as first-time parents, nor quite as inclined to see their child as uniquely perfect and gifted . . . It's no wonder younger siblings often fail to measure up . . .

She was gifted, she thinks. She is. She could have been a singer, should have been, if it hadn't been for what happened that first term at the Conservatoire. She's angry about it, is the truth, bitter. Hates the deep-rooted feeling in her that she hasn't fulfilled her promise. And although she's so proud of her sisters – so proud that Nancy's a doctor, so proud of Eva's giddy journey, of her youngest sister's quiet fuck-you resilience – although she loves the reflected glory, she sometimes worries that *she* is the sibling who failed to measure up.

Pretty soon Alex is googling frantically, thumbs flying. *Like a woman possessed.* The phrase strikes her. It goes through her mind that this is more intense even, more frenzied, than her tracking of Matt. Her tracking (*stalking . . . ?*) of Matt and of his wife, of their lives. There's the same feeling of shame. Of dread at what she might find.

> . . . If you had a choice, she reads, don't ever choose to be the middle of three – you don't have the status of being the oldest, or the comfort of being the baby . . .
> . . . Parents without the resources to educate the whole brood will most commonly invest in the firstborn – even if a later-born shows a greater aptitude for learning . . .

She knows she's digging deeper and deeper into the rabbit hole, and she isn't sure what she hopes to figure out. That isn't true. She knows exactly what she wants: she wants an answer to what she saw on Lucy's TikTok, an answer to what happened that day and what it means. She wants to know that she's her dad's favourite – or, at least, that he doesn't *have* a favourite. Does she want that? She's so confused.

. . . Research indicates that when parents treat siblings differently, they foster feelings of injustice, competition, and comparison, with both favoured and less favoured offspring exhibiting poorer mental health . . .

. . . It's particularly interesting that siblings continue to engage in such a high degree of social comparison well into their middle years . . .

. . . recent research contrasting mothers' and fathers' differentiation among their adult children has shown that fathers' favouritism has more negative effects on sibling relations than does mothers' favouritism . . .

. . . both men and women were more likely to have a favourite child if their own fathers had favourites . . .

'Where's Dolly?' At the other end of the room, the door has swung open, and her mum's standing there. For a moment she panics: where is Dolly? Touches her body, at her breastbone, at her hip, reflexively, like she might find her there. Before she remembers.

'Nancy's got her.' Her head is still half in her Google search, as she clicks the side of her phone to clear the screen. Pushes the hair from her face to disguise the fact she's done it. She has the feeling she's been rumbled, as if she's nine years old and eaten all the Chinese lanterns – even though it wasn't her idea in the first place.

'Christ, it's hot in here. How can you stand it?' Her mum moves towards her, along the edge of the pool. Her mum who demands to be noticed. Her flamboyance, her noisiness, her messiness that has always made

Alex feel other. 'I could jump in the pool like *this*!' Her mum indicates the bright tapestry of her outfit, from her hooped earrings threaded with coral beads, all the way down to her pink Turkish slippers, the *indoor shoes* she insisted on bringing despite the under-floor heating. There's the sugary, vanilla-pod smell of her perfume, as she bumps Alex's hip with her own, like, shuffle up.

Alex notices awkwardness in her mum's movement, as she seats herself on the narrow ledge that doesn't really have room for two. Swallows the fact of it, the low-level alarm, because she doesn't want to acknowledge it, doesn't want to know. Her mum is breathing a little heavily too, as she puts a hand on Alex's forearm. 'I see everything you're doing, you know, darling,' she says. 'I see the work you put in. I remember how hard it is.'

It isn't like her mum to talk this way, and Alex feels suddenly, inexplicably, as if she might cry. If she let herself, if she started, she thinks maybe she wouldn't be able to stop.

'And I see that Luc doesn't show up sometimes.' Her mum is picking her words as if they're breakable, Alex can tell. 'The burden's on you, and it doesn't go unnoticed, not by me anyway, and trust me, I know that feeling well.' She says it in a tone that makes Alex look up. 'I know it too, *too* well.'

Their eyes meet briefly, and it's almost uncomfortable – it *is* uncomfortable – because there's something weighted, different, in the way her mum is looking at her. And Alex is all set to ask what she means, to get her to elaborate, but the question jams in her mouth. In her head, her aching head, snatches of the whispered argument she overheard the other morning. *Just what the hell, Patrick? You want to dredge the whole thing up? You think that'll benefit anyone?* Her mind is scrambling, trying to join the dots.

'He loves you, you know.' It's a change of tack, and Vivienne doesn't look at her as she says it. Alex feels the child in her rise. She almost can't believe she's heard right. Because they don't do this, they don't go there. Is her mum going there? Neither of her parents has ever told her they love her: it's just the way it is, a generational thing. She's always assumed it's the language of romance for them, the vernacular of lovers. *He loves you, you know.* Why is her mum saying it? It shouldn't need to be said; it sounds like she's protesting too much. It's so stuffy in here. Stifling. Alex feels if she stood up she might faint.

'I would hate you to think . . .' her mum goes on. 'Y'know . . .'

Alex waits, stares straight ahead. The gurgle of the pool filter sounds like a soft strangling.

'Okay, good!' her mum says, after a pause, and she pats Alex's leg, a full stop. 'I'll leave you to it.' She manoeuvres herself with difficulty off the ledge. 'Fuck's sake,' she curses, as she straightens. 'Excuse my bloody French.'

Vivienne's almost at the door when she turns. Her dress is the same shade of green as the saltwater pool. She is a force, Alex thinks, standing there. A Goddess Mermaid. The way she holds herself, her head on her neck, her neck on her shoulders, her shoulders on her body. The blaze of knowledge in her eyes. A champion bareback riding queen.

'You should probably apologize to Eva,' she says, and when Alex doesn't reply, 'the whole we-don't-need-your-charity thing?' Her mum makes an elaborate gesture with her arms to imply there was more, quite a lot more. And then she disappears through the door, leaving an invisible theatre of unsaid words inscribed in the air.

Alex waits for the suck of the airlock before she moves. Her headache is really starting to take hold now, a heavy *thunk* of pain with each step. She needs paracetamol. She needs water. She needs to load up on carbs. She wonders if she can take something from the kitchen and make it to her bedroom without being seen. She wonders where her children are. Moving past a ceramic planter, she bangs her toe. Tears burn in her eyes.

She's always thought Nancy was the difficult one, the loose cannon, but now that she looks again, she thinks maybe she's been missing something this entire time, because is Eva playing favourites? Has this been her game all along? Her youngest sister is the expert at games, after all. She has the bank balance to prove it. Alex is hurt still, and angry and upset, but even so, she knows her mum is right. The truth is she can't bear to think about everything she said last night. Her *little outburst*, she imagines the Wilsons would call it, and, oh, God, why did she get so drunk? She should apologize, obviously she should. She knows this. It's just she isn't good at saying sorry; she finds it too hard. She doesn't want to admit to anyone – to *herself* – that she's done anything wrong. And, anyway, is she really to blame?

This whole thing with her dad, whatever it is, has

made her feel she's come unhooked. There's cloudiness now where before there were hard lines, no variables. The rules – the rules of her family – have always been sharp, defined, established, predictable. Fixed like music, or maths, and they were good. They worked. But something is happening that's unravelling everything she thought she knew, and she wants someone to tell her that things can be put right, back to the way they were.

There are toys along the edge of the pool, floats and dive sticks, a limp rubber ring that's lost most of its air, and she twitches, but she won't pick them up. She walks past an abandoned towel, a damp scrunch of swimsuit left on a sunbed, a single white sock. She won't touch them. Why should she? Why should she continue to pick up the pieces of everyone else's messy, messed-up lives? Let them do it themselves. She's had it with putting everyone else back together, with putting herself last; she no longer cares. An image of Matt jumps into her mind. A picture of him. The one where he's standing against a backdrop of towering Jurassic palms, a pair of sunglasses pushed up onto his head. Who does Matt put first? she wonders. And as she's thinking it, she sees Zoë, as if she's flicked the page in a photograph album. Matt's wife is wearing a white bikini top and low-slung sarong, no stretch marks. And she's looking into the camera, and out from the photograph. Her eyes are light, laughing, like there's a private joke, and Alex isn't in on it.

It's so hot in here, unbearably hot. In one quick movement, Alex yanks her T-shirt up and over her head, flings it as far as she can across the room. Standing there in her bra, she watches the dark flop of material as it lands, tries not to think about the fact that it will crease, lying there on the floor in this damp heat. Then she plunges her foot into the pool, kicks wildly, disrupts the surface. She almost loses her balance, as water arcs through the air. And it should look beautiful, the dazzling shatter of it, but it seems to her sharp, violent, broken. A manifestation of the scream she's pushing down inside herself. Pushing all the way down, with such force, it's making her whole body shake.

Eva, Summer 2008

Eva's at the counter, holding the box of prototypes in front of her like a shield, and she's acutely aware of the other customers in the shop. She knows she's red in the face, because she's just done her spiel to the woman at the till, and she can feel the burn in her cheeks.

'So you came up with the idea while you were trying to help your seven-year-old with a maths problem?' the woman says now, and Eva nods enthusiastically, stupidly, like her head is on a spring. Like one of those dumb nodding-dog toys that's probably stocked somewhere in this shop, which is full of Playmobil and plastic princesses and hundred-piece puzzles. She feels as if she has the googly eyes twanging from her sockets too.

'Your *seven*-year-old?' the woman says, and Eva knows what's coming. Because this is the woman's takeaway from their five-minute conversation, from Eva's carefully crafted pitch. What else? 'You barely look old enough to have a baby!' The woman is looking at Eva with comedy shock. She has enormous hair, wide and frizzy, and a pair of pushed-up glasses, holding it back.

If she wasn't already flushed, Eva knows she'd feel herself go. She knows, too, that the woman thinks she's flattering her. There's the usual shrivelling that happens somewhere between her sternum and her stomach, and she hates herself for it. 'Thanks,' she says, too brightly. She can't look at the woman as she speaks.

Already this week, three people have expressed their disbelief at her having a child of Lucy's age. It sounds like a compliment, but it isn't. Not to her. To her it sounds like, 'You had her too young.' The baby with the baby: this is how she thinks people see her. Her own family. It's how she sees herself. Like she hasn't moved on from childhood games with Alex and Nancy, when they'd let her join in – but she was only allowed to be the baby. Or the dog. It didn't last long, the feeling that, for once, she'd leaped ahead. Her sisters, who she worships, would never have been so stupid. They would never have allowed this to happen to them. Even though way back at the beginning, after the initial shock had worn off, her dad had joked (was he joking?) that he might've expected it from Nancy, not from her.

Eva is constantly amazed at the things people will say in front of her daughter, as if Lucy isn't there. Implying, with barely a trace of subtlety, that her child must have been an accident, or – more than once – someone just coming right out and saying it, usually with a wink, like they've made a hilarious joke. Worse was pity. Endless variations on 'Oh, and you had that fantastic opportunity at the ad agency too . . .' or 'I guess you'll be clubbing in your forties when the rest of us are knee deep in toddlers!' *She can hear you, you know*, Eva has wanted to say a thousand times.

She'd thought she might catch up, the older she got, that people would stop saying it, but that hasn't happened. It makes her feel less-than, foolish. It makes her feel her small family is somehow void, wrong, not as good as other families. And, yes, she and Carlos haven't lasted, but he's involved and they don't hate each other, not even close, and they do a good job, she knows this. Okay, she's found it hard to make mum friends, mostly people mistake her for the nanny, but she has energy. Hell, she can run like Princess Di in the parents' race on sports day. She'd nearly burst into tears the first time she won, when Lucy had run onto the track straight after, thrown her skinny arms around Eva. And she's present, she's here, she's doing it. So why does she feel such a failure? Why does she feel she needs to apologize for them?

Pushing her feet into the floor, she makes herself look at the woman with the huge hair. She offers up one of the prototypes, and the woman takes it. 'Feel free to open it and have a look.' Eva leans a little way over the counter. 'It's just a zip-fastening and then you're away!'

The woman takes the eight chunky dice from the little pouch, that Eva has hand-sewn into the shape of an eight-leaf clover, which is a thing. She found it in her parents' Royal Horticultural Society encyclopedia of plants and flowers. Eva watches as she weighs each one in her hand, lines them up on the counter. Together the colours of the cubes shade like a sunset. They look like a design piece, Eva thinks. She would display them on her mantelpiece – well, her mum and dad's mantelpiece, but that's not the point – and, no matter what, she's proud. No matter that she's pretty sure the woman with the huge hair is going through the motions, that she won't take the game, that she isn't taking Eva – who looks far too young to have a seven-year-old child – seriously.

'Hmm, unfortunately . . .' she hears the woman say, and Eva's already reaching for the dice to pack them away. A smile fixed on her face, she's thinking she'll try somewhere else, it's not over, she's not giving up that easily, when the woman says it again, 'Unfortunate.' She's stretching out the word, kind of weirdly, and it's a moment before Eva realizes that the woman behind the counter means Unfortune8!. She's saying the name of the game. Her game.

'I like it.' The woman cups both hands around the dice and shakes them. Eva loves the sound they make. It sounds, to her, like rainy holidays and Sundays at home.

'It's neat,' the woman's saying. 'Compelling. I think it could work.' And Eva is nodding again, like her head might spring from her crazy, boingy neck.

'Can you leave me with five? On a sale or return basis?' When the woman grins at her, Eva notices she has a gap between her two front teeth like Eva's mum. She thinks it must be a sign, a good one.

'Yes,' she says. 'Of course, no problem. I'd love to. Are you sure?' It's all she can do not to launch herself across the counter and kiss this woman – this wonderful toyshop woman, who's prepared to take a chance on her – all over her magical, Mary Poppins face.

Eva, Wednesday morning

The smell in the glass house is getting worse. It's spreading. Beyond the hallway outside the pool room, and through the atrium that's filled with glossy plants and the U of concrete benches Eva's been using for her warm-ups, her stretches. In the TV lounge now, it's pretty foul, although Jay is sleeping in there still; she guesses he's used to a berth on a super-yacht, chemical toilets and cooped-up living that she imagines can get pretty fresh sometimes. Eva can taste it on her tongue, as she stands in the kitchen, whizzing up a protein shake in the blender. It's like nothing she's ever smelt before, a little eggy, a little fishy, a little like petrol, and she knows she can't ignore it much longer, will have to get the rental people on to it. If the others knew how much this place had cost to hire for the week, they'd be making a lot more noise about it. An eye-popping amount, Eva thinks, for what it is. More silly sums of money she can't ever imagine she'll get used to spending. Alex, of course, has had her rubber gloves out, T-shirt pulled up over her nose, and some kind of eco-friendly cleaner, scrubbing fruitlessly at the walls, the floor, muttering about *Amityville Horror*. But now even Alex seems to have given up on it; she seems to have given up on being herself, full stop.

The truth is, Eva's been avoiding her eldest sister, ever

since Alex went full on batshit at her in the restaurant with the Wilsons last night. Which is quite *the feat* in a house made of glass. Eva's tried to bury it, but there's the residue of her anger at what happened, the whole business with the bill. How Alex had humiliated her. How her sister had humiliated herself. But there's the stupid guilt, too, that she doesn't want to think about. That, anyway, should be her dad's guilt, and is nothing to do with her. But even so, she's starting to ask herself, Is it true? Is she his favourite? Because if she's completely honest, she's noticed how he shines a light on her in small ways. She's always assumed it was a youngest thing. A baby-of-the-family thing. Something her dad did to boost her, elevate her, and she liked it. Did she play up to it? Encourage it? Like every single person on the planet, she's hardwired for parental approval – she isn't going to beat herself up about that. Eva chucks a handful of blueberries into the blender, sprinkles in some chia seeds. She is definitely beating herself up about that, because have her sisters felt it too? Do they resent her? Blame her? If she wanted it before, she certainly doesn't now. Or, rather, she wants it and doesn't want it. And she can't say any of this, she can't confide in anyone, not even her mum. To say it might make it true. Truer even than the glaring truth of what happened at the naming ceremony, of what her dad did. What he didn't do.

'Eva!' Lucy puts her head round the door, raising her voice above the sound of the blender. When Eva doesn't instantly respond, she says it again. 'E-*vaaa*!' This new thing her child does, of calling her by her first name.

206

It started as a joke, and Eva found it kind of funny at first – a knowing humour that made her proud, even as she batted it away – but now it's stuck, and she hates it. It's a distancing, Eva knows this, a necessary pushing away. Knowing doesn't make it any easier to take.

Eva switches off the blender at the wall, gives her daughter a look. 'I think you mean *Mum*?' she says.

'Yeah, yeah . . . Have you seen my bikini top?' Lucy skates her eyes around the kitchen, like she might have dumped it on the counter, the stone floor, over the back of one of the high stools at the island, any and all of which are entirely possible. 'Y'know, the coral one? Have you seen it?' She manages to make the question sound accusatory.

Eva unscrews the plastic jar from the top of the blender, wipes a drip from the edge with her finger. And then there's her mother's voice, except coming out of her own mouth: 'When did you last have it?'

'Oh, slay, *Mum*.' Lucy rolls her eyes, as if it's entirely Eva's fault that she's discarded half her belongings in little piles around the house. Then she pushes out her lips, in that pouty, Instagram way, and it takes all of Eva's strength not to tell her please to stop, that she's basically aping porn.

'Someone's obviously moved it. God, I wish people would leave my stuff alone!' Her daughter makes a low growling noise, turns and leaves the room. Leaves Eva feeling like growling too, but also – and she knows it's ludicrous – like maybe the exchange was somehow her fault, that she should have handled it better. Eva brings the protein shake to her lips and starts to drink. Direct from the jar, like she's a junkie getting her fix. But she's misjudged the consistency so the liquid splashes her face. And it's dribbling down her neck when she hears the scream.

Instantly she knows something's wrong, that this isn't one of the kids messing around. She isn't sure how she knows this, just that there's fear, or pain, in the shape of the sound. Is it Lucy? Eva bangs the jar onto the counter, moves through the kitchen, like she's going at an assault course, and out into the corridor. 'Lucy?' she calls, and she's heading towards the pool room, trying to figure out where the sound has come from. Because her daughter was looking for her bikini, after all, it makes sense that's where she'd be. As she moves along the corridor, past the pink and blue paintings, the window seat, she's straining to listen, trying to stay calm, but she's thinking of her mum now, her dad. She's thinking heart attacks and strokes and a long-ago argument, when she hears a second scream. The door to Alex's room is ajar; the sound has come from there.

Nobody notices her enter. Alex is kneeling on the floor at the end of her bed. Her head is bent over Dolly, and the baby is crying and crying, and that must be a good thing, Eva thinks automatically, as she moves towards them. Crying is a good thing. Stillness, floppiness, those are the things you don't want. Those are the terrifying things, and crying is okay, it's almost always okay, she's pretty sure. Eden is standing behind his mum, and he looks as though he's been struck.

'What happened?' Eva raises her voice above the cries. 'Alex? Is Dolly okay?'

Eden looks up at her, drags a hand across his eyes, and she can see that he's saying something, but she can't make out what.

'Alex?' Eva's chest is tight. Why isn't her sister saying anything? She moves closer, crouches down, scans the baby. There's no blood, no bruising, nothing to see. But even so, she's afraid to touch her, afraid that if she does the baby might break.

'Rosa pushed her off,' Eden says, in a louder voice this time.

'What?' Eva frowns up at him.

'Dolly scratched Rosa's face and Rosa pushed her off the bed,' Eden tells her, his voice coming in gulps.

'Jesus!' Eva glances, without thinking, at her niece, who's hovering next to the loveseat that's across the room. She looks as though she's trying to blend in with it, trying to make herself as small as she possibly can, although she can't actually sit on the seat because it's covered with tech, all lined up neatly and charging.

'Is Dolly okay, Alex?' Eva tries to keep the concern from her voice. 'Where's Luc?'

Alex is talking to the baby, starting tentatively to press different parts of her body. She doesn't look up.

'Should I get Nancy?' Eva stands. She looks from the bed to the floor, assessing. The bed is huge, but it's low, and there's a thick wool rug, a bedspread that's fallen off the end. 'Is this where she landed?' Eva asks.

If Alex hears her, she doesn't show it.

Eva puts a hand on Eden's head. 'Don't worry, okay?' she tells him. 'Dolly just wants you all to know she's a bit pissed off.' Eva uses the swear word on purpose, a deliberate transgression in front of the kids; she's trying, for their sakes, to keep it light. She has no idea if what she's saying is true.

Her nephew has his thumb in his mouth, and he speaks round the slippery side of it. 'Mum came in and caught Rosa doing it.'

'Shut up, Eden!' Rosa hisses, between clenched teeth. It's the first time she's spoken.

Eva needs to find Nancy. They need to get the baby checked over, and Nancy will know what to do. 'Okay!' she says, too cheerily. 'I'm going to find *Dr Fisher!*' She's using the kids as a conduit: it's Alex she's really talking to.

'Okay . . .' she says again, and she's turning to go, but it's as if someone has pressed pause. Eva realizes that Dolly has stopped crying. The baby's eyes are bright, her face patched pink. There are shuddering breaths in and out of her mouth still, but they are indignant breaths, Eva sees. They are *What the hell? Who let this happen?* breaths. Looking at her, Eva's heart squeezes. She knows how it feels to be Dolly. She knows how it is to be the third child, the youngest. She knows what it is to be the baby. Or the dog.

As if she's reading her auntie's thoughts – as if in solidarity – Dolly puts her small fist to her mouth, and blows a pitiful raspberry. The alarm that has lodged in Eva's throat eases a little.

'She's stopped crying,' she says, to herself as much as anyone. Then, to her sister, 'She seems okay, Alex, don't you thi–'

'Lucy was supposed to be looking after her.'

Her sister's voice is flat. Eva stops.

'Yes,' Rosa pipes up. 'She was.'

'What do you mean?' Eva glances first at her sister, then her niece. Rosa is standing a little taller now, in front of the loveseat.

'She was meant to be in charge.' Rosa is tripping over herself to say it. 'Auntie Nancy was looking after her, and Lucy after that.' Eva sees in her face a child who can hardly believe her luck.

'Lucy's a narcissi who might want to pop a few more clothes on,' Rosa adds, and she glances at her mum, at Alex, for approval as she says it.

Eva frowns. It's a moment before she understands what her niece has said, before she understands that she's doubling down. The words aren't Rosa's, obviously. They're something she will have overheard. Eva looks from Rosa to her sister. Alex won't meet her eye. Narcis-si*st*, she wants to tell her niece. The word is 'narcissist', you little idiot. Inside, she feels the *whump* of rage ignite.

'Rosa, this isn't Lucy's fault.' Eva keeps her tone even, but her fists are balled, nails digging into her palms. 'You need to take responsibility for what you've done.'

'She's eight,' Alex says tightly.

'My point exactly.' Eva watches as her sister lays Dolly on the rug and stands. She registers surprise that her sister has done this: Dolly seems vulnerable, left lying there like that, so soon after what's happened. Out of the corner of her eye, she sees Rosa fold her arms across her chest.

Eva has no idea if her argument is with her sister, her niece or both; she has no idea why she's being dragged into this. She only knows that their exchange is pulsing with danger. That they are crossing a line. That, although it would sound mild to almost anyone else, in her family this is a gargantuan transgression. It pretty much qualifies as a shouting match. *We don't need your charity!* She hears Alex's words in her head, all the things her sister said at the meal with the Wilsons when she was drunk. So drunk she could barely stand by the time they got her out of there. But right now they aren't drunk. They are here in this moment, stone-cold sober, no excuses.

Rosa is too old for this, Eva thinks. She's eight, not five. She's in junior school. Eva remembers how Lucy was at this age. Skipping out, shiny with enthusiasm, onto the stage in class shows, her hair matted at the back, like she'd been rolling down hills to get there. Unloading the dishwasher in the new flat, where they lived, just the two of them, standing on a chair for the cupboards she couldn't reach. And Eva knows her daughter was always mature, independent. She had to be because *families come in all shapes and sizes* . . . She hadn't been able to see it at the time, but looking back it makes her want to cry with pride, cry that she wasted her time worrying about what other people thought of them. That sometimes – too often – she couldn't see the merits in them. You've had it so easy, Rosa, she wants to say. You have a mum, a dad, two siblings, and you all live together. It's nuclear, plus one. It's better than nuclear. This is not my child's fault, she thinks. We are a valid family, she thinks. Don't you dare blame my child for this.

'Lucy wouldn't have pushed a baby off the bed when she was eight,' she says quietly. She's looking at the floor as she says it, then takes a breath. She's pretty sure she can smell the foul smell in here now: it's starting to seep through every single wall. 'And she's not a narcissist. She's a teenager.'

Before Eva knows what's happened, before she can think, something slams into her face from the side. She has her hand up to her cheek, which is hot and throbbing, and she's blinking wildly, because she can't quite believe it. She can't quite process the fact that her sister has just slapped her.

Alex has taken several steps back, and Eva can see that she's trembling. The kids are wide-eyed, stunned, silent.

'Don't worry,' her sister says, and her voice is thin with bitten-down rage. 'Mum will leap to Lucy's defence. You won't have to ask twice. Your family pretty much has it sewn up, what with their "Special Relationship".' Alex flicks her fingers, like knives, putting inverted commas around the words. 'I mean, the US/UK alliance has *nothing* on them. *Nada.* Zero. And then there's dear darling *Daddy* and your good self, which –'

But Eva doesn't hear the rest. There's a ringing in her ears, as she crosses the space between them. Wrenching her sister's arm with both hands, she opens her mouth wide like she's about to scream. Then, it's like time has collapsed in on itself, and she bites down hard through the fabric of Alex's shirt. All she can think about is Nancy's peach dressing-gown, the one she coveted, with the appliquéd cupcake on the back. How she'd gripped her sister's wrist through the squeaky material, with her teeth – her new teeth that were still growing in where the baby ones had been – and hadn't let go. Like she was a dog in a cartoon (again and always the dog . . .), going at the postman's flapping trouser leg, hanging on for dear life. And even though a part of her knows she's ridiculous – standing here, in this glass room, in this glass house, with the washing powder and salt taste of her sister's shirt in her mouth – she isn't about to let go now either. The truth is, she feels as if she couldn't stop herself if she wanted to. She won't stop, not until she's sure she's left her mark.

Nancy, Spring 2009

Nancy's late and Leon won't be happy. She's left Georgie crying with the nanny, and she could kick herself, because she should have come straight from the hospital, instead of going home first. Leon is grandiosely describing tonight's performance as a premiere, which, technically, it is. But Nancy's been to enough of these avant-garde things to know it's basically a vanity project that no one is expecting will be particularly well attended; if Nancy didn't have to go she absolutely wouldn't. She'd rather be at home, snuggled into her daughter's narrow bed among the tangle of soft toys, reading bedtime stories, salivating at the thought of the Cookies & Cream Häagen Dazs in the freezer she'd eat in front of the TV afterwards, straight from the tub, watching whatever she wanted. Instead she's lost. In the maze of the Barbican, where everything looks the same, and the brutalist architecture, the looming, shadowed blockiness of it, is matching her mood.

She's coming up to the outdoor café that's next to the rectangle of green water, across from the girls' school, when the man passes her. There's a glimmer of recognition; she's pretty sure she sees him register it too. He's tall, with hair that's just the right side of over-styled, and he has on chinos and a light blue shirt. He looks more fastidious, more *hygienic* than most of the frayed-round-the-edges guys at the hospital – he looks like the kind of man who probably smells of citrus aftershave – so she doesn't think he's someone from work. And she's racking her brains, as she skirts the edge of the concrete pond, trying to place him, when she hears him call her name.

He's already walking back towards her when she stops and turns.

'Matt.' He has his hand on his chest to signal that this is his name. 'Matt Dempster?'

And then she's shaking her head and smiling, even though she's late and strung out, and she knows she should make her excuses and keep going, because how long has it been since she's seen him? *Matt Dempster*. Her sister's ex-boyfriend. Alex's improbably beautiful first love. It's like her teenage years are rushing back to her, there among the hard edges and grey-brown slabs of this place, which seems at a remove from the rest of the city, the rest of the world in this moment. She can almost smell the clandestine scent of the Silk Cut they pretty much chain-smoked in the Dartmouth Arms, the tumblers of warm, sticky Bacardi and Coke, the White Musk perfume they all wore that came in tiny bottles from the Body Shop.

'Matt Dempster!' She sticks her tongue into the side of her mouth, gestures with her hand from the top of his manicured head, all the way down his body to his polished brown brogues. 'What happened to you? You're all grown-up.'

He's carrying a jacket and switches it to one hand, reaches out and squeezes her arm. 'Smoke and mirrors, Nancy Fisher,' he says. 'Never judge a book, you know that . . . How are you?'

'Late,' she says. Because she has no idea how she is, and it's the first thing that comes to her. That and the chaotic cram of the past two decades in her mind. 'I'm late for my husband's "recital".' She says it like it isn't, in fact, a recital, like she's mocking it, and she isn't sure why she does this.

'You have a husband?' Matt opens his eyes wide, feigning shock.

'Oh, okay,' Nancy says. 'You didn't think anyone would be reckless enough?'

Matt looks confused. 'No,' he says, 'not at all. Definitely not. It's just, in my mind, you're like, sixteen years old.' He holds his hand at waist height, as if that's how tall she was the last time he saw her.

'A child bride.'

'Basically.' He shrugs, laughs.

She has a sudden memory of him leaning against the kitchen door frame in the Dartmouth Park house, his arm around her sister's shoulders. She burned with how much she wanted that. Not him. She hadn't wanted him, not specifically, that would've been weird. She just wanted someone, anyone, it didn't matter who. It was the fire and romance that seduced her. The eighties teen-movie lie of it. The expression on Alex's face, as she glanced up at him, the soft, half-melted look that made Nancy a little queasy. Like her sister was an acolyte in thrall to a charismatic cult leader, like it didn't get much better than this.

Matt is still stupidly good-looking, Nancy thinks. Just a little pouchy around the mouth, the eyes now. And she's cataloguing him, thinking how she'll describe him when she reports back to Alex, when she realizes – and it makes her suddenly horribly self-conscious – that he'll be assessing her too. Judging her face, her body, her clothes, seeing in an instant how she's aged these past years, charting her personal journey of decay. Because it shows, she knows it shows, dramatically so, when you haven't seen someone for this length of time. She touches a hand to her face.

'How's your sister? How's Lexi?' Matt grins at the mention of Alex's name – his pet name for her – and, in that moment, Nancy sees seventeen-year-old him.

'She's good.' Nancy wants to pull a hand through her hair, except she doesn't want him to thinks she's vain, that she's doing it for him. She knows her hair looks better off her face. 'Um . . . teaching music in south London. Bossing random teens around, these days, instead of her sisters. *As well as* her sisters,' she corrects herself, and he laughs.

There's a pause, a nothing pause, but still it feels awkward. Then, in a rush, they start speaking at the same time.

'You go.' Nancy inclines her head a little.

'No, I just . . . Married?' His voice is light, but there's something weighted in the way he looks at her as he says it.

'Alex?'

He nods.

'Yeah, she's –'

'Matt!' A woman is coming up behind him, and she's waving, even though he has his back to her and can't see. *Put together* is the phrase that jumps into Nancy's mind. The woman is small and neat, radiating a glossy perfection, a casually nailed stylishness that looks expensive and time-consuming. Nancy glances down at the front of her top, at the place where she splattered bolognese sauce earlier, heating dinner for Georgie. She'd got most of it off with a damp tea towel – no time to change. As the woman approaches, Nancy covers the stain with her hand.

She smiles as Matt introduces his wife, Zoë. They're going out for dinner at St John. Date night, he supplies, and his wife makes a face as he says it, which is a relief and also annoying. Because Nancy would have liked to bitch about this to Alex. Mimed sticking her fingers down her throat, at the enforced, saccharine bleurgh of it. She smiles some more and nods and studies Zoë. Is this woman more attractive than her sister? Than her? Nancy feels shame slide through her, because why is she doing this, thinking this? She's better than that, worth more. They're all worth more – she, Alex, Matt's wife, all of them, all of the women. And she, of all people, should have more perspective. In clinic this morning, she saw a woman in her thirties, not much older than her, who has stage-two cancer. The woman doesn't know yet, not quite. Nancy has laid the groundwork for telling her; she'll be more explicit at her next appointment – she's found it more bearable, or rather less unbearable, when she gives the bad news to her patients, her women, in increments. For the patients, but also for her. It isn't unethical; it doesn't make a difference to their wait time. Just it means they aren't punched in the face with the news of it – not quite so violently anyway. It should give her more perspective, but it doesn't. Most of the time it's just lowering these days, anxiety-inducing. She doesn't feel the hero people tell her she is. Generally, she just feels tired. Tired and overwhelmed and worried. Paranoid. Paranoid that cancer, which seems to her to be everywhere, might come for her next.

Opposite her, Zoë glances at her husband, taps her watch. 'We have a reservation,' she tells Nancy apologetically.

'No, you're all good.' Nancy blinks, gestures with the flat of her palm, like *Off you go!* 'I'm fantastically late anyhow, so . . .'

Matt leans in towards her, kisses her cheek. And she's right, he smells of citrus. What else? 'It was so great to see you,' he says.

'Likewise,' she tells him. 'And nice to meet you.' Nancy smiles again at his wife.

As they walk away, he calls back over his shoulder, 'Say hi to your sisters!' And she isn't sure, but she thinks maybe she sees him wink.

Who ended things between the two of them? Between Alex and Matt? She's trying to remember and she can't. She thinks maybe it was Alex, but she isn't sure why.

The story of them had loomed so large, and now there are blanks where the narrative should be. She's revving her brain, but she can't access the information; she can't believe she's forgotten. How many moments like this has she lost? Is this what dementia feels like? The inability to reclaim the hours, weeks, years that made you *you*, that make up a life. There's a queasiness in her, standing here grasping at the past that's just out of reach, a sense that if she could just *think* hard enough, she'd find the answers.

She takes her cardigan from her bag; she's cold. She's stuffed in the itchy blue one by accident, but she pulls it on anyway because it's like, all of a sudden, there's a draught blowing up through the Barbican tunnel, bouncing off the tower blocks and around the concrete concourse. As if in leaving, Matt has taken the warmth of the day with him. There's a space, something hollow, where he'd been. And she knows it's nostalgia: she knows that what she's remembering – those parts she can remember – isn't real world. She knows there was heartbreak and angst and powerlessness in those years. She knows she spent an insane amount of her time feeling angry, sad, misunderstood, but even so . . . What happened to the fierce, heady hope? The promise of a star-strewn future? Of unrelenting love and lust and fulfilment?

As she moves off, in what she thinks, hopes, is the direction of the venue, she starts to think about Leon, about Leon and love and lust and lack. About the thing that happened a fortnight ago that's been poking at her since.

She was in their bedroom, hers and Leon's, getting undressed. Georgie was asleep and it was a Friday night, no work the next day. She had on good underwear, newish, expensive, matching for once. Hot, if she's being honest, and she studied herself in the mirror. Sucking in her stomach, turning a little one way, then the other, tipping her body, tensing the muscles in her thighs to tighten them up a bit. And she looked good. She isn't kidding herself to think that – even she could see it. Because of the half-light maybe? For a woman who'd had a baby? Maybe. Because she'd had most of a bottle of wine? Definitely. But she was admiring herself – her *body* – for once. She was about to unhook her bra, take it off and put on her pyjama top, when she heard Leon's tread on the stairs. Pausing, she listened. Glanced again at her reflection. She wanted him to see her like this. To *see* her full stop. She wanted him to desire her. To be unable to resist her, to keep his hands off her.

When he came into the room, he didn't even look. He knocked a towel off the end of the door, bent to retrieve it, and she waited. 'Have you seen my glasses?' he asked, straightening. And she felt suddenly unnatural, standing there. Like a pose-able doll. A fake. Like she didn't know how to position herself, what to do with her hands, while he looked past her, around her, through her. While she waited for him to notice her. But it didn't matter because he didn't so much as glance at her. 'The black ones?' he said, as he moved across the room, started rummaging in a drawer. She wrapped her arms around her body, concealing herself, made a sound like

'No.' Then she counted on her fingers the number of weeks since they'd last had sex. But she already knew the answer was thirteen. Thirteen weeks this time. Unlucky number thirteen: she was keeping track.

It's crossed her mind that maybe he's been unfaithful. She's pretty sure she could be having an affair and she swears he wouldn't notice; she isn't honestly sure he'd even care. 'Did you check the mantelpiece?' she asked, because a part of her just wanted him out of there. But as he moved towards the door, she blurted his name. Then when he glanced round, 'Should we have sex?' She couldn't look him in the eye as she said it.

Leon pulled a quizzical face. 'What?' he said, as if she'd suggested something outlandish, before his expression dissolved into a grimace of apology, or pity, or panic, she wasn't sure which. 'It's just I'm in the middle of getting this cadenza down . . .' He trailed off, a school kid making a dog-ate-my-homework excuse. And Nancy shrugged, like no big deal, felt shame prickle her chest, under her arms, around her hairline, the tips of her fingers.

She stops outside the café. Wonders for a wild second whether she could turn around and go home, back to her daughter. Whether she could skip the concert entirely. She could tell Leon she had period pain, a migraine, that there was a body on the tube line, something, anything . . . She glances over her shoulder. Matt and his wife have disappeared. She thinks about the evening stretched in front of them. Imagines bottles of chilled wine and shared starters, manicured hands linked across a table they won't have to clean. Then she's thinking about the past, about who she was then, about where that person went – and there's a fizzing in her that's getting louder as she stands there, so that she wonders if the people at the outdoor tables might be able to hear.

The tables are packed, but her eye falls on a couple, a man and a woman, who are maybe in their twenties. They're across from each other, but half out of their seats, and they're kissing crazily – more eating than kissing – like no one is watching. Or maybe like everyone is watching. She's surrounded, Nancy thinks. Desire is everywhere. These people are everywhere, flaunting it, taunting her, and she's about to move off when she feels eyes on her. There's a waitress across the café, hair piled high on her head, plates stacked up her arms, and she's looking at Nancy. The waitress glances sideways at the couple, rolls her eyes. It's as if a private joke has passed between them, and Nancy laughs out loud. And that's when she decides: she's going to do it. It feels so easy, she doesn't know why she hasn't made the decision before. Hitching her bag onto her shoulder, she turns, starts to walk back the way she came. She puts a swing into her hips, and there's Aretha pumping in her head, as she takes bold, unrepentant steps away from her husband, towards home.

Alex, Wednesday noon

As she comes out onto the front deck, Alex is holding her arm where Eva bit her. The midday sun is burning a hole in the sky, and the light off the white marble paving hurts her eyes; she can't look directly at the ground.

'Hey, Alex!'

Her throat tightens. She's making her escape, and thought no one was out here. The deck stretches the length of the house and, squinting, she sees two figures at the far end. It's a moment before her eyes adjust, and she's able to make out Scott and his son. They're moving their arms in the air, turning their bodies like they're running out of battery juice, or they're enacting the slo-mo sequence of an action movie.

'Qigong!' Scott calls, as he lifts a leg performatively, moves it an inch, places his foot back on the blinding deck. 'It's beautiful. Restorative. Wanna join?'

No, she does not *wanna join*. You look like a dick, she wants to say. And surely you shouldn't be speaking, ruining the zen of it. At least your son has the presence of mind to look vaguely embarrassed. Alex smooths her thumb across the place on her arm where she can still see her sister's toothmarks, and carries on walking, as if Scott hasn't spoken at all, as if she can't see him, hasn't heard him. She's done. And they might as well know it.

She's had it with her sister, with her niece, with her dad. She's had it with her husband, with the whole bloody family. She's had it with humanist naming ceremonies and holding it together, with to-do lists and people-pleasing and bleaching the kitchen. She's through with cold-water swimming and her gut bloody biome. And with never *ever* forgetting a birthday.

'Alex?' Scott calls after her.

She stops, faces him, Eva's boyfriend. Her B-Tech Wim Hof. Scott, who can ram his singing bowls where the sun don't shine. Scott, who treats every single passing fad as if it's an extreme sport. A paid-up member of the conspirituality crew (who doesn't appear to *pay* very much towards his own lifestyle), she bets he's a few scrolls short of throwing in his lot with the alt-right. Alex shades her eyes, squints into the sharp light, considering him. He's balancing on one leg, wobbling wildly.

'All these hobbies, Scott,' she calls, and her voice is sweet, too sweet, it sounds like it's spiked with sugar, 'don't leave much time for your "portfolio career", do they?' She frowns, 'Hmmm, remind me,' she goes on, 'what was it that attracted you to my *multimillionaire* sister?'

Stumbling across the grass, with the sun on her head and Scott's shocked expression imprinted on her mind, Alex doesn't look back. She's headed to the carport, and nothing's going to stop her. She's going to DM Matt and she doesn't care about the consequences. The baby's with Luc, who finally showed up once the drama was done, after Nancy had checked Dolly over and reassured them all. But they must watch for signs of concussion. 'Theme of the holiday . . .' Nancy had laughed, squeezed Alex's arm right on the place where Eva had bitten her, made Alex wince. Luc hadn't said where he'd been, just that he'd been 'taking some time for himself', his exact words. She'd plonked the baby in his arms and walked out.

As she crosses the track, she allows the thought in: she didn't feel the right feelings when Dolly was crying. Knowing the baby – *her* baby – had fallen off the bed, knowing she could have been seriously hurt, knowing that Rosa had tried to harm her, she'd felt numb, was how she'd felt. Foggy. Detached. All she could think was that it was another problem she'd need to deal with, yet another thing to add to the list. And does it mean Rosa needs therapy? Because they can't afford it, no way, and the thought of it all, of what it might mean, exhausts her. But more than that, she's scared. Scared about the gap where her emotions – her fear, her love – should have been. The same gap she felt when she was planning the naming ceremony, and on the day itself. A barely there suspicion in her that maybe she was overcompensating somehow. She is scared, too, that her anger just now was a cover, that it had been misdirection, a trick. The truth is that when she'd slapped Eva, she'd been trying to knock some feeling – some *sense* – into herself.

Something seems off as Alex comes into the carport. It's dark after the bright sunshine outside, and the cars are heavy shadows, but it's more than that. There's the ticking of an engine just turned over, the smell of petrol,

227

and then, moving out from behind the charging station, coming towards her, like he's been lying in wait, her dad.

'Jesus Christ!' Alex puts a hand to her chest.

'Sorry,' he says. 'Sorry ... I didn't mean to scare you ... '

'Are you for real?' she wants to say. 'Lurking in here, hiding, you didn't want to scare me?' But the words won't form in her mouth. She feels trapped.

'I need to talk to you, Alex.' He stops next to Nancy's car, like he's afraid to come any closer. 'This whole thing, with the tree ... It isn't what it seems.'

Alex shakes her head. She doesn't want to do this – she can't do this.

'Please, Alex,' he says. 'It's important. Don't make me beg.'

She feels as though everything has been tipped up. Like they're in a topsy-turvy place, and all the rules have been rewritten. This isn't them. This isn't what they do. This is not how they speak to each other. It's like vertigo.

'Alex, I know what it looked like, but you have to understand ... '

He's wearing the stupid jerkin, and for a split second she registers how hopeless he looks, how vulnerable. She wants to cover her ears, to make him stop.

The year she qualified as a teacher he called her every evening for two months straight. Those long nights of lesson planning that nearly killed her. The phone would go at six p.m. in the Hammersmith flat, and she'd know it would be him, her dad. *Okay*, he'd say, *your first hour of*

work starts now. I'll call you back in sixty minutes. Be strong!
You'll be rewarded . . . He knew she couldn't stop thinking about the Conservatoire – about where she might have been if she'd stayed on. On the worst days, he'd call her back every hour. Each hour with a new, terrible joke he'd picked from the book they kept in the bathroom, curling at its edges in the damp, and that no one ever read. And somehow she got through the year that way.

'Please, darling,' her dad says.

She fires her key fob at the car. She can't look at him.

'I . . .' He falters, gives up.

She doesn't say, 'Why did you do it? Do you love me? Do fathers have favourites? Is she your favourite?'

'Alex, tell me, how am I supposed to get through to you if you won't listen?' He's positioned himself so that he's standing in front of the Volvo, blocking the driver's door so she can't get in. 'You're wrong if you think –'

'You're in my way,' she says tightly. And she stares straight ahead.

'Okay, Alex.' He shrugs. There is something pathetic in the way he says it, in his stance.

Her mind is scrambling as he walks away. Flicking from the TikTok post to the naming day to the plunging cedar. Is that it? she thinks. Is that the best you can do? She is suddenly furious. She wants him to try harder. To make it up to her. *Don't make me beg* . . . She would like him to beg – she is *willing* him to. To convince her she didn't see what she saw. Even now she has hope.

He's a silhouette in the entrance, his back to her, when she pulls open the car door. He's leaving; he isn't going to fight for her. He's leaving without looking back, and a part of her feels that maybe – although she hadn't realized it – he'd already left. That he left a long time ago.

Tears bloom in her eyes as she climbs into the Volvo, starts the engine. And then she's driving fast down the track, the car bumping from side to side, throwing her around in her seat. Her hands on the steering wheel are her dad's hands. There's the shock of recognition: she hadn't known she knew his hands like her own. Her fingers are becoming her father's fingers. Her skin, her knuckles, all his. So why does he feel like a stranger?

Something has changed in her as she parks at the side of the road. Within seconds she's in Matt's DMs, cursor flashing. She's imagined herself doing this a thousand times this past year, ever since she saw the picture of him on Yasmin D's Instagram post. Yasmin D from school, who she doesn't like – *never* liked – but even so they're social-media 'friends'. She was pregnant and fat and unhappy at the time, and spending her evenings doom-scrolling, once the kids were in bed. It was the first picture she'd seen of him in a decade, more, and she's seen how many since? A silly number. Too many.

Alex is so sure about what she's doing, she isn't even fumbling, as she starts to tap out a message. hi, it's been a hot sec. twenty years give or take i'm guessing . . . ? would be good to hear your news. better late than never i say. hit me up!

Before she can change her mind, she presses send. Her heart is thumping in her temples, and for a moment she thinks that what she's feeling is panic, regret, mortification. And she's all set to toss her phone into the back seat, into the boot, out of the car window – to put distance between herself and this dangerous device – so that she can pretend she hasn't done it, that none of this has happened. But then she pauses, meets her own gaze in the rear-view mirror, looks at herself. Really looks into her own eyes. Then, as if she's in conversation with her reflection, she raises her eyebrows and starts to laugh, long and loud into the quiet of the car. Because she feels as if she's just injected Coca-Cola or electricity or sunshine into her veins. For the first time in she doesn't know how long, she feels alive.

Alex, Summer 2012

Alex is trying on straw hats in the market, smiling from time to time at the woman behind the stall, while she waits for Luc. He's at Carrefour buying baguette and cheese that they'll eat on the church steps in the shade for lunch. It's only eleven in the morning, but Alex is starving. A hunger in her, in her body and in her bones, that feels like something new, insatiable. They flew in last night, to this island in the west, where it's flat and manicured and chic. Where Luc had come for the *grandes vacances* as a child – him and his family and half of Paris. They were giddy, both of them, as they walked down the path at the Dartmouth Park house yesterday. Away from Rosa and Eden, who they'd left in the kitchen, making macaroni collages and drinking pink lemonade, with her mum. The first time they've left them to come abroad. 'Quick, run!' Luc said, as they went through the gate, and he grabbed her hand, and they didn't stop until they turned the corner, out of breath and laughing.

Already this morning they've had blissful, noisy sex with the bedroom door wide open, eaten fresh croissants and chocolatines, and cycled out past the salt marshes. Past little pyramids of dirty white, all lined up, she could taste in the air. After lunch, Luc's going to take her to a beach where he's promised she'll find sea glass, the size of a baby's fist, in cobalts and emeralds and ambers. And something has shifted. Something that – with the kids and with work and with life in general – she hasn't had time to process she's lost. *They*'ve lost. Here on this island, which might be magical, time has gone backwards. It's the two of them again, the way they were at the beginning, in the before. Here, they are different people, *good* different. Lighter. Funnier. Like if the wind got up they might blow away, giggling.

'Alex!'

She turns when she hears her name, one hand on the brim of the hat she's trying on, to keep it in place. Scanning the crowd, she spots him. He's standing in front of a green-shuttered building that looks like something from a French fairytale. The words 'Maison de la Musique' are inscribed on the stone façade, and it goes through her head that she must take a photo to show her sixth-form students. It'll be a good composition stimulus, she thinks. Luc smiles as their eyes catch, and although he's across the street, and it's busy, there's a sudden stillness; she has the sense he's holding her face in his hands. Next moment, his mouth is moving. She can see that he's saying something, but she can't hear him for the hum of people, and the stallholder demonstrating a knife sharpener to a gaggle of customers. Alex cups a hand to her ear, pulls a quizzical face.

'JE T'AIME, ALEXANDRA!'

People turn as he shouts it, and Alex blinks, tries to process what's happened. Like, did he really just do that?

'I LOVE YOU,' Luc yells now, in English this time,

and is he drunk? Because this is not him. Luc doesn't do public displays, and he doesn't do romantic, and he certainly doesn't do *wildly* publicly romantic.

Colour burns in Alex's cheeks. She can feel eyes on her. People – the woman behind the stall – following Luc's line of sight, as her husband comes towards her. Alex tips the hat that isn't hers down over her forehead and squeezes her eyes shut because she's dying of embarrassment. But also . . . also she feels like maybe she's stumbled onto the set of a Nora Ephron movie, and she is the heroine, she's Meg Ryan. Her sisters will explode when she tells them. They won't believe her. 'Luc?' they'll say. '*Luc?*' And they'll look sideways at each other, like, if there's one thing we know, Luc is no frickin' Billy Crystal. And then Nancy will start on about the multiverse and quantum physics and the simulation hypothesis.

'I love you, Alex Fisher.' He's standing in front of her now, speaking quietly. So quietly she imagines she's the only one to hear it this time. He's used her maiden name, and it makes her feel that he's seeing her. Really seeing her.

'Yup, I'm getting that . . .' She looks up at him. She can feel that her face is hot still. 'So's everyone else.'

'There's a wine-tasting stand just outside Carrefour,' Luc says, by way of explanation. 'It's good wine, rosé, local.' He shrugs, but he has that same look on his face, like she is the only person in the market, he can only see her, they are alone. 'I just saw you there, doing your thing, and you looked so fucking beautiful.'

234

'So you *are* drunk.' She smiles.

He starts to say something more, but she puts her mouth on his and kisses him. She can taste the wine on his tongue. As his arms go round her, the straw hat slips from her head, and she's too late to stop it falling to the ground.

Flustered, Alex bends to retrieve it, and she's apologizing to the woman behind the stall, expecting her to be annoyed, anticipating that now she'll have to offer to buy the hat, although it isn't the right shape for her face. Instead, the woman starts to clap, and the enamel bracelets on her wrists clatter one against the other. '*Ooh, là là*,' she says, or maybe Alex just imagines it, this French cliché, because of the strange moment she's in. And then there's more. More applause, as all around them passers-by start to join in. A scattered chorus of clapping, as Alex hands the hat back to the woman behind the stall – and it doesn't quite feel real, none of it does. Like the tables and tarpaulins and bicycles and shopping bags are just for show. And now Alex knows for sure that she, that *they* have slipped through the gaps in something, in time. That they've returned to a point, or vaulted sideways or forwards or upwards, because who really knows how it goes . . . the confusingly kaleidoscopic 3D maze of love and marriage and parenthood and life? Who knows when and how you'll find your way back to something or someone you hadn't understood you'd half lost?

Alex makes as if to take a small bow, to lean into this whole thing. But already people are turning away, moving off, getting on with their lives. And she finds, anyway, that she doesn't care what anyone thinks. There's no film, no performance. *This*. This is the thing, this moment. Here and now, just the two of them, and their shared history rushing in at her, filling her up.

She can smell the fresh bread that's poking from Luc's backpack, and she reaches out, breaks off the crusted end.

'*Je t'aime aussi*,' she says, as she splits the bread, hands half to him, 'whoever you are and whatever you've done with my husband . . .' Then she bumps her shoulder against his. 'Okay, I'm starving, let's eat.'

Nancy, Wednesday afternoon

Nancy can hear the music the instant she comes through the door. As if she's passed through a portal from the silence of the mountain outside, the percussion of the rare toads that seem to be everywhere, to this: the cheesiest club track she thinks she's ever heard, piped through the expensive sound system. The walls are practically shaking, and it's like whoever's at the volume control is trying to blast away the tension, the fissures that have opened up these past few days. In her hands, the plastic bags from the Spar are cutting in, like cheese wire. 'I'll reuse them . . .' she'd said, grinning guiltily at the uninterested checkout woman. Nancy can feel the bass in the pit of her stomach. And despite herself – despite everything that's gone on – as she walks down the hallway, dumps the bags on the kitchen counter, there's a rush in her, a headiness.

There's no one in the kitchen, no one in the lounge, no one in the bedrooms she passes, as far as she can see. And it's starting to feel as if maybe she's the butt of a practical joke, or that something has gone wrong, because where the hell is everyone? At the pool room, the little rectangular window is all steamed up.

Her daughter is the first person she sees as she enters. Like her mothering instinct is a heat-seeking missile,

237

tuning out everything else in its path. Georgie is in the pool, goggles pushed onto her forehead, cheeks wet and pink.

'You're here, sweetheart! When did you arrive?' Nancy has to shout to make herself heard over the music. 'No one told me!' She pats her pockets, checking reflexively for her phone.

Georgie grins and waves. 'We're having a pool party,' she calls, and Nancy can tell she's giddy with it all, with the glass house and her cousins and the holiday that isn't.

The urge to take her child in her arms, to hold her, is like hunger. But as Nancy moves towards the pool, Georgie adjusts her goggles – all fingers and thumbs and over-excitement – and dives underwater. For a second, Nancy considers jumping in fully clothed, swimming to her daughter and trapping her in a sodden embrace; she can almost feel herself springing off her back heel. In her head, on a loop: I love you, you're here, I love you, you're here, I love you.

'Surprise . . .'

She turns and Nik is standing right behind her. Nik, who she's used to seeing at the hospital, or on the tube when their shifts align, in the pub when there's a leaving do. He looks incongruous here, though, parachuted into the middle of her fucked-up family holiday. As if he's been badly superimposed onto a photograph. And even though she's been expecting him, she's known all day that he was on his way with Georgie, it's like something in her is speeding up a little at the fact of him here, out of place, in this other part of her life.

'So your dad loaned me his trunks,' he says, before she can speak. And he makes a chopping motion with both hands in the direction of his groin, like he's the dancer in a boy-band.

The swimming shorts are far too big for him, sagging in the middle and shiny with wear, and Nancy puts a hand over her mouth as she laughs.

'I couldn't say no,' he tells her now. 'I mean, like, seriously. *Literally*. He would not take no for an answer . . .'

His mouth is close to her ear, because of the volume of the music. They're both laughing now, and she has a sudden urge to turn and kiss him. To kiss him on his familiar, laughing mouth. It comes from nowhere this feeling, and she takes a step back, away from him, shakes her head to dislodge the thought. Then she pulls a face. 'Welcome to the madhouse!' She can't quite look at him as she says it. 'Um, you don't have to be mad to holiday here, but it helps . . . or something . . . and why the fuck is this music so loud?'

She's never felt self-conscious with Nik like this before, and it's a reason to look away from him. That, and she's trying to figure out what's going on. She's surprised to see Rosa, if she's honest, jumping and hooting in the pool. When she left, to pick up some things for dinner, it was in the aftermath of yet another crisis. Now it seems like she's found herself at an Ibizan rave. Classic Family Fisher, she thinks, and rolls her eyes minutely. Something goes wrong? Sweep that shit straight under the carpet.

Alongside the kids, Lucy's in the pool, and Nik's niece,

Priya, who looks a little older than Georgie. Scott's son is in the water too, doing some splashy lengths of crawl, but mostly resting at either end from what she can see, propped showily on his elbows, his waxed chest pushed out. Over by the window, Scott is waggling his phone, trying to get signal, while Eva's reading on one of the loungers. Looking, in her sporty one-piece, as if her body has been digitally enhanced. Sculpted thighs and strong calves, and on her ankle, the little bird tattoo. Nancy has a matching one, on her much fatter ankle, which is unshaven so it's like the wings are sprouting real feathers. She feels herself sag a little.

'Thank you for bringing Georgie.' She faces Nik. 'I think it's pretty obvious she's been desperate to see me.'

He laughs again at that, and she sees his teeth, the unzipped zip of them, and it goes through her mind that she'd like to know how it would feel to poke her tongue through the gaps. Jesus. It's like she's on heat. It's the music, she thinks, she's going to blame that. The pumping strike-at-the-heart-of-your-youth whoosh of it that's making her a little loopy. That and the fact it's been so long since she's had sex, or even masturbated. She's surprised by how good it feels to have him here. Good and weird and still kind of awkward. But she thinks maybe it's relief. That already he's defused things – the music, the pool party, the apparent collective amnesia about what's gone before – for her, for everyone.

'Any time,' he tells her. 'Your kid is definitely one of the better ones.'

She wants to say, I still can't believe you've done this

for us. Instead, she finds herself saying, 'Yup, very much above and beyond, except you clearly didn't drive at seventy in the slow lane as per instruction.' She's joking, but also she's trying to stop her mind going there. To the fact of her daughter in someone else's car, to the pictures in her head of burned-out metal on a hard shoulder, a tailback of rubbernecking motorists. And, my God, she's ridiculous. *Riddled with neuroses*, her mum would say, if she knew. One of her very favourite phrases. She's used it several times this week already to describe Stella Wilson.

'So Dad found out Nik's a radiographer.' Eva joins them, wrapping a towel around her shoulders like a cape. 'He's angling for a quickie scan for his dodgy knee.'

'Hence the trunks?' Nancy says. 'The generous loan thereof . . .'

'Hence the trunks,' her sister says.

Nancy shrugs her arms out of her coat. She's boiling. 'Where's everyone else?' she asks. 'Is Dolly okay?'

'Um, not sure, and yes,' Eva says. 'Dolly's completely fine. She's a third child. Resilient. She has to be.' She shoots up her eyebrows; she isn't smiling.

Nancy studies her sister's face. There was an atmosphere earlier as she checked the baby over. Eva had come to fetch her, then hung back in the doorway. She'd been quiet, monosyllabic, and Nancy had assumed it was concern. When Alex tried to make a joke about social services, her voice was tight and it didn't land, and behind her, Nancy heard Eva make a huffing sound in her throat. Then her younger sister walked out of the room, without saying a word. 'Did something happen with you and Alex?' she asks now.

There's a scream and a splash then, and all three of them look towards the pool.

'No dive-bombing, Georgie!' Nancy yells.

'No running, no ducking, no shouting, no smoking, no heavy petting . . .' Eva ticks off the list on her fingers, as she says it. 'Christ, those swimming galas.' She adjusts her towel. 'Mum hated them. She used to bring a book to alleviate the boredom.'

'No, she didn't.' Nancy frowns. She remembers her mum up out of her seat and cheering them on. Louder, more vivacious, more *fun* than all the other mums. 'You're wrong.' They're shouting still, above the music, so it comes across as combative, more combative than it otherwise would.

'I'm not. Ask her.'

'I don't need to ask her,' Nancy says. She can't let it go. 'I already know you're wrong.' She sounds to her own ears, like Alex. It's the sort of thing her elder sister would say. She's annoyed. Like, does Eva think she has the monopoly on their memories? On their parents full stop?

They stand looking across at the pool. Nancy does and doesn't want to ask again about what may or may not have happened earlier between her sisters, whether there's an issue. She watches Lucy throw a dive stick for Nik's niece, then another for Georgie. She's very sweet with her younger cousins, which feels like a clash given the thong she's got slicing her buttocks in two, the microscopic bikini top she might as well not be wearing, and has Eva not said anything to her about that?

'Big moment bringing the boyfriend on the family holiday, I'm guessing?' Nik says it like he's trying to fill a gap, as if he's sensed a bit of an atmosphere between her and her sister. Then he blows out of the side of his mouth, like *phew*, rather you than me.

Eva laughs uneasily, as if he's made a joke that's missed. 'You mean Scott?' She gestures towards the window at the end of the room, where Scott is still jabbing away at his phone. 'Nah, he's been around a while.'

'No, I meant Lucy – is that your daughter's name?' Nik nods in the direction of the water. 'And the guy with Dwayne "The Rock" shoulders . . . who's putting us all to shame,' he adds.

There's a second when Nancy has no idea what Nik is talking about, none whatsoever. And then, suddenly, she does.

'Wait, what? No!' Eva's saying. 'Nope, no. Ew, absolutely not. That's Jay, Scott's son,' she tells Nik. 'God, no. I mean, sorry, but the guy's a dick!'

As her sister shouts this, the music cuts out, finally. So that the words THE GUY'S A DICK! shriek into the silence. Everyone in the pool room turns to look. There's a pause, and then the kids start to giggle.

'Trump,' Eva says, and she's still talking too loudly. Overcompensating now. 'We're discussing Trump, excuse my French.' Her face is flushed, as she looks from Scott to Jay, and back again, as if somehow they know, like she doesn't think they're buying it for a second, as if they can see straight through her.

Nancy can tell that Nik is trying not to laugh. He's twisting his mouth, as though his nose is itching, and he won't meet her eye. He's going to set her off. She can feel the surge in her, like the time in the canteen when the old man who sits at the till had his bad wig on so wonkily it was obscuring his eye. They couldn't stop, the pair of them, and it had been mortifying, and she'd felt so mean, but also, also . . . after they'd paid for their food, walked away to a far-off table, she'd felt something flare in her. Something transgressive, absurd, joyous. A sparking adrenaline binding them.

'So are you swimming?' she asks. She wants to save him. From her sister, from himself.

He looks unsure, or maybe he doesn't quite trust himself to speak yet.

'Oh, okay, you don't want to mess up your luscious locks, am I right?' She loves this joke between them: it makes her laugh. It could run and run as far as she's concerned. '*Exquisite*,' she whispers, and reaches out, as if to stroke his hair, but something stops her touching him. Because, yes, she's teasing him, but there's something else too. She realizes in this moment that a part of her wants to know how it might feel.

'Am *I* swimming?' he says, and starts to walk towards the pool. 'Are *you*?'

At the edge of the pool, Nik stretches his arms above his head. His T-shirt rides up as he does it, exposing a band of smooth skin at his waist.

'Diet Coke break . . .' Eva murmurs.

Nancy watches as he peels off his T-shirt, and it almost feels indecent.

'He's even managing to rock Dad's shorts, for fuck's sake,' Eva says. 'You didn't tell me he was a *hunk*, Nance.'

'NO DIVING!' Nancy shouts, at the same moment as Nik splits the surface of the water. She finds she's holding her breath, as she waits for him to come up. And when he does, he's laughing and looking at her, shaking water from his ears.

'No shouting!' he calls back.

Eva, Spring 2015

Nancy has gone first, which is a surprise to no one. They could hardly keep her out of the tip-back chair that reminds Eva of the dentist, except it's black wipe-down vinyl, not white. Nancy had headed straight to it, when they'd walked through the door, and she's already on first-name terms with the tattooist, Michaela. She's talking non-stop, and Eva is starting to wonder if it's more a reflection of her sister's nerves than the gregarious nature she's always been able to switch on, no matter where they are, who they're with.

'So, yes, okay, we were drunk when we decided to do this,' Nancy's saying, and she gestures towards Eva and Alex. 'We're sober now, obviously, but *do* you tattoo people if they're pissed? Or . . .' Is it just Eva's imagination or does the little room smell of blood? Blood and bleach, like a crime scene. It's certainly making her heart speed up. She wonders what the tattooist is thinking. Is she asking herself why these three women have decided to do this? Eva suspects she's seen it all before, that she and her sisters are a tragic cliché, three women trying to swerve a middle age that's coming for them anyway. They can inject all the ink they like into their skin. Hell, they could get a sleeve, *two* sleeves, they could cover their entire bodies in permanent pictures, like David Beckham, and they still won't ever be twenty-one again.

'Do you have sisters, Michaela?' she hears Nancy say.

Eva tries to focus on the fact that, in her day-to-day life, she is a woman in charge of fifty-plus people. She's CEO of a business – her *own* business – and in the past year she's had three offers from FTSE 100 companies to buy her out. She's done all this as a single mother; she is capable. She's capable of getting a small tattoo done. And, yes, she's also the third child, the youngest sibling. There's always her shadow self, there in the background, trying to derail her, but she can do this, she will. She should have gone first, she thinks, glancing at Nancy. The anticipation is the worst, she knows this.

Alex is across the room, studying the example tattoos on the studio walls, as if she's weighing up which she might pick. Eva isn't sure why she's doing this, since they've decided on the design already. They're each getting a tiny beautiful bird, the one from the Lotto game they had when they were kids. The Lilac-breasted Roller, from the board they all coveted, and they've decided they'll get all the colours inked in: the cobalt, the turquoise, the mustard, the lilac, the emerald, the yellow, the blush and the grey.

'In terms of placement,' the tattooist says, as she presses the design to Nancy's ankle, 'I'd suggest here?' She fits a head torch, adjusts the thick elastic strap. 'And we're numbering them, yes?' She points at the sisters in turn. 'One, two and three?' Then she pulls on a pair of black latex gloves.

It looks so intimate. The way this near-stranger is leaning in close to her sister's body, working on her skin. The concentration on her face, the way she's finessing the marks she's making, the complex artistry in it. Intimate but also slightly sci-fi, as if the tattooist is performing some kind of dystopian surgery.

'Is it normal that I feel sick?' Nancy asks quietly.

'Very.' The tattooist nods. 'Just try to breathe through it.'

'Remind me why we're doing this again,' Nancy says, and her voice is thin. 'Do you think it's because none of us is having any sex? Like we're just trying to *feel*, and something – anything – is better than nothing.' She's half laughing, but Eva knows, because they talked about it at the bar in Steeles, the same night they'd decided to get the tattoos done, that Nancy and Leon haven't slept together in months. 'Sorry,' her sister adds, glancing at the tattooist. 'I'm just trying to distract myself . . . Ow, fuck! Ouch!'

'A takeaway in front of the telly? Or a night of unbridled passion?' Alex comes towards them. 'I mean, no contest. Right?'

'A book in bed and a bar of Dairy Milk, family size?' Nancy says. 'Or your husband with his face in your twat *and* you don't even have to give him a blow-job in return? Sorry.' She apologizes again to the tattooist.

'Wouldn't even have to be family size,' Alex murmurs.

'Speak for yourselves . . .' Eva says. The words are out before she has time to engage her brain. She'll regret saying it, she knows, but a part of her wants to share it with them. Or maybe she wants the tattooist to know she isn't past it, that she's still got it. (Has she still got it?) This woman she doesn't know, and likely won't see again, and why does she even care?

'Wait, what?' Alex grabs her arm. 'Say more.'

'Hinge.' Eva mimes swiping right. 'I joined. Would not recommend for finding everlasting love, but . . .' She lets the sentence trail. Transactional, is the word she'd use. Just another item on the agenda. Because she's so busy with the business and with Lucy, it's all she has time for. Although . . . although, you never know. A friend of a friend found the love of her life this way. It happens. It could happen.

'Why didn't you say anything?' Alex asks. 'At Steeles? This is headline news, Eva!'

'Don't tell Dad, okay?' Eva says. 'Please. He'll be on the *internet*, searching up horror stories. She says 'internet' like it's a novel concept.

'Please God tell me you're using industrial-strength condoms.' Nancy lifts her head a little. 'I know someone – more than one person – who got *the* nastiest – ouch!'

Nancy's looking pretty pale by the time her tattoo is done, but she smiles as she gets down from the chair. 'Kind of weird to put weight on that leg,' she says.

The tattooist puts out a hand to steady her. 'Okay, who's next?'

Eva turns to Alex. 'You're the eldest,' she says, and she flattens her palm, gestures towards the chair.

Alex shakes her head; she doesn't speak.

Eva's about to double down, but the look on Alex's

face stops her. Her sister's neck is red all of a sudden, like the capillaries have gone pop, her eyes a little glossed.

The atmosphere in the room tilts and shifts.

'Woah, woah, woah,' Nancy comes towards them, hobbling. 'Wait, this was *not* the deal. The whole point is we all –'

'Don't,' Alex interrupts. She sounds annoyed, angry even; it's the pinch-lipped tone Eva knows so well. But studying her sister, Eva sees that she's shoulder-hunched, turned in on herself. Her voice, when she speaks, is barely audible.

'I can't,' Alex says, and waves a hand vaguely in the direction of the floor. 'I thought I could but I can't, I'm sorry, it's –' She gestures again at the floor, or maybe her feet.

Alex never apologizes, is the first thing Eva thinks. And then – it just takes her a moment to catch up – she understands. She understands that her sister is referencing the accident. She's meaning the camping trip, the fire pit, the burns, the skin grafts, the endless hospital appointments that they rarely talk about. Eva has a sense of it all, something built into the fabric – the history – of their family, even though she wasn't yet born when it happened. Alex's burned feet that have never healed, not properly. They are still shiny and pink, raw-looking in places. Eva didn't like seeing them when she was younger, and it made her feel ashamed. It still does.

'Oh, Alex.' Nancy puts a hand on her sister's arm. 'You should have said.'

'I just did.' Alex half rolls her eyes, smiles a little, but her voice is soft still, and Eva can see that she's battling to recover herself. For a strange moment, it's as if Alex is the youngest of the three. It's discombobulating. *Out of the order of things*, her mum would say.

'Yup, it's a no from me,' Alex says, and she gestures towards the black vinyl chair, the tattoo pen, the walls of the studio. She's trying to make a joke, but the intonation is off, and the words dribble and fade.

'It's okay,' Eva tells her sister. 'I mean, it's not obligatory, right? In fact, it's a bloody stupid idea.' She looks apologetically at the tattooist. 'It's pretty much on a par with "Let's eat the Chinese lanterns!"' She juts her chin towards her middle sister. 'Another Nancy Fisher brainwave . . . So don't worry at all.'

But even as she's saying it, she's wondering. Is it a bad omen that Alex isn't going through with it? Stupidly, it feels weighted, symbolic. Like if this were to happen in a fairytale it would jinx things.

'You're not the first to change her mind, hon,' the tattooist says, and as she turns, her head torch shines in Eva's eyes, dazzling her momentarily. 'And you won't be the last, so don't sweat it, okay?'

Nancy's ankle is wrapped in clingfilm, and through it Eva can see the little Lilac-breasted Roller, perfectly drawn. It's red around the edges, swollen, and there are droplets of blood and ink that look as if they might be part of the design, but it stuns her. She finds she's having to hold on to herself, or she might cry. Her mind flashes to the five of them, to her family, cross-legged on the swirled yellow carpet in the lounge, the one her mum loved but they all thought was hideous. There's the Lotto box in the middle of their circle, Alex with the red velvet pouch calling the cards, and her dad waving his empty board, laughing and shouting, *It's a fix! This is a stitch-up! Don't think I'm taking this lying down, girls . . .*

It's like she's watching a film on playback, except she knows how the moment feels, the solid, safe foundation underneath and around her, the giggle in her chest that's going to spill. There are chunks spliced out, though. Missing pieces, like she's glimpsing someone else's life, and where did those people go? She looks at her sisters, not so they'd know she was looking. Alex has come straight from school, and she has a lanyard round her neck still, that reads Ms Fisher, Head of Music. She's wearing the navy silk shirt Eva knows she wears on Fridays. Nancy, on the other hand, spent the day in bed, bingeing *Grey's Anatomy*. She's on a ten-day fortnight, and did her makeup on the tube: red lips, thick mascara and her hair clipped up. She looks like an opera singer, not a doctor, Eva thinks. They are here with her now, these strange, familiar people from her past, and also they're not. Her sisters are exactly the same and entirely different, and how can both things be true? It makes Eva feel she has mislaid something, a favourite sweater she no longer wears, but would like to find anyway, because it's soft and worn and she knows it would still fit her perfectly.

'Right, I'm ready!' Eva says, with a peppiness she isn't feeling. 'Let's do this!'

The tattooist points her electronic pen towards the

ceiling, and there's the thin buzzing sound, as though she's a cowboy in a western, firing celebratory bullets in the air. Adrenaline hits the back of Eva's throat, hums behind her eyes.

'Do you think David Beckham's had his penis done?' she says, as she seats herself in the tattooist's chair. 'Genuine question. I mean, is that a thing? I'm imagining the World Cup on his shaft.'

'Eva!' Nancy screeches.

Eva smiles as she shuffles herself into position, lays her head back against the cushioned headrest.

'Please don't use the word "shaft",' Alex says.

Alex, Wednesday afternoon

She'd only intended to head to the shop to pick up some jars of baby food, and a bumper pack of wipes, so Alex has no idea how she's ended up here, at a service station, forty miles down the motorway. That isn't true. She knows exactly why, and she thinks that maybe she's losing her mind. But it feels good. Her whole body is buzzing still – it's been buzzing the entire way here, as if her body was jacked into the Volvo's power source. There was a moment, at some point along the way, when the sky split in two, white sunshine beneath and a wide, grey block above. A Rothko sky, right before the downpour. In the end, the rain was so bad, she had to take a break from the road. If it hadn't been for that – for the concentration it was taking just to see past the water sluicing across her windscreen – she thinks she could have kept right on, all the way to London, all three hundred miles of it, without stopping.

There's a woman sitting across from her, at one of the unwiped tables, reading a copy of *New Scientist* and drinking tea with the string and paper tag hanging down. Alex is eating a chicken sandwich, although she has no appetite. She's convinced that she's visibly jittery. Pushing her fingers into the greasy paper, she tries to stem the tremor in her hands. She doesn't want the woman to interrogate her, to ask if she's okay, because what will she say? She thinks if she opens her mouth to talk, goldfish or dahlias or a pigeon-blood ruby might slip out.

There are seven missed calls from Luc on her phone, but she doesn't care. He's left messages too, but she has no intention of listening to them. Her thoughts are running on a single track, and she isn't about to deviate from that. Across from her, the woman gets up and leaves. Alex rests her sandwich in its paper on the dirty table. Bunching her hair in her fist, she squeezes out rainwater, lets it dribble to the floor. She is sick of fitting in, making do, sacrificing herself for others.

Her leg has started to jump now, like the adrenaline is spreading through her body. It's out of sync with the too-bright music she can hear from the arcade, which sounds like cheap dopamine. Gripping her thigh to still it, Alex looks again at her DMs – even though she's read the message maybe thirty times already, and knows, word for word, what it says.

> wait, lexi?! is this really you? it has indeed been a hot sec.
> fucking decades . . . is it insane to say i've missed you? M

He sent it minutes after she'd messaged him earlier, although she didn't see his reply for hours. By the time she got back to the house, she'd regretted what she'd done, had felt seared with embarrassment. Didn't check her phone until she headed out for the baby supplies. The baby supplies that she never got; she didn't even make it into the shop. *Is it insane to say I've missed you?* Alex has had the words running on a loop in her mind, her foot pressed hard on the accelerator in the fast lane, the windscreen wipers going a hundred miles an hour, the shining road in front of her, like freedom. *This.* This is what she's imagined. A thousand times this past year. Scrolling through Matt's perfect life, she's wanted to message him, talk to him, see him, touch him. She's wanted to trace the lines of his dumb tattoo with her fingers, wanted to kiss him, to fuck him, be fucked by him. And now? *Lexi?* she reads. It's a moniker from another time. *Lexi.* He is the only person who calls her that.

Eva, Wednesday afternoon

'Alex has run away,' Nancy announces, as Eva comes into the room on the hunt for some painkillers: her ankles won't stop throbbing.

'Don't blame her,' Eva says. 'Do you have any ibuprofen?' She bends over, presses at the tendons where it isn't too sore to the touch; she thinks maybe it's the weather that's getting to her ligaments, her bones. The crazy, depressing rain, which has blackened the sky and turned the glass house dark. That it's showing up as pain in her body, the storm that's coming, that's almost certainly coming. Amber weather warnings that could turn red. *That could result in loss of life*, as Scott is all too eager to point out.

'Are we having a party?' Eva cranes her neck up from where she's folded over her knees. Because Luc is here too, in Nancy's bedroom, which strikes her as a little odd, and Nancy's friend Nik. Like, why are they all gathered in here, and not in the lounge or kitchen, or in the pool room? The baby's propped against a pile of cushions in the middle of the floor. She has a dummy wedged into her mouth, although Eva knows Alex doesn't approve of dummies, and she's watching Bluey on a laptop.

'I'm serious,' Nancy says. 'Alex has gone.' She's articulating the words, as if each one has a full stop in between: Alex. Has. Gone.

Eva straightens. 'What do you mean?'

'I mean she's on her way back to London.'

Eva looks from Nancy to the baby to Luc. 'You sure?'

'Oh, she was kind enough to text.' Nancy comes towards her, holds out her phone for Eva to take.

The message on the screen is short, almost non-existent. But, Eva can't help it, a tiny voice in her head – her third-child voice – is asking, Why didn't she text *me*? Why am I the last to know?

Headed home. I'll text when I get there

No sign-off, no kiss. Which in their vernacular is basically a 'screw you'.

'What the actual fuck?' Eva hands the phone back to her sister, frowns. 'Does Mum know?'

Nancy shakes her head. 'We're slightly hiding from the grown-ups,' she says.

'But we're not worried?' Eva inclines her chin in the direction of the baby. 'I mean, we're not *worried* worried? Like she hasn't been in a car crash, or joined a cult, or offed herself, or kidnapped Dad. Has anyone told Rosa and Eden?'

'Not yet,' Luc says. He looks tired.

'Shit!' Eva seats herself on the end of the bed.

'Right?' Nancy clicks her tongue. 'This holiday just gets better and better . . .'

All Eva can think is that she had a fight with her sister, a physical fight, and now her sister – her *forty-five-year-old* sister – has run off, like they're maybe five and nine years old, not grown adults with kids and jobs and houses and

258

pensions. Like this is something Eden and Rosa would do. And time is doing something strange in this place, something more than the usual micro-regressions that happen when her family gets together. This place is strange full stop, she thinks. Her mind flicks again to what her mum had said that day on the beach after they'd bumped into the Wilsons, a day that feels for ever ago already. *This place is bloody weird*, she'd heard Vivienne say. *Why does it feel like the past is treading on my heels here?*

'I bit her earlier,' Eva blurts.

'I'm sorry, what?' Nancy blinks her eyes, and then she laughs. 'You did what?'

Eva fixes her with a look. 'I mean, she slapped me first, and then . . .'

Nancy's friend Nik snorts, covers his mouth with a hand, mumbles an apology.

'I knew it!' Nancy says. 'I knew something had happened. Jesus Christ, Eva. I mean, this is just a bloody shit-show at this point. I can't even . . .'

From nowhere Eva starts to laugh, although she knows it isn't funny. It isn't funny at all. And then – it's like she's infected her sister – Nancy is laughing too, and Nik, although he's trying not to show it. The kind of laughter that happens in church or one time – horrendously, unstoppably – at a dance show when Lucy, aged four, appeared on stage in a top hat and whirling a cane. Because what else is there to do? She is so exhausted by everything that's gone on. And is she to blame? This holiday was her idea after all. It wouldn't have happened if it wasn't for her. None of this would have happened. Nancy has tears running down her face now, and she's letting them flow, making no attempt to wipe them away. There's a thin line between laughter and pain, Eva thinks. Is that a quote from something? She's pretty sure she read it somewhere. 'I swear to God . . .' she starts to say, and her voice is wobbly with laughter. Or maybe pain. '. . . if I wake up and find you've escaped, Nance . . .'

'This is not funny.' Luc puts his body between them, as if that way he might make them stop. His voice is raised and his accent more pronounced than usual. 'Your sister . . .' He gestures wildly around the room. 'I've had enough.'

'Enough of what?'

They turn. Vivienne is standing in the doorway. Despite the heat in the house, she's wearing the green mohair cardigan that's more like a blanket, and Patrick's right behind her. No one's laughing any more. Eva feels as if she's been caught doing something she shouldn't, as she glances from her mum to her dad. He's got his glasses pushed up on his head, a pencil behind his ear, as though he's been knee-deep in the crossword, as though he's oblivious to everything that's been going on, to everything he's set in motion. This is your fault, not mine, Eva wants to tell him. This whole thing, this holiday that isn't. Alex leaving like this. It's all your fault.

'Your daughter has run away,' Luc tells them. *Your daughter.* As though Alex – the mother of his children – is their problem not his, as if he wants nothing to do with her sister. The baby starts crying, and when Luc makes no move to comfort her, Eva squats down, reaches for the dummy spat out on the rug, plugs it back in.

'She's halfway down the motorway, apparently,' Nancy murmurs.

Silence stretches around the room, around the entire glass house it feels to Eva. But for the sound of a tinny cartoon dog, coming from the laptop on the floor. And she's just about to say something, to break the awful deadlock because she can't bear it any longer, when her mum takes a long, audible breath.

'Well, okay, then,' Vivienne says, in a tone that suggests it is very much not okay. 'I'm going outside for some air.'

'It's pissing down out there, Mum,' Nancy says. 'You'll get soaked.'

'Oh, I've survived worse.' Vivienne pulls her cardigan around her, as if that will see off the worst of it.

'Mum, I really –' Eva starts to say.

'What she means is,' her dad raises his voice to talk across her, 'she's going out for a cigarette.'

For a moment, Eva thinks she's misheard him.

But then her dad brings two fingers to his mouth in a V, blows out an imaginary puff of smoke. 'When your mother says she needs air, what she means is she wants a fag.'

'Shut up, Patrick!' Her mum is looking at her dad as if she'd like to slap him.

'Oh, for God's sake, Vivienne.' Her dad comes further into the room. 'They all know you smoke.'

Eva glances at Nancy, then back at her parents.

'*What?*' her dad says now, arms wide in appeal. 'They all *know*, Vivienne.'

There's a pause, a gap in things. And maybe it's Eva's imagination but the smell in the house, the awful smell that's getting worse by the day, seems all at once unbearable.

Nancy's the first to speak. 'Nope,' her sister says, and the word skips from her mouth, with a casualness that doesn't match the expression in her eyes. 'No, in fact, we didn't know.' Then she claps her hands together, fixes a dangerous smile on her face. 'Wonderful!' she says. 'Is there anything else this family's hiding?'

Eva feels sick. The baby's starting to cry again, and she's aware of Nancy's friend standing there, looking like he's trying to shrink himself to nothing, and why doesn't Luc pick up his daughter? *Is there anything else this family's hiding?* Yes, she thinks. Yes yes yes. And she's picturing Scott up a mountain and between her legs and in an expensive suit, making promises she knows they won't keep. Scott, who's in the den right now, watching *Lethal Weapon* of all the films he could choose, with a shiny new ring on his pinky finger. I THINK I MADE A MISTAKE! For a split second she almost shouts it. Because why not? Her mum, her beloved mum, who she wants to think is going to live for ever, is a *smoker*. It feels like a dirty word. Her mind is skating backwards over all the unseen things. All the things she'd thought she knew. What else is there? What else don't they know?

'What about us?' She hears Nancy say, and her sister sounds like a child. 'You're lopping a decade off your life,

Mum, and that's if you're lucky. I mean, do you have any idea about the medical implications of this? At *your* age? You're about to turn seventy. I can show you the stats if you want. It's absolutely bloody . . . Christ, what is it with this family being so goddamn furtive? Why can't you all just –'

'People in glass houses, Nancy.'

Her mum says it quietly, but something in her tone makes Eva glance up. Dolly takes a shuddering breath, jams a fist into her mouth.

Vivienne looks from Nancy to Eva to Patrick. She looks like someone who has had enough. 'People in glass houses,' she says again, and tips her head towards the wall of glass that runs the length of the bedroom, 'shouldn't throw stones. Should they?' she whispers. And then she turns, and leaves the room. Leaves them all standing there, silenced.

Eva, Christmas Eve 1982

It's the night before Christmas and Eva is supposed to be in bed. Instead, she's sitting on the stairs, and she's listening; she can't sleep. She doesn't believe in Father Christmas any more, so she isn't worried he won't come. *Santa is a lie that mums and dads tell their children to make them behave*, Alex told her two days ago, and Eva felt the same way she feels when she does a drawing and gets it wrong and has to screw up the paper. The same fight with her body not to cry. Because she felt so stupid that even though she's six years old she didn't know, tried to pretend that she did. Eva's sitting in the middle of the stairs, not at the edge. There's the gap you could fall through, between the banister and the steps – the gap that's been there since the house was in flats, when other people used to live here – and it feels wider than ever in the dark. She dreams of it, this gap. Her tummy all the way up in her mouth, and falling, falling like Alice.

The door to the lounge is open a little, wide enough that she can see in, but can't be seen. Her mummy is saying something about the police, and then she's saying something about being rich. She says this bit twice, so Eva knows it must be important, even though it doesn't make sense, and she's using her cross voice, even though this is supposed to be one of the happiest days of the year. She's been using her cross voice for quite a long time now, the one they don't hear very often, and Eva wishes she would stop.

'And it was your *brainwave* to have the neighbours over for drinks,' Eva hears her mum say, and it makes her think of the picture on the classroom wall at school, of the bobbly pink cloud inside the cartoon man's head. And she's imagining the pink cloud taking a trip to the seaside, having a swim, when suddenly her mum is walking across the lounge, swishing past the open door. Eva tucks her head down, making herself as small as she possibly can, peeks out through her hair that's all in her eyes. Her mum is wearing the bright red dress, the one she sometimes lets Eva dress up in. Scarlet, she calls it, and Eva loves that word. She's got the earrings on too, the candy-cane ones with glitter that Eva chose with her dad from the black-and-white shop round the corner from Hamleys. 'As a surprise from you and your sisters,' he'd said. But really they were from her and her dad.

In the lounge, her mummy's voice is getting louder. It's like she isn't even trying not to wake them up, even though Eva's already awake, but her mum doesn't know that. She can hear a gulpy sound too, the same noise Helen and Katy's cat makes when it's sick, and she doesn't want to hear any more. So she puts her hands over her ears, and thinks about the broken fairy on top of the tree, whose wing got all bent up in the box in the attic. She can see the fairy reflected in the mirror through the door, the little bandage she helped her dad wrap round it, which Nancy said was stupid. And she wants to go and get her sisters, to bring them down here and into the lounge to make her mum and dad stop. But Alex and Nancy are asleep with their empty stockings at the ends of their beds, and she's here all alone, and anyway her legs are so tired she doesn't think she can move them.

Outside in the street, a woman starts singing, loud enough that Eva can hear, even though she's covering her ears still. The woman is singing 'We Wish You A Merry Christmas', except not in tune, like when Felippo sings stupidly in assembly at school and gets sent to the headmaster. Next thing, there's a crash and a shout from inside the house. From the lounge, but she can't tell whether it's her mum or her dad or someone else who's shouted. Shiny coloured baubles jump from the Christmas tree and smash as they hit the yellow carpet, and Eva feels like maybe pieces of the glass have flown out of the door and got into her eyes because they feel all sting-y and hot. And she's just about to get up off the stairs and tiptoe back to her bedroom, because she's scared now and doesn't want to be here, when her mum appears in the hallway. She looks straight at Eva, and Eva knows that now, *now* this whole thing will stop, that her mum will run up the stairs to where she's sitting, that she'll pick her up, and kiss her, like bright stars all over her face, and there'll be the perfume up Eva's nose that smells like vanilla ice cream, as she puts her back into bed.

So she doesn't understand why her mummy isn't stopping. Why she's turning away, and running down the hall and out of the front door, even though there's slushy grey snow out there that looks dirty and not at all like proper Christmas, and is worse than having no snow at all, Alex thinks, and Eva thinks so too. And there's the sound like the cat being sick still from the lounge, and her mummy keeps on going, down the path, but she hasn't noticed that she doesn't have any shoes on. Not even the flat pointed pink ones that Eva wears when she's playing poor princesses, and that her mummy uses to take out the kitchen bin when it starts to smell.

Vivienne, Wednesday afternoon

Vivienne feels free. Yes, it's raining, but she's grabbed a waterproof coat on the way out, a heavy one that she thinks belongs to – Eva's bloke? Whose name escapes her at this precise moment, but he's into all that outdoor stuff, so she assumes it's a good one (not least because Eva likely paid for it), and it's big on her, swamps her really, so that's good, and there's a hood that she bets makes her look like a hag, which is even better. 'Don't come near me!' she imagines screeching at anyone who might care to approach her, out here in the gloom. 'I'll turn you into one of those toads on the signs, the chatterbox ones, or whatever the hell they're called, the ones that are going extinct!' Although she can't think she's going to be bumping into anyone, because her daughter was right . . . Which one? Alex, Nancy, Eva . . . She cycles through their names, gives up. Whichever one of them said it was pissing down wasn't wrong. It's windy too, but it's not a problem: she's only planning on walking down the track, clearing her head – she can handle a bit of rain, can't she? She's seen a lot worse, and the truth is she's enjoying the feel of it on her face, the sharp spattering against her skin that's making her feel fresh and new, like she's waking up from something, even though she can't say what exactly.

Alex, Christmas Eve 1982

Alex has come out onto the landing because she can hear arguing downstairs in the lounge. She's pretty sure it's her mum and dad, which doesn't make sense because they hardly ever argue, not like Cerys's parents who shout at each other all the time. Straight away she sees Eva, who's sitting hunched over, halfway down the stairs. When Alex steps on the floorboard that twangs, her little sister turns and presses a finger to her lips. Her cheeks look hot, and her hair is straggling across her face, like it hasn't been brushed in a week.

'Ssh!' Eva says, and it comes out loud, because she's six and still can't whisper. And Alex scrunches up her face, even though she doubts her mum and dad will hear them, because her mum's shouting is way louder than Eva's ssh.

Alex comes to sit on the stairs behind her sister, tucks her nightie under her legs. There are goosebumps all up her arms because it's cold out in the hall, and because of the shouting, and don't her mum and dad realize it's *Christmas Eve*? Through the gap in the door, she can see the clock on the wall, the gold one her mum got from the charity shop. The twirly hands show ten past one. What has happened since they went to bed? Alex rewinds her mind by an hour, two, thinking back to the end of the party. They stayed up late, even Eva, and all the people at the party had gone. Nancy was overtired and broke the glass hummingbird, but no one got cross, and her dad promised to glue it back together in the morning. And she doesn't understand it, because right before they went to bed, when they'd put out the things next to the fire-place, like they do every year – one of the fancy glasses with whisky in the bottom, a mince pie on a china plate, and a carrot for the reindeer – her mum and dad had seemed normal. They'd smelt of wine and weird spices when they'd kissed her goodnight, and she'd told them ugh, because she hates it when they drink alcohol, and they'd both laughed.

'*You*'re policing *me*?' she hears her mum say, and it sounds like there are tears in her voice. 'Well, fuck me, that is rich! I've heard it all now!' Alex puts her hand on Eva's shoulder. She wants to whisper in her sister's ear that it's okay, even though it isn't okay, and she knows Eva doesn't like swearing – *she* doesn't like swearing. She's about to say it, when a woman starts singing out in the street. She's singing 'Jingle Bells', but the version with all the rude words. Alex thinks maybe it's the same woman who usually sings the opera song from the Just One Cornetto advert, waking them all up in the middle of the night. And then her mum appears for a second, moving past the open door to the lounge. She's wear-ing her black dress, the one with the little purple roses all over it. The one she used to let Alex dress up in, all bunched up on the floor and drooping down to her tummy, but she felt like a grown-up, a queen. And she has on the long necklace with black glossy beads. She looks like someone else's mum, Alex thinks, or a film star.

'This is all on you, Patrick,' her mum is saying now. 'All of it. I'm not to blame, you are. And you always will be.' And then she says it again, like her dad might not have heard her the first time.

'WHAT DO YOU WANT ME TO DO?' Her dad's voice is an explosion. He sounds angry, which he never does, not really. Or maybe not angry, but a mixture of angry and sad, which makes Alex feel afraid, even more so than she is already. In the mirror she sees him lurch forwards, and she's about to grab Eva and run back upstairs, because she doesn't want to hear any more – she doesn't want her sister to hear any more – when there's a noise like something ripping in two. Through the crack in the door, she sees the Christmas tree, the entire tree, tip and crash to the floor. And all she can think is how she hates that stupid star on top, the emergency star they bought in Oxfam. How maybe if the fairy hadn't got squashed in the attic and her wings all bent up, they wouldn't have had to throw her away, and then maybe . . . maybe none of this would be happening. And she hopes someone is going to clear up the Christmas tree and make it right again in time for tomorrow, because she can't stand mess, and it's making her feet horribly itchy, with all the decorations flung everywhere, and water from the plant pot soaking into the yellow carpet that Nancy says is the same colour as diarrhoea.

Then, from nowhere, Nancy appears in the middle

of the hallway. And if Alex actually believed in fairies still, she would think her sister had been magicked there. Because she knows – she's pretty sure she knows – that Nancy was asleep in her bed when she left the room just now. They're all three of them sleeping together, like they always do at Christmas, because it makes it more fun.

Next thing, her mum is running up the stairs with Nancy by the hand, yelling at the three of them to get back into bed NOW, or they won't get any presents in their stockings because she can't do everything and be blamed for everything, and she's not even trying to pretend about Father Christmas, which is so unfair on Eva, who doesn't know yet that he isn't real.

Nancy, Wednesday evening

No one's made tea and the kids have gone feral, and Nancy is having a hard time trying not to blame Alex for all of it. That isn't true: she *is* blaming Alex, and also her dad, and the whole bloody lot of them, if she's being honest. The kids are watching shit on telly that they shouldn't be, on the cinema-sized screen in the lounge that unfurls at the touch of a button. Rosa and Eden are on their backs with their legs the wrong way up the glass wall, shouting about the Upside Down. If they're worried about their mum, it doesn't show. Someone has streaked mud across the pristine stone sofas, and there's a red glove stuck on top of the expensive sculpture they've all been told not to touch.

'Get down, please,' Nancy says to Georgie and Nik's niece, who are balancing on tiptoe on the coffee-table. She says it with a smile because of Priya, and she indicates the sofas.

'I'm starving,' Georgie says. 'When's tea?'

This is not a holiday, Nancy thinks, as she leaves the room and nearly trips over a discarded pair of trousers. Literally nothing about it feels fun or rebellious or free-ing. Not even the carte-blanche holiday drinking, which takes the edge off but mostly makes her feel permanently headachy, hung-over. It's not at all enjoyable, and there is no bullshit bohemian narrative – no double-page spread in a high-end lifestyle magazine – that will convince her otherwise. Firefighting is what it is. She's been trying to style the whole thing out, the whole mess of it all, the mess of her family, which seems to have come as such a surprise to her sisters, but to her feels like a continuum of something she's always known was there. She's been trying to quash it, to push it down deep, but Nancy knows, and it's disquieting knowledge, that she, too, is reaching her limit.

In the kitchen, her sister is pulling a carton of twelve eggs from the fridge. Nik is alongside her, behind the counter. Nancy's surprised all over again to see him here. There's that feeling still that's like those hybrid taxidermy animals she saw one time at the Saatchi Gallery – a fawn sprouting bat wings, the head of a peacock grafted to a penguin's body, half a dog and a flamingo jammed together. Except not as macabre, obviously not. Just the sense of a slightly upended reality, things not quite how they should be. A sense that, at any moment, anything might happen.

Nik holds up a whisk and a wooden spoon, waves them around loose-armed. '*Sesame Street*?' He winks. 'Or was it *The Muppets*? Either way you've got yourself a dream cheffing team.' He makes as if to bop Eva on the shoulder with the whisk as he says it, at the same time as Eva turns and hands him a packet of butter. There's a choreography in their movements that trips her.

'Nik and Priya are staying for dinner,' Eva tells her.

'Such as it is . . . It's not safe to drive in this insane weather.' Her sister gestures, without looking, towards the glass wall. 'He was making noises about escaping, but I couldn't allow it.'

'Very "Misery" of you . . .' Nancy murmurs. And what is she, fourteen? Because she wants to say, 'He's *my* friend, not yours.' She can't help it, she feels displaced, standing here on the wrong side of the counter.

'We're going scrambled eggs,' Eva says. 'For ease and speed.' She waggles a four-pint container of milk at Nik, who takes it from her, sets it on the counter next to the butter, the eggs. And Nancy glances from one to the other, remembering her sister's Diet-Coke-break comment by the pool. *You didn't tell me he was a hunk, Nance . . .*

'Yup, eggs are perfect,' Nancy says, in a voice she knows suggests otherwise. She sounds sulky, is how she sounds. It's not just the kids who are overtired . . . She imagines her mum saying this. Her mum, or maybe Alex, who is God knows where right now, but always and for ever no stranger to a spot of hypocrisy. Nancy casts around for the warm glass of wine she left in here earlier. Is Eva attracted to Nik?

'The sooner we can get these bloody kids into bed, the better,' she says. 'The place looks like a squat, and where the frick is Alex and her Type A personality when you need her?'

'Have you heard from her?' Eva starts cracking eggs into a bowl.

Nancy shakes her head. Then she looks at Nik, winds a finger by her temple like, yes, my family is crazy. 'We'll let you go as soon as we've fed you and the weather sorts itself out, I promise,' she tells him.

'*If* the weather sorts itself out,' Eva says. 'It was looking brutal when I checked the app. Colour-coded warnings and the cutest little tornado graphic.' She pauses. 'It's only local, though, right? Alex wouldn't drive in this.'

Nancy takes cutlery from the drawer, plates from the shelf, and starts to set the table. Nik and her sister are talking behind her, about a TV show she hasn't seen. 'Excuse me,' she says, moving past them to fill the jug with water at the tap. She feels like she's butting in, feels like an interloper. Is *Nik* attracted to Eva? Nancy sets the jug on the table, begins counting glasses. And she's clearing her throat, about to make a comment, to ask them who's in the show, what it's about, when Luc comes into the kitchen with the baby.

There's a moment when nobody speaks. If they're waiting for him to go first, to say something about Alex, he doesn't. Instead he asks Eva would she please pass him a jar of baby food from the cupboard, one of the plastic spoons. He doesn't say anything else, and he doesn't look at them when he takes the things from Eva.

'Dolly seems fine,' Nancy says, as he settles himself at the end of the table, with the baby on his lap.

Luc shrugs, unscrews the lid of the jar. And Nancy thinks maybe it's the first time she's seen him do this – feed his own daughter – since they arrived. She glances at Eva, widens her eyes, just a little, and Eva does the same.

'So this is where you're all hiding!' Scott swings into the room. 'Jesus, this weather!'

He starts to talk gleefully about convective precipitation and flash flooding and the Gulf Stream, but even so Nancy's almost relieved to see him because he's broken the atmosphere; he's saved them. Except that he's basically in his pants – although he calls them cycling shorts – and even though she's trying not to look, her eyes keep straying to the bulge at his crotch. It's like those fuck-me baboons with the livid, red bottoms, about that subtle. Is *this* what you see in him, Eva? she thinks, because, God, there has to be something. And she tries to catch Nik's eye: she knows he'll find it funny too. But Nik is loading bread into the toaster, signalling to Eva that he's got more slices coming up.

'Ooh, smells great!' Scott interrupts himself. 'What's for dinner?' He says it like somehow he's being magnanimous, like he's a yoga guru (one of the sex-cult ones) popping in to see to his flock. His *yogis*.

'I don't know, Scott. What are you making?' Nancy keeps her voice flat, and she thinks maybe she sees Eva pause. She wants to say, Have you spotted that Nik's in here helping, and he's only been here five minutes? PS, she'd like to add, you seem to have forgotten to get dressed. She's going to say it, this last bit, it'll make Nik laugh, she knows, and she wants to make him laugh; she wants to get his attention, to share a private joke with him. She's about to say it, when her dad appears in the doorway. All the men, Nancy thinks, showing up

277

hungry. 'Eye roll . . .' she starts to say, but there's a look on his face that stops her.

Frowning, her dad rubs the island of hair in the centre of his scalp, throws a glance around the kitchen. He seems confused, or cross, or in a rush, she isn't sure which.

'Has anyone seen your mother?' he asks.

Vivienne, Wednesday evening

She's come further than she intended, but she definitely knows the way back. There's rain on her face, in her mouth, her shoes, and it's in the trees. Weighted branches hang low across the path and her ears are blocked with the sound of it, like television static blasting full volume. In Vivienne's head, the story of Hansel and Gretel, a trail of breadcrumbs, of white stones in the moonlight. It was Eva's favourite book. Or Nancy's? Alex's? She can see the dog-eared, cardboard cover, remembers how hungry it always made her, that gingerbread cottage, studded with sweets. Another long-ago story: Vivienne squashed into a narrow bed, exhausted but happy, book held up and out so her children could see. Where did that woman go? Those babies? Did it really happen?

She tugs at the zip on the borrowed coat. Rain is getting in where it gapes at her throat. Everything is slick and shining and running with water, so that the path that's thick with leaves, the solid trunks of the trees look as if they are moving, undulating, alive. She'll just walk to the waterfall. Then she'll turn back. Because it's getting dark – it *is* dark – and she isn't stupid, unlike Alex, who has decided, in her wisdom, to drive hundreds of miles in this weather. Vivienne claws her toes in her damp shoes. Nobody tells you. She could shout it into the empty forest. Nobody tells you you'll be worrying about them for ever. For *ever*. She's fumbling in her pocket as she's thinking this, drawing out a cigarette. At least, no one tells you until it's too late, and then there's no return. Rain spatters the cigarette paper instantly, and she's trying to be quick, flick, flick, flicking the lighter, but it won't catch, and it won't catch . . . and then – miracle! – it does, it bloody does! *Do you have any idea about the medical implications of this, Mum? At your age?* Nancy's words ring in her ears, as she pulls the smoke deep into her lungs, but they all know her middle daughter's a hypochondriac, and, yes, okay, she's a doctor, she supposes, but it's the odd cigarette, it's not going to kill her. There are all those people who smoke twenty a day and live until ninety and – and – and . . .

It goes through her mind that she is running away too. Like Alex. Like her eldest and most sensible daughter, and now there's the cliché – the whole birth-order thing – and is it even true? Her fingers are freezing, and the end of the cigarette has blown brown. It tastes like hell, but she's smoking it anyway. She intends to smoke it right down to the filter, and by that time she thinks she'll have reached the waterfall. Of course she isn't running away, of course not. She's just out for a walk, taking a break from it all, trying to dislodge the feeling in her stomach that's building and building and getting more difficult to ignore. Like maybe if it rains harder and harder, maybe if it rains hard enough, the feeling, the fact of it, will wash away, and she won't have to think any more about what she knows, or rather what she doesn't know, or what she might know.

The rain is getting heavier, if that's possible. There's the smell of it too, which is making her think of her girls when they were children. Of circles of breath on the kitchen window, knee-high puddles and muddy fingers and worms dug up in the garden. If she could have anything, Vivienne thinks, if, right now, the wild, dark forest could rise up, magical, and grant her one wish, it would be this: that the past would stay in the past. Because she feels – has felt since she got here – that her secrets are tracking her, stalking her, waiting in the shadows. Little by little, piece by piece, catching up with her. And although she's shocked at what Alex has done, although – if she's honest – she's hurt that her daughter has run out on her seventieth-birthday celebrations (which, in any case, she didn't want to have, and if anyone had thought to ask her she'd have told them so), a part of her doesn't blame Alex for leaving.

Nancy, Christmas Eve 1982

Nancy is hiding in the cupboard under the stairs. She has on the peach dressing-gown she got for her birthday, and she's way too hot in it. Her knees are pulled up to her chin, and in her lap are the chocolate decorations, the ones that are supposed to hang on the tree, but that she stole just now from the kitchen dresser. The door to the cupboard is open a crack, because she didn't have time to close it properly, and now she doesn't dare to move, hardly dares breathe, because it's the middle of the night, and she shouldn't be up – when she checked the clock on the cooker just now, it showed twelve fifty-five a.m. All the people from the party are gone, but at the front door, her mum is talking in a low voice to a man Nancy can see but doesn't know. He was at the party earlier, and she thinks he's something to do with the Wilsons, although he doesn't look anything like them. He's tall with reddish hair and a short, fuzzy beard, and has an accent that she thinks is maybe Canadian, like Mr Ford's, the teacher in class seven.

There'd been the rattle of the letterbox as Nancy had come out of the kitchen and into the hall. She'd been clutching the chocolates, and she'd known straight away, because her mum and dad were in the lounge still, that she wouldn't make it back upstairs in time. That if she tried, she'd get caught red-handed. Looking at the pile of shiny foil in her lap, the fiddly, glittery strings that are supposed to be tied to the Christmas-tree branches, she feels sick with shame. Like she's gobbled down all the chocolate already, although she hasn't so much as nibbled a corner, and now she doesn't want to. It's the last thing she wants.

Nancy can't hear what her mum is saying to the man at the door, but she's doing a lot of laughing. *Mum's drunk,* Alex had whispered into the dark bedroom earlier, after they'd laid out their stockings, switched off the lights. Their mum had been singing carols in a silly voice, as she pulled the door to. Switching the words of 'God Rest Ye Merry, Gentlemen' for 'I love you little Fisher girls . . .' And Nancy wonders if her sister was right. From where she's sitting, she can make out the bottom part of her mum's green velvet dress, the one that matches the Christmas tree and makes her boobs poke out at the top, and that Eva sometimes wears for dressing-up, when she's allowed.

'Is this what you're after?' Her dad's voice makes her jump. She can't see him, but he sounds as if he's right there, just the other side of the cupboard door. Nancy tries to shrink herself without moving; she shuts her eyes.

'Oh, bravo, Patrick,' she hears her mum say. 'I was just looking for those.'

'In the doorway?' her dad says, at the same time as her mum starts talking loud and fast.

'John-Paul needs his glasses to read the Delia recipe

tomorrow . . . Long-sighted, isn't it? He'll be up at five, putting the turkey in, and didn't think we'd appreciate a knock then!' And her mum is laughing again, but it's the laugh that isn't a laugh, that she does in shops sometimes and on the phone, and sometimes when she's talking to Helen and Katy's mum.

After the front door shuts there's quiet. It's quiet for so long, that Nancy almost starts to believe that maybe her parents have left the house too. But when she opens her eyes, she can still see her mum's dress through the gap, her bare feet and red-painted toenails.

Then she hears her dad blow out a noisy breath.

'What's going on, Vivienne?' he says, and Nancy doesn't like the way he sounds.

'You've had too much to drink, Patrick,' her mum says. '*We*'ve had too much to drink, okay?'

'Yup, not an answer. What's going on?' Her dad says it louder this time, and Nancy feels her head go hot. She doesn't want to be here. She wants to be upstairs in Alex's bedroom, with her stocking that's actually a pillowcase at the end of the blow-up bed that has tape over the hole where the air leaks out and always deflates in the night.

'Please, Patrick. It's Christmas Eve,' her mum says now.

'The most wonderful time of the year!'

'Ssh, the girls. Keep your voice down,' she hears her mum say.

'I don't give a fuck, Vivienne. What's going on?'

There's the sound of something, a bunch of keys, Nancy thinks, hitting the hallway floor.

'Oh, okay, so we're doing this, are we?' Her mum's voice has changed, and Nancy watches through the gap, as her feet with the red-painted toenails, her legs, the bottom half of her beautiful green dress move down the hall towards the lounge; she's almost marching.

'You want to get into it, Patrick?' her mum shouts suddenly, and Nancy flinches, bangs her head against the sharp underside of the stair. Tears jump into her eyes.

Her mum has stopped inches from where she's sitting. Nancy can see a hairy patch on her mum's bare ankle that she must have missed with the razor she keeps in a mug by the bath.

'Let's do this! I'm ready.' Her mum is shouting still. 'You know what, Patrick? I've been ready for a long, *long* time.'

Alex, Wednesday evening

There are flood warnings all along the motorway. One sign, then another, and another. Signs that say, SLOW DOWN! And it feels, to Alex, like an existential command. Because she's wired and exhausted both, if that's possible. It is possible, she knows, because this is the way she operates now, constantly. She thinks if she shut her eyes, here in the fast lane that's limping along at twenty miles an hour, she'd fall asleep instantly. Then wake up seconds later, her to-do list drilling into her head. Slow down? *She* wishes. It's like the content she gets pushed on Instagram. The smug, bossy, cloud-cuckoo-land stuff that seems to be reading her spinning mind, like, *If you think you're too busy to meditate, then you need to meditate!* Or *Self-care is not selfish, Mums! Remember to put your own oxygen mask on first!* The kind of sanctimonious claptrap that Scott likes to spout, and that – even as she's dismissing it – gets to her. More and more and more to add to the long, long list of all the things she isn't doing that she should be.

She's got the satnav on her phone, which is propped in the holder on the dashboard, and she's hoping it might offer up an alternative route into London. She's got a mad plan, a mad half-plan, really, she's still working out the detail, but one way or another she's determined to see it through. *Put your own oxygen mask on first*, she's thinking, and for once, she's doing just that, she's ticking that little fucker off the list at least, and it feels good. Alex whoops into the car, starts to poke at the buttons on the stereo, one eye on the road, trying to find a track to match her mood. Trying to find a track that she and Matt would have listened to back then – some Prince, or Guns N' Roses, or Deee-Lite or Belinda Carlisle, because Matt had a massive crush on her. They both did: the woman was literally perfect. *Is it insane to say I missed you?* His words have accessed a part of her she'd thought she'd lost. A secret, pulsing space that's like swimming underwater in a sun-dazzled pool.

On her phone, a text pings through. Another text from Luc, she's lost count of how many now.

We need to talk. It can't wait

Alex flicks away the message. 'Well, it'll *have* to wait,' she announces, as if she has an audience sitting in the back seat of her car. 'I'm putting my own oxygen mask on first, Luc, okay?'

Another text pings into the car.

The kids are asking for you

Fuck, she thinks. Fuck. She finds Heart FM, cranks up the volume. On her wrist, the faint impression of her sister's toothmarks. Did that really happen? She isn't going to think about her children. She won't. She doesn't want to turn her thoughts to what Rosa has done, to what it means. She doesn't want to think about therapy and bills and difficult conversations. She refuses to dwell on the fact that she's left her baby – her baby who makes her feel . . . what? She can't find the word. Her baby who makes her feel *nothing*. Almost nothing. Is that right? Alex blinks. She won't go there. She'll steer her mind back to the message from Matt. *Is it insane to say I missed you . . . ?* Alex tries to pin the words in place, to keep them there, to drown out the rest, but it isn't working. 'Here's a thought.' She's talking aloud again, like a crazy person, addressing her husband, who's two hundred miles away in a glass house in the middle of nowhere. '*You* can bang some fish fingers in the oven and change some goddamn nappies for once. I feel like it won't kill you, and I believe they are, in fact, *your children too!*'

The song on the radio is filling the car, and she's going to sing along. She doesn't know the words, but she knows the track – what is it? She thinks of her old students, of her quest to teach them perfect pitch. Of her conviction that she could do it, that she will do it when she gets back to work. It's just, somewhere along the way, she stopped singing for herself. Alex turns the dial up another notch, and starts to la-la-la it. Her mouth is wide open and she's letting the sound out; she's letting it out loud. She has to because of the rain that's like bullets on the car, the churning in her mind. So she sees, but doesn't hear, the next text come through. A flurry of messages now, one after another, like he can't wait to send them.

Okay Alex I'm done

I don't want this

This marriage isn't working

Her first instinct is to laugh. Like maybe he heard what she said about the fish fingers, and the thought of taking charge of the domestics for five minutes pushed him over the edge. Well, *that* escalated quickly, she imagines herself telling her sisters, before the thought trips her. She won't do that now. She can't. Okay, she thinks, okay . . . and she breathes in through her nose, out through her mouth, twice, three times. She's tempted to read the texts aloud, to mimic his accent, here in the car where no one can hear her, to make it super *'Allo 'Allo!* but then she feels her throat shut. *I don't want this* . . . What does he mean exactly? Does he mean he doesn't want *her*?

Alex slams her foot on the brake as the car in front of her stops suddenly. Her body jolts forward then back, as the seatbelt smacks her torso. 'You idiot!' she shouts, and she gestures, palm-splayed, through the windscreen. A voice in her head: It's your fault, Alex. *I don't want this* . . . His words have unnerved her. She doesn't want to admit it but it's true. Shaking her head, Alex blitzes the thoughts. She needs to refocus, to concentrate. She isn't the first woman to do this, and she won't be the last – she's seen *Thelma and Louise*. And there was that story in the *Ham & High* not so long ago. The one about the woman who abandoned her car in gridlocked traffic on a boiling hot day and walked away, left it there. Lost her shit in general and got arrested in the end, Alex is pretty sure. Did she get Tasered? Maybe she's made up that last detail, but whichever way, what Alex is doing is a minor infraction in comparison. Nothing in the whole scheme of things. A blip.

The petrol gauge has dipped, and how has she not noticed? She likes to keep it above half a tank, minimum, at least three-quarters full for preference, but it's showing she has less than a quarter of a tank left. Alex winces. Then recalibrates. She sits up straighter, rolls back her shoulders, pushes out her chest. I am the kind of person who lets her petrol tank run on empty, she thinks. I am the kind of person who . . . who does what? She doesn't know exactly, but she does know it has to do with Matt. And she knows she's going to do it before she changes her mind. That she isn't going to let anything stop her. *If you're too busy to meditate*, Alex thinks, then you need to self-medi*cate*! Because she knows – she's certain – there's something more, something better. Something that will plug the gap in her, the lack. She doesn't want to become the kind of person who cries in cafés when songs from her past play through tinny speakers.

The traffic is speeding up again, the road fogged with rain. Alex has her foot flat to the floor, the music up loud when, from nowhere, everything slips. The steering wheel spins through her fingers, the car veers to the left, starts to aquaplane. Alex jerks the wheel. There's the drag of tyres through water, her heart firing, and her dad's voice in her head: *Steer into it*, she hears him say, and she sees the two of them, in the front of the family car, the green Ford, L-plates on, and him in the passenger seat, driving round and round the Inner Circle at Regent's Park. Her beloved dad who, when it came down to it, didn't try to save her. *If you ever lose control, steer into it* . . . And she does, she is. That's exactly what she's doing. The motorway is a pool or a lake, or it's the ocean and she's swimming, lungs bursting, deep, deep underwater.

And then, and then . . . it's like the sun's come out. The windscreen clears and she can see. She can see the cars in front of her, and to the side, the road unspooling ahead. Two hands on the wheel, she's moving forward, her feet light on the pedals. She is parting the waves, her whole body sparking, and she has never felt more powerful.

Nancy, Wednesday evening

Nancy has hold of the huge golfing umbrella, the one they took from the glass house, but the wind is so strong it's wrenching her arm; it's all she can do to stop it blowing away. She and Nik have been walking for what feels like for ever, but has probably been less than twenty minutes. They were joking at first, like, *Whose idea was this again?* and *Raining? Are you sure?* But these past few minutes they've fallen silent. They've got their phone torches on, and they're scanning the woods. Dark shapes loom, then recede, and none of them is her mum. There's the pulse behind her eyes that she thinks must be to do with the looking, with staring so hard, afraid to blink in case she misses something. The others – her dad, Eva and Scott – have headed towards the mountain. She wonders how far they've gone, whether they've found her yet. And she's asking herself why they didn't call rescue services for help. How long should they leave it?

'I'm sorry,' Nancy says, turning towards Nik, and she has to raise her voice above the sound of the rain. 'This is completely and utterly insane.' She waves her arm around, and the light on her phone swoops and dips in and out of the trees, across the path. 'The whole *Blair Witch* thing. I don't know why we're doing it. I'm sure Mum's totally fine – she's probably sitting in a nice cosy pub somewhere, and I don't bloody blame her, and I'm . . .' She means to say, 'I'm sorry you've been dragged into this whole psychodrama,' but she finds she can't speak. She has the urge to give in. To give up and go back to the glass house. To go *home*, like Alex has. It would be easier. She's so sick of it all, of keeping everything in, of caring too much. Of fighting just to stand still.

'Nancy, wait.' Nik stops a little in front of her. He has rain on his face, and his hair is flat against his scalp. He takes hold of the umbrella, and his fist grazes hers as she relinquishes it. 'Trust me when I say this is the most excitement I've had in a long time.' He pushes the hair back from his forehead; he's smiling. 'I love a good jump scare, you know that.' He keeps his eyes on her. Behind and around him leaves are ripping from the trees, stripping them bare. 'We'll find her, okay?' he says.

They start to walk again, and Nancy blows out a breath, makes her lips vibrate.

'Did you tell them yet?' he asks. 'Your family? About the suspension?'

She shakes her head.

'I believe in you,' Nik says. He says it in a self-helpy way, and winks at her, but she can see that he means it. 'The work thing is just due process. You have nothing to worry about, trust me.' He pauses, tips his head back. 'Listen, I know what it is to feel like everything's gone to shit, okay,' he says. 'Don't judge me, because I'm telling you this against my better judgement and for your benefit, but I – Christ, I hate this expression – I had my *heart broken*, I suppose.' He says the words 'heart broken' in a goofy voice, raising his eyebrows, like don't you dare come at me. 'Long story, long time ago, but someone cheated on me and it wrecked me. And then it didn't, so I –'

'I thought she died!' The words punch the space between them.

'What?' Nik looks confused.

'Oh, God,' Nancy says. 'Sorry. It's just . . . that's what I heard at the hospital. Sorry.'

'Ha!' He rolls his eyes. 'You know what, though, metaphorically speaking, I guess she kind of did. It felt a bit that way, for a while, not to be dramatic . . . We were together for seven years, and her timing was *extra shit*.' He pulls a face, makes a circle with his thumb and forefinger, as if to suggest his ex totally nailed it. 'Anyway, massive overshare, my apologies, but I guess the moral of the story is, um . . .'

'Things get better?' Nancy says hopefully.

'Things get better.'

He looks at her, and she looks back at him. His eyes are crazily dark, like they're all pupil, no iris, it seems to Nancy, and there's rain running down his forehead, his cheeks, but he makes no move to wipe it away. The moment stretches. They aren't laughing or smiling, as they usually are, and it's going on too long. Nancy wants to reach out and touch him, to wipe the rain from his face, or feel the line of his brow bone, or push her thumb against his bottom lip, she doesn't know which, but one of those things, something, anything that has to do with the feel of his skin against her fingers. Instead, she drops her eyes to the ground. She feels like all her breath, all the blood in her body has lodged in the back of her throat.

'Nik, I –' she starts to say, at the same instant he opens his mouth, and shouts into the wind.

'VIVIENNE!' he bellows. 'Don't leave us hanging! There's a gin and tonic with your name on it back at the house!'

Nancy bursts out laughing, a pressure valve released, and she swerves the torch towards him, catches him in its beam. She sees that the words out of his mouth don't match the expression on his face. She knows him, she can read him, and it makes her afraid. The crease between his eyebrows, the clench of his jaw, he can't hide it. And she feels she's misread the situation entirely, that it has nothing to do with her, to do with them. Nik thinks something has happened to her mum.

Vivienne, Wednesday evening

Vivienne hasn't thought this through. She's cold. She's freezing, truthfully, and her body has started to shudder these past few minutes; she can't get warm. She should have kept walking, she knows, but something has locked in her – in her knees and her hips and her elbows, in her *bones* – and she's taking a breather. Just a short one, gathering herself. *Fail to prepare, prepare to fail,* she thinks. One of Alex's incredibly annoying mantras. Or Eva? Definitely not Nancy. Nancy who throws herself, like a bomb, into the middle of everything, always has. If only she'd stopped on her way out to change her shoes, none of this would have happened. It's wet underfoot and slippy, yes, true. But also she's convinced the tree root snaked out from nowhere and caught her by the ankle. It moved, is what she thinks. Does she think that? She's just going to sit here for another few minutes, rest the ankle before she tests it again. There's a shooting pain in her temple, but she's pretty sure she didn't hit her head when she fell; she's pretty certain about that.

Vivienne, Autumn 1975

Vivienne hasn't thought this through. They've barely been here five minutes, and she's already asking herself why they've come. A camping trip, with two kids aged three and under, and a bunch of people she doesn't know particularly well. An old friend of Patrick's and his wife, and friends of theirs, and no one else has children. She's exhausted and they haven't even started. They were hanging wallpaper at ten o'clock last night, and it feels like the house will never be done, like they've been renovating it for ever. She has to remind herself it was cheap. The cheapest house in NW5, as Patrick likes to tell everyone. That turning three damp, greasy flats into a home is worth it, it's definitely worth it, it will be worth it in the end, because they get to live in Dartmouth Park.

They've argued in the car on the way down, she and Patrick. Loudly, nastily, until Alex started to cry. And then, with ten miles of the journey left to go, Nancy threw up, all down herself, like a punishment. There's the smell of sick filling Vivienne's nostrils still; she can taste it at the edges of her tongue. So now she's taking a moment, in the small on-site shop that's also Reception, gathering herself, her energy, trying to pull her smile from somewhere before she faces the friends that aren't really friends. She's done the driving, after all. All six hours

297

of it. Patrick can manage the kids without her for once. Taking a small jar of Nescafé from the shelf, she checks the price. It's like they're trying to pretend nothing has changed, she thinks. Or, rather, it's like *Patrick* is trying to pretend nothing's changed, that they are still young and free and sexy as hell, riding horses bareback around a circus ring.

Later, afterwards, she'll understand that she heard the screams and already knew. But in the moment, she glances across at the woman behind the desk, the one with frizzy brown hair, who's busy changing a till roll, and doesn't seem to have heard a thing. Maybe it's nothing, Vivienne thinks. Just kids letting loose in the adventure playground that's pictured in the brochure. But her pulse picks up a little as she replaces the jar of coffee, moves towards the exit. 'Thank you!' she calls to the woman behind the desk, so that she won't think Vivienne has come in, stolen something and left. Even though she's a married mother of two, she still feels this. The woman glances up, smiles, says something Vivienne doesn't catch.

She isn't running, exactly, as she crosses the patch of grass in front of the shop headed towards the tents, but she's moving pretty fast. She's just going to check, she thinks, that everything's okay, and then she'll head back, grab a few things. She's wearing the silver hoops in her ears, with the big wooden beads, and they're banging against her cheeks out of time with her steps. Grit is getting into her sandals, between her toes and under her heels. The scream comes again as Vivienne weaves through the car park, and it's not the good kind of screaming, not the fun kind. And now she's running, and she isn't noticing the earrings any more; she couldn't care less about the scratch of dirt in her shoes.

As she comes through the gap between the tents, she sees them all, standing in a circle, like maybe they're at a drinks party, except their stances are off – they're all angles and points. She's scanning, scanning for Patrick, and where is he? It's taking too long to find him. Then the circle shifts and he's there, in the middle of the group, with Alex in his arms, not Nancy, which isn't how it should be and it throws her, because Nancy's the baby, not Alex. There's something wrong, too, in the way Patrick is holding their child, like she might break. Something in the set of his shoulders and in the rigidity of Alex's small legs, her bare feet, size seven, measured at Clarks a fortnight ago. And although Vivienne knows she's still running towards them, towards her husband, her daughter, this group of near-strangers, it's like she's in the dream when she's trying to get away, but her legs won't move so she can only watch as her child opens her mouth, her eyes, too wide.

Vivienne has never heard her daughter make a sound like this before. It isn't right this sound, it's beyond not right. And someone is shouting now, more than one person, about fire and skin and blisters. And all she can think is she must get Alex's piece of pink blanket from the car, the one her daughter can't sleep without. She has to get it. If only she can get it, her little girl will stop making the strange, awful noise and everything will be okay.

Alex, Wednesday evening

Alex is breathing too fast. There's a horrible looseness in her stomach, and her feet in the footwell are itching, from the rain that got into her shoes when she stopped at the service station. It's soaked into her socks, stained the leather, but it's more than that, she knows, this feeling, this *itch*. It's the fact she's parked across the road from her ex-boyfriend's house, as though, after nearly three decades, she's just dropped by for a visit, as if this is completely normal behaviour. Also the fact that she's driven hundreds of miles to get here, to this dark, empty street in a rabbit warren of streets – even though he's not expecting her, has no idea she's coming. And the fact that she knows where he lives, although he hasn't told her his address. Because she's stalked him so thoroughly over social media this past year, spent hours, days, scouring his photos and captions and locations and Google Earth and Street View and Rightmove and Zoopla and – and – and . . . piecing together the online clues to find his house. His three-storey Edwardian townhouse that she can see right now through her steamed-up window, *IRL*, as her students would say, *in real life*. She even knows how much he paid for it. How much *they* paid for it. An eye-watering £2.2 million. She knows, too, that they've done an extensive renovation – they've dug out the basement, knocked down internal walls, converted the loft. It's perfect, the house. With its cocktail bar and walk-in fridge, its double vanities and AC. And his life, also perfect. All of it perfect, from what she can see, from what she has seen.

Alex stamps one foot on top of the other, trying to scratch away the itch that's making her lips fizz. The street is dark, empty, oily with rain. She wonders what her sisters would say if they knew she was here. Imagines herself asking, 'Is this all a bit Glenn Close of me?' Making them laugh, except would they? Is it all a bit Glenn Close of her? She checks her face in the rear-view mirror. Pulls a lipstick she never wears from her bag, draws on a confident mouth. Will he be pleased to see her? *It has indeed been a hot sec . . .* she thinks, and she leans across the passenger seat, wipes a circle in the condensation on the window, so she can see out better. When she checks her palm, it's streaked with dirt.

The blinds in the upstairs windows are lowered, yellow light pushing at their edges. The downstairs bay is dark, the lights off. Matt is probably in the kitchen at the back of the house, she thinks. There's an open-plan den and a wall-mounted TV, orange Togo sofas where they all hang out with Friday-night drinks, non-alcoholic for the girls. Is it weird that she knows this? Alex feels in her bag for her breath spray, the one she uses at school after coffee breaks in the staff room, removes the lid, squirts inside both cheeks. Eyeing the path, which she knows is laid with reclaimed tiles that almost-but-not-quite match the originals, she assesses. She isn't about to march on up to the front door and press the bell, of course she isn't: she hasn't gone mad. They'll no doubt have Ring anyhow, and does she want pictures of herself all over their security footage? No, she does not. What does she want?

She wants to unsee the images in her mind of the tree falling at the naming ceremony, her dad dropping his camera, how he launched himself towards Eva. She wants to unthink what Rosa did to her baby sister in the glass house. She wants to wipe clean the whole awful holiday that's exposed the fault lines in her family, that's ruined them. She wants to be loved, cherished, desired, *noticed*. She wants to do something for herself, for once in her life, and screw everyone else. That's what she wants. She's so sick of sugar-coating and bowing and scraping and tidying up after others – literally, metaphorically. She's sick to death of smoothing things over, making everything right. Of not rocking the boat. She hasn't come all this way just to turn back. She's done, she's ready.

Scooping her mobile from her lap, she finds Matt in her DMs – the little circular photograph of him in a trilby hat, looking a bit Jude Law. Before she can change her mind, she presses the phone icon at the top of the screen. Simple! Her whole body is thumping as the ring tone starts up. Two rings, three, four ... What is she doing? She's going to hang up.

'Hold on . . .' she hears, and it's a moment before she understands that it's Matt, that he's on the line. 'Hold on,' he tells her again. Matt tells her. In that voice. His voice that sounds just the same as it always did, only she'd forgotten. 'Give me a second . . .' He's drawing out the syllables, and she imagines him saving a file on his computer, or half unknotting his tie, lifting it up and over his head, dropping it onto a bedroom chair. Alex feels his words, his breath on the line, in the pit of her. Is he there? In the house? She looks out through the car window, thinks she's going to be sick.

'Okay, we're good,' he says now, and, as he says it, the downstairs lounge explodes into light. Boom! And there he is. He's there, framed in the bay and standing in the front room of his house, phone held up to his ear.

'Are you still there?' he asks, and somehow she manages to tell him yes.

'Hey, hi,' he says then. 'Wow, is this real?' She can hear humour in his tone. 'I haven't heard from you since Friends Reunited . . .'

God, he's beautiful. She'd forgotten the ridiculousness of his beauty. The fact that other girls – other *boys* – would sneak glances at him wherever they went. Or not sneak even, just brazenly eye him up, as though she didn't exist. Better-looking, sexier girls, so that she'd felt permanently as if she was on borrowed time. He has on a shirt that's popped at one collar, and his hair – his full head of hair – is just the right side of 'I ran my fingers through it when I got up and left it at that, no big deal' . . .

'It's real.' She laughs. 'I think.'

'Lexi,' he says. 'Lexi. Fisher.'

Her name in his mouth sounds exciting, full, hot . . . It sounds like the name of a missing person she once knew.

'Matt Dempster,' she says. 'How the heck are you?'

'I've been thinking about you all day,' he says, and he turns away from the window as he says it. 'About us back then and, oh, my God, do you remember . . .'

He starts to cross and re-cross the room, splurging on their past, their youth. They talk about snake-bite black in the Dartmouth Arms, about Rowans Bowling in Finsbury Park, about late-night kebabs from the dodgy chip shop that was surely a drugs front. They talk about people they knew and parties they went to and presents they exchanged. Some of it she remembers and some she doesn't, and it's bizarre, the sense that he's filling in parts of her past that she's forgotten. It makes her feel untethered, like she's come loose from herself. Like she's drunk a magic potion that's erased half of her mind. Like she's being rewritten. The same way she felt the time she blacked out after downing a bottle of Blue Nun, lost the memories from the night before. Had to reconstruct what had happened from the versions her friends regaled her with. 'How do you know?' she wants to say. And 'Are you sure?'

They do not talk about the present. He doesn't mention his family, his children, and neither does she. They are talking as though none of those things – those people – ever happened. As if they're seventeen again, or eighteen, nineteen, sharing cigarettes in the summer grass at Waterlow Park. At one point he comes to lean against a piano, which looks to her like a baby grand. She knows that both his daughters play, that one got a distinction at grade eight. 'And do you remember . . .' he asks, and he starts to say something about a Billy Idol gig, about a boy they called Fingers. Sounds, images, colours are tugging at her, but she can't gather the shapes into a solid form.

She won't tell him yet that she's here, outside his house. She probably won't tell him at all. Maybe she'll ask where he lives, these days, say she's nearby. Coincidence! Because he's flirting with her, she knows. This, she does remember. This lexicon, the long-ago vocabulary that's like a mother tongue. The language she used to dream in. It's making her giddy to hear him talk, and there's a sudden impatience in her, an urgency: she wants to move things on. She's going to move things on. She's going to say it. She hasn't come all this way not to say it. They are his words, after all. He'll get it, he'll know. She knows he'll know.

'Is it insane to say I've missed you?' she blurts.

There's a pause, a chasm of silence down the line. She waits for him to acknowledge what she's said, to bear witness to this, their private code. In her ears, the sound of her heart banging in her chest. She's pretty sure Matt must be able to hear it too – she thinks anyone passing on the opposite side of the street would hear it. She watches as Matt moves across the room, stops in front of an outsize print, a couple in a car, which makes her think of Lichtenstein. Seconds pass, entire minutes, days, decades it feels like, and she glances at the clock on the dashboard. Tries to anchor herself. She understands he needs to catch up – that she has been living *this whole thing* in her imagination for a year, while he's been what? Living his life. It's going to take him a moment to process the shift, she gets that, she does get it, of course she does. 'Matt?' she tries. Because even though he's holding the phone to his ear still, there's a chance, she thinks, that they've been disconnected.

'Yes, sorry, hi,' he says, and he clears his throat.

'I'm round the corner from your house just now, in fact,' she hears herself tell him. It's like she has no control over what she's saying, none.

Through the window, she sees him half bend at the waist, then straighten. What is he doing?

'Ouch, fuck!' he says – she *sees* him say it, and a wincing sound comes down the line. 'Sorry . . . I'm multi-tasking here. I just burned myself putting something in the oven. Ouch,' he says again. 'Sorry, ow . . . I'm literally here in an apron, slaving over a hot stove, if you can believe it . . .'

No, I can't believe it, Alex thinks, watching him through the window. He's waggling a hand, as if what he's saying is true, and he really has hurt himself. As if he's so deep in the lie he can feel the burn. It goes through her mind to tell him, 'Very method', like this is a joke they're both in on, like she herself isn't burning with shame inside. But she understands that might give her away.

'Right, kids to feed,' he says now. The first time he's mentioned them, and he's doing it on purpose. To make a point, to let her know, she understands this.

'You have children?' she asks, as if she isn't acutely aware of that fact. Her mind is scampering. Despite everything, she wants to keep him on the line. She doesn't want to let go of this, whatever it is. First her dad, she thinks. Now Matt. She isn't stupid; she feels so stupid.

'Two teens, God help us!' he says, and his voice has taken on a formality, a polite distancing, a *grown-upness* that wasn't there before.

He doesn't ask her the question back, and she doesn't volunteer the information. She doesn't want to tell him about Rosa and Eden and Dolly. She doesn't want to think about them, about Luc. 'When did we get so old?' she murmurs. 'Who even were we? Where did we go? How did this happen?' She tries to laugh, to inject her words with humour, but each syllable is dragged lead.

He turns then, so that he's facing the window again. The light in the room glares behind him. It seems to her he's peering through the glass. Can he see her? Does he know she's there? Alex shrinks in her seat.

'Okay, that's the alarm,' he says now, although there is no alarm, she knows. 'This has been so nice, but I need two hands for the next bit.' And it's true he does, he needs both hands, because he's adjusting his hair while he holds the phone. Spiking it a little one way, smoothing it another, and Alex sees that he's looking at himself in the window – that he can't see beyond his own image in the glass.

She's vaguely aware of him telling her bye, a few dribbled platitudes, imagines him thinking, *Whoa, this shit got real. I'm out* ... And she almost can't look, except she can't pull her eyes away, as he hangs up the phone, throws it onto the sofa, like he wants rid of it, wants rid of *her*. Then he crosses to the door, flicks off the light, plunges the room into darkness.

Eva, Wednesday evening

Eva had the dream again last night. The one where she's in a hotel room that opens out into a public corridor on either side, both to the left and to the right. There are no doors between her room and the corridors, no privacy. Anyone passing could just walk in. There is a door in the middle of the wall, but there isn't a way to lock it. In the dream, she doesn't ask for help or to switch rooms: she's trying to figure it out herself, even though she's scared and alone and knows she can't fix it. Eva's got the same panicky, stuck, looped-up feeling now, as the three of them – she, Scott and her dad – approach the first tarn. They're sticking close together because the rain is so dense up here, the sky so dark, she can hardly see a hand in front of her face.

'Mum!' she shouts, and her voice out here sounds too, too loud and, at the same time, impossibly quiet.

'Vivienne,' her dad calls from behind her. And she can hear that he's out of breath, struggling, reduced.

'Slow down, Dad,' she says, over her shoulder. 'Let's all slow down a bit, okay?'

He shouldn't be here, she thinks. They shouldn't have let him come. There was a moment, in the hall at the glass house, when he'd looked from her to Nancy, and opted to head to the mountain. 'It's where Mum'll be,' he'd said, in a rush, and did she just imagine it, or had she seen Nancy stiffen? Because it felt, in that moment, as though he was choosing her all over again. Eva grips her toes inside her trainers. She's slowed her pace, but she's fighting the urge to break into a run.

There were all the dumb modelling assignments, she knows. So, yes, they spent a lot of time together, in cars and on trains, planes, bored stiff doing word searches and telling jokes and eating crisps and waiting, waiting . . . in airports and warehouses and stately homes and skate parks. And she's the youngest, so it's true he came to her defence in arguments sometimes. Most of the time? That time she bit Nancy through her dressing-gown. 'You shouldn't have been teasing her . . .' she remembers her dad telling Nancy, and her sister's screeched response, 'I'm *bleeding*! There are *toothmarks*! Are you *serious*?' Before she slammed out of the room in tears, breaking the hinge on the door that they never got fixed.

The golden child . . . A series of memories seize her. It's what Stella Wilson used to call her, and she hadn't understood it. She'd thought it had to do with Katy's picture book about King Midas, the shining, seductive, sinister pages that thrilled her. Is she the golden child? She has always hated that expression. If she is, she doesn't want it. Is that true? She does and doesn't want it, this poison accolade. Rising above her is the dark mountain peak that, from a distance, looks like the apex of a near-perfect triangle. She imagines herself balanced on top of it, scanning the land, finding her mum, drawing her family back together. *The golden child*. She thinks maybe she wants it more than she doesn't want it, and it makes her ashamed, because has she encouraged it? She licks the rain from her lips: she's thirsty. Another thing she wants: she wants to believe her dad is above favourites, that he's better than that.

'Eva,' her dad calls. 'Can we . . .'

She stops and turns. Her dad looks up at her from where he's bent over his knees. 'You're going quite fast.' He wipes his face with his coat sleeve. 'All those protein shakes . . .'

He's trying to make a joke of it, but she can see he needs to take a break. She can see in his eyes that are pinkish at the rims, in the liver spots on his face, in his vanishing island of hair how old he's got, and how did this happen? She's remembering the version of him who'd grab her arm in the street when they heard police sirens, shouting, 'I've got her, Officer! Quick! Over here!' then poking her in the ribs, until they were both collapsed on the pavement, laughing, and where did that person go?

'Okay, Dad,' she says, 'no problem.' Although it is a problem, it is. Because how are they supposed to find her mum going at this pace? They should have brought Jay instead, Lucy even. They'd tried to get her dad to stay behind, but he'd insisted.

As soon as she gets the chance she's going to talk to Nancy about his energy levels, his fitness for his age, like should he have a check-up? When did he last have blood tests? Any kind of screening? She wants to ask her sister about her mum, too, about the forgetfulness they've mostly been ignoring, laughing off. About the fact that her mum's done this, gone off like this, and is it outside the normal ranges? Eva can pay for them to go private, that isn't a problem: it's just a question of raising it, of persuading them. And, oh, God, she isn't ready for this. She doesn't like these shifting roles, this strange new territory. The subtle, scary dance, the realignment of the status quo. She isn't ready.

'Did someone say protein?' Scott has stopped just behind her dad, and is pulling something from his pocket. 'Peanut butter and oat, sir?' Scott hands a cereal bar to her dad, with a smug expression, like he's thought of everything. As if they're choosing to be here, choosing to be out in a rainstorm doing an extreme hike, and all is as it should be. *Sir?* Eva thinks. *Sir?* It sets her teeth on edge. Her *husband* sets her teeth on edge. She has accidentally married a fucking Boy-Scout-on-steroids.

She can hardly bear to watch as her dad fumbles with the cellophane. It's all she can do not to snatch the bar from his hands, rip it open herself. She would like to go on alone. The swelling in her ankles has gone down, she has a dressing on her heel, and she thinks she could go all night, even in these conditions. It'd still be half the time it takes to do an ultra. She thinks she could go until she finds her mum – she knows she could. She can push the fear from her mind; she has the stamina, physical and mental. There's a reason people over forty are more likely to win the endurance races. Also, she knows the route, more or less, because she's run up here once already – two days ago, three? She isn't sure exactly. The days have all jammed together. But it had been early and cold and Arthurian. There'd been thick mist over the tarn, two smooth black rocks piercing the white. But she doesn't want to think about that. About the freezing water, the slipperiness of the rocks, how easy it would be to get into trouble out here, in these conditions. How easy it would be for her mum to lose her way, to trip, to fall, to . . .

'Why don't I do this myself?' she blurts, and turns to Scott. 'You could go back with Dad, and I could cover the ground faster. I do this all the time, I think it makes sense, and . . .'

Scott shakes his head, before she's even finished her sentence, and Eva's opening her mouth to protest when her phone starts to bleep.

'Signal!' she says, to herself as much as anyone. And she squints, checking the screen, as message after message comes through. There's the sound of them, sharp and loud and insistent in the dark, and her fingers tighten on the handset, because the notifications aren't stopping. She waits; she feels dizzy.

'Is it Mum?' Her dad leans in, unsteadily, towards her.

She breathes in, breathes out. 'Twelve missed calls,' she tells him, but she can't look at him as she says it. 'From Nancy.'

Vivienne, Winter 1975

Patrick leaves her on a Tuesday while the girls are at play-group, bowls of cornflake sludge still on the side. She's in the kitchen, trying to find the hospital letter, think-ing, When will this ever end? Because they've always just been to an appointment, or they're about to go to one, and in between her head is filled with sterile dressings and skin grafts and scarring, and there's the constant thrum in her chest. So at first she doesn't register what he's said. Afterwards, when she trips, and trips again, over this moment, she'll think of Pompeii. Of calcified ash and pumice and everything permanently suspended as it was in that instant: a carton of orange juice sticky on the table, a cloth dumped in the milky sink, the clock on the wall showing twenty past nine.

'It's too much,' is the first thing he says. Or, at least, it's the first thing she hears. Opaque and indistinct, and he's looking at the spice rack, or beyond the spice rack at the fridge or the window to the garden, she can't tell. Either way he isn't looking at her. 'I can't do it any more,' he murmurs, and his voice is flat, it's dead. It's the same voice he uses more often than not these days when they speak – if they speak: there's so much else to do all the time. She thinks her voice is the same. It sounds that way in her head when she addresses him, heavy and thick and slow.

'The responsibility . . .' he says. 'I just can't.'

Now he looks at her. He has on the old cricket jumper that's frayed at the wrists and that he wears on days when he has no client meetings. His hair needs a wash. For a moment, Vivienne thinks he's smiling, because his eyes are crinkled at the edges. She wonders if this is some bizarre, elaborate joke, he's just hit the wrong note. But then she sees he's wincing. Wincing not smiling. *Drowning not waving*, she thinks. And he's looking at her like he knows she'll understand what he's saying – what he's proposing – and that it's reasonable, it's right, it's the only thing he can do. She sees all this, and she doesn't understand. She does not.

'It should have been put out,' he whispers. And she knows, she knows because it's there constantly, at the edges of everything, pretty much all she thinks about – still now – that he's talking about the fire, about the embers of the open barbecue that looked like nothing, like grey sand. About the third-degree burns, the skin and blisters and pain, and Alex's perfect ruined feet that . . . She stops the thought. She won't go there.

'I couldn't have known,' he's saying. 'It shouldn't have been left.'

Five minutes, she wants to say. She wants to shout it. She almost does. I left you in charge for five fucking minutes.

'It's too much,' he says again, and he keeps saying it over and over.

She puts her head down and moves past him. 'Have you seen the hospital letter?' she asks. 'I can't find it.' And she starts to rifle through a pile on the end of the table, all fingers and thumbs, although she's already searched it twice.

He comes towards her, takes hold of her upper arms. 'Did you hear me?'

She would like to shake him off. Instead, she makes herself go slack. There's the smell of stale cooking, the greasy grill pan she needs to see to, which she was too tired to wash up last night. In her ears, the hiccuping tick of the clock on the wall. It's been losing time these past few months, another thing she needs to fix.

'Vivienne?'

'Are you having an affair?' She stares him straight in the face as she says it. 'Is that what this is?'

He lets go her arms, takes a step back. 'You don't get it, do you?' He's almost crying, but she would like to bang his head against the wall behind him, because why is he feeling so sorry for himself? If she had the strength, she thinks she might do this. He has his head in his hands now, and it's like he's really lost the plot . . . and is it cold in here? It feels really cold, even though she has on her thick green cardy, the one Alex wears, buttoned right up over her head, when she's playing caterpillar-butterfly. Alex, who she needs to pick up in less than three hours, Nancy too, and she has so much to get through before then, she hardly knows where to start, and she still hasn't found the letter, even though she's looked in all the places she knows it would be.

315

She moves back across the kitchen. She's going to search again in the drawer, under the sink, that's full of batteries and nails and washing pegs and rusty screwdrivers, and where she knows damn well the letter isn't, but she's yanking out the drawer to the end of its rails anyway. And isn't it obvious? Although she's trying her best to keep it inside – she's doing it for the girls – isn't it obvious? It should be bloody obvious that she's beyond overwhelmed and she doesn't have time, she does not have time . . . and why can't he see that? The Sellotape is there in the drawer, the brand-new roll she bought to wrap the present for the birthday party Alex is going to tomorrow, which is another thing she needs to do, but for now . . . for now, she'd like to bite off a strip with her teeth, stick it over his mouth to stop him saying what he's trying to say, and why is he doing this? Why why why?

'I'm leaving,' she hears Patrick murmur, and when he clears his throat, the sound goes through her. '*Leaving leaving*.'

Vivienne swings round to look at him, narrows her eyes. 'What does that even mean?'

'I love you, I'm sorry,' he whispers.

She lets go of the drawer, and it crashes to the floor, spitting its contents across the kitchen tiles.

'I don't have fucking time for this!' she screams.

Vivienne, Wednesday evening

Vivienne should not have sat down under this tree. That was her mistake. She should have kept going, not taken a breather. She knows this. She is old enough to know better. She's about to turn seventy, for goodness' sake. Seventy. It's such a preposterous number. How can it possibly apply to her? The ground is slippery, pooled with water, and the wet has seeped through to her skin, or at least she thinks it has – she can't tell exactly because every inch of her is numb. She thought she'd be okay to rest for a second, but she wasn't, she isn't, and now she can't get back up. Blind faith, that's what she has sometimes, and it surprises her, this ability to trick herself, to insulate herself from the truth. Take the time that Patrick left. Bolted, abandoned her, ran away. It sounds so dramatic. It *was* dramatic, although it took her a little while to catch up. She's thinking more and more of the past, these days. The truth is it feels easier sometimes. Even when it's harder, if that makes sense, and she isn't sure it does and, oh, her head hurts.

She didn't believe at first that he'd go through with it. But as days passed, then weeks, months, she understood that he wasn't coming back. He saw the girls sporadically, or maybe they had an arrangement, she can't remember. Whatever it was, it would never have been enough. Her silent fury – her fear – filled her head, painting over the detail. She only knows she did what she had to in order to get by, in order to *survive*. If she told the children anything, she told them, 'Daddy's at work,' and they accepted it as truth, as children do – even if deep down they knew things weren't as they should have been. Did they know that? She has no idea. They were so young, so, so young they hadn't learned yet not to trust. She wouldn't have them go to the grotty flat where he'd set himself up, like a punishment, and anyway, he never asked to have them. But, after a while, he started to come several evenings a week to see them. Didn't stay long, left as soon as they were in bed, and she had insisted on that. And then some Sundays too, for a couple of hours, and she'd hide, with her rage, in their bedroom – in *her* bedroom; she gritted her teeth and did it for her daughters.

He never once came to the hospital, though, from the moment he left, until he came back, not once. He'd been the one in charge when Alex had jumped barefoot into the fire, but Vivienne picked up the pieces, and she picked them up alone. It was bad, but it could have been worse. A part of her – the part beneath the anger, which was desperately sad, impotent – was relieved that he wanted to see his children at all. They loved him; she loved him, despite everything.

This, Vivienne thinks now, this is the past that's coming for them, here in this place. This is the past that's always been there, just she and Patrick have tried to mute it, to shun it, outrun it. To pretend it never happened. *This* is

why . . . the thing in the woods at Betty's naming ceremony that she doesn't want to think about. She squeezes
shut her eyes, clamps her jaw. It's why Patrick chose Eva.
Or, rather, it's why he didn't choose the others. Because
of the promise he made. The promise he kept too well.

'They need to know, Patrick,' Vivienne says. Because
here he is, sitting in the rain next to her, white in the dark,
soaked to the bone and trembling like she is. Where did
he come from? He doesn't reply and she's too tired to
say it again. But she's going to make him tell them. As
soon as they get back to the glass house: it's gone on too
long. She's going to tell him she was wrong to say she
didn't want to dredge it all up, that it needs to be said.
That their silence is costing the family too much.

Her husband isn't talking, like he normally does. Still,
she's glad she's not alone out here, and she reaches out
to touch him. Finds thin air. 'Patrick?' she says. Grop-
ing around her, she hits her hand against the tree, once,
twice, scraping her knuckles, then pats the sodden
ground he'd been sitting on. Where did he go?

And now, and now . . . when she turns her head, and
it's slow because she's stiff from the cold and the wet, she
sees two figures walking towards her. They come and go,
in and out of her vision, or maybe she's opening and closing her eyes, because of the sharp rain that's like pinpricks
against her eyeballs. They are there and then they're not,
the people, the pair, and is she hallucinating? 'Over here,'
she calls, or she thinks she does, but also she has the sense
that her lips aren't moving, that her mouth has frozen shut.

Vivienne, Spring 1976

It happens in the spring. Season of fertility and renewal and new beginnings – and Vivienne is drunk when she gets home. No, not drunk, *tipsy*. A little blurry at the edges, and she's thinking how nice it feels, as she lets herself in at the front door. That she's forgotten how to do this, be this. She's been to Covent Garden, to the Punch & Judy, to see her old school friend, Anna, the first time she's been out in the evening since the accident, since Patrick decided he was leaving and not coming back. He's here tonight, though. She can hear canned laughter on the TV, the volume turned up higher than she'd have it, because she's always listening out for the girls just in case. He's babysitting them. Not babysitting, she corrects herself. They're his kids too. She's lost count of how many months it's been – she doesn't want to know – but it's both strange and oddly familiar, the sound of someone else awake in her house past seven p.m.

Vivienne dumps her bag in the hall, steps out of her shoes, which are killing her feet, and checks her face in the mirror. The colour is high in her cheeks, from the night air and the wine. And her eyes are bright, also from the wine, and the air, and she thinks she looks good, pretty, with her hair in a ponytail, like she used to wear at school. Again, the wine is softening her usual critique so she's moved to perform a small curtsy to herself, followed by a wink. In the lounge, Patrick laughs, and she thinks for a second that somehow he's seen her do this, then just as quickly realizes he must not have heard her come in.

She's aware, as she enters the lounge, that she's moving too carefully, because of the alcohol, yes, but also because he is here. And she's annoyed at herself that she doesn't quite know how to be in her own house, in *their* house. The house they've dismantled and put back together, and where he no longer lives.

He's grinning at something on screen when he notices her, and covers his mouth with his hand, like she's caught him. Starts to get to his feet.

'Girls been okay?' she asks, and he nods.

'I mean, I read *Not Now, Bernard* about a hundred times,' he says. 'But it's a beguiling narrative, so . . .'

'Do you want a drink?' Vivienne asks, and she has no idea why she's said it. Maybe because of the moment in the hall when she heard him laugh, or the way he was smiling when she came into the room. Maybe because she's remembering him reading to their babies, to Alex and Nancy. Wearing his daughters like limbs, and doing all the voices, making them giggle around the soggy edges of thumbs in their mouths. 'A *drink* drink,' she adds, and she crosses her eyes, tilts her head a little.

It's a moment before he responds, and she can tell he's surprised she's asked him. 'Sounds good,' he says, and he smooths down his hair, in the way that he does.

Vivienne crosses to the drinks cabinet. 'Do you remember?' she says, and she gestures at the black

321

lacquered cupboard they'd bought at the charity shop. 'We carried it all the way home, you were worried you'd get a hernia.' She laughs. Her hands are clumsy and the bottles clank together as she takes out the single malt, the Tia Maria, the vermouth, reaches all the way into the back. 'Brandy?' she asks. 'It's the expensive stuff.'

He fetches two glasses from the kitchen, holds them while she pours. 'Make mine a Spanish double,' he says, without meeting her eye. It's an old joke. A holiday they took a thousand years ago, a tarpaulin bar on the beach in northern Spain, a hippie bartender who poured spirits like wine.

They drink, standing there, and she feels the brandy flame in her. She feels as if she's stepping back into their past.

'Listen!' Patrick says, and he starts to run his finger around the rim of his glass, circle upon circle, trying to make it sing. 'Wait, hold on . . .' He licks the finger, tries again. 'Any second now . . .'

'Oh dear.' Vivienne clicks the side of her mouth. And then she runs her finger around her own glass, once, twice, until it starts to chime. 'Ha!' She laughs. 'I guess some of us just have it.' And she dips her finger in the brandy, sucks the alcohol from the tip, draws a jubilant point in the air.

'I miss you,' he says. He looks at her for a long time.

'Stay,' she tells him, and although she sways a little on her legs as she says it, she knows enough, in that instant, to know it's what she wants.

*

Afterwards, they lie on their backs on the yellow carpet she loves – the one she found on the King's Road and that they're still paying off. Rather than look at each other, they stare at the ceiling. It would feel too much, too *intimate*, to gaze into her husband's eyes. How is it she feels sober now? Entirely sober, when for those stretched moments she'd forgotten herself. She'd forgotten to hate him. It had felt to her like coming home. Vivienne presses her palms into the carpet. She wants to smoke. She's desperate to smoke, but the cigarettes are in her bag, and her bag is in the hall, and she feels like Alex playing hide and seek – like she's covering her eyes and believing she can't be seen. A sense that, as long as she doesn't move a muscle, it isn't real, what's happened, she isn't really here. And she doesn't want to be here, lying on the carpet, with her husband who left her. She doesn't want it to be real, because the thing is . . . the thing is . . .

'I'm told you're the woman I need in my life right now,' was the first thing the man said to her, when she opened the door to him a week ago now. To a *handsome auburn-haired stranger*, she's imagined herself telling someone since, except there's no one she'd tell, of course she wouldn't. He was facing away from her, and turned, with a smile, as he delivered his line. 'I've locked myself out. Like an idiot,' he added, 'and apparently you have the spare key. I'm John-Paul, your neighbour's . . . Stella Wilson's cousin.' He put inverted commas around the word *cousin* with his intonation, then shook his head. 'I don't know why I said it like that – she is, in fact, my cousin.' He pulled a face, and something had passed between them, a look, a transgression. The shared knowledge that Stella Wilson is, in fact, a bit of a pain in the arse. 'I'm over from Canada,' he went on, 'heading back tomorrow, and I can give more details if you need to know that I'm the real deal, not some kind of, I don't know . . . charming thief.'

She lifted an eyebrow. 'There's nothing remotely valuable inside,' she said, and invited him in.

She's entirely unsure how it happened. She only knows he didn't need to ask twice. He didn't need to ask at all. Stella's key wasn't in the kitchen drawer where she thought it was, and she hunted and hunted, turning over piles of crap, searching everywhere, feeling increasingly useless, out of control. Like in front of this man, observed by this near-stranger, she was demonstrating the mess of her life, laying bare her failings. And she apologized, and apologized again, moving from room to room, growing increasingly, stupidly frantic, until she started to cry, quietly, surreptitiously, she thought, but he saw it. Instead of leaving, he approached her, wiped her tears with the sleeve of his shirt, like it was something he'd done before. And when she kissed him, he didn't stop her. They didn't stop – she doesn't think she *could* have stopped. They didn't make it past the hall, and the sex didn't last long, but it felt good, better than good. As if she'd shaken the stagnant atoms of her body into a whole new form.

After that, they gave up looking for the key. Shared a cigarette, sitting on the bottom step of the stairs, and then he got up to leave. 'I hope you don't feel I took advantage of you,' he said, at the front door, one hand on the latch. 'I mean, you were upset, and . . .'

Vivienne looked him straight in the eye, adjusted her top with a deliberate snap. 'Oh, I never say no to an orgasm on a Wednesday morning. I hope *you* don't feel I took advantage of you.'

Laughing, he rubbed the stubble at his jaw, pulled open the door. 'In reference to your earlier comment,' he said, glancing back over his shoulder, 'I would respectfully suggest that there is, in fact, something – *someone* – of great value in this house. I just hope she knows it.'

Next to her, Patrick props himself up on an elbow. 'Hey,' he says, and she turns her head to look at him. 'You were miles away. Where did you go?' There's sweat above his top lip, along his hair line.

Me, she thinks. Where did *I* go?

He's smiling at her, shaking his head.

She wants to say, 'You're the one who left, Patrick, where did *you* go? I've been here *the whole time.*'

'Fuck,' she whispers. 'What am I doing?' And she's already starting to scrabble back into her clothes, which are half-on half-off, as Patrick sits up, confused. He looks ridiculous, sitting there, with his socks pulled up to his calves, his penis drooping on the expensive yellow carpet. It isn't difficult, in this moment, to say what she's going to say. 'Okay, you should go,' she tells him, and she bundles his shirt in her hands, shoves it at him. 'Fuck,' she says again, as he opens his mouth to speak, and he stops, frowns instead. Vivienne feels light-headed. She's laddered her tights – or, rather, *he* has – all the way from the toe to the knee. Rather than look at her husband, she studies the intricate pattern, the holes and loose threads, her exposed skin in the gaps, which looks pink, raw. 'The girls will expect you on Tuesday,' she says, and the words on her tongue sound formal, the language of separation, of family courts, of expensive, dispassionate lawyers. 'You can see yourself out.'

Eva, Wednesday evening

Her mum is okay, her mum is okay, her mum is okay is all Eva can think, as she comes across the lawn, past the copper seat, towards the carport. She's run on ahead, feet heavy in her sodden trainers, but her heart a thousand times lighter, leaving Scott to walk back more slowly with her dad. She hadn't known how worried she was – hadn't let herself go there – until they'd found her, Nancy and Nik. Very, very cold, her sister had said on the phone, and a little confused maybe, but fine. When Eva had tried to reply, her voice had split and she'd had to pause. *I've checked her vitals, okay?* Nancy had reassured her. *She's a tough old bird, don't worry . . .*

Lucy will be relieved, Eva thinks now, the first time she's allowed herself to think this too. They have a special bond, her mum and her daughter, she knows: she sees it. Everyone must see it, and it's crossed her mind that she'd hate it if her mum was that way with one of the other grandkids. It's different, and not just because Lucy's the eldest. It's different because of everything – because Eva was barely more than a kid when her mum, her brilliant, bright, maddening mum, stepped in and wrapped her arms around them both, didn't let go, not until Eva was ready.

Mum will leap to Lucy's defence. You won't have to ask

327

twice . . . Eva hears Alex's voice in her head, touches her cheek involuntarily, feels again the force of her sister's palm against her face. Tries to push from her mind that awful moment in the bedroom, the shock of the slap that feels as if it happened in a past life. Is Lucy her mum's favourite? Is it a thing? Is *she* her dad's favourite? Do parents really have favourites? She wouldn't know, has no idea. She has only one, just Lucy – more than enough, she likes to tease her. There's nothing and no one to compare.

The dressing on her heel has slipped again, and she stops at the carport, bends to adjust it. Later, when she thinks back to this moment – the moment just before she sees her – Eva will not be able to quash the sense that thinking about her daughter somehow wills her into being. She'll remember her coat zip dragging against her throat, the metallic smell of the saturated ground as she glances up at the glass house, at the cut-out yellow rectangle glaring in the dark.

Eva sees her straight away, through the section of glass wall that gives onto the lounge – although it takes her a second, longer than that, to process what she's witnessing. There's the ugly, pointed sculpture that reaches almost to the ceiling, and next to it, her daughter. Her daughter and someone else, two figures that could be one. They look bedraggled, wet, like they've just come in from the rain outside. Except Lucy is wearing a bikini and he's in shorts. They've come from the pool. Her daughter's head is tilted back, and he – Eva squints, her eyes blurred with rain – he has his mouth clamped against her neck, his hands covering her breasts. And this isn't right, it can't be right, it cannot, *cannot* be happening.

Big moment bringing the boyfriend on the family holiday . . . Nik's words slam into her mind, and she wants to scream. She wants to run at the glass, to throw her weight against it. She wants to make this stop. She'd thought she had hundreds of miles left in her, that she could scale a million mountains if that was what it took to find her mum, but right here, right now, she finds she isn't able to move. The flesh and muscle and bone of her has seized up; she's fixed in place, stuck.

The glass house is a stage, and the pair are spotlit – *floodlit* – and she doesn't want to see this, but there's nowhere else to look, and how has this happened? Because Lucy can't stand him, Scott's son. No, Eva thinks. No. There's been a mistake, she thinks, or maybe she says it, as she stands there watching this thing that she can't unsee. Watching her daughter push her mouth against his – against her *stepbrother's* mouth – although she isn't aware of that fact, has no idea. And in that moment, Eva realizes she's known all along this would happen.

Alex, Wednesday evening

Alex just wants to go home. Not to the Balham house that's painted all in one colour – in Julie's Dream – and fitted with storage solutions in every room. They got a man in to do it, and he'd laid down a dust sheet, his first day on the job, and said, *You could eat your dinner off this floor, it's so clean.* And it's true, you could. Alex sprays and wipes the plastic mat under the high chair after every meal. Making wider and wider circles, until sometimes, on her hands and knees, she's done the whole kitchen. She has to force herself to stop, not to continue through the rest of the house. No, she doesn't want to go back there yet: she isn't ready to return. She wants to go home. *Home* home.

When she starts the engine, the sound explodes into the quiet of the street. Her body tenses, and she shoots a look at Matt's house. Imagines him appearing on the doorstep, like, what the hell? The lounge window is dark still, but she's panicking anyway, that he'll come out and find her here, and her humiliation will be complete.

Her feet are clumsy on the pedals, as she pulls out into the road. At some point the rain must have stopped, and she hadn't noticed. She flicks the wipers, once, twice, to clear the windscreen. There's a feeling in her gut like she's eaten something bad. She's going to drive to the

Dartmouth Park house. She has the key she never gave back. She'll sleep in her childhood bedroom that's now a guest room, but where her initials are still scratched on the inside of the wardrobe. She'll raid the drinks cabinet, drink her way through the gin, the vodka, the whisky, all the way to the bottle of Tia Maria that's been there since the seventies. She'll eat cornflakes out of the packet, in front of the TV.

Alex makes a turn and then another turn, and then she's on the high street. She drives past the cinema, turns right at the church, stops at the junction by the hospital. And she's flicking on her indicator to make a left, when she sees a yellow diversion sign blocking the road she wants to take. 'Shit,' she murmurs, and slows the car, glances down the street, assessing, as she drives by.

Each time Alex gets to a road she wants to take, there's a yellow sign. A yellow sign or a flood-warning sign or a no-entry sign, like the council is having to mix it up, because they're running out of the right kind of messaging. Alex has never seen so many roads closed, which is saying something, and she starts to laugh, because it's all beginning to feel a little too meta. Yes, she's *on diversion*, she thinks, that's exactly where she is. It couldn't be more apt. She can't get to where she's going. She's been on diversion this past year, longer. She's come so far in the wrong direction, she doesn't know where she is any more; she hardly knows *who* she is.

The Matt she saw tonight, with his artfully dishevelled hair, his shirt popped at one side of the collar, the slow roll of his shoulders as he turned to face the window, is someone she knows both intimately and not at all. She knows, for example, she remembers, that he has three moles in a triangle close to his navel. She also knows – she understands now – that he is a near-stranger. Alex has had sex with this man, touched every inch of his body – she has had his cock in her mouth and it doesn't get much more intimate than that – and also she hasn't. Because isn't it the case, scientifically speaking, that every cell of him will have died and regenerated in the years since then, since she last fucked him? That he is a different version of himself now from the person she knew. That they both are. And she feels so stupid because what was she expecting? Checking her rear-view mirror, Alex watches the road recede behind her. She has built an obsession from Instagram posts and unstable memories; a house of cards from nostalgia and trickery, envy and delusion.

Nancy, Wednesday evening

Nik is waiting in the corridor, sitting forward on the window seat, when Nancy comes out of her mum's room.

'How is she?' he asks. He's keeping his voice low, respectful, like this is the night shift at the hospital. He makes to get up, but she signals for him to stay.

'Trying to style it out,' Nancy says, 'which is *very* Vivienne of her.'

'Like mother, like daughter . . .'

'Good one,' she says, and bumps down on the seat. She is all of a sudden exhausted, and what time is it? It could be nine in the evening or two in the morning, she has no idea, none.

'She's okay, though, is she?' He isn't letting it go, and she nods, *Yes*. She doesn't say her own heart has just about settled, after the shock of finding her there in the forest, the state she was in. The rushing fear, the burst of relief. Nancy can still feel the adrenaline jumping around her body. And she's about to thank him for his help because, praise God, he was there, keeping it light; she wasn't alone. Tell him he's free, finally, to leave this glass madhouse, just as soon as the weather clears and *if* he can find his niece, when his expression turns serious.

'Listen, Nancy . . .' He pauses, pulls his hands through his hair.

It goes through her mind to tell him, *because you're worth it!*, this tired joke of hers. Instinct pushes the words to the front of her mouth, but she stops herself: he's acting a little weird, and she feels like maybe it wouldn't land.

'I haven't been entirely honest with you,' Nik says now.

Nancy presses her fingers into the seat, feels her nails scrape the upholstery.

'Ugh . . .' He tips his head up to the ceiling, like he can't hold her gaze. 'Why am I doing this?'

'I don't know, Nik,' she says, with a breeziness she isn't feeling. 'You're really picking your moment.'

When he looks at her, she sees his Adam's apple rise, then fall, as he swallows. It's like their faces, their eyes, their mouths are too close together. Or not close enough.

'I don't have cousins who live nearby, okay.' He says it in a rush, and it takes her a moment to process the words. 'I know I told you I did, but I don't. I wanted to . . . I wanted us to –'

There's a slam, like books falling from a shelf, and then a shout.

'WHY WOULD ANYONE BUILD A GLASS HOUSE? THERE'S *LITERALLY* NO ESCAPE!'

From the corner of her eye, Nancy sees a flash of colour down the hallway. When she turns her head to look, there's Lucy backing out of the lounge, yelling. She's in a bikini, like she's been for a swim, had a citrus

334

sauna maybe, as though the crisis of her granny's disappearance has entirely passed her by. 'YOU DON'T UNDERSTAND!' she's shouting. 'WHY DO YOU HATE JOY AND FUN?'

Nancy glances at the door to her mum's room. Then she's up and out of her seat, moving quickly along the hallway towards her niece. 'Lucy?' She puts a restraining hand on her arm. 'Can you just . . .' Pressing a finger against her lips, she lowers her voice to a whisper. 'Granny's just resting, okay? The kids are in bed too.'

Lucy snatches her arm away. Her skinny body is stippled with goosebumps. Nancy takes in her sister in the lounge, standing in front of the long, low sofa, her raincoat and trainers still on. Scott's son is in there too, over by the glass wall that's reflecting the room, the people, the objects in it, back at them, like there's another identical space beyond the first. He's wearing swimming shorts, like he's come from the pool too, and he looks uncomfortable, trapped against the glass. He looks as though he's wishing he could walk through it and escape into the phantom lounge.

'Eva?' Nancy moves a little way into the room. Her sister's clothes are dark, weighted, dripping still. Her whole body looks weighted, as though something is dragging at her shoulders, forcing her head down.

'Is Mum okay?' Eva asks, and Nancy nods.

'We've put in a call to the paramedics, but they've said she's not a priority. Which she isn't, she's fine. Belligerent, honestly.' She tries to laugh.

Tears gloss her sister's eyes. Nancy watches as Eva

feels for the sofa behind her, then sits, puts her head into her hands. 'I've had it,' she says, and her voice comes out muffled, thin. 'I just can't, Nancy. I can't any more.'

'Slay, *Eva* . . .' Lucy's voice, from the hallway, is slurred with sarcasm.

There's the sound of the front door opening, closing, voices coming from the lobby.

'Oh, terrific . . .' Eva murmurs.

'What's going on?' Nancy asks now. 'Eva, what's happened?'

When her sister doesn't respond, she turns to Lucy. Holds out her hands, palms up. She registers Nik, hovering in the hallway, near the pink and blue paintings. Don't go, she thinks. She almost says it. Just give me a minute . . .

'Fantastic, we're celebrating!' Scott marches into the room, shaking his head, like a dog fresh out of a pond. 'I've got some Lithuanian tea with a surprising kick. I can do a brew, if anyone wants to – Why are you still in your coat?' He comes to a stop. 'Eva? Am I missing something?' He frowns. 'Is it Vivienne?'

'No, Mum's fi–' Nancy starts to say, at the exact same moment as Eva replies: 'I don't know, Scott, *are* you missing something?' Her face is pink. Nancy knows this look: her sister is angry. 'I know I was,' Eva says. 'Maybe ask your *son*.' She spits 'son', as if she wants the word out of her mouth.

Nancy looks from Eva to Scott. Glances from her niece to Jay. They are standing there nearly naked, like they've stumbled into the wrong room, the wrong house, the wrong holiday. The wrong family. And it's obvious, blindingly obvious, and how hadn't she seen it before? She'd been thinking about her mum, that's how, and Nik and, Jesus, *fuck*, they're practically related, they basically are related, Lucy and Jay. Out in the hallway, Lucy is sucking in her lips, like she's trying not to shout, or cry, and Nancy almost feels sorry for them – she *does* feel sorry for them – standing there, exposed and vulnerable like this. And, oh, God, Eva.

'Where's Mum?' Her dad appears in the doorway, shuffles into the room. His socks are two-tone with rain, and Nancy can smell him from where she's standing. A damp, oniony smell that makes her want to cover her nose. He hasn't read the room, and she doesn't know how to fill him in. Where would she even begin?

Jay heaves an audible sigh, like he is *so over all of this*. 'We had a little thing, okay?' He's smoothing the front of his waxed chest as he says it, but Nancy sees that his hands are a little unsteady. 'It's no big deal. Everyone needs to just chill.'

'Why is he even here?' her sister says, coldly. She says it as though Jay isn't, in fact, there at all.

'Wow.' Scott runs his eyes around the people in the room, as if he's gathering witnesses, galvanizing support. Like, you all heard that right?

'I'm not following,' her dad says. 'Where's Viv—?'

'I got fired from the boats.' Jay shrugs. 'I had time on my hands.'

'Mm-hm.' Eva pushes herself up off the sofa. 'Yeah, I didn't mean it *quite* so literally. Fun fact, though, Jay.'

She looks at Scott. 'And super-interesting that your dad didn't think to mention it.'

As if he hasn't heard her, Scott's son ploughs on: 'I'm thinking of setting up my own business. Along the lines of your thing.' He tips his head in Eva's direction. 'But probably a bit more high-end.'

'Ha!' Eva shrieks. 'Oh, okay, yup!' She puffs out her cheeks, makes her eyes go all stare-y and wide.

What is happening to her sister? This is not the Eva Nancy knows. She has rarely seen her act this way.

'I hate you so much.' Lucy's words swell and settle in the room. She isn't shouting any more and it's almost worse. She's eyeing Eva as she says it again: 'I hate you.' A simple statement of fact. She looks as though she might break if you touched her; she looks young, is how she looks, as she wraps her arms around her body, turns and walks away, down the hall.

'Always so dramatic, Lucy!' Scott calls after her.

'Don't you dare talk to her like that.' Eva won't look at him. She makes to follow her daughter, but Scott puts up a hand to block her.

'In answer to your question, Eva,' he says, 'have you met my son Jay? *Son* being the operative word in that sentence. That's why he's here.' The sarcasm is new on him. It shouldn't suit him, but it does. It's like he's broken character, Nancy thinks. Does he get what's happened? Has he understood what's gone on between his son and his girlfriend's daughter?

There's a dangerous pause. Nancy waits for her sister to push past him, to follow Lucy out of the room.

Because why is she still standing there, opposite Scott, who's twisting and twisting the ugly gold band on his pinky finger? Like maybe he thinks he's fucking Gollum, or a member of the Mob. A phone starts to ring into the silence. It's the jaunty generic ringtone that comes as standard, and Nancy thinks it might be hers: she thinks she probably left it in her coat pocket in the hall. Then remembers there's no signal there. Even so, her fingers twitch reflexively, and she glances across to the corridor, like should she go and check? And she sees that Nik isn't out there any more. He's gone.

'My son,' Scott says again, and he doesn't take his eyes from her sister's face. '*Your* stepson, Eva.'

For a moment, Nancy doesn't understand. She thinks she must have heard wrong, or that Scott is playing fast and loose with the word 'stepson'. As in, he might as well be your stepson because we're a couple. Then she registers her sister's expression. A look on this face she knows like her own. Better than her own. The same look she had when she'd borrowed Nancy's Clinique moisturizer or her burgundy pixie boots or her beloved Lenny Kravitz album without asking. She looks guilty. And Nancy understands that it's true.

If Scott knows he's just thrown a bomb into the room, he doesn't show it. He bounces a little on the balls of his feet.

'You *married* him?' Nancy scans her sister's hand for a wedding band, finds nothing. 'Tell me you didn't, Eva.'

'I'm not following,' her dad says. 'Eva?'

'What the actual fuck?' Jay has moved away from the

glass wall, and he's gripping the back of the sofa with both hands. 'Dad?'

Somewhere in the house, another phone starts up. It sounds close by, but it can't be, and everyone else is ignoring it. Eva would be saying something by now, Nancy thinks, correcting her if Scott was lying. If there was anything to correct. Telling them she has no idea what he's talking about. She can feel that her T-shirt, her bra, her knickers are damp where the rain soaked through. It's making her cold and she's starting to shiver. How could her sister keep this from her?

'Traditionally families tend to congratulate the bride and groom,' Scott says.

And, reeling though she is, Nancy can see that he isn't even trying to stop this thing erupting. Before this, Scott was just a nuisance, but this . . . this is different. This is new, a reveal. He's a fake, she thinks. She'd like to shout it. He's a fake and she knew it. *She* knew it, Alex knew it, they all knew it. What was Eva thinking?

'Please God say there's a pre-nup . . .' Nancy's talking to herself as much as to her sister.

Eva starts to say something, but Scott cuts across her. 'Do you have any idea how rude you are?' he says. 'I mean, as a family.'

Nancy closes her eyes, opens them. She tries to count to ten. She's not going to say it; she's going to say it. 'Do *you* have any idea how much of a dick you are? Genuine question.' She makes a pinching motion with her thumb and forefinger. 'A dick, and a little bit of a gold-digger.'

'Totally unnecessary, Nancy!' Her dad rounds on her,

and for a long moment, she can't believe the words out of his mouth. It's like she hears them in slow motion. 'For God's sake, why the hell do you always make things worse?'

All of a sudden the smell is there, the awful smell that's been spreading through the house this whole holiday. Until this moment, it hadn't reached as far as the lounge, but here it is now. It's in the room, up her nose and coating her throat, and it's stronger, much stronger than before. Her eyes start to water as she faces her dad. 'Are you serious?' Nancy whispers. She can't believe it. 'Me? I'm the fuck-up here? Still now?' She pauses, waits. Despite everything, she waits for him to tell her sorry, he got it wrong this time; he got her wrong.

When he doesn't answer, she shakes her head. 'It's not a virtue to say nothing,' she says, and she starts to cough. She feels she might be choking. Choking on the smell that's getting worse and worse, and why is no one saying anything? Can't they smell it too? She bends over her knees, and her eyes are streaming. 'Is no one else smelling this?'

'It's the dead frogs,' Jay mumbles. He's looking at his dad still as he says it. 'Toads, whatever. There's a ton of them floating in the pool – we thought they were toys. It's disgusting.' He half gags. 'And in the air vents, all rotten.'

'Oh, Christ!' she hears someone say, she doesn't know who, at the same time as her sister asks, 'Nancy? Are you okay?'

And, no, she's not, she's not okay, but she doesn't

know how to tell them this. They all think she's so bol-shie. A *gobshite*, they'd call her, fierce, and not in a good way. But she runs away from the difficult conversations too, just as they do. *Why the hell do you always make things worse?* She has tried so hard not to let this happen, to swerve the trap she falls into again and again and again, to bypass the pain of it, but it's happened anyway.

Straightening, she fixes her eyes on her dad's. The coughing has eased, and she wants him to listen, to hear her. 'I just try to tell the truth,' she says quietly. The words trigger something in her, and she feels all at once poised, unassailable, as though she's walking a high wire across the Grand Canyon without so much as a tremor, like she's out for a stroll in the park. 'I'm not fourteen years old any more,' she tells him. 'I'm a woman, a mother, a fucking good doctor. I'm someone who understands what a scapegoat looks like.' She pauses. She can see the pores on his cheeks, the veins around his nose, his tufted ears that are larger, thicker than they used to be. 'I'm not a bad person, and whatever this is, it's not on me.'

She's saying it for herself as much as them; she's saying it because the truth is she still struggles to believe it. She's saying it for her daughter and for Dolly, for her sisters – every version of them, she's saying it for her family. Because she wants to break open the secrets, the things they don't acknowledge, don't say. She would like, finally, to upend the fixed stories of who they are, to rewrite the stealthily poisonous narrative of them. 'I'm not sorry,' Nancy says now. 'I'm not sorry I won't paper over the cracks of other people's shitty behaviour.'

When her dad doesn't respond, when no one says anything, Nancy holds up her hands. As she does, she catches sight of the movement of her palms, fingers spread, reflected back at her in the glass wall. The black glass wall that's casting her – casting all of them – as doubles, doppelgängers, facsimiles of themselves. They're a little wider, a little longer, a little darker; it's them and also it isn't. And, staring at the figures copied there, Nancy gets the sense that the glass is starting to move. Inch by inch, closing in on her, shrinking the space.

She doesn't want to be here. She's going to fetch Georgie and leave. She's going to leave just like Alex. 'Okay, I'm done,' she says, to everyone, and no one, and starts to walk out.

'Wait!' Her sister is in front of her, blocking her. 'Stay, don't go. Don't leave. Please . . .' Eva turns to their dad. 'I don't want this! I never wanted it. It's bullshit!' She's shouting as if the words have been building in her for weeks, months, decades. 'What kind of father picks favourites?'

There's silence in the room. Nancy wants to cover her ears; she wants him to deny it.

'What is all this?' Luc has materialized in the doorway. He has the baby in his arms and she's crying. 'You woke her,' he says, and he's frowning. Then he puts his lips close to the baby's bright cheeks. 'Ssh.' He blows the sound against her skin. 'Ssh, *petite*.'

And seeing the baby's hot little face, her yellow sleep suit that's ringed with damp at the neck, Nancy's mind flashes to Georgie, to her own baby. She knows how it would feel to reach out and touch the hair that's fuzzy with static at the back of her niece's head. She imagines fine strands stuck to the soft sheet of her travel cot, the warm dent where her small body has just been. And she's vaguely aware that Eva is starting to talk again, and that her phone is going, or someone else's, she can't tell, but it's making her brain jump. It seems that every time one phone stops, another starts, or is she going mad? And now Scott's son is moving away from the window, making his way around the side of the sofa. 'Dad?' he's saying, and his voice is high-pitched. He sounds like a boy, not a man. 'Dad? Is it true?' The baby's cry is getting louder and louder, and the phones won't stop ringing, and Nancy needs to get out of here, she needs to check on her mum, on Georgie, and where is Nik?

'NO ONE'S LISTENING TO ME!'

Eva screams it. She's screaming the words that take Nancy back to another time, another place. Her little sister is at the dinner table and in the den; she's in the garden and the street, in the supermarket, the park, and she's down the road at Helen and Katy's house, bunches bouncing either side of her head, in indignation . . . *No one's listening to me!*

Eva has her arms around the ugly, pointed sculpture, the one they told the kids *on pain of death*, they must not touch. Before Nancy understands what's happening, her sister has lifted it, this sculpture that is taller, heavier than she is, and with a howl, she launches it at the glass wall.

It's as if someone has pressed pause. Spidery cracks spread like tentacles across the dark glass. Then, piece by fractured piece, the wall shatters and falls. The entire side of the room, the house, is gone. The sound of it is extraordinary, how Nancy imagines a landslide would sound, or the Snow Queen's frozen lake, splintering into a thousand icy shards. It takes her a moment to realize there's nothing left. That the people in the room are no longer looking at themselves looking back at them: their reflections have been sucked out into the night. The mirror has broken; they've disappeared.

'Patrick.'

When Vivienne says his name, Nancy turns – they all turn – from the ruined wall of the glass house, the crystal mess of it. It's cold, freezing cold, with the room open to the elements as it is, but if she feels it, Vivienne doesn't show it. She's standing there, serene, her bright pink Turkish slippers on her feet. Her hair is combed and there's nothing to suggest she's been out in the rain; she's even applied lipstick. She doesn't reference the broken glass; she doesn't even glance at it, not once. Her focus is on her husband, entirely and unwaveringly on him.

'You need to tell them, Patrick,' she says, and her voice is steady, quietly resolute. 'You need to tell them that you left us. It's time.'

Vivienne, Autumn 1976

Half of the lounge is filled with presents – almost half. Bright-wrapped, like it's Christmas or someone's birthday, except it isn't. It's taken Patrick two trips in the car to get them here, and now Vivienne's watching him, pacing the room, chewing a thumbnail while he waits for the girls, who are having tea down the road at Stella's. They take it in turns on Fridays. She'll have Katy and Helen next week.

'It's too much, Patrick,' Vivienne says, for the third, maybe fourth time, and she's trying to tamp down the annoyance – the anger – she's feeling. The chemical smell of the wrap is making her head ache. That, and the nausea from the morning sickness, which is worse this time round than it was with the other two. It's lasted five months so far – although at the beginning it took her a while, more than a while, to catch on to what it was. For weeks she thought she was ill, a bug she couldn't shake, and had she been kidding herself? She adjusts the photograph on the fireplace, the one of the girls sitting in a cardboard box. At any moment she knows she might have to bolt from the room to be sick. 'Why are you doing this?' she says.

'You know why.' He comes towards her, places a hand on her stomach.

Vivienne shakes her head minutely, and when he

doesn't move his hand, she does it for him. Not yet, she thinks. She tries to communicate this with her eyes. It's too soon – she isn't ready, not even close. Truthfully, she isn't sure she'll ever be ready.

He knots his empty hands in front of him, as if he doesn't know what to do with himself. 'It's a fresh start,' he says. 'I want to mark it.'

She lifts the green glass bird from the mantelpiece, wipes dust from the smooth curve of its back with her finger. Nothing about this whole thing feels like a fresh start to her. It feels like a precarious compromise, or a trick. She feels as though she's about to jump off a cliff without a safety harness. 'You're spoiling them,' she tells him. 'They're babies, Patrick. This is – it's crazy.'

She hasn't told him yet that he'll be sleeping in the box room. At least until the baby comes, and likely after. She's doing this for the children – letting him move back in. That's the only reason. The reason that tipped her in the end. And also, she supposes, although she can hardly bear to admit it to herself, because she doesn't know how she would cope with a newborn – with three kids under five – alone. She refuses to ask herself whether she still loves him, she won't go there; it hardly matters either way when she can't trust him.

'I want them to know I love them,' Patrick says now, and she wonders, for a fleeting moment, whether he's read her thoughts somehow.

Vivienne eyes the presents, the obscene pile that's stretching all the way from the bamboo shelving unit to the sofa. This isn't what love looks like, she wants to say.

Patrick has made promises these last few weeks, since she told him. Since she'd decided what she was going to do or, rather, what she *wasn't* going to do. Promises upon promises upon promises. Near religious in his zeal. 'I have to see you now, right now! Don't say no,' he'd pleaded with her on the phone, the morning after she'd broken the news. 'I'll keep ringing back until you say you'll meet me.' He hadn't said much the night before – she hadn't given him the chance. Told him quickly in the hallway as he was leaving, Alex calling her from upstairs to come and kiss them goodnight . . . *By the way, I'm pregnant*. Like it was an afterthought. Then she'd shouted up to Alex that she was coming, held open the front door, shut it behind him.

He'd phoned at eight the following day, and she'd left the girls with Stella, claiming a work emergency. Gone to find him in the strange little chintzy café in the upstairs room of someone's house in Highgate. 'I haven't slept,' he'd told her, as he'd risen from a table in the corner. And he looked like he hadn't, his hair going in all directions, white crust at the corners of his mouth.

She'd found it hard to focus as he'd talked at her, breathlessly, desperately, barely breaking off when the waitress came to take her order, brought her coffee with a little biscuit wrapped in plastic on the side. 'I've changed my mind, Vivienne,' he'd said. 'I want to come back. Please tell me it's not too late. It will all be different this time.' He'd tried to take her hand across the table, and when she'd pulled away, it didn't deter him.

He'd had an epiphany. This new baby – this new

life – was his second chance. It meant he'd get to go round again, and it would be perfect this time. He would make it up to her, to them. He would dedicate his life to this if she'd let him. He would never, *never* let them down again. He'd redeem himself. She'd only have to watch, she'd see. This third baby would be the making of them. The making of their family. *Lucky Number Three*.

'I feel like it was meant to happen,' he'd said, as she'd drained her cup, got up to leave. Told him she needed some time. 'Can't you see that too?'

Vivienne replaces the glass bird on the mantelpiece, next to the photo of the girls. She doesn't let herself think about the other man, the one who came before. She hasn't heard from him since, and neither has she contacted him, although she could. She has told herself that maybe it never happened, those moments of fast desire in the hallway – it had been over in minutes, after all. It's almost easy to believe she dreamed the whole thing.

Alex, Wednesday evening

When Alex arrives, at last, in Dartmouth Park, there's a no-entry sign set up temporarily at the end of her street, blue and white police tape stretched between the corner houses. They're blocking her access and she can't see a way round it. She'll have to get out of the car and move them. There's an uneasy feeling in her, but she bangs on her hazards, dismisses it. Her mind is focused on a single point: she needs to get into the house.

Pulling on her jacket, she steps from the car, realizing, as she does, that she hasn't moved from the driver's seat since she left the service station hundreds of miles back up the motorway. She arches her back, hears her neck crack. It's taken her an hour to get here from Matt's house. An hour for a drive that should take twenty minutes, no more than forty, even in rush-hour. A crazy, tortuous route, because so many roads are flooded; she's never seen anything like it. Even so, it didn't occur to her until she got here that her road might be affected too.

She stops at the police tape, assesses. The streetlights are on, but she can't make out her house. The road is long and bends to the left, and the house is all the way down the other end, towards the bottom of the hill. Alex would give anything to be inside right now; she imagines herself unlocking the front door, the tricky little push and pull where the key sticks, crossing into the hall-way that will smell of stale garlic and spilled coffee and something a little too sweet. She's going to stand in a hot shower until her skin turns pink, then find her mum's dressing-gown, the thick one with the towelling lining, the green silk trim, that she knows will be hanging on the back of the bedroom door.

Alex starts to move the sign. It's heavy, with sandbags weighting it down, but she's pretty sure she can drag it to the edge of the street, move it back into place once she's gained access. There'll be red wine in a box on the kitchen dresser, she thinks, as her fingers slip on the wet metal. She'll start with that while she goes through the cupboards. Maybe she could cook some pasta to have with it. There's always penne in the glass jar with the cork lid, a multipack of tinned tomatoes. She'll add out-of-date spices from the rack on the wall that's been wonky for decades, little wooden pegs poking out at its edges. Much like the house itself – that's pretty wonky too. Shambling and worn, it's definitely seen better days. She smiles at the thought of it, of the picked-off wall-paper and curling carpets. The faded sofa in the lounge, where the slats dig in if you sit in the wrong spot, but it's the comfiest place in the world.

In the morning she'll call Luc. The thought jumps into her head. There have been no more texts from him, no missed calls. She tries to picture him in the glass house, with her family – with *their* family – and finds she can't. She can only summon an impression in her mind of angles and points and sterile, sharp edges. A feeling in her like she can't breathe, like he can't, that he's trapped in there. That they all are, *Lepidoptera* in a museum-quality display case.

Alex rests the sign on the ground, flexes her fingers. There's the blast of a horn behind her, and when she turns, a car swerves out into the road where she's double-parked. 'Screw you,' Alex murmurs, as the driver accelerates past. If she were Nancy, she would have yelled it. Pausing, she wipes her hands on her top, tips back her head, takes in the sky. Despite the light pollution, she thinks she can make out stars, bright points with smoky trails. Distant burning suns.

Another place, another time, another house: the Maison de la Musique, the fairytale building on the island in the west of France. Green-shuttered, and her husband standing on the steps, shouting across the crowd. *'Je t'aime, Alexandra! I love you . . .'* She hears his voice in her head, and did it even happen? The memory seems to belong to someone else's life. A different version of her, of them. But she knows she isn't making it up: it's not a false memory. She knows because of the *chapeau*, the hat. The straw hat that doesn't suit her, but that's packed carefully in paper in the loft. The one Luc went back for and bought to surprise her.

Okay, Alex, I'm done . . . As she bends again to the sign, the words assault her. *This marriage isn't working . . . I don't want this . . .* There's a gap at her waist, between her waistband and her jacket, her top that's ridden up. It's exposed her flesh, and she starts to shiver.

'Hey, you can't move that!' The shout comes from

down the street, and when she glances up, there's a police officer in a hi-vis vest coming up the hill towards her. 'No entry here,' he calls, and he makes a brisk shooing motion with his hands, like she's maybe five years old, or a stray.

Alex straightens. 'Is it flooded?' she asks. 'How badly?'

'Are you a resident?' he says as he nears her, and she can hear he's a little out of breath.

'Well, no,' she tells him, 'but . . .'

He starts to move the sign back to where it was.

'How bad is it?' she asks again, and the pulse is going in her neck.

Pausing, he adjusts his hi-vis vest. She notices a nick at his throat where he's cut himself shaving. 'Put it this way,' he says, 'you can't come through, not even on foot. It's like a lake down at the bottom. Pretty unlucky, to be honest, because it's all fairly localized. My colleague, who's –'

'My mum and dad live here,' she blurts. 'They're away, but I have the key.' She starts to pat her pockets, like she'll have to prove it somehow. Pulls out a mint in a twist of plastic, a packet of tissues, a hair elastic, her mobile. 'I'm going to phone them,' she tells him. 'Let me just phone them. They'll tell you I'm basically a resident. I don't know why I said I wasn't.' Words are coming fast out of her mouth, but she isn't really aware of what she's saying. 'What I mean is, I grew up here, hold on . . . Just wait, please . . . Give me a minute, okay?'

She doesn't really know what she's doing. She both wants and doesn't want to push past this man to get to the house, *her* house. She isn't going to think about what she might find. Her fingers are unsteady, fumbling as she pokes at the screen, from the cold and the wet, and she's all at once aware of her hazards going behind her, the beat and flare of them, making her heart speed up. Alex tries her mum's number first, and it rings out. What did she expect? Her mum never *ever* picks up. Next she tries Nancy, but the phone rings and rings, until she gives up.

The man in the hi-vis vest is saying something long and involved about water and electric shock, waiting times, rats and disease, but she's calling her family on rotation and she can't focus. Why is no one picking up? What's wrong with them? Her thumb hovers over Luc's number, then away. She isn't ready to talk to him yet. Now isn't the moment. She just needs to get this sorted, and then she will, she will . . .

'Look, I'm going to have to ask you to move your car.' The police officer waves a hand over her phone screen, forcing her to acknowledge him. 'I'm afraid I can't let you leave it double-parked like that. I've overlooked it, but it's in contravention, obviously, and we've got enough problems this evening. We don't need –'

She's dialling numbers still – like if she can only speak to someone, it will sort this whole thing out, it will save her. 'I need to contact them,' she says, without looking up. 'They need to know.' Come on, Nancy, she thinks. Come on, Eva. She's trying not to imagine the house, what might have happened. All their stuff, the years, the decades of their lives. The little wooden box, with the secret compartment, on the shelf in the hallway. The clay lady she made when she was nine, with her unintentionally scary eyes, which they keep still on the kitchen windowsill. The books and records and pictures and photographs; her mum and dad's wedding portrait on the mantelpiece, the Cary Grant and Grace Kelly romance of it. She'd leave fingerprints on its silver frame, staring and staring at the black-and-white image, trying to understand that these impossibly beautiful, laughing people – these people who came from a time before she was born – were her parents.

'Okay, you're not listening, madam. I'm going to have to ask –'

With her phone to her ear, Alex turns and walks the short distance to her car, grabs her bag from the back seat, starts to rifle through it. Grit from the seams catches under her fingernails as she checks each compartment. And she's getting that panicky feeling because where is the key? Why can't she find it? She's always so organized. What is happening to her? Her neck, her face, her whole head are hot, and tears are pushing up from nowhere. And then it's there, in the zip-up pocket at the back of the lining, which she's already checked, the orange key fob with her mum's writing on the little piece of card that slides in under the transparent window. 'I've got it!' she shouts, and she moves towards the man in the hi-vis vest, leaving the car door wide on its hinges. The man shakes his head, one hand on the sign. As if this is his street, not hers, and he doesn't care that she has a key – she could have a whole bunch of keys. He won't allow her to pass.

'Let me through,' she says, when she reaches him, and she can hear the choke in her throat as she speaks. 'It's my house. It's my home.' Alex grips the cordon, which feels like nothing, almost nothing, in her hands. But all the same, she doesn't want to let go. She won't let go, she can't. She looks him right in the eyes. She thinks maybe she's crying. He's shaking his head still, but she isn't giving up. She just wants to go home. That's all she wants. It's so simple. Can she please just go home?

II

Eva, Thursday morning

Standing in a pair of borrowed wellies in the lounge, Eva reaches out and takes hold of her sisters' hands. No one is saying anything, and she doesn't look at them as she does this. She knows, like her, they're unable to speak. The floodwater is brown, filthy. It comes up as far as the windowsill in the bay, all the way to the letterbox on the front door. It's higher than her knees, so the wellies are useless: they've filled up with water, and she's aware of the discomfort of this, but at the same time, entirely detached from it. The room seems to have been tipped on its side: the sofa is half submerged, and the bamboo shelving unit gives the impression it's sliding down the wall. There are things – belongings – floating around them, but she doesn't want to acknowledge it. She can't. Eva has seen scenes like this on TV; this is the sort of thing that happens in other places to other people.

Her head is bursting, dizzy still with all that her dad, her mum, told them last night. She has no idea how to slot this new version of her parents into her memories. She always thought they were as solid as couples came, Vivienne and Patrick, Patrick and Vivienne – there was no reason to think anything else. Her whole life she has trusted them completely. And now this feeling she can't escape: that her childhood was founded on a lie. A lie of omission, and she's trying to process it, rewriting and rewriting the story of them. At the same time as she's standing here looking, *not looking*, at what has happened to the house where she grew up, the house where Lucy lived for the first eight years of her life. It's impossible to calculate the extent of the damage, the ruin.

Out of the corner of her eye, Eva can see a photograph floating in front of the fireplace – or, at least, where she knows the fireplace *is*, except it's underwater. She thinks it's the one of the Elvis show, of the three of them with Helen and Katy; she knows it is – she can tell by the frame. The print Stella Wilson gave to them, and that must have been on the shelf for thirty years, longer. Her past – *their* past – is stitched into the fabric of this place. It's on every surface and in the drawers, hanging on the back of the doors, trapped under the fridge, and it's burned into the curtain in her old bedroom, where she scorched a hole when she was a teenager, smoking out of the window.

Next to her Nancy clears her throat. Then she squeezes Eva's hand, releases it. 'Well, thank fuck it's all over for Mum's yellow carpet,' she says. 'Every cloud . . .' Her voice comes out a little too loud, a tell. Eva fixes her eyes on the green glass bird, the one from the mantelpiece, that's lying on its side on the tipped-up arm of the sofa. Stranded where it shouldn't be. She doesn't look at Nancy – she can't still, she doesn't trust herself. It's like the damp has got into her chest, her mouth, under her tongue, and it's making it difficult to breathe. But she could kiss her sister for this. For trying to make it better for them.

Slipping her fingers from Alex's, she rubs her face, presses her knuckles into her eyelids. She's exhausted. They'd decided, in the end, not to drive down overnight, instead setting an alarm for six that morning. At a point, she'd left a message for the high-end rental firm, told them there was an emergency in London, and that they'd need to get on to a glazier for a *fairly big job* at the glass house, that she would cover all the costs, just send her the bill, please. But also that they'd need to discuss compensation in the coming days because of the problem with the dead natterjacks and were they aware of that? The rotten smell they'd had to endure, the toad corpses in the pool, blocking the air-con units, and who knows what else? Then she'd driven the Tesla at ninety miles an hour down the motorway, Lucy sulking in the back, Beats clamped over her ears the whole way home.

Eva hadn't stopped once. She'd driven crazily, desperately, even though she knew it was already too late. As if somehow, if she drove fast enough, she might be able to save everything. And then, when it came to it – after she'd dropped Lucy home, and pulled up at the end of the street in Dartmouth Park – she hadn't wanted to get out of the car: she'd felt all of a sudden that she couldn't face it. So she'd waited. She'd waited until Nancy had shown up, blank-faced, twenty minutes later, and Alex soon after, hugging a pair of spare wellies to her chest. A peace-offering. They'd walked down the hill in silence, held each other's elbows as they waded into the water, gone in together.

'We should get the band back together,' Alex says

now, and holding up her arms, bent at the elbows like *Don't shoot*, she starts to move through the water. She's wearing blue jogging bottoms, and with each step, the material darkens, a tidemark bleeding further and further up her thigh. 'Ugh,' she says, as she lifts the Elvis photograph from the water, wipes her fingers on her top. Dishevelled, is how her sister looks. She looks like maybe she slept in the car, which is about as un-Alex as you could get. The thought makes Eva ache inside, but also, she can feel herself smiling a little.

'Look at us,' Alex says. 'I love us here. Absolute geeks that we are . . .' She's studying the photograph as she says it, and doesn't look up. 'Your nosebleed, Eva.' Alex touches her finger and thumb to her lips. 'That was the *pièce de résistance.* The showstopper. Literally.' It's nothing really, a quip, a handful of words, but Eva knows. The same way she knows that, although they can't see their feet underwater right now, they're rooted, she and her sisters. She doesn't have to see it to know it.

It was my fault. Her dad's voice comes at her from the night before. *What happened to your sister, to Alex. And then . . . afterwards . . . I couldn't handle it, and I'm so ashamed to say it out loud.* Eva has never heard her dad talk that way before, and she'd wanted to tell him to stop, because she almost couldn't bear it.

'Oh, God,' Alex says, and she's fishing another frame from the water. When she turns it over Eva sees it's her mum and dad's wedding portrait. 'The water's got in under the glass,' Alex says. 'I love this photo. Is there another copy? I think this is the only one . . .' Slowly, her sister starts to make her way back towards them. With each step, the water sluices dangerously. There's a smell too, a gassy, sewage smell that swells and dips. She thinks if she let herself, if she gave in to it, she'd be sick.

'Why don't we remember that he wasn't there?' Nancy murmurs. 'That it was just Mum.'

'We were babies, pretty much,' Alex is using her sleeve, blotting the photograph. 'And you were just a twinkle in their eye . . .' She glances at Eva, says this last bit in a bad Cockney accent.

You were my second chance, Eva. His voice is in her head again. *If that makes sense? My chance to get it right.* This half-explanation that's complicated and confusing, and does she believe him? She wants to. But she's struggling to reconcile her dad – her dad who she knows from his tread on the stairs, from the way he smooths down his hair when he catches sight of himself, from how he twitches his thumbs absentmindedly when he's listening, or maybe not listening – with this man he's described. Because who was he, that person? The person who left her sisters, her mum? Eva's grappling to rearrange the scattered pieces of their past, to fit them into place. Is there anything else they don't know?

'I was always jealous of you, you know?' she tells Alex now. It's true, but she isn't sure why she says it. To try to make it all better somehow?

Her sister stops wiping the photograph; she looks surprised. 'I was never jealous of you.'

'Oh, no offence!' Nancy goggles her eyes, like *some-one* needs to step in on Alex's behalf. 'She has no idea,'

Nancy says to Eva, and laughs. 'She doesn't know her own power.'

'I don't want you to hate me.' The words are out of Eva's mouth before she can stop them. She looks from Alex to Nancy, and the tears come then. She's been holding them back since they walked through the front door. She can't keep it in any longer.

Her sisters are looking at her as though she's said something in a foreign language, words they don't understand.

There's a pause, before Nancy shakes her head. 'What? No! Eva –'

Next thing, they're standing in the middle of the lounge, arms around each other. There's the damp heat of her sisters, the smell of shampoo, the itch of Nancy's jumper against her jaw, and a decade and a half slides from under her in that instant. To the rainy night at the Hammersmith flat her sisters shared. Steamed-up windows and her clothes drenched through to her underwear, and her baby – her baby, who was Lucy, although she didn't know it yet – barely more than a frightened thought in her. She can feel her sisters' palms, their fingers pressing into her back. The flesh and bone of them, made from the same body she is. They're three, and they're one, and it's strange – it's *unfathomable* – and it's solace all at once.

'Scott's stayed up there.' She mumbles it into the clutch of them. 'He's booked himself onto a silent walking retreat.' She says it because she wants them to know; she says it because she wants to break the moment, to give them something, make them laugh. 'They all carry

364

laminated cards that they whip out if anyone tries to talk to them . . .'

'Oh, *please!*' Nancy releases them, slaps a hand to her forehead.

'Can you get it annulled?' Alex asks. 'Genuine question.'

And it makes Eva squirm a little, this reference to the marriage – *her* marriage – the wedding she didn't invite them to.

'Not if you've had sex,' Nancy says.

'Ew.' Alex screws up her nose.

'Could he prove it?' Nancy turns to her. '*Intercourse,* I mean.' She says "intercourse" in a silly, staccato voice, like they're maybe fourteen.

'Nope.' Alex covers her ears. 'No. Stop.'

'I don't think it counts anyhow,' Nancy says. 'If your sisters weren't there to witness it.' She shoots a look at Eva.

'What? The sex?' Eva says.

'Funny,' Nancy says. 'Very, *very* funny.'

'There's a pre-nup okay,' Eva murmurs. 'I'm not a total idiot.'

She won't tell them yet, what she's decided, what she's pretty sure she's decided. She needs the space to think. But she's already started the process with Scott, of letting him know. *I need some time,* she'd told him last night. She's aware there's no room for subtlety with him. In the end she'll just have to come out and say it. It isn't the Jay thing. It's given her a reason – half a reason, yes, but the fact is she'd known already there was so much that wasn't right with them. She'd known since the start. And the truth is, Scott hadn't seemed all that surprised; he hadn't seemed especially *bothered*, if she's being entirely honest with herself. When the time comes, she's going to bill it as a 'conscious uncoupling'. He's a Coldplay fan, and happy to admit it. He thinks Goop is *ahead of the curve*. She'll present it to him, she'll sell it. Then make him think it was his idea.

'And Lucy?' Alex asks now.

Eva takes a deep breath in through her nose. Another thing in the arsenal of things she doesn't want to think about.

'Yes, how's she doing?' Nancy says. 'I mean in relation to her, um . . . *stepbrother?*' She takes a step back as she says it. Brown water whooshes around their knees. 'Please don't bite me!' Her sister clamps her arms across her torso, like she's protecting herself, and laughs. 'Don't go smashing up the windows, either. I beg of you . . .' With her arms squashed against her body still, Nancy forces her hands into prayer.

Eva can see that Alex is laughing too, or rather, trying not to.

'Seriously, don't!' Nancy's laughing so hard now at her own joke, she can hardly get the words out. 'Alex will twat you one if you do . . .'

Alex rolls her eyes, flicks a little water at Nancy.

'Wait, what's this?' Eva makes as if she's peering at something she's holding in her hands. Then slowly, slowly, she pulls one hand from the other, flips up her middle finger, brandishes it first at Nancy, then Alex, and they're laughing, all of them now. The three of them, standing among the wreckage.

This, Eva thinks. This is the vernacular of sisters. It's childish and absurd and funny and infuriating and painful, and it's beautiful. They are under her skin and in her heart, these women, her sisters. She has no choice in the matter. And despite everything, she'd rather be standing here right now than anywhere else. A cocktail by the pool in Mustique doesn't come close. She wants to let them know this, she needs to. So she does the only thing she can. 'Fuck you both very much,' she tells them. She's laughing still, as she says it, and she can feel that her eyes are bright. In her head, she means something entirely different. In her head she's saying, I love you.

Nancy, Thursday morning

There is something biblical here, is all Nancy can think, one hand on the floating fridge in a vain attempt to steady herself. A kind of half-body baptism, a twisted christening, a muddied cleansing that feels like a test. She couldn't have imagined, when the call came through from Alex last night, that it would be as bad as it is. They're trying to salvage as much as they can, but they keep stopping, restarting, distracted by the past that's drifting out from where it's been stored. Hidden, forgotten, things she barely remembered they had, and coming at them now, like a sideways punch, a left hook they can't duck.

Eva's upstairs gathering towels from the bathroom, the airing cupboard, and over by the kitchen sink, Alex is holding up another photograph for Nancy to see. This one she's peeled from between the ruined pages of *Delia Smith's Christmas*. 'The three of us, and I'm guessing nineteen eighty- . . . seven?' her sister says. 'Iconic hair, Nance.'

'Show me.' Nancy comes towards her, takes the photo from her sister. The ink has slid, blurring the colours in the bottom corner. 'Christ!' she says. '*No one* should have that many layers. What was the hairdresser thinking?' She knows this picture, she remembers it, and she hates herself here. Buttoned up to her throat in an electric blue shirt that's cheap and shiny. She looks cheap and shiny. And fat. Was she fat?

'You know, it was super-shit, being the ugly one.' The words are out before her brain has engaged; she's never said anything like this before. It's one of the unspoken things, and she doesn't know why she's said it exactly. Does she want her sister to agree? To disagree? She thinks maybe it's to do with the house, the damage, that's unravelling everything, stripping them back. And although she put quote marks round the words when she said them – *the ugly one* – she meant it.

'I'm sorry, what?' Alex says, and Nancy braces herself, waiting for the platitudes. *Of course you weren't . . . Nobody thought that . . . Don't be stupid . . .* Instead, her older sister frowns a little, blinks like she hasn't understood. 'Are you serious?' Alex says. 'I always thought *I* was the ugly one.'

Nancy doesn't know what to say. She has known her whole life that she was the least attractive of the three. She's known this, lived with it, thought it was an accepted truth, a *fact*. Something everyone knew. And now, and now . . .

'I always thought: at least I have the good teeth,' Alex says now.

'Right?' Nancy laughs. 'That's not nothing.'

Her sister flashes a too-wide smile.

'Shit,' Nancy says, and she's shaking her head. She can't believe it; she doesn't believe it, except that she knows her sister, and she sees in her face that she means every word. What a waste, she thinks. What a waste of time, of *everything*. In all these years, how have they not shared this?

Eva comes into the room, towels bundled in her arms. 'What are we talking about?'

'The million-dollar question, obviously.' Alex gestures at the devastation around them. 'Here we are with all of . . . *this*, poring over a single photograph, still asking ourselves, are we pretty enough?'

Eva looks at Nancy. 'I'll tell you who definitely thinks you're pretty enough.'

'Please don't . . .' Nancy hands the photograph back to Alex.

'He's in love with you,' Eva says. 'You do realize that?'

'Who?' Nancy asks, but she knows.

'*Who?*' Alex rolls her eyes. 'Like, sure I'll drive *three hundred miles* up the motorway to drop off your daughter. Not a problem!'

'Make it happen, Nance.' Eva wades through the water, dumps the towels next to the sink. 'I like him for you. Great hair.'

'*Great* hair,' Nancy agrees.

She doesn't tell them about the text that came through as she pulled up in the car earlier. The one she hasn't replied to yet, but that made her grin at herself like a lunatic in the rear-view mirror. Hard to fault our high-end NHS lunchtime dining, Nik had written, but would you want to get dinner one time? Somewhere that doesn't smell of disinfectant and death? And it's a little weird, kind of wild that it's him, that it's Nik, but also – and it's the only way she can describe it – it's like taking off her bra after a long day

370

at work, or letting herself cry at a schmaltzy film so she won't get a headache, or drinking a bottle of wine by herself and feeling no shame.

'Also, Mum likes him,' Eva says.

'And right now nobody cares what Dad thinks.' Alex has her back to her, moving cookbooks, one by one, to a high cupboard. 'So.'

It was instinct, what happened in the forest. That's what he'd said. Impulse. Habit. A reflex. That makes it worse, not better, she'd told him. His words are ringing and ringing in her still. *I don't know how to explain it to make you understand . . . it felt like it was happening all over again, the fire pit, Alex, that we'd re-wound forty years . . . I know there's no way to make it okay . . . I can only tell you it doesn't mean anything . . .*

Another forest, another time, and there's the four of them. Her sisters and her dad, running, running through the trees, out of breath and stumbling in their wellies, and shrieking with laughter. *Quick!* her dad's shouting, and he has the mischievous look in his eyes, the one Nancy loves, the look that says he doesn't play by the rules, not like other dads. *Quick, kids, she's coming! Betty Bumsucker's behind us, run! Don't look back!*

She shouldn't look back. She shouldn't, but she can't help it. There's a sense that something has been ripped from her. That her version of events – her whole *self* – has been upended. Like the table and chairs, the fridge, the sofa in the lounge, like the entire ground floor of her childhood home. She has felt it, over the years, his leaning away from her sometimes. She thought she had, at least. And she's asked herself a thousand times, Am I difficult to love? Am I to blame? *I don't have a favourite, I just don't*, her dad had told them last night. *I know it's the worst moment to ask for your trust, but please trust me on this* . . . She thinks again of the almost-accident. Nothing happened, she tells herself. Nothing happened, but also everything happened. Everything she can't unsee, and doesn't understand, and she's so sick of these secrets her family is keeping. She's sick of the secrets *she* is keeping.

'Okay, I have something to tell you,' she blurts, and her sisters turn to look at her. Before they have a chance to speak – before she has a chance to change her mind – she ploughs on: 'I thought it would go away, but it hasn't, and please don't tell Mum and Dad, or do tell them, I don't know –'

'You're pregnant!' Eva says, wedging a towel into the gap next to the washing-machine.

'Not unless it was an immaculate conception . . .' Eva's comment has derailed her, and she feels suddenly ashamed. The truth is she's felt ashamed all along, although it isn't her fault, and she knows this. She can't look at them, as she opens her mouth, lets the words out. 'I've been suspended from work. It's a long story, and I don't want to talk about it, but it's bullshit, basically.' She stops. Waits for them to judge her. It's what she's expecting, that here she is, the fuck-up, fucking up again. The difficult woman, being difficult again.

Alex and Eva are clamouring to speak, but it isn't what she'd anticipated. They don't ask what's happened, what she's done or hasn't done, just leap to her defence.

They're outraged, her sisters, on her behalf, and they look ridiculous, insane. Up to their knees in stinking, muddy water, and gesticulating the way they are. And standing there, listening, Nancy feels something let loose in her; she feels vindicated. 'Look,' Eva says, at a point, 'I'm thinking of starting something new, Nance. Early days, but I've got investors interested, people who backed Unfortune8! right at the start. A running thing, and it's kind of cool. So if it all goes tits up at the hospital . . . no pun intended . . .' And for a moment Nancy wonders, What if? Her mind flicks again to Nik. She could make a change, she could change everything. Why not?

And then Alex is moving past the cooker and towards her. New sweary Alex, who Nancy kind of prefers, and she's putting a hand on her arm. Telling them they can finish this conversation back at Eva's, that she's fucking freezing, and it's time to take her perfect goddamn teeth out of here, there's really nothing more they can do for now. And Nancy hadn't noticed, but she is shivering too, trembling. From the cold, and also, she thinks, from her sisters' furious kindness, their unquestioning belief in her.

'Wait, Mum wanted pictures!' Alex stops, turns around. 'She wanted to know how bad it was.'

'Ha, no!' Nancy shakes her head.

'Absolutely no way,' Eva says.

'*Nothing a pair of Marigolds and a squirt of Flash won't sort out . . .*' Nancy takes a pretend drag on an imaginary cigarette.

'Nah-ah,' Alex pulls a face. 'Not ready to laugh about the smoking yet, and probably never . . .'

They look around the kitchen, all three of them then, as if they might have forgotten something. Like they're visitors here, and they want to make sure they're not leaving anything behind.

'Most of it will dry out just fine,' Eva murmurs.

They all nod. They all know it isn't true.

Alex, Thursday morning

Luc is coming down the hill as Alex wades out of the water. She isn't expecting him, and it's like she's found herself at the apex of a rollercoaster, a feeling in her that's both fear and anticipation, excitement even; she can't tell exactly. Unmoored is how she feels. Luc has the baby strapped to his chest, facing out. She's wearing the sky blue snowsuit, and kicking her legs, they're going like pistons, and Alex's body is remembering. Remembering what it is to hold her baby's soft, small feet, feel her delicate hump of belly under her hands.

Balancing on one foot, then the other, Alex empties water from her boots. She locked the front door while her sisters went on ahead, and she watches now as they greet Luc on the street, cover their niece with kisses, squeeze her cheeks, her toes in the blue snowsuit. There's a sudden, unbearable urgency in Alex. Something visceral, unbidden, in the pit of her: she wants to reach out and touch her daughter; she needs to do this.

There was a moment yesterday evening, standing with the police tape against her chest, when she thought about her babies – how she'd brought them to the house after they were born. Wearing little knitted caps on their impossibly small heads, and slumped tiny in their car seats. How she'd breathed out as she'd walked through the door. She thought about the games, stacked haphazardly on the bamboo unit – Cluedo and Operation and Bird Lotto and Sorry! – that she used to play with her sisters, and that Rosa and Eden have played now too. And she understood that she wants the same for Dolly. She wants her youngest child to know the house like they've all known it. She wants her to jump on the same beds, pick flowers in the same garden, play Sardines with her mum, who always, *always* hides in their old den at the top of the house. It snares her, this thought; it undoes her.

She had a dream last night about a woman driving a London bus. An angry woman, with bleached blonde hair, who had on a black velvet ballgown. A woman who was both in control and very much not in control. Who was maybe drunk, or perhaps just furious. In the dream, Alex was on the bus, a passenger, but also somehow she was the driver, terrified about crashing and dying, because what would happen to her children? And she's feeling something not unlike that now, walking towards her husband, because why is he here?

Okay, Alex, I'm done. I don't want this.

Alex has the sense, as she approaches, that somehow she's forfeited a right: that she isn't allowed to come too close to her baby, her child. But it's like the pull of nicotine, alcohol, desire – she can't stop herself, she won't. 'Um-mmm,' the baby's saying, and it's the noise she makes when she's teething, but also . . . also, it sounds like maybe she's saying *Mama.* The hood of the snowsuit looks huge on her, it's down over one eye, and her fat, sky blue arms are sticking out at angles in the sling. Alex doesn't look at Luc as she kisses her baby, gazes into her eyes. Then she kisses her again and again and again.

'Hi,' Alex murmurs. 'Hi, little one.' Behind her breast-bone a feeling like she might burst, something that's happy and sad all at once.

I'll never forgive myself for what happened, her dad said on the call last night. He was on speakerphone, her mum in the background, and his voice echoed, came and went . . . *the burns, the surgeries, my cowardice . . . I've never apologized, and I should have. This is me apologizing, okay? I'm so sorry, darling.*

Alex sat in her spotless kitchen, at her spotless table, a glass of water in front of her that she didn't drink, and tears running down her face as she listened.

'I thought I'd broken things. I don't know how to explain it,' he said.

'You mean you resented me?' she asked. 'I don't want you to resent me.'

'No, Alex. God, no.' She heard the scrape in his voice as he said it. 'I thought I'd ruined everything, that it was done. That I'd never be able to make it up to you. To Nancy. And the guilt was . . .' He stopped talking then, for the longest time. And then, in a rush of sentences, of sound: 'The thing is, Eva was my chance to redeem myself. To show your mum, to show you all. I thought if I could be the perfect dad to her, somehow it would re-set things, or erase my mistakes, or make things right, and it's the faultiest logic, I know, and –'

She pressed the phone hard against her ear, her jaw, as though if she could just hear him more clearly, she could better understand what he was trying to say. If she pressed hard enough, would he say the words she wanted to hear? Could she will him to say it?

'I never knew,' she told him, when he finished. 'I didn't see it.' And she must have moved in her seat in some way, knocked the glass of water with her elbow maybe, because it tipped; and she watched the clear liquid pool across the table, drip steadily onto the floor. 'I didn't see it,' she said again, to herself as much as him.

Next to her, Luc clears his throat. 'You took the car,' he says.

She nods, adjusts the baby's hood that's down over her eyes again; she finds she can't look at him.

'Should I be worried, Alex?'

She wedges the side of her thumb into the baby's mouth. Feels the strong suck and pull of her hot, sore gums, the scratch of new teeth. 'I was going to call you,' she says. 'But then . . .' She gestures behind her at the road, the lake of it, that's rendered the street strange, unfamiliar, other. 'And all the stuff with Dad . . .' She trails off. Should he be worried? She doesn't know the answer. Should *she*? She has no idea, because who can ever really know what happens next?

'We figured it out,' he tells her, and she glances up at him now, confused.

'The drive back, I mean. As you can see . . .' Luc motions with his hands towards the tarmac, then to the houses either side of them.

There's a pause. Alex knows she needs to say something, to try to explain, but she can't. It's too big what she has to say, and it's tangled and messy and difficult. The pause is going on too long, and Alex wants to shield herself, because she's waiting for him to say, *I can't do this.*

Sliding his palms under the straps of the sling, Luc shifts the weight of their daughter. He looks as though he's about to leave; she's certain he's going to leave, and she wants to grip his arms to stop him, to keep him here.

'Your mum spoke to me,' he says.

'Oh, God.' Alex puffs out her cheeks.

'Yeah, she basically told me off.' He lets go the straps, fixes his eyes on her. She thinks she sees the shadow of a smile. 'Made me feel like one of my students. The whole shit sandwich, you know. Like I was one of the real problem kids.'

'Oh . . .' She raises her eyebrows.

'She's right.' He says it quietly, firmly. 'I need to do more . . . for you. Sorry, not for *you*,' he corrects himself. He looks a little panic-stricken, she thinks. 'I need to do more for us, our family. It's not your responsibility, the kids, the house, *toutes les choses*. Obviously, I know that.'

Alex waits for him to say more, but he doesn't. Her mum has spoken to him, she thinks, and she tries to imagine it. Her mum, whose marriage she always thought was superior to theirs, hers and Luc's. This whole time, she's known it was wilder, sexier, stronger, *better*. But now . . . Everything is altering, shifting, changing. Her mind flashes to Matt. To his timeline, his posts, his stories, to the multiple curated snapshots documenting his too-perfect life. These things are never as they seem, she knows, but it isn't enough to know it.

Luc is so close to her: it's nothing, no distance, it's inches. But also it's like she's about to vault an endless ocean. Her entire body is in her throat, as she leans her forehead against his shoulder. Lightly, uncertainly. There's the heat of him through his shirt, the sharp beat of his blood, or maybe hers.

'It's been a difficult year,' she whispers.

She hears him inhale, exhale.

'*Je sais*, I know.'

He puts his arms around her, and she lets him. She feels, all of a sudden, as if she couldn't have held up her weight any longer. The baby is sandwiched between them, mumbling in consonants and vowels that sound like drunken giggles, a crazy, experimental language that's all promise. 'Alex Fisher . . .' Luc says, and his words are hot against her hair. He says it like he's checking it's still her.

'I was thinking about the Music House,' she tells him, 'the Maison de la Musique, and you on the steps, calling across the market. Did that happen?'

He takes her face in his hands then, and kisses her. He barely kisses her, as if he thinks she might stop him. She can taste his breath in and out of his mouth, and there's the almost-press of his lips against hers. And how can something that's almost nothing make her feel so full?

Standing here, at the edge of the flood, it's like they're back at the beginning. Except there's every second of every day, every month of every year, every year of every decade they've spent together too. They are a million miles apart and in each other's bones all at once:

380

he's her husband, the father of her children, and at the same time he's someone she can hardly grasp – and how is that possible?

His mouth is on hers still, when he starts to speak, like he's afraid to break apart. 'I missed you,' he murmurs, and his teeth knock against hers. 'I miss you, Alex. We need you. Come back to us.'

Nine Months Later, Vivienne

Vivienne is feeling a little light-headed. She has the new nicotine patch stuck to her upper arm, and she's wondering if that's what's making her feel this way. Or maybe it's the 'Sold' sign, jammed into the flower bed in the front garden of her home. Or that Patrick texted while she was at the food and wine shop, to let her know her daughters, her beloved girls, are inside waiting for her. She's holding a bottle of boxed champagne. In her bag are bright green olives in a plastic tub, a grab bag of Twiglets that were on special, sherbet-filled Flying Saucers for old times' sake. They're celebrating her birthday finally – the ridiculous number she doesn't want to think about, just the five of them, her request.

She walks down the path, leans against the wall of the house, takes a breath, two. The patch is a little itchy at the edges, and, setting the champagne on the step, she pats the skin around it, although she'd like to scratch. She's thinking about yesterday's appointment. How she'd paused on the way out of the doctor's office. 'I've been a bit forgetful,' she'd told the woman, who looked younger than her daughters. She'd said it quickly, before she changed her mind. 'There's been a lot on, I'm sure it's nothing.' And the doctor, who she's never seen before, had asked her to come back in, to take a seat. There'd been a softness in the way she'd said it, a kindness that felt overdone, and then Nancy's words in her head, *Patients always raise the thing they're actually worried about on the way out . . .*

But Vivienne's not worried, it's just a slipping sometimes, she's sure it's normal. Health anxiety is all the rage, these days, after all, and she's probably being a bit of a hypochondriac, like her middle daughter – *Ssh!* she thinks, don't mention it. The fact is, all it takes is a UTI to send you bonkers when you get to this age. She hasn't said anything to Patrick yet. Why would she? But she'll take the tests. She has nothing to lose, might as well get her vitamin levels checked, all that jazz.

Vivienne pulls a weed from the dirt at the edge of the step. She hadn't wanted the Sold sign. It feels too final, too real. But the estate agent had pushed, and Patrick and the girls had outvoted her. It's the end, she thinks, so why does it feel like the start of something?

The way I see it . . . she hears Alex say authoritatively. Seven-year-old Alex, who's the other side of the bedroom door, chatting with her sisters after lights out. It's Easter, and it's late, the girls are stuffed with chocolate – they all are – and she's about to shush them, but instead she listens. 'The way I see it,' her eldest daughter says again, making sure she's got the attention of her younger sisters, 'life is a long line all planned out. You don't want to waste it.' There's a thoughtful pause, and Vivienne can picture their earnest faces.

Then Nancy says, 'The thing I'm most happy about is that I'm alive. But I'd prefer to be a butterfly.'

Eva tries to say something next, but Alex gets in first. 'I want to get a place in Heaven,' she tells her sisters, and Vivienne smiles, shakes her head, because they aren't religious, but they've been talking at school about the Easter story, all the gore and supernatural thrill of it, and it has hooked her children.

Next thing, there's the twang of bed springs, a light thump of feet across the carpet. 'I want to be God,' Eva announces, in her little high voice. 'I'm going to be God.' And Vivienne laughs outside the door – she can't help it. 'Get back into bed, Eva!' she hears Alex hiss.

Vivienne glances up at the bedroom window, the square room at the front of the house that her children used to share. Bunkbeds and a single, and Beatrix Potter curtains, a wall frieze of *Where The Wild Things Are*. They're having this same conversation still, her girls, she knows. The same conversation, but different. They've been talking, talking their whole lives, sharing the secrets of their hearts, and Vivienne loves the fact of it – that they have each other, no matter what. It makes her less afraid.

She takes the keys from her bag. She'll go inside in a moment, she will. It's just there's the last of the light out here, the kind of quiet calm that shouldn't belong in the city. It's been months since they stayed at the glass house, almost a year now, but everything is a little precarious still, with Patrick and the girls. Not so anyone would notice, particularly, just her. She watches when they're together, and she sees. Does he have a favourite? Vivienne has wondered this. Is Eva his favourite? She doesn't think so; she guesses they'll never know. Something else she'll never know: when exactly she conceived her youngest child.

Running her thumb over the jagged edge of her keys, she thinks back. To another key, a lost key, and to the day he turned up on her doorstep, the *auburn-haired stranger*. To John-Paul. She has almost removed it from her memory, convinced herself of its insignificance, but it's there, flickering at the edges of her. She saw him again, just the one time, years later, when he came for drinks on Christmas Eve with the Wilsons. He'd been staying with Stella; she thinks maybe he'd split from his wife. They'd had a row about it afterwards, her and Patrick, an awful row, with all the kids out of bed, she hardly remembers why. Because she'd talked to him too long at the party? Leaked something in her body language? Because she and Patrick were drunk? She tries not to think about it, but she has wondered, of course she has. Whether Eva is his.

A flash of memory: the kids in the lounge, all three of them teenagers. Watching *Ricki Lake* or *Kilroy* or *Trisha*, one of those shows, and scrolling across the bottom of the screen, the words, *Who's the Daddy?!* Vivienne remembers hovering in the background, tutting at the whipped-up nonsense of it, the exploitative bullshit, the trashy timbre, and these young kids, too young really to be parents. Like Eva would be, only she didn't know that then. And yet something had struck her. 'It takes more than sperm to make a dad . . .' Trisha or Kilroy or Ricki had announced, to whoops and lassoed arms in the studio, and needled as she was, she'd known it was right. A truth. Or maybe she'd only wanted to think that. If you pretend long enough, does it become a truth of sorts?

Vivienne lets herself into the house. It sounds as if there are forty people in there, not four. The radio's on, music blasting, and they don't hear her come in. From where she's standing, she can see through to the kitchen. Alex has her trouser leg rolled up, showing them the tattoo. '. . . more painful than childbirth, thank you for telling me,' she's saying to her sisters. Vivienne pictures the lilac bird on her daughter's ankle, the same one the other two have. A matching set now. She thought she'd hate the look of them, the tattoos, but she doesn't.

It smells a little damp in here still, but she can see from the hallway, they've lit candles, and there's a cake on the worktop that she knows Nancy's made. They had the kitchen redone after the flood. Glossy and white, but they salvaged the table, Superglued the spice rack. They'll take them to the new, smaller place, the Victorian terrace in Highbury Barn they're buying from a young family who've outgrown it. When it comes down to it, you have to decide what to hold on to, and when to let go, she thinks. She's been thinking this a lot lately.

'I'm sorry, is that my jumper you're wearing?' Vivienne hears one of her daughters say. Nancy or maybe Alex: they sound so similar, she can't tell who's who some-times. 'Oh, my God, take it off, you're stretching it . . .' Without their children, they become children again, her girls. In this house. She can see Patrick, leaning against the cooker, arms folded, watching them. He's rolling his eyes, but he's awestruck – he can't disguise it. It's there, in the soft, hopeless expression on his face. She feels it too. Awestruck by her children. That is the word.

Vivienne moves down the hallway towards them. It's gone through her mind that it might be the last time they eat dinner here, in this kitchen, the five of them like this. But she won't dwell on it, she will not. Because here they are, right now. This is it, *this* is the moment. This is them, her family.

In the doorway, Vivienne clears her throat. 'Let's make a toast,' she says. She has to raise her voice so they can hear her. When her daughters turn to look, when Patrick does, she holds up the champagne, waggles the box. Then, smiling, she walks into the room.

Acknowledgements

Thank you thank you, to the one and only Hellie Ogden. The kind of woman who (among many other very super and professional things) texts a photo of herself, midway through a work chat, Taylor Swift-ready in a Stetson & sequin jacket combo. No higher praise, really.

Thank you, wonderful Lily Cooper! For your cheerleading, your commitment, your discerning eye, and on-point book recommendations. Also your bonus French-ness ;) Thank you, fabulous Team Penguin Michael Joseph, especially Annie Moore for marketing magnificence, and Lee Motley for creating a *dream* cover. Thank you, Gaby Young, Maddy Woodfield, Louise Moore, Max Hitchcock, Clare Parker, Nick Lowndes, Colin Brush, Hazel Orme, Alice Mottram, Judie Ovens and Eugenie Woodhouse, and Clio Cornish for helping to birth this book, as well as your *actual* baby. Thank you, glorious rights team: Chantal Noel, Sarah Scarlett, Lucy Beresford-Knox, Beth Wood, Agnes Watters, Madeleine Stephenson, Lucie Deacon, Olivia Diomedes and Jake Dickson. Thank you, Akua Akowuah, Kelly Mason, Bronwen Davies and Christina Ellicot, sales sensations! And thank you, amazing Ma'suma Amiri, Claudia Ballard and everyone at WME.

Thank you, Caroline Zancan! For making it feel as though you're down the road in town, rather than across the other side of the Atlantic. What a total joy it is to work with you. Thank you for your thoughtfulness, your warmth, your humour, your smarts and for championing this story. I'm ridiculously happy to be sitting next to the other books on your fabulous list, and I *love* that I inadvertently wrote your family (ish). Thank you, Caitlin Mulrooney-Lyski, for being my guide, unflappably, and for your general publicity excellence. Thank you, Andrew Miller, and superb Team Holt: Leela Gebo, Amber Cherichetti, Alyssa Weinberg, Sonja Flancher, Jane Haxby, Hannah Campbell, Meryl Levavi, Janel Brown, Jason Reigal, Nicolette Seeback Ruggiero and Jay Miceli.

Thank you, my brilliant, unstoppable Dodwell Claxton women, and all who sail with us. Thank you, Cath and Jules, 1 & 3, for the talking we've been doing our whole lives. Thank you, Mum (who's definitely still worrying about us), for your love. Thank you, Margaret and Chris Begg, *world-class* in-laws. Thank you, Cass, Ione and Lucia, my favourite children. And thank you, Si, my favourite husband.